IRRESISTIBLE PASSION

"Think about what I am, Viva. Everything I own I can carry in my saddlebags. I've got nothing, and you're a rich lady from New Orleans."

"Rio, what a man carries in his saddlebags isn't what makes him what he is. It's what he does, how he acts, that's important."

"Like making a bed so he can seduce you in comfort instead of on the hard ground?"

"Is that what you were doing?" A little bubble of laughter forced its way through her tears. Warmth began to coil inside her. In a slow, husky whisper she asked, "Then what are we waiting for?"

His mouth was on hers in an instant, tasting the salt of her tears. She met him with her own fury, her own passion. Whatever they had started was beyond stopping now. She was no more in control than he. She did not want to be . . .

CAPTURE THE GLOW
OF ZEBRA'S HEARTFIRES

LINDA HILTON
DESIRE'S SLAVE

ZEBRA BOOKS
KENSINGTON PUBLISHING CORP.

*With love and "Thanks!" to my parents,
Don and Elaine Wheeler, who have
always had a house full of books—
from your crazy daughter who said
she wanted to write them.*

ZEBRA BOOKS

are published by

Kensington Publishing Corp.
475 Park Avenue South
New York, NY 10016

First printing: April, 1992

Printed in the United States of America

Chapter One

As the riverboat *Carolina* approached the Sacramento dock, Genevieve Marie du Prés leaned over the rail and swallowed a brief pang of homesickness. The bustle, the noise, the smell, the shouts of impatient men all reminded her of New Orleans. With a firm shake of her head and a blink of her eyes, she forced the feeling out of her mind. Home was too far away to think about now.

Genevieve settled her now worn blue wool cloak around her shoulders and forced herself to concentrate on the future instead of the past. In just a few minutes she'd be on solid ground again, and ready to make what she fully expected to be the last leg of a very long journey.

It was a beautiful morning, crisp with the smell of autumn and wood smoke, and Genevieve considered herself to have accomplished much in having come so far. Best of all, the enormous task she had set herself was nearly completed. Perhaps even today would see the end of it. Then she could indeed head home, back to New Orleans and the serene life that had been so inconveniently interrupted.

The *Carolina* slowed and began to edge toward the pier. Other passengers who had come out onto the deck now moved toward the rail where Genevieve had stood since dawn. Voices murmured behind her

5

with a subdued excitement. The crowd pressed against her, preventing any attempt she might have made to escape.

Genevieve turned her head slightly as instinct prompted a warning expression to her face. But instead of staring down an apologetic victim of gold fever, she found a man's shirt button no more than a few inches from her nose.

"I beg your pardon, sir," she began in her most haughty voice.

Whatever she might have said after that was lost in astonishment as she gazed upwards to find the face that belonged to the wearer of that plain wooden button.

He was tall and broad shouldered, and Genevieve knew she had seen him somewhere before, though she could not remember where or when. Surely, she thought in an instant of shock, it would be nearly impossible to forget someone like him.

He didn't look at her, despite her mild scolding, and for that she was grateful. She would have been more than just humiliated if he had seen the way she stared. But she simply could not help it.

This vaguely familiar stranger was the most beautiful male creature she had ever seen.

He had pushed his dusty, flat brimmed hat back on his head, revealing a lock of wavy black hair that drooped boyishly over his forehead. His eyes, shaded by thick dark lashes, were a startling blue in his tanned face. With all the appreciation of an artist, Genevieve studied those bronzed features, knowing that this man could have modeled for any of the greatest sculptors of the world. Fine, arched brows, the high cheekbones of a Greek or Spaniard, a proud nose that might even have been broken once, a sensuous mouth that could smile and melt any woman's heart, a hard, square jaw that when set would warn any man not to take *this* man lightly.

"You got a problem, lady?" he asked suddenly,

6

giving Genevieve the full force of his blue gaze.

She was caught and she knew it.

"I was afraid of being crushed," she managed to respond while she tried unsuccessfully not to blush. She doubted that he noticed. He had already turned back to his determined contemplation of the approaching shoreline.

"It's always like this. 'Specially on a morning arrival."

He spoke matter of factly, as though she were expected to understand and therefore accept the press of unfamiliar, unwashed bodies.

That thought prompted another, and Genevieve was finally able to attach a name to this remarkable specimen.

"You're Mr. Jackson, the scout from the wagon train, aren't you," she said, unable to keep a trace of amazement — and disappointment — from her voice.

He nodded but didn't change the direction of his stare. Nor did he say anything.

Which meant that either he knew who Genevieve was and didn't need his knowledge confirmed, or he didn't know and didn't care.

And she couldn't for the life of her imagine why *she* cared.

So she turned her own attention back to the dock, which had grown considerably closer in just the past few moments. She could see the individual men waiting to grasp the ropes that would be thrown from the *Carolina* to make her fast. Already there was a row of drays and other vehicles waiting for prospective fares.

"Excuse me, Mr. Jackson, when we dock would you be so good as to procure me a carriage and load my luggage into it?"

"Sorry. I got things to do."

That was it. He didn't even look at her when he said it. She wanted to kick him, or stomp on his foot, but she suspected either action would inflict

7

far more pain to her than to him.

Besides, she was no longer the pampered little girl who had left New Orleans six months ago. She could handle these things herself now.

She braced herself for the bump of the boat touching the dock, but that didn't save her from the increased pressure of all those bodies behind her. A flush spread upwards from her throat when she realized that handsome, insolent Mr. Jackson was pressed with intimate tightness to her back. She could feel those buttons through her cloak and gown and even her undergarments.

Rio Jackson felt everything, too. What would normally have brought a grin of anticipated pleasure to his lips now generated only a grim line of determination.

In his line of work, Rio didn't meet many women like the one whose tight little bottom was pushed smack up against his thighs. Most of the women who came to California were as crazed with the fever as the men they accompanied. Once in a while there was a grumbling wife dragged along by a husband with dreams of riches, but that kind of woman held no attraction for Rio. He more frequently found himself in the company of a greedy but willing creature whose only interest lay in getting as much of the wealth coming out of the mountains and streams as she could without having to scratch for it herself.

The dark-haired beauty whose violet eyes had lavished him with such scorn a few minutes ago reminded him more of the pampered bitches he'd known in San Antonio. Only this one was from New Orleans, with a lilt of a French accent instead of Spanish in her insults.

As the jolt of the *Carolina* hitting the dock pushed Rio more firmly against the girl's posterior, he had to stifle a groan. The sooner he got off this boat and picked up his pay, the sooner he could find one of those willing creatures and ease the ache aroused by arrogant Mademoiselle Genevieve Marie du Prés.

Despite the frantic rush to disembark, the crowd on the dock dissipated slowly. Genevieve waited and watched, fascinated by the activity, the chaos. After the long dreary months with the wagon train, she savored the vitality of this first day in Sacramento.

Many of her fellow passengers hurried off the riverboat and headed toward the town itself, with no other luggage than what they carried on their backs or in their hands. Nearly all these were men, and she knew they had but one goal: to reach the goldfields and stake their claims as quickly as possible. She shook her head sadly, and whispered a silent prayer that she didn't have to follow them.

She did not, she reflected, endure hardship gracefully.

The sun was well up and the day had turned pleasantly warm when the dock was clear enough for her to consider venturing off the deck of the *Carolina*. Shifting her valise to her other hand, she moved slowly away from the rail and headed toward the gangplank.

A dozen men awaited her, all clamoring loudly enough to deafen her.

"Here, Miss, here, I'll take ye wherever ye want to go."

"Get yer luggage, Miss?"

"I know every hotel and boardin' house in Sacramento, Miss. Get ye the best rates, too."

"Cheapest transportation to the goldfields, honey."

". . . Get ye up there in two days time."

She stopped and stood stock still, letting her eyes wander over the crowd until her own silence stilled their chatter. The whole dock seemed to have quieted, save for the distant shouts of stevedores unloading freight.

When she had their complete attention, Genevieve opened her reticule and removed a carefully folded sheet of paper.

"Gentlemen, I am looking for two things in this fair city," she began. She pushed the hood of her cloak back, for it had grown too warm in the past hour, and she knew her audience would not be completely unimpressed by the full measure of her looks.

"You name it, honey, you got it," one of the men quipped.

She ignored him, except for a quick glance with those bright blue-violet eyes. She shuttered that glance behind a long sweep of ebony lashes, just as she had been taught by her mama.

"I require lodging at a suitable hotel," she said, with appropriate emphasis on that next to last word. "And then I would like any information you can find regarding the whereabouts of this man."

She unfolded the paper and held it up for all of them to see.

"His name is Jean-Louis Marmont," she went on to explain. "He is twenty-seven years old, approximately five feet ten inches in height, with blond hair and grey eyes."

The men around her turned to each other and muttered amongst themselves for a moment, then the quipster stepped forward and pushed his hat to the back of his head.

"This Jawn-Louie, he talk with a French accent, kinda like yours only worse?"

The man would never die from a surfeit of tact.

"Yes, he does. Like myself, he is from New Orleans."

Another of her would-be employees said, "That's gotta be Frenchy, Joe. Sports a fancy walkin' stick to cover a bit of a gimp?"

Genevieve felt another blush warm her throat. Jean-Louis was very self-conscious about his uneven gait and everyone in New Orleans took great pains

10

to avoid mentioning or even thinking about it.

"He was injured in a riding accident," she replied, falling back on the convenient lie that had become such a habit many believed it and had forgotten the truth.

The man with the hat stepped back and gave her a rather bold, quickly assessing gaze.

"It sure sounds like the same guy, but he ain't goin' by that fancy moniker now. Calls himself Johnny LeSaint these days." Again his eyes wandered up and down, taking in every detail of the young woman from her severely coifed blue-black hair to the dusty hem of her plain grey gown.

"Is something wrong, sir?" Genevieve prompted.

"Well, you'll have to excuse me, miss, but you just don't look like Frenchy's type."

She had no idea what he meant nor did she have the time to ask for clarification. Good God, Jean-Louis was right here in Sacramento! The realization hit her with enough of a shock to stop her heart for a beat or two.

What difference did it make if some dockworker thought she wasn't Jean-Louis' type? She was engaged to be married to him, or had been until he up and left her to chase some crazy notion of honor and integrity in this wilderness called California. But all that was behind them now.

She hadn't travelled all these thousands of miles to be told she wasn't suited for the man who had, less than a year ago, literally gone on his knees and begged her to become his wife. She had sneaked out of her parents' house, stowed away on a Mississippi riverboat, bribed her way into the wagon train, endured uncounted dangers and indignities as the wagons wended their way across the prairies and mountains, and finally suffered the snub of that insolent Mr. Jackson, all for one reason and one reason alone: to find her fiance and bring him back to New Orleans where he belonged.

11

While refolding her sketched portrait of Jean-Louis, Genevieve calmed her racing heart and then wiped her sweating palms on her skirt under the concealment of her cloak. With calm restored, she addressed her audience again.

"Whether you consider me a proper companion for this man calling himself Johnny LeSaint or not, it is important that I meet with him as soon as possible." There, she had her voice under control so it didn't rise to an excited squeak. And her knees weren't trembling anymore either. "If there is one of you who can transport me and my luggage to a respectable hotel and give me directions to find Mr. LeSaint, I would be much obliged."

There was a moment of tense silence, then the quick-tongued man tipped his hat forward once more and let out a short bark of a laugh.

"Hell's bells, boys, if the lady wants to see Frenchy, that's her business. I ain't gonna turn down a payin' customer just 'cause I don't approve of her destination. Hell, I don't approve of all these idiots traipsin' off into the mountains with no more sense than God gave a daffodil neither, but it don't stop me from takin' their money!"

He doffed the hat entirely and swept it with a flourish in front of Genevieve.

"At your service, ma'am," he mocked, but without malice. "The Parkland ain't Sacramento's finest, but it's clean and decent and won't cost you an arm and a leg neither."

Another wagon clattered by, forcing Rio to pull his horse off to one side or risk an accident. The big palomino was skittish after two days aboard the *Carolina,* and Rio admitted to himself that he wasn't paying close enough attention to his horse to guarantee he could control him in an emergency.

His mind was fully occupied with other things.

12

The uncanny sense of direction and memory for landmarks that had landed him the job bringing gold seekers to California brought him unerringly to the bank building he had visited only once before in his life. Like Sacramento, the building had grown from the wooden-fronted structure that had occupied the site last spring. Now the Miners and Merchants Bank boasted a two-story granite facade complete with fluted columns and leaded glass windows. Rio contemplated the new opulence with a skeptical eye, then dismounted and tied the fractious golden stallion to the hitching rail.

Inside, the bank was busy, but even the sounds of business were muted under the vaulted ceiling. Rio squelched an urge to tiptoe to the teller's cage.

He pulled the letter from his pocket and pushed it under the grille.

The teller took a pair of wire-rimmed spectacles from the top of his balding head and slowly read the letter. Rio noticed the little man's lips moved with each word.

"This will be just a moment, Mr. Jackson." The teller eyed him suspiciously over the rims of those glasses. "Mr. Bruckner will have to approve the disbursal of these funds."

Rio bit back a retort. He'd been through this before, but it was humiliating none the less. Still, there was five hundred dollars waiting for him at the end of it; he could put up with a sneer or two for that kind of cash.

He drummed his fingers on the marble counter and stared up at the ceiling, lost in shadows even at midday. Then Paul Bruckner's voice shattered the staid, businesslike quiet.

"Rio! For God's sake, man, why didn't you let me know you were coming?"

As tall as Rio but slender and fair, the banker clasped his arms around his friend's massive shoulders, then held him at arm's length and grinned.

"Damn you, old man, you get handsomer all the time. If my Angie weren't in a family way, I'd be afraid to take you home to her."

A man shouldn't blush, but Rio felt his cheeks grow warm. Thank God months on the trail had bronzed his skin to a color that hid the rush of red, the same rush that had tinged that little New Orleans strumpet's cheeks that morning.

"Paul," Rio cautioned, "your customers are beginning to stare."

Bruckner chuckled and relaxed his grip on Rio's shoulders.

"If more of my customers were women, I'm sure you wouldn't mind their stares. Come on, we'll take this little piece of paper into my office and get your money for you."

Rio removed his hat and followed Paul Bruckner's energetic strides up a flight of marble stairs to an office overlooking the main bank lobby.

"You will come home with me tonight, won't you, Rio?" the young banker asked. He sat down behind a massive, richly carved mahogany desk and reached for a pen.

"I got things to do."

Rio longed to run a finger around his collar. Even though the top button was undone, he felt as if he were being slowly strangled. The room seemed to close in on him, its oak panelled walls threatening to converge and crush the air out of his lungs.

Paul looked up, pen in hand poised over the piece of paper.

"Is that a refusal?" he asked quietly.

Rio twisted his hat in his hands and stared at the toes of his dusty boots. "Yeah, I guess it is."

Bruckner affixed his signature to the bottom of the letter and then slid the paper across the desk. Rio looked at it but didn't pick it up.

"Why? Angie gets a big kick showing off the new house, and we don't get a whole lot of visitors who haven't already had the grand tour."

There was no guile in Paul Bruckner, which made it hard for Rio to dislike him, even when he was as persistent as he was being right now. But Paul was a banker, educated, polished, at ease in every situation. All the things Rio Jackson wasn't, and could never be.

He reached for the paper and Paul's pen. It took a minute to find the familiar letters printed where he was to sign. Slowly, carefully, he copied them, aware as he did so that Paul discreetly looked away.

But it was better than having to make a wavering "X", which was the way Rio Jackson had signed his name up until a year ago.

"Thanks, Paul," he whispered. The awkward moment was passing. his self confidence starting to return. "Keep that invitation open."

They both knew he'd never accept it, but this was a way for both to save face.

"Is there anything I can do for you, Rio?"

"You done quite enough." he replied, taking the letter into his hand. He set his hat back on his head and walked with long easy strides to the door, then turned to face the young banker again. "Yeah, there is something you could do for me. Steer me towards the best hotel in town, and the fanciest whorehouse."

Genevieve surveyed her accommodations with a critical eye and was not disappointed. Though not luxurious, the second floor room at the Parkland Hotel offered a large, comfortable bed, maple wardrobe and washstand, lace curtains at the window overlooking the street, and a bright braided rug on the floor.

"Bath's at the end of the corridor," the porter informed her. "I'll see to it you got extra towels, Miss, if you'll give me five minutes."

15

He slid her trunk into the middle of the room, then made way for another man to bring in the second. Genevieve dropped a coin into each outstretched palm and then waited until they had left her alone.

Exhausted, she fell backwards onto the bed. With no effort at all, she could fall asleep right now, before noon, and sleep until the next day. The desire to close her eyes and do just that tempted her strongly, but she did not give in to it. Even now, word of her arrival in Sacramento might have reached Jean-Louis, and she did not want to risk his deciding to run away again.

She gave a moment's consideration to the possibility of confronting him immediately. That course of action had its merits: the element of surprise might give her an advantage in persuading him to return with her at once to New Orleans.

The lessons and habits of a lifetime, however, made the decision for her. Genevieve Marie du Prés, who had turned down eight proposals of marriage in one evening, who had received gifts and flowers and poetry nearly every day from dozens of admirers, who had her pick of the eligible men in three states, could not possibly face her fugitive fiance until she had bathed, washed and curled her hair, and hung the wrinkles out of her blue satin gown.

There was nothing she could do about the golden tint six months in the sun had given her skin. After her bath — she had soaked until the water was cold and stagnant and her hands were as wrinkled as her gown — Genevieve studied her reflection in the little mirror over her washstand. At least the sun hadn't put freckles across her nose. And, as she turned slowly from one side to the other, she couldn't say she was displeased with her heightened color.

What Jean-Louis would think of it was another matter.

16

"He can be dealt with," she told her reflection firmly. "Haven't I always dealt with him?"

Before the image in the glass could remind her that she had not been able to deal with Jean-Louis when he left her in New Orleans, Genevieve turned away from the mirror.

Two hours later, dressed in the blue gown, with a matching lace-trimmed parasol to shade her from further depredations of the sun, Genevieve Marie du Prés stepped out the door of the Parkland Hotel in Sacramento, California. It was 3:45 in the afternoon.

The street was busy, but no more so than any major thoroughfare in New Orleans. Genevieve glanced to her right and left, then stepped smartly into the soft dust. She had already committed to memory the direction the slightly befuddled hotel clerk had given her.

"You sure you want the Maison de Versailles?" he had asked when she first requested instructions. At her insistence, he shrugged and told her, "North two blocks, then turn right. It's about the third place, not much on the outside, so be careful you don't miss it."

Genevieve was quite certain she would not miss it.

Rio lay back in the big copper tub with a contented sigh. Closing his eyes, he groped under the water for the cloth and lathered it lavishly. He intended to soak and scrub until there wasn't a speck of Missouri, Kansas, Nebraska, or any other state or territory left on his body.

"Shave, too?" Lo Pau, the Chinese attendant, asked as he stropped the razor Rio had left on the washstand.

"Sure, why not. Don't want to scratch the ladies."

A man could get used to all this luxury, Rio told himself. It's a shame everything cost so damn much.

After the hotel room, the bath and shave, and the dinner he had ordered sent to his room, he hoped he'd have enough left to afford a night's entertainment. Bruckner had told him the new establishment going by the florid name of Maison de Versailles was reputed to be expensive, but happily married Paul couldn't speak from personal experience.

Hell, everything else in Sacramento was sky high, why shouldn't the whores charge more? Rio frowned, drawing a hiss from Lo Pau.

"No make face, Mr. Jackson," he cautioned. "No want cut your throat."

Rio almost laughed, but Lo Pau quickly plied the razor again.

So Rio just smiled to himself and submitted to the expert ministrations of the wiry Chinese. What a difference this was from the last time someone had come close to cutting Rio Jackson's throat open. From a dusty back street in San Antonio to a luxury hotel in Sacramento. And this time the blue-eyed, black-haired boy hadn't had to fight his way out from under the blade held at his chin.

The bullies had learned to respect him after that, after he had trounced their leader in a less-than-fair fight. But the black eye, the broken nose, and the bruises that left him stiff for a week had taught Rio a painful lesson, too. One he never had and never would forget. All the perfumed baths and shaves by pigtailed Chinamen, all the fancy clothes and fancy women, wouldn't change Rio Jackson from what he was, what he'd always been.

He wiped the last of the shaving soap from his face and then stood to let Lo Pau wrap a big soft towel around him. Accepting a lavish tip from the tall man, Lo Pau bowed respectfully and backed out of the room. He closed the door with a soft click of the latch.

Rio took a second towel and ducked his head into it to dry his freshly trimmed hair. He felt good to be clean, free of shaggy hair hanging over his collar, free of the last of the beard he had clumsily shaved off his first night on the *Carolina*. Checking his reflection in the long mirror, he allowed himself a satisfied grin.

The San Antonio bullies hadn't been able to take away his looks. Broken nose and all, Rio knew few women were immune to him. Even that haughty little New Orleans witch on the boat this morning. He had seen the look of admiration in her eyes when she turned and found him scrunched right behind her. Then she had recognized him as the scout who had brought her wagon train from Missouri to California, and she'd given him a long stare of disgust.

"Bet I could change your mind," he muttered as he finished drying his skin and reached for the clean clothes laid out on the bed.

But he knew he'd never have the chance to alter the proud beauty's way of thinking, so he might just as well put her sleek ebony hair, her violet blue eyes, her—*all* of her out of his mind right now. It'd be one thing if he could dress up in a linen shirt with gold studs and a natty fawn-colored coat like the one Paul Bruckner had worn in the bank. The best Rio Jackson, half-Mexican wagon train scout, could muster was clean cotton shirt and black whipcord pants.

Clothes didn't matter, not tonight, he reminded himself. In just a few minutes he'd sit down to a fine meal, to be enjoyed in complete and blessed privacy. No one would see or care if he used the right fork or knife or held his wine glass properly. And when he had licked the last of the butter-drenched lobster from his fingers and crunched the last shrimp tail with belly-warming satisfaction, Rio Jackson would stroll on down the street to the latest addition to Sacramento's growing collection of bawdyhouses. Its name was French, and Paul had said the guy who ran it talked like a real Frenchman, though Rio had

19

his doubts. Then again, anything was possible in Sacramento these days. Hell, he might even get laid by a real French whore at the Maison de Versailles.

Chapter Two

Genevieve blamed her error on pride which wouldn't allow her to appear too curious, too unsure of her whereabouts. Rather than examine closely every door she passed, she depended on discreet sidelong glances, and they weren't enough. She didn't find the entrance to the Maison de Versailles until she had strolled past it three times.

There being neither bell nor knocker, she placed her hand firmly on the handle and twisted. It turned more easily than she expected; she could have pushed the door open and walked right in. Instead, she paused for just a moment and mumbled a quick prayer that Jean-Louis would be at this place and that she could put an end to her quest tonight.

As she nudged the door inward, she took one of those instinctive glances around, as though assailed by a sudden and unaccountable guilt. Further down the street she saw a tall, broad-shouldered man swing down from an open carriage, and for a split second her heart rose into her throat. When he turned toward her, however, she saw that he was not so much broad as fat, and his full beard was a dingy red sprinkled liberally with grey.

Relieved, Genevieve ducked into the Maison de Versailles and wondered why she had been so worried about being noticed by someone as inconsequential as a wagon train scout.

Her worry vanished almost instantly, to be replaced by an ever increasing sense of amazement.

She had taken two or three steps inside the building, just enough to allow the door to swing shut behind her. It closed so silently she did not even have the snap of a latch or the squeak of hinges to warn her. Deprived of the afternoon sunlight, she was plunged into a moment's darkness, until her eyes adjusted and she became aware of a soft dim light.

It was lamplight, filtered through the gauze of a beaded curtain separating the unlit vestibule where she waited from a larger room. Of the interior of this room, Genevieve could see little, save for two chairs covered in red leather, one on either side of a marble-topped gilt table on which rested a lamp with a red glass shade. A brass spittoon occupied the corner behind one of the chairs, but beyond that, Genevieve could see nothing. She walked closer, cautious, curious, but not yet afraid.

Just as she raised a hand to push aside the curtain, she felt the soft brush of moving air at her back that signalled the entrance of another person into the vestibule, from a side door Genevieve had not seen.

"May I help you?" a soft, feminine voice asked.

Genevieve turned, suddenly aware that this person stood between her and the door to the street.

They stood in silence for a long minute, while Genevieve's eyes further adapted to the dark and while the other woman waited for a reply to her question.

"Is this the Maison de Versailles?" Genevieve asked slowly, keeping as much of her thoughts out of her voice as possible. She knew she must not appear eager or afraid or curious or shocked.

"It is." Yes, there was a trace of an accent in the woman's voice, but Genevieve could not tell if it were genuine. "I am Yvonne, and though the Maison is not usually open until seven o'clock in the evening, I will try to help you as best I can."

The accent was good, but it was not genuine. Nor, Genevieve decided, was much else about this Yvonne. The brassy blonde hair owed its color to art, not nature, and the cunningly applied cosmetics hid a good many more years than Yvonne would probably admit to. A low-cut black gown that revealed generous amounts of bosom and shoulders also revealed the softness of flesh that had lost the resilience of youth.

"Come, we will be more comfortable in the blue salon," she invited, holding aside the shimmering curtain to allow Genevieve to precede her. "To your left, please."

Genevieve passed, then waited for her guide. She had already noticed the glittering stones so prominently displayed on Yvonne's hands. Imitations, every one, and cheap ones at that.

Yvonne had hurried Genevieve so quickly through the red room that she had no time to satisfy her curiosity. The adjoining room, which she assumed from the sapphire tones of the furnishings to be the blue salon, was probably little different.

Opulent to the point of garishness, it threatened to overwhelm her. Velvet draperies festooned with gold braid and tassels hung over two tall windows, shutting out the afternoon sun. A pair of lamps shed soft light that did little to relieve the oppressive atmosphere.

A long sofa dominated the room, upholstered in deep blue damask. Yvonne glided to it and sank down languorously at one end, then, when Genevieve held back, the older woman nodded an invitation to join her.

"Are you thinking you have come to the wrong place?" Yvonne asked, accurately guessing Genevieve's thoughts.

Was it possible? she asked herself. No, she had

23

shown the men on the wharf Jean-Louis' portrait, and they had identified him beyond any doubt. Yvonne had already confirmed that this was indeed the Maison de Versailles, and who else but Jean-Louis would name his business establishment after the palace he had fallen in love with when he and Genevieve had visited it together a few years ago?

Even if it were the wrong place, Genevieve Marie du Prés was not going to be intimidated into leaving until she had found out for sure.

She took the sketched portrait from her reticule once more and handed it to Yvonne.

"I am looking for this man," she said firmly. "I understand he may be using the name Johnny Le-Saint, though his real name is Jean-Louis Marmont. I was told he is the owner of this establishment."

Yvonne glanced absently at the portrait, then laid it on the sofa beside her. She did not give it back to Genevieve, nor did she display any intention of doing so. Well, it didn't matter. She could keep it if she liked: Genevieve had only to draw another.

"So, you are looking for Johnny LeSaint. And why are you looking for him?"

Genevieve tilted her chin up.

"That is business I will discuss only with him."

Yvonne threw her head back and laughed, a hoarse, unattractive bray like an angry mule.

When she had stopped laughing, she turned an angry gaze on Genevieve.

"What kind of 'establishment' do you think this is?" she asked, all trace of accent gone.

Genevieve Marie du Prés had encountered many dangers in the past six months. She had been cold and hungry and thirsty and hot and tired beyond any endurance she might have thought she possessed. She had lied, and she had bribed men to break rules of their own making, and she had come very close to stealing and even to murder. On many of those nights on the prairie she had cried herself to

24

sleep, not from homesickness, but from frustration and impatience. She had been prepared to face bloodthirsty savages, venomous reptiles, man-eating beasts, and a host of other dangers that never materialized.

She had known privation and apprehension, but never fear.

She felt it now, as her mind grabbed hold of the thought that had hovered just out of reach since the moment she set foot through that unmarked door.

Yvonne's malicious answer to her own question sent a shiver down Genevieve's spine.

"You are in the biggest, most expensive, most exotic whorehouse in Sacramento, honey. You just sit down here and wait a minute, and I'll go get Johnny for you."

The man who had stunned the male population of New Orleans by persuading the elusive Genevieve Marie du Prés to accept his proposal of marriage stroked with one hand the silken red hair of a half-dressed, over-eager whore while he stared at the creased portrait of himself held in the other.

"It's not possible," he repeated, for the tenth or eleventh time. He looked up at Yvonne, who rested one hip on the edge of Jean-Louis' walnut desk. "Did she say her name was Genevieve?"

"No, you fool. And I didn't ask her. I didn't have to. Christ, you've talked about the bitch often enough. Don't you think I'd know her when she set foot in my parlor?"

"*My* parlor now," he corrected. He shoved the red-head off his lap and waved her absently out of his presence. She pouted for a moment, then, when Yvonne repeated Jean-Louis' gesture, escaped through a sliding door. "How did she ever find me? How did she ever get here?"

Yvonne shrugged.

"Same as the others. Same as you, maybe."

"Not by boat, it would have taken her longer. She had to come overland, wagon train probably." He shook his head. "No, not her. Not the banker's spoiled daughter. More likely she hired a carriage for the whole trip."

He got to his feet and reached automatically for the gold-headed ivory cane that was never far away. Its thudding accompaniment to his pacing on the worn carpet punctuated his anger and served to focus his thoughts.

"She is in the blue room, no?" he asked, almost lapsing back into the French he had been raised to speak.

"Yes, but she's not locked in. I don't think she'll leave, though."

Jean-Louis snorted a knowing laugh.

"She's capable of anything, especially what you don't think she'll do. She came all the way out here, to California, to find me."

"Whatever for," Yvonne muttered, the words silenced by the thud of Jean-Louis' cane.

"If she had just married me when I wanted her to, none of this would have happened," he lamented. "But no, she wanted a long engagement, with lots of parties."

Yvonne draped herself on the little settee where Jean-Louis had been fondling the redhead. At least one of them ought to be comfortable. He'd probably pace until he grumbled about his knee. That's the way it usually went when things didn't go his way.

She had heard the story often enough in the past two months to be able to recite it with him. Drunk or sober, he rarely changed a word of it.

"My father and hers, they were partners, but in name only. Victor du Prés had the fine house, the rich wife, the golden touch with money. All his investments prospered, until he was wealthy beyond imagining."

26

It sounded almost like a fairy tale, but Yvonne put it down to Johnny's flair for the dramatic, a Gallic flourish with which he did almost everything.

"For my father, life wasn't so generous. Etienne Marmont's ventures failed more often than not. But could his wife and son suffer? Of course not. Because Victor du Prés expected us to live as he and his family did, until it was more than we could afford. Yes, my father embezzled, but only because Victor and that virginal whore of his daughter drove my father to it!"

Yvonne yawned, as much out of exhaustion as boredom. She'd had little enough sleep last night, then had to rise early to prepare for the evening's entertainment. Johnny boasted he had done it all on his own, but she knew better. After all, she had been in this business twenty years. She had lost the building to him in a carefully manipulated poker game so he could be responsible for the mortgage. If her gamble paid off, she'd win everything back and be sitting pretty once again. If not, well, Frenchy could pay the bills for a while, even if Yvonne and the girls had to skip town and start over again. They'd done it before.

He paced for another minute or two, then paused, leaning heavily on the cane. Yvonne watched him from beneath droopy lids. The leering grin that slowly spread over his face told her he was thinking something nasty.

"You'd better not stand there too long," she reminded him. "She's likely to get tired of waiting."

The Frenchman's misty-colored eyes hardened.

"She'll wait as long as I want her to."

Yvonne translated that to mean he was worried and would rush to see if his visitor had indeed left.

"In fact, I believe Mademoiselle du Prés will be staying for quite a while." Had he been looking at Yvonne, Jean Louis would have noticed the look of warning she threw at him. But he had complicated

27

plans to be set in motion, and so he focused on the gold head of his walking stick rather than the woman. "Move Serafina to Number Three, if you can get the lazy slut to walk that far. Then clean Number Five thoroughly. Fresh linens, fresh flowers."

"Serafina won't like it."

"Then put her out on the street and tell her to peddle her ass elsewhere!" Jean-Louis exploded. "Be glad I'm not asking for *your* room!"

Yvonne had already thought of that.

"You'll want supper taken to Number Five as well?" she asked.

He shook his head.

"No, just champagne. Genevieve loves champagne."

The blonde madame got to her feet and smoothed the flounces of her black dress. It was none of her business if Johnny wanted to seduce the little strumpet. Yvonne herself had no interest in him. Oh, she liked younger men, the younger the better, and the man who called himself Johnny LeSaint couldn't be but half her age. But Yvonne's experience demanded that her lovers be capable of performing like men, not like boys, and she had already found the Frenchman lacking.

As she headed to comply with Johnny's orders, she wondered again why on earth the impetuous Miss du Prés had come halfway across the continent in search of this man.

Yvonne had just stepped into the hallway and was about to pull the door shut behind her when Johnny called to her.

"Yes?" she purred.

"Buster Kulkey was invited to our little soiree, wasn't he?"

Ordinarily, Yvonne would have done no more than wrinkle her nose in disgust at the mention of that name. This time she felt a sheen of sweat break

28

out on her brow and between her shoulder blades.

"Yes, of course he was," she answered.

Johnny smiled, and Yvonne knew there was wickedness behind that smile.

"Very good. Now, see that Number Five is readied, and send a bottle of our best champagne to the blue salon."

Rio stepped into the night air and filled his lungs with its freshness. The sun was just going down, leaving Sacramento bathed in that fine golden glow of twilight. It seemed almost a crime to disturb the peace of the hour with the city's noise, but Rio knew there was no stopping progress. Especially in Sacramento.

Still, he himself could take a moment to enjoy the fading of the day, the kindling of the first points of starlight. Somewhere behind the mountains, a big fat golden moon was rising. He had watched it last night, just short of its fullness, while he paced the riverboat's deck. Too many nights spent under open skies left him restless in the tiny cabin, and he had strolled impatiently for hours, until sheer exhaustion helped him fall asleep long past midnight.

Tonight he'd seek a more welcome kind of exhaustion.

Bruckner's description of the place was surprisingly accurate for a man who claimed never to have been there. The entrance door was plain, windowless, and only a small bronze plaque just above eye level identified the establishment. Rio examined the raised letters for a moment, then looked to see if any other building on the block had so discreet a sign. He found none.

In the vestibule, a small room itself with closed doors leading to the right and left as well as the arched entry to a red-decorated salon, Rio removed his hat and waited patiently. He barely had time to glance around and appreciate his surroundings when a voluptuous blonde, well past her prime, came out of the salon to greet the newcomer.

He stood still, hat in hand, a vague smile on his face, until she had finished her appraisal. She might not be too impressed by his clothes, but if she was like most women in her profession, she'd know there were all kinds of riches beneath.

"Welcome, monsieur," she purred, "to la Maison de Versailles. You have chosen the perfect evening for your first visit."

He raised an eyebrow, but said nothing. The woman gave him another appreciative once-over before leading him into the red room.

The bottom immediately dropped out of his stomach.

The place was gaudy beyond belief. Everything, from floor to ceiling, chairs to chandeliers, was swathed, upholstered, draped or painted scarlet and gold. Pleasure didn't come cheaply in a place like this. When contemplating the cost of purchased ecstasy, Rio had earlier only wondered if he really wanted to waste good, hard-earned gold to the tune of a hundred dollars for a night with a whore. Now, following the plump madame, he doubted that hundred would buy him even an hour in the Maison de Versailles, much less a whole night.

Though there were no other patrons in the salon, the evidence of empty whiskey glasses and cigar stubs told Rio the room had only recently been vacated. The acrid stink of tobacco smoke still hung in the air.

Rio's guide pulled open a pair of heavy doors that gave access to another room, as splendid as the first. Here he saw gaming tables, though these had been pushed against the walls. Neat rows of gilt chairs now filled the space, and not a one was empty.

Thirty-five, maybe forty men, of varying ages, descriptions, and finances, fidgeted impatiently. Some still puffed on their cigars, sending ribbons of smoke to the plaster ceiling. Some chatted with their companions. Lusty chuckles were not uncommon.

"I'm afraid you are too late for a good seat, monsieur," the buxom proprietress apologized. "But the auction should take only a few minutes."

"Auction?" Good God, what had he stumbled into? An illegal slave market in Sacramento?

"You didn't know? Ah, well, then I must explain quickly, for it is nearly time to begin."

Yvonne wondered if she were wasting her time with this one. He didn't look like he could afford the least expensive of her girls, let alone one of the new additions. But one look at his breadth of shoulder, the lean length of thigh and calf, the rugged planes of his face, the startling blue of his eyes, and she knew she couldn't turn him away.

"I have three new 'ladies' joining us tonight, and I always give my regular clients the first opportunity to enjoy their special charms," she explained. "They will go to the highest bidders, then I will open the house for normal business."

Rio swallowed and felt an uncomfortable knot form at the back of his throat. Something about this whole procedure repulsed him, yet he made no move to leave, for beneath the repulsion lurked an intense fascination.

"I'm not one of your regular customers," he remarked.

She smiled and ran the tip of her tongue over brightly rouged lips.

"Perhaps you will be, after tonight."

She gave him another sweeping appraisal.

"If you will excuse me, monsieur? Please, there is whiskey and champagne. Be my guest for this evening."

She touched two fingers to her lips, then reached up to transfer the kiss suggestively to his own. The

31

gesture left him wary, but with no doubt as to her intentions.

Because of his height, Rio had no trouble seeing over the heads of the men seated in front of him to the low platform to which the madame slowly walked. As she took her place at its center, the crowd grew silent. Rio looked around and found the whiskey she had offered. Still entranced by the erotic "business" about to be conducted, he filled a glass and leaned comfortably against the back wall to watch.

Some of his fascination faded when the first woman appeared on the block. He must have been expecting a lush, exotic virgin, he laughed to himself, because the scantily clad redhead displayed herself with such practiced abandon that though she might be "new' to this house of joy, she was a veteran of the trade.

Eager to spend their wealth on fresh flesh, the men quickly pushed the bid to five hundred dollars. Rio shrugged. He might not be able to buy himself an evening's companionship here, but the whiskey was good — and free — and there was always the possibility that the madame might offer herself at a similar price. She wouldn't be the first. So while she slowed the bidding to let the redhead shamelessly strut her stuff before the randy crowd, Rio sipped his whiskey and studied his competition.

A clock somewhere struck twice, signaling the half hour. Genevieve stifled a yawn and the urge to press her fingertips to her throbbing temples. She had long ago dismissed any feeling of joy at having found her betrothed. Now, after two and a half hours in his company, she felt only weary, disappointed, and confused.

"Jean-Louis, I must take my leave now," she insisted. She had listened to him long enough, hearing pathetic excuses, whining complaints, and blatant lies until her head ached with the effort of trying to justify his unprincipled actions. "I believe it would be in your best interest to accompany me. The sooner we return to New Orleans, the sooner we can put this whole sordid episode behind us and get on with our lives."

She had never before uttered such stilted, insincere nonsense. But never before had she been forced to endure such an insult to her intelligence as the charade Jean-Louis had played for her this afternoon.

If it weren't that she'd have to admit her mission a failure, she thought his refusal to return with her might actually come as a relief. Even so, his announcement took her by surprise.

"I think not, my dear," he said in an odd tone of voice, much different from the grovelling whine she had come to loathe. He took out a silver cased watch and snapped it open, then shut it with satisfied finality. "Come, drink up, else I'm afraid you will wish later on you'd had more."

That was the last straw. After an afternoon spent on an uncomfortable sofa in an oppressively gaudy salon in a house of prostitution, Genevieve could not stand another trial to her patience.

"You are talking nonsense, Jean-Louis," she accused.

"Am I?"

She picked up her reticule and stood.

"Yes, you are. And I am leaving at once."

He rose, too, and for an instant Genevieve suffered a rush of nervous fear. Seated, Jean-Louis seemed no taller than she, and the absurdity of his claims and complaints left her feeling so much older and wiser than he that she had begun to look upon him as one would a child, immature and selfish. Standing, he was once again an adult, taller than she by half a foot or more. And though not a muscular man, Jean-Louis was still male, still stronger than she.

33

But he had always been a weakling, easily manipulated, too cowardly to stand up for himself. Genevieve simply turned her back to him and walked toward the door.

He told her, "It's locked," and plopped back onto the sofa, stretching one arm casually along its back. "Now, remove that hideous gown and whatever petticoats you have on under it."

She whirled to face him.

"Jean-Louis, have you lost your mind?"

He ignored her and went on as though she had not spoken at all.

"I can't decide whether you should take down your hair or leave it up. Some men would undoubtedly find it exciting unbound, but you might be tempted to hide your charms behind it." He seemed to ponder the alternatives a moment, then said in a mocking, syrupy voice, "Do co-operate, Genevieve, and don't force me to remove your clothing for you. Before you even think of screaming or doing something equally foolish, let me point out that the room across the hall is presently occupied by thirty six of the most loyal and enthusiastic patrons of the Maison de Versailles. They are enjoying an auction, my dear, of two very lovely, very willing, very provocative young women. Under such influence, those gentlemen will most likely not be in the proper frame of mind to rescue you."

An eerie blackness descended over Genevieve. It closed in on her, narrowing her field of vision until all she saw was the man who lounged on the blue sofa. Her heart pounded, and the blood roared in her ears like thunder. She knew she was going to faint, and in a way she welcomed the oblivion as preferable to the horror Jean-Louis offered her.

No, she refused to take that cowardly way out. She had not come this far only to shrink in the face of the first real danger she encountered. She forced her knees to stop quivering, and pushed back the

34

cloud of unconsciousness that would have engulfed her.

She reached behind her to begin unfastening the long row of buttons down the back of the dress. She had to stall, think of a way to escape. Jean-Louis himself was incapable of chasing her, and she could not imagine that any peace officer would return her to a brothel once she had told her story. Once beyond the confines of the Maison de Versailles, she would be safe—and free.

"Please hurry, Genevieve," Jean-Louis ordered without so much as glancing her way. "We are on a very strict schedule this evening. Yvonne will be here at precisely 6:45 to take you to the auction block."

Genevieve's heart fell to her toes. She had counted on Jean-Louis to be her only escort. Yvonne might be female, but she was not hampered with a shattered knee. Nor, Genevieve was certain, did Yvonne possess an overabundance of scruples. The blonde madame would no doubt do everything in her power to turn a tidy profit from the sale of another young body.

There was nothing to be done but go along with Jean-Louis and his diabolical plan—for now. With a deep breath to calm her fears and steel her nerves, Genevieve slipped the first button of her dress from its loop. Several doors had been closed behind her, but that did not mean another might not open in front of her. She would have to be vigilant so that she did not miss any such opportunity that came her way.

The redhead went for a cool nine hundred dollars. Raucous cheers greeted Yvonne's cry of "Sold!" and the high bidder's companions clapped him enviously on the back as he staggered to the dais to claim his purchase.

Rio shook his head and reached for the whiskey

35

bottle to refill his glass. He had a hundred dollars in gold in his pocket, plus some odd bits of change, but it would never be enough for this place. Still, the evening was young, and the entertainment was free.

The second girl was a blonde, young but fleshy, and almost too eager. Perhaps, Rio thought, they get a cut of what they bring in, and that's why they try so hard to get the price up. But it was clear from the beginning that this one would never fetch what the redhead had.

He was right. Less than five minutes later, Yvonne turned the girl over to a bearded young man with the deceptive appearance of a religious zealot for a mere four hundred fifty dollars, in gold. If the girl looked disappointed, her purchaser did not.

Yvonne excused herself for a moment to bring on the last of the evening's merchandise. Rio finished his drink and would have left, but one of the other patrons walked up to him and engaged him in conversation.

"New in town, ain't ya."

He was a big man, nearly as tall as Rio but heavier, with a substantial roll of fat overhanging his belt.

Rio decided it was safer to lie than contradict the man.

"Yeah," he agreed.

"Buster Kulkey," his companion said, extending a meaty hand with half the index finger missing.

"Jackson," was all Rio would say as he shook Kulkey's hand.

The big man grinned conspiratorially.

"You waitin' for the last one, too?" he asked. "There was only s'posed to be two of 'em tonight, but Yvonne always was one for surprises. And she saves the best for last, too."

Rio nodded but said nothing. Kulkey poured his own glass full, then topped off Rio's as well.

"Hope you got lots of cash, Mr. Jackson, 'cause

36

she's bound to go high." He laughed, displaying broken, rotten teeth. "I'd wish you luck, but I'm plannin' to out bid you, so I guess I'll keep my luck to myself!"

Kulkey staggered away then, still laughing, to join a small circle of men he obviously knew well.

Rio tossed down the rest of the whiskey and held his breath to savor the fiery explosion when it hit his stomach. The stink of Buster Kulkey's big, unwashed body lingered even over the cigar smoke and whiskey fumes. Reaching into his pocket, Rio muttered an angry curse under his breath. His hundred dollars was nothing compared to what a lucky bastard like Kulkey could put up to buy what he could never get for free.

The others moved back to their chairs for the final sale of the auction, but Rio turned his back on the ugly proceedings. It had lost all its appeal, even as a showcase for succulent female flesh. The blonde had been overweight for all her youth, and the redhead had been too cold, too professional, to suit his personal tastes.

He should leave. The whiskey was putting a bad taste in his mouth, and he had lost his sick fascination for this peddling of pleasure.

One more glass of whiskey, just enough to dull his senses for the time it would take to sneak out of the auction hall. Then, as he tipped his head up to swallow it, he caught sight of the movement at the front of the room. The freshly cut hairs at the back of his neck raised in a chill, and his hand slid instinctively to the gun at his hip.

Chapter Three

Genevieve swallowed a cry of sheer terror as she stepped into the room, Jean-Louis' hand supporting hers in mocking imitation of courtly manners. No one could see that he gripped her little finger in his until the pain brought uncontrollable tears to her eyes.

If she had drunk all the champagne he tried to force on her, she would undoubtedly have been sick right then and there. As it was, her stomach revolted at the sight of these leering, slavering beasts who dressed as men. She choked down the nausea lest it cloud her thinking. Above all else, she must keep her mind clear and alert.

"You are doing very well," Jean-Louis whispered through a tight, artificial smile. "And remember, it isn't forever. Just until you've repaid me everything your father squeezed from mine."

She had already tried offering him the money, deliverable when they returned to New Orleans, but he only laughed at her.

"It's not the money, my dear, it's the suffering, the wondering how much longer it can go on," he had informed her. "That's why I won't even tell you how much you owe me."

They approached the dais, with Yvonne walking ahead of them. Genevieve could already hear the whispers around her, hungry whispers, ugly whispers. She was cold, but sweat trickled between her breasts and down her back. Words pleading for mercy threatened to fly from her throat, but she choked them back. There was no mercy in this room, only the vilest of evil emotions.

She shivered, but to hide it and the fear it represented, Genevieve shook her head and let the cascade of her unbound hair ripple around her like a cloak. It concealed so little, yet gave her comfort all the same. She wasn't defeated yet, she reminded herself, and tilted her chin even higher.

Then, when Yvonne opened the bidding, Genevieve turned her gaze to the men who would try to own her. She fixed each and every one of them with the challenge of her glare, daring them to vanquish her spirit even as they mastered her body.

There were fewer than she had at first thought, though the odds against her were still astronomical: Three rows of twelve chairs each, arranged with an aisle down the middle leading to a pair of double doors. Closed tightly now, the doors opened outward, probably into the red salon. Beside them stood a small sideboard laid out with an assortment of whiskey bottles and glasses. Another patron of this sink of iniquity was calmly pouring himself a drink when a man in the front row suddenly called out, "Five hundred dollars!"

Genevieve swung her eyes to the first bidder, skewering him with the force of her gaze.

"Six!" another cried.

She tried to locate the source of that second bid, but almost immediately a third voice raised the amount to seven hundred dollars. Before she could put a face with that bid, two more had been shouted, and her value was an even thousand dollars.

There was a half second's silence, and Genevieve held her breath, wondering if the degrading experience had come to an end so quickly. She soon learned it had not.

A huge bear of a man from the last row got to his feet and was walking toward her. His gait was uneven, the result of too much drink, but he never faltered.

"Three thousand dollars, and that's the last bid, Yvonne," Buster Kulkey announced. "I want this one, and ain't nobody here can outbid me for her, so let's not waste nobody's time."

Genevieve heard the voice, heard the groans from the audience, and heard the transfer of a small leather sack of gold coins into Yvonne's hand. But she saw nothing of what happened no more than two feet from her, for the tall man at the back of the room had captured all her attention.

At first Rio simply didn't believe it. The prim and proper New Orleans aristocrat couldn't have been an act, and there was no other way to reconcile the Miss du Prés he had known all those months on the wagon train with the half-naked harlot presented for the delectation of a roomful of drooling lechers.

She certainly was delectable. He had come here tonight with pleasures of the flesh on his mind, but the way his body reacted to the sight of this proud beauty surprised him.

She stood as tall and straight as she could, with her shoulders thrust back in an air of defiance. Did she know such a stance emphasized the fullness of her breasts over the edge of her corset? Did she have any idea what the shimmer of her hair in the bright lamplight did to the itch in a man's fingers to slide through those long, free waves?

Then he saw her eyes, stabbing each of her would-be lovers with arrows of unmitigated hatred. She didn't fight, didn't even try to hide her near nakedness, but she wasn't here willingly.

He closed his hand around the butt of the Colt

40

revolver at his right hip and slowly withdrew it from its holster. Buster Kulkey was already reaching for the girl's hand, offered by the grinning pimp with the gold-headed cane. With no conscious effort at all, Rio calculated where to place each of his six shots, how to get the girl to the door, and which escape route offered the greatest chance of success.

A scream froze in Genevieve's throat. Her whole body seemed turned to ice, even the hand that was surrounded by the big man's rough fingers. The ringing in her ears almost drowned out the sound of angry mutterings from the crowd, but it made no difference. She didn't need to hear, only see.

This time she recognized Mr. Jackson the instant she saw his tall frame leaning against the door jamb. For that first instant she had thought all hope gone, as the blue-eyed half-breed tipped back his whiskey and swallowed. Then she met his eyes.

Was that subtle nod of his head a signal? She felt Jean-Louis release her hand, though the other was still trapped in her purchaser's big paw. Oh, God, Jackson *had* signalled, but what did he mean?

She was terrified, no matter how hard she tried to hide it behind that shroud of blue-black hair, but Rio had watched her long enough and often enough during their cross-country trek to know she was stubborn, too. And reckless. If ever there was a time for Genevieve Marie du Prés to be reckless, this was it.

"C'mon, Frenchy," Buster Kulkey urged when Genevieve dragged her feet. "You and me's got business to tend to upstairs."

She had to slow him down as much as possible. That was what the nod from the scout had told her. Delay the inevitable, and maybe you can avoid it completely, she told herself. But Kulkey was driven by a blind lust that would not be denied, and he was growing impatient.

Ten steps separated her from Jackson and the

41

doors. He moved, lazily, to open them for Kulkey's convenience, then swung back with a slightly crooked grin on his face. Genevieve groaned, thinking him drunk, and stumbled to her knees.

Buster Kulkey loosed an obscenity and bent down to jerk the girl to her feet. When he looked up, the long barrel of a Colt revolver greeted him, six inches from his belly.

"I'll take the girl," Rio told him in a soft voice. He didn't wait for Kulkey to comply; he reached for Genevieve's hand without ever taking his eyes or the barrel of the Colt from Kulkey.

She looked at that strong brown hand and almost took it, but the open doors beckoned. From the red salon to the street was no more than a few strides, and she didn't need Jackson's help to get that far.

But Kulkey hadn't released her other hand.

"I paid three thousand bucks for her, and I ain't givin' her up without a fi — "

The gun never wavered as Rio backhanded Kulkey, splitting the fat man's lip open and loosening his vise-like grip on the girl's hand.

Ten seconds had elapsed since Rio confronted Kulkey; he knew he had no more than five left.

"Now!" he ordered the stunned Genevieve.

She grabbed his hand, then cried out when he pulled her roughly to her feet and slung her toward the barely open doors. Before she had any chance to recover from the shock, he was beside her, in the red salon, slamming the doors with a thud that shook the whole building.

"Get the other door!" he hissed at her. Damn, didn't she realize they had seconds, not hours, not even minutes? Already there were heavy bodies pushing against the doors while Rio struggled with the key he remembered Yvonne had left on this side of them.

"The other is locked, from the inside," Genevieve told him.

42

For a split second they stared at each other, breathless, uncertain, on the edge of panic. Then Rio grinned and grabbed for her hand as he bolted toward the exit.

"Let's get outta here!" he suggested. He grasped the edge of the beaded curtain and ripped it loose from the ceiling.

He had just pulled the door to the street open when the crash of splintering wood exploded behind them. Genevieve jumped ahead of him with no further encouragement necessary.

She sucked crisp October air into her lungs and turned instinctively in the direction of the Parkland Hotel. She had taken only one step when strong arms encircled her waist and lifted her off the ground.

"Put me down!" she screamed. She lashed out with her feet, but they kicked only air. Before she could scream again, those arms hoisted her up and over a broad, hard shoulder, knocking the wind out of her. Something cold and heavy descended over her head and shoulders, and when she tried to raise her head, she found herself peering through the beaded fabric her rescuer had torn from the whorehouse doorway.

"I ain't gonna fight with you, lady," Rio explained. He dodged a slow-moving wagon and hurried across the busy street. "That fella Kulkey is gonna have that door broke down in a blink of an eye, and that's all the time we got to get out of sight."

"Then put me down," Genevieve begged, each of his steps jarring a gasp from her. She had given up trying to escape because she had to concentrate on breathing and hanging on. "Surely I can run faster than you can carry me."

"Maybe, but we ain't goin' far. Now, shut up, unless you want me to put you down and you can fight it out with Kulkey yourself."

43

Reluctantly, she acquiesced, but she wondered if she had escaped one kind of bondage only to land in another. Surely there could be nothing dignified in being carried about Sacramento like a sack of potatoes over some madman's shoulder.

What had made her trust this Jackson anyway? Genevieve groaned and cursed out loud. He was a patron of that place, no better than any of the other lecherous animals. Worse, because he hadn't even paid for her services. He was a common thief!

No, not common at all, she reminded herself. The image came back to her of the man who had stood behind her on the deck of the riverboat only that morning. Until she'd remembered who he was, he had sent a queer thrill through her. Even now, with his shoulder bruising her ribs and his long-fingered hand clasping the back of her thigh most improperly, Genevieve felt an odd excitement.

She had thought to keep track of where he took her, but she soon found it impossible to keep her head tilted at the angle necessary. Even if he had motives as low as those of men like Kulkey, at least she wouldn't have to fight three dozen of him. She was trying to think of various ways to protect herself from just one attacker when suddenly he stopped, paused a moment, then turned so abruptly Genevieve thought certain she'd fall.

"It's all right," he whispered. "Hang on; I'm gonna set you down, but you might be a bit dizzy."

He slid her down the length of him until her toes touched solid ground again. All around her was darkness, and even after she had clawed her way free of the tangled curtain, she still could see nothing. And she had no idea where she was.

"Where are we?" she demanded.

Whether from being bounced upside down so long or from discovering herself quite totally blind, Genevieve was every bit as dizzy as Jackson had predicted. Involuntarily, she grasped the steady hands

44

offered to her and did not fight when he pulled her against him.

"Where we are is in an alley behind the place we just left."

She pushed away from him and looked up in the direction she expected his face to be, though she could see nothing.

"What? Are you crazy?"

He clamped a hand over her mouth.

"I told you to shut up! The last place they'll look is in their own back yard."

That, she thought, was probably true, but it didn't make her any more comfortable.

And he reminded her, "Just how far do you think you'd get runnin' around Sacramento in this?"

She felt his fingers lift the silky fabric of her skimpy camisole and rub the two layers together. Again, he was right. Anyone looking for her would have little trouble finding passersby who remembered seeing a woman clad only in silk underwear running through the streets.

It was almost enough to make her laugh, if she hadn't been the fugitive.

He eased her away from him, and for the first time since running out of the Maison de Versailles, Genevieve felt the chill autumn air on her naked skin. She shivered and sought again the warmth of the man's nearness.

"Here, take my coat," Jackson offered. "I'm gonna see if I can't find somethin' else for you to wear."

He draped the coat, still warm from his own body, around her bare shoulders. She welcomed it, but felt alone and abandoned when he no longer touched her.

"Don't go," she whispered to the dark, not knowing if he was still there.

For the first time, he heard fear in her voice. He wished he could see her now. He imagined her eyes enormous and dark in that little oval face, the tumble of her hair tangled and wild, her lips soft and parted, her nostrils flared and quivering with each breath. Blinking the image away, he extended a searching finger to graze her cheek.

"I won't be gone long," he assured her. Her skin was like velvet; he let his hand linger to cup her chin while he told her, "Everybody'll be out lookin' for us; nobody'll notice me sneakin' in the back door and takin' a bit of the laundry."

He made it sound so simple, like a child's prank, but Genevieve couldn't ignore the warning that hummed in her veins.

"Jean-Louis won't leave. He'll be waiting inside." Her fingers closed around his hand. "We have to go now, get as far away as we can," she pleaded, turning in the darkness to run blindly, if necessary, so long as she did not stay in that place so close to the danger.

And then they heard the voices, angry masculine voices, coming not from one end of the alley or the other but from within the building.

"She's gotta be here, Frenchy, and you're gonna find her or else," Buster Kulkey threatened, only a flimsy wooden door separating him from the girl he sought. "Nobody's seen a half-nekkid whore on the street, so my guess is you staged this whole thing."

"For the love of God, Buster, you've searched the whole place. Where could I have hidden her?"

The whine had returned to Jean-Louis' voice, but this time it held terror, and perhaps pain.

Rio wasn't about to wait for the Frenchman's reply. He knew the next place to look would be the alley.

Without a word, he took the girl's hand to lead her down the narrow, rubbish-strewn passage between two rows of buildings. He could barely see and prayed they didn't step on a sleeping cat or disturb an angry drunk. The light was so bad that he

46

found himself stretching a hand out in front of him, almost feeling his way along.

Then there was light ahead, just enough to see the shape of a man leaning against a wall at the entrance to the alley. Rio halted, frozen midstride, and pulled Genevieve back.

"Is it one of them?" she whispered.

"Can't tell."

But when the loiterer struck a match on the sole of his boot and touched it to the end of a thick cigar, Genevieve knew she had seen that face before. She shrank back, seeking the shield of the shadows.

"He was there, at the auction."

Resignation tinged her voice. She was trapped, defeated, as much as she hated to admit it.

Rio took her shoulders in his hands, amazed at how tiny she was, how lost inside his coat, and gently shook her.

"Wait," he ordered. "Don't move. Understand?"

Before she could argue, or ask a question, he leaned her gently against a brick wall and moved off toward the man at the end of the alley.

He stayed within the shadows, able to see a little now that some light trickled into the alley. The man with the cigar was a tall, skinny drink of water, a gambler maybe. Probably hadn't done an honest day's work in his adult life. A man like that could be bribed, but Rio doubted his hundred dollars would be enough, especially if this was one of Kulkey's cronies.

He slipped up almost behind the sentry, near enough to tap him on the shoulder before dodging back into the shadows.

With a nasal whine in his voice, Rio whispered, "Hey, I think they're here." The smoker turned and took a single step into the alley toward the unfamiliar voice. "Buster's gonna flush 'em out from the other end, so we—"

It was just enough to put the man at his ease, and

47

then Rio slammed his fist into an unsuspecting belly. The cigar dropped with a shower of red sparks as the tall man doubled over with a soft grunt. When Rio's fist came down on the back of his head, he toppled without another sound.

Stunned, Genevieve came out of her hiding place. Instinct almost drew her to check on the fallen man to see if he was still alive, but another, deeper urge forced her to step over his inert form and take the hand stretched out to her. Then there was nothing left to do but run.

"Not much further now," Rio encouraged. "We're almost there."

She was limping badly and holding her side against the stitch that first long run had given her. Twice they had had to outrun the hue and cry set up by Kulkey's minions, and both times Rio had been certain they'd never make it. Only sheer and simple luck had saved them, first in the form of a slow-moving wagon that concealed their movements as they darted across a street, and second when a startled tomcat attacked their pursuer.

But the flight had taken its toll on the girl. She had twisted an ankle, though not badly, but it still slowed her. And the coat that kept her from freezing to death also made running even more difficult. The sleeves hung past her hands, and she had never had time to button it.

Somehow, however, they had escaped the lights and alleys of downtown Sacramento and made their way into the quiet of a residential neighborhood. Now, too, the moon was up, and there was light enough to see by, as well as plenty of shadows for concealment.

And Rio knew exactly where he was headed.

"I've got to rest," Genevieve begged, pushing a long tangled strand of hair out of her eyes. Her an-

48

kle throbbed, and she hugged the ache under her ribs. Every breath burned her lungs and throat, yet the pain didn't stop her from trying to drink in more and more air. It seemed she couldn't get enough.

"Not yet. I got a friend lives here, one, maybe two more houses. Want me to carry you?"

She shook her head.

"No, I can make it."

She was a stubborn one, but he already knew that.

"C'mon, then. I ain't got all day."

He turned and headed up the road, toward the house Bruckner had described so carefully, with such pride. If the girl wanted to follow, well, she ought to be able to see well enough by now. In the moonlight his white shirt glowed as bright as a torch.

One step at a time, Genevieve forced herself after him. How long had they been running? An hour? Two? She had lost all track of time, except to note the moon that had finally risen above the trees. It could not be very late. The windows of the houses they trudged past were still warm with yellow light.

These weren't the mansions of the wealthy, but they were still substantial homes, new as was everything in Sacramento. Genevieve glanced occasionally at them, wondering if she would ever know the security of home again. Even when her escort paused and waited for her to catch up to him so he could take her hand and lead her around to the back of one of the houses, she was struggling to dredge up the memories of the calm, serene, secure life she had left so many months ago.

The memories wouldn't come. Frustrated and frightened, she was barely aware that she stumbled and fell to her hands and knees, that someone lifted her bodily and cradled her in his arms. She clung to him and buried her face against him.

And she knew nothing else until he shook her roughly and told her, "Knock on the door."

She had to unwind her arms from around his neck to do so.

"Louder."

She rapped again, three times.

"Is that the best you can do?"

"I am not accustomed to breaking down the back doors of respectable people, if that's what you expect of me."

Rio frowned. Her little fist didn't make enough noise to attract a watchdog, much less a man relaxing in his parlor with his wife. The front door probably had a fancy brass knocker, but Rio didn't dare approach from that direction. Not with a half-naked woman in his arms.

"Try again. And this time remember we still got Kulkey on our tail."

She balled her fist and pounded with the edge of her hand, not her knuckles, with better results.

A young woman opened the door, a small lamp in her hand.

"This the Bruckner house?" Rio asked.

She nodded, and Rio realized she was only a maid, not Paul's wife. From the looks of her robe and rumpled hair, she had been in bed, and he felt slightly guilty for disturbing her. But only slightly.

"Look, you go tell Mr. Bruckner that—"

"What's going on, Emmie?" a masculine voice interrupted from inside the house. "Who are you— Rio!"

Paul Bruckner pushed past his servant and pulled the door all the way open.

"Good God, what in heaven's name is going on?" he asked as his guest sidled into a dark room filled with the scents of lye soap and wet wooden tubs. "Emmie, don't just stand there. Go get Mrs. Bruckner."

"I'm already here, Paul."

Rio turned to the tall, elegant woman whose protruding belly preceded her. She, too, held a light, a single tall candle whose flame flickered in the air currents.

"You'll pardon us, Mrs. Bruckner, for barging in on you this time of night," he began. "But there's a gentleman by the name of Kulkey—"

"Buster? What's he done this time?" Paul interrupted.

Genevieve looked from one face to another and wished she could disappear into a hole in the floor. These were civilized people, the kind she had left in New Orleans, and here she was, dressed only in a whore's underwear and a man's unbuttoned coat. She didn't know what to do with her arms; wrapping them around her rescuer's neck was unacceptably intimate, but there really was nowhere else to put them, unless she wanted them to flop at odd angles in those absurdly long sleeves. She couldn't even find her hands in order to close up the front of the coat.

Her legs were even more exposed, bare from the tops of her shoes almost to the tops of her thighs. To try to cross them would only bring more attention to them, so she lay still, fighting the furious, humiliating blush that suffused her face.

Then Rio gently shifted her and set her on her feet, keeping her turned toward him until she could arrange the coat to cover the most of her skin possible.

"Kulkey, ah, tried to buy her," he answered. Damn it, why did Paul's wife have to stand there, looking so poised and unaffected? How was a man supposed to explain to another man how he got into this mess, with the other man's wife takin' in every damn word?

Angela Bruckner raised a questioning eyebrow to her husband, and that seemed to alert Paul to the gravity of the situation. A moment ago he had been just a startled private citizen; now the businessman in him took over.

"Emmie, you can go on back to bed now," he told

51

the maid as he ushered everyone further into the house and closed the door behind him. From the laundry room they passed into a kitchen still smelling of roast beef and vegetables. "Angela, I think the young lady Mr. Jackson has brought with him could use some, er, assistance from you. Why don't you find her something a bit more comfortable to wear on this chilly evening and then wait for us in the parlor. Rio and I will be in the library."

Genevieve turned her attention to the woman who had just been so peremptorily dismissed. She was surprised to see Angela's brow remain raised.

"I believe, Mr. Bruckner, that I will find the young lady something more comfortable to wear, but I will not wait for you in the parlor," she told him with a voice filled with determination. "And I expect *you,* Rio Jackson, to hold every detail of this story until your friend and I have joined you and my husband in the library."

Jean-Louis rubbed his knee, but the pain persisted. He had walked too damn far, and too damn fast, with the expected results.

"I told you, Johnny, I want that girl," Buster Kulkey reiterated. He looked absurd, his awkward bulk sprawled on the delicate settee, and Jean-Louis actually had a moment's sympathy for Genevieve. "You promised her to me, and I want her."

He sounded like a petulant little boy, which in some ways he was, for all his fifty odd years.

"I didn't promise her. I simply said she would be offered for sale."

"Same thing. I paid for her, so you got to deliver."

Jean-Louis sighed. Kulkey was being too damned impatient.

"She's not going to get away," Jean-Louis repeated yet again. "You have a man watching her hotel. If she goes anywhere near it, they will apprehend her.

She has no money." He lifted the little blue reticule and shook it. "If she attempts to secure other lodgings, she will be unable to pay for them."

"What about that half-breed she was with? He musta had money or he wouldn'ta been here. He could get her a hotel room."

"Possibly, but not likely. We'll post a watch at every decent hotel in the city. She may not notice, but he will, and he'll soon realize she's more trouble than she's worth. More than likely, he'll get rid of her soon enough and we'll find her when he does."

"You better."

Chapter Four

Refilling Rio's brandy snifter, Paul shook his head in sheer amazement.

"Not too many men in Sacramento would take on Buster Kulkey, and fewer would survive the confrontation."

Rio sipped the fiery brandy slowly this time. Any minute now Angela would return with the fugitive, and he needed plenty of fortification.

He felt uncomfortable, especially in this cozy, book-filled room. He had known, from Paul's description of the place, what it would be like, but in the back of his mind, Rio had only the image of the little cottage Paul and Angela had moved into on their arrival in Sacramento a year ago. They, like Miss du Prés, had been his charges on a wagon train from Missouri to the gold fields. They were newly-weds then, looking forward to their first real home since leaving their parents' nests. Unlike most of the travellers to California, however, the young Bruckners were not pioneers, setting out into the unknown with only dreams. Paul, who had grown up in a banking family, had taken a position with one of the more prosperous banks in Sacramento. In a year he had risen to vice-president, and built this home on the edge of town for his wife and the child soon to be born.

All of the things Rio Jackson could never aspire to.

Paul settled himself on the sofa again and crossed one ankle over his knee before resuming his questioning of his guest, in open defiance of his wife's orders.

"What I don't understand is why Yvonne let you keep your gun. Two prostitutes were shot up pretty bad last week when a gunfight broke out in one of the brothels, and since then they've been careful to make sure the customers check their firearms at the door."

Rio shrugged and couldn't hide a little grin as he remembered the way Yvonne had studied him.

"I think she had the hots for me is why."

"Probably," Paul agreed with a chuckle of his own. "I swear, Rio, you have the damnedest luck when it comes to women."

Damnedest is right, Rio wanted to echo, but with bitterness, not self congratulations.

He was spared having to make any reply at all by the arrival of Angela Bruckner and a considerably better dressed Genevieve Marie du Prés. As expected, Angela took immediate charge of the situation.

"Since Mr. Jackson failed to do the honors earlier, Genevieve, I'd like you to meet my husband, Paul. Paul, Miss Genevieve Marie du Prés, of New Orleans. You may have heard of her father, Victor du Prés, one of the partners in the Louisiana Commercial Bank."

Paul, who had got to his feet the minute his wife and her companion stepped into the room, extended a hand to Genevieve. Rio scowled and took another swallow of brandy.

"Very pleased to meet you, Miss du Prés," Paul greeted.

Genevieve blushed, but she did not smile. Good

God, what kind of lout was Jackson, anyway? His friends had been kind enough to take a total stranger into their midst at his request, and he didn't have the courtesy to rise when his hostess entered the room.

She wondered how he had ever become acquainted with the Bruckners, much less well enough to call them friends.

But friends they must indeed be, because neither Angela nor her husband took any notice of Rio's breach of manners.

"You men are all alike," Angela scolded gently as she eased herself into the comfort of a deep, well cushioned chair. "You think just because we happen to be female, we ought to be able to share clothes. Do you ever take into consideration the fact that Miss du Prés is several inches shorter than I, that she has more bosom than I ever hope to have, and a waist I'd never achieve with the tightest corset? Oh, no, you just assume—"

"That's one of my shirts!" Paul Bruckner exclaimed.

Genevieve wondered if she would have been less humiliated had she kept the silken undergarments. A crimson flush burned her face, and for the first time this horrible evening, she felt tears threaten to spill down her cheeks.

"A shirt is a small price to pay in return for what we owe this gentleman," Angela insisted. She paused, letting her admonition sink in, then before she could speak again, the banging of a brass knocker on the front door interrupted her.

Genevieve's blush turned to a ghostly pallor. She knew the urgency behind that kind of summons. When the New Orleans police came looking for her father, they had wasted no time with polite taps on the door.

"Open up, Mr. Bruckner," a gruff voice shouted,

with no respect for the neighborhood or the hour.

"My room," Angela whispered as she offered her hand to Rio while Paul, with a grim nod, headed for the door. "And don't forget the glasses."

Genevieve scooped up the extra brandy and sherry glass that would have betrayed their presence, then followed Angela and Rio through the house to a back stairway. They climbed in the dark, in silence except for Angela's labored breathing, until they reached the second floor.

She stopped and leaned against the wall, unable to go another step. But a slow grin spread across her face even as her eyes closed and a furrow of pain crinkled her brow.

"You do have the damnedest luck with women, Rio Jackson," Angela breathed. "What better place to hide than the bedroom of a woman who's havin' a baby."

Now it was Rio who blanched, but his panic lasted only a fraction of a second. Angela was much taller than Genevieve and her condition had added several pounds to her weight, but Rio scooped her up as easily as Genevieve had picked up a couple of wine glasses.

"The doctor warned me about the stairs," Angela explained.

Genevieve held the bedroom door open, revealing a tiny pile of silken garments in the middle of the floor. Other clothes were strewn on the bed, including Rio's coat. She looked around for a place in which to hide the evidence of her presence.

At least her mind was functioning again. Embarrassment was one thing, survival another.

Setting the two glasses on the dressing table, Genevieve began to issue orders.

"Put Mrs. Bruckner in the bed," she instructed Rio without the slightest hesitation. "I'll get these clothes out of sight."

57

With gestures instead of words, she told him to put his coat back on rather than waste time trying to find a place to stash it. The silken souvenirs from the Maison de Versailles went into Angela's bureau, where they were indistinguishable from her own expensive lingerie.

The door to the hallway, however, remained open, and for good reason. Voices from the downstairs vestibule travelled clearly up the front stairs.

"Good evening, constable," Paul greeted expansively as he pulled the door open. If his voice was any louder than normal, the police officer apparently did not notice it, for his was equally clear.

"Evenin', Mr. Bruckner. Sorry to disturb you, but we got a bit of a problem."

"Oh, God, not the bank?"

Genevieve murmured a quick prayer of thanks. Paul Bruckner's quick-thinking response to the constable's presence not only bought an extra few minutes of time. It threw an added light of innocence on him, and on his household.

"No, no, nothin' like that," the officer hastened to assure him. "Sorry, Mr. Bruckner. Lord, I never thought to fright you like that. You gonna be all right?"

Paul's chuckle sounded weak.

"Yes, yes, I'll be fine. It's just that my first thought was for the bank, and well, I'm afraid I worry too much about it."

"Well, see, what we come about was some trouble downtown that we think might've spilled over into your neighborhood."

"What kind of trouble?"

Having tucked the last of Angela's clothes into her wardrobe, Genevieve froze and almost held her breath while she listened to the conversation.

The constable cleared his throat before explaining, "Well, I know it sounds crazy, but there was a kidnapping at Yvonne's bawdyhouse, the one that danged Frenchman took over a couple months ago. One of the, er, customers said he thought he recognized the kidnapper as a man he saw in your bank this morning. Tall fella, black hair, maybe a half-breed Mexican."

"That could be any one of a dozen of my customers," Paul replied. "And I certainly don't take personal responsibility for every person who walks into my bank."

With brandy in hand, Rio strolled into the vestibule and asked, "Is something wrong, Paul?"

In the bedroom at the top of the stairs, Genevieve's heart jumped into her throat. What arrogant foolishness was this madman playing now?

"No, nothing of importance," she heard the banker reply. She thought he sounded just a little drunk, like her father when he had been celebrating with too much champagne. "It seems there's been a bit of a row over at one of the bawdyhouses and Officer Perry here believes someone from the bank may have been involved."

"Oh, no, Mr. Bruckner," the policeman hastened to correct. "Not someone *workin'* in the bank. Mighta been one o' your customers."

The suspicion in the officer's voice was obvious, even to Genevieve listening upstairs. She could imagine him even now giving Jackson a visual once-over. Good Lord, she hoped the scout wasn't stupid enough to antagonize his accuser. But what little she knew of Rio Jackson did not reassure her. He was arrogant and altogether too sure of himself. And she had seen him drinking, which probably added to that self-confidence.

But when Rio responded, he betrayed no such cockiness.

With what sounded like genuine perplexity, he asked, "Why would you come here looking for one

59

of Mr. Bruckner's customers?"

"Well, Mr. Kulkey and some o' his friends said they tailed the kidnapper a ways in this direction. I seen lights here, and we kinda put two and two together and—"

"Obviously you didn't come up with four," Paul interrupted. "As you can see, the only people here are myself and Mr. Jackson, celebrating his completion of another trek across the prairies. Mrs. Bruckner is upstairs asleep, and the maid is in her quarters, sleeping also. Would you care to have a look around?"

Genevieve bit her lip and wished she could warn Bruckner to go lightly with his pretense of being drunk. It might not be good for his reputation in the community, for one thing, but of more immediate concern was that the police officer might think him too inebriated to know what he was talking about.

When Paul spoke again, he seemed more in control.

"Mr. Jackson has been here all evening, Officer Perry. I can vouch for that. And I can also vouch for his conduct, if need be. He saved my life and my wife's last year; I'd lie for him if necessary, and I don't think anyone in this city would take Buster Kulkey's word over mine."

The policeman's voice dropped to a mumble that Genevieve could not understand, but she suspected he was reluctantly giving in to Paul's incontrovertible logic. The banker confirmed her suspicion when his next words were spoken in a tone that did much more than merely hint at farewell.

"Wherever the kidnapper is, you can rest assured he isn't here, Officer Perry, so you'd best resume your search elsewhere. I shall certainly let you know if I see anyone answering that description in the neighborhood. Good night."

Genevieve let out a long-held breath and sagged

against the door frame. The front door shut with a soft thud, then for a long moment there was only silence.

"Is he gone?" Angela whispered.

"Yes, I think so." Tears started to well in Genevieve's eyes, tears of relief, and the fear she had not dared to feel before.

She was still struggling against those tears when Rio and Paul Bruckner quietly mounted the gracefully curved staircase. Instead of smiles of success, however, both men looked as serious as if the constable were right behind them.

"What's wrong?" she blurted, fear once again taking hold of her.

With none of the bravado that had marked his voice a few minutes ago, Paul answered, "We've got to get you two out of here. The sooner the better."

He strode past Genevieve into the bedroom, where Angela was throwing back the covers and awkwardly pushing herself out of the bed. Genevieve turned, but she did not enter the room, as though afraid it would become more prison than sanctuary.

"That should be no problem," she said as she squared her shoulders inside the over-sized shirt. "I shall simply return to my hotel. I may have difficulty explaining the loss of my room key and the change in my attire, but I'm sure I can—"

"Impossible," Rio cut her off. His blue gaze skewered her, condemning her without words for the trouble she had caused him.

"Nothing, Mr. Jackson, is impossible. I need only—"

"You need only," he echoed in blatant mockery, "set one foot outside this house to have that beer-bellied peacekeeper or one of his cohorts escort you back to the Maison de Versailles."

He was dead serious. She read it in his eyes, in his

arrogant stance, in the way he seemed to dare her to argue with him.

And she wanted to argue. She wanted to tell him exactly what she thought of him, of his bullying tactics. But when she opened her mouth to spit the words at him, all that came out was laughter, bubbling, delightful, musical laughter.

It was nerves. It had to be. Nerves and exhaustion and fear and confusion and a sudden overwhelming sense that for the first time in her life, Genevieve Marie du Prés was not in control of *anything* at all. Ever since she could remember, she had taken charge of every situation in which she found herself. Now, facing a man who just might not succumb to her wiles or knuckle under to her superior logic, she dissolved into giggles.

"That's it, go ahead and laugh, you spoiled, ungrateful little—"

"Rio!" Angela exclaimed, effectively halting a flood of vulgarities. She pushed past him to kneel beside Genevieve, who had somehow slid to the floor, where she sat, cross-legged, leaning against the door frame, half in and half out of the bedroom. "Now, my dear, I know it may seem like a simple matter of just marching back to your hotel," she soothed, "but I do think perhaps you ought to give the gentlemen a fair hearing."

Angela was undoubtedly right. So was Jackson, painful as it was for Genevieve to admit that. She was most assuredly spoiled, and probably ungrateful as well, but it still hurt to have someone like him point it out to her. Especially when she owed him a great deal of gratitude.

Slowly, the giggling subsided, though it left Genevieve with a painful case of hiccoughs. She got to her feet and helped Angela to rise, then stood, feeling chastened as well as vulnerable.

"I think I figured out a way to get you outta this

mess," Rio said quietly. "But we gotta move fast, before they got time to get organized and start thinking with their heads instead of their—"

He caught himself just in time. The whiskey and the brandy had loosened him up, made him forget the fragile veneer of civilization he donned during his stay in Sacramento. He saw the color rise in the girl's cheeks and knew that she understood exactly what he had left unsaid. Maybe she was less of an innocent than he thought.

"Please, wait just a moment, Mr. Jackson," she said in a voice that let him know she was thinking about every word. She might not be arguing with him now, but if he gave her answers she didn't like, she wouldn't hesitate to let him know. "Just exactly why is it that we can't stay here until morning, walk back to our respective hotels, and go about our respective business tomorrow? Neither of us has broken any laws that I know of. I certainly do not consider myself to have been kidnapped, at least not by you, Mr. Jackson, and I do not see how this Mr. Kulkey could claim that I had been without my corroboration."

He shook his head. She really was innocent. Or just naive.

"I don't know why I waste time explaining this all to you. Ought to be plain as the nose on your face."

"Well, it isn't. Indulge me."

He was aware that Paul had slipped an arm around Angela and was herding her back towards her bed, but that awareness remained on the fringe of Rio's consciousness. Far clearer was the presence of Genevieve Marie du Prés in her baggy shirt, belted skirt, and dainty high-heeled shoes. The liquor, the aftermath of excitement, and the provocative sight of a woman whose charms had already been displayed for his enjoyment all combined to remind him he had not completed his night's planned entertainment.

Oh, yes, he would love to indulge her, but not in the way she intended.

He cleared his throat and took one small step nearer to her.

"You and me are gonna be outta this house before sunup," he began. "And we ain't gonna draw attention to the fact, neither. Paul Bruckner lied to save my sorry hide, and I won't repay him by lettin' anybody know he lied. Dishonest bankers don't have much of a future in this town."

He had a point, and a good one.

"And how do you propose we leave here without being seen?"

"In a few minutes, Mr. Bruckner is going to go to bed, and put out all the lights in his house. In about half an hour, he's going to get up again, 'cause he couldn't sleep for worryin' about his bank. In fact, he's gonna be so worried that he decides to take a look at it, in the middle of the night, just to make sure everything's all right."

A plan so simple should have no trouble succeeding. It hardly took Rio five minutes to outline, and when he had finished, he folded his arms across his chest with a smile of self-congratulations.

Genevieve allowed him only a second or two of his smug enjoyment.

With no trace of amusement in her calm, haughty voice, she said, "Surely you jest, Mr. Jackson."

The smile disappeared. Black brows knit over eyes that turned icy.

"I have only just arrived in Sacramento," she continued, without acknowledging or even letting on that she noticed his increasing anger. "I have had but one bath, which is nowhere near enough to wash away the sweat and dust of half a continent. I have not yet slept in a real bed, which is something I have dreamed of since the day your wagon train left Missouri."

His temper was difficult to ignore, rising like a creek in spring spate about to burst its banks. But now that some semblance of calm had returned to her existence, Genevieve was not going to relinquish control without a fight.

"Therefore, Mr. Jackson, I find your suggestion that I get on a horse this very instant and ride immediately for San Francisco utterly untenable. Even more so, your instruction that upon arrival in San Francisco, I purchase passage aboard the first eastbound ship and head home to New Orleans."

He was close to an explosion, but she dared to taunt him further by taking a step in his direction.

"And you seem to have forgotten, Mr. Jackson, that I have no money with which to buy my passage. What little I brought with me this evening remains in my reticule, which was left behind at the Maison de Versailles." Speaking the name of that iniquitous establishment sent a tremor through her, but she shrugged it off. She could not afford to dwell on past terrors. "I have a considerable sum in my hotel room, but you have already pointed out that you think it would be unsafe for me to return there. In that case, would you point out just exactly how I am to buy this passage homeward?"

She mimicked his stance, though she immediately regretted folding her arms across her chest. There seemed to be no way to do it that didn't call attention to the outline of her bosom under the loose-fitting shirt.

Rio knew it, too. She saw the gleam come into his eyes, fighting for supremacy over the firmly ensconced fury. Tantalized or not, however, he stuck to his logic.

"You can't go back to that hotel yourself, but Kulkey ain't gonna touch your stuff. If that Jean-Louis has it in his head to go claim it, he won't be doin' nothin' 'til tomorrow. By then, Paul here will give a letter from you to the manager."

"That still doesn't solve the problem of the money."

"I'll give you a draft on my bank," Paul interrupted.

Rio shook his head. "Not a draft. Cash. Don't want anything they might be able to trace."

The banker nodded in agreement before turning to plead once again, "Miss du Prés, Rio is absolutely right. You can't stay here, and the sooner you're on your way to San Francisco, the better your chance of eluding Buster's henchmen altogether."

She opened her mouth to ask a vaguely sarcastic question, but one look at Bruckner's deadly serious expression gave her the answer she did not want. She glanced back to Jackson and found the same message in his dark eyes and set mouth.

She wanted to ask them for time, even ten minutes, to think this over. It seemed so unfair, after all the interminably long days and nights with the wagon train, to have to make up her mind in only a few seconds. Just last night, waiting for the riverboat to reach Sacramento, she had suffered the frustration of impatience. No amount of wishes or prayers had hurried the time along. Now, when she desperately needed time, there was none to be had.

Yet there was still something to be said for hasty decisions: they forced one into action and required one to live with the consequences. No one knew that better than Genevieve Marie du Prés. She had had six months to reflect upon a moment of impulsiveness that set her stubborn feet on an impossible journey. Not once in all that time had she envisioned such an ignominious end to her adventure.

She squared her shoulders and lifted her head with a defiant toss of her unbound hair. When she spoke, however, there was a distinct quaver in her voice.

"How soon can we be on our way?"

Chapter Five

If anyone followed Paul Bruckner from his house to the bank at the ungodly hour of half past midnight, they left him alone when he returned. Watching from a darkened upstairs window as Paul strolled with unfeigned weariness up the street toward the house, Rio breathed a sigh of relief. He turned away and leaned back against the wall. Genevieve took his place, careful not to disturb the white lace curtains.

"You ready?"

His question was not unexpected. During the two hours since Bruckner had left the house in a state of obvious agitation, neither Rio nor Genevieve had spoken a single word. They had waited in the dark, tensely aware of each other's presence but not able to put any of the feelings into words. It was difficult to stand watch for more than a few minutes at a time, so they had alternated turns at the window. The moonlit darkness strained the eyes, and the almost silence strained the ears, but nothing could match the strain to nerves.

"As ready as I can be," she answered. "There wasn't much I could do."

"No, guess not."

He moved again to stand behind her and peer over her head to stare out the window. Two stories below, Paul Bruckner mounted the steps to his front porch and fumbled for a key. He did not look up.

Genevieve drew in a long, slow breath. In the past two hours she had thought of a thousand things she should say—apologies, explanations, confessions— but she had said nothing. Now the man into whose hands she was putting her life stood just inches behind her. She could feel his warmth in contrast to the cool of the darkened pane of glass in front of her. The last thing she wanted now was his nearness.

She had wanted to be alone, completely alone, after Paul left, but Rio insisted that they stay together. Angela, exhausted but determined to see this thing through, agreed. If anything happened, they would have a better chance if they were together rather than separated in the unfamiliar house.

Genevieve refused to think about what could happen. The problem was that the only way to avoid worrying about the future was to dwell on the past, and that was hardly encouraging.

He didn't move behind her. She knew he was waiting until Paul was inside the house. If no one had followed him, then they would descend the dark stairs and meet Paul on the landing, but not before Rio deemed it safe. He had made it quite clear before Paul left that Genevieve was to follow orders, not give them and not even question them.

The night was so quiet that they easily heard the turning of the key in the lock, the click of the latch, the creak of the door as it swung open and then shut again. Still Rio didn't move. Genevieve could feel his breath against her hair, he was that close to her, unmoving, patient, controlled.

A cry of mingled emotions strangled in her throat, to emerge as a muffled sigh as she tilted her head back to contain the tears. She found the solidity of his shoulder, and though common sense urged her to withdraw immediately, instinct pushed her even closer to him.

"Not now," he whispered with an angry hiss that accomplished what twenty-one years of her mama's admonitions had not. She stiffened, putting that scant inch or two between their bodies once more. "I don't see nobody followin' Paul, so we might as well git while we can. C'mon."

What in God's name had she got herself into this time, Genevieve wondered, as she let him lead the way through the darkened room. This morning all had seemed so simple, and in a few short hours everything had changed, from bad to worse to impossible, until she found herself facing a nightmare beyond comprehension. What did she know of this man Rio Jackson? That he was a good scout? Well, she surmised he was since he had brought the wagon train from Missouri to California without significant incident. That he was a respecter of respectable womanhood? Possibly, but she had after all encountered him in a brothel.

She reminded herself that he had encountered her there, too.

There was no time for more questions. Rio opened the door and slipped out into a hallway even darker than the room they left behind, for here there was not even a glimmer of moonlight. Genevieve instinctively felt for his hand. He clasped hers in return, but more with impatience than reassurance.

She nearly fell going down the stairs; her stumble drew a muttered curse from the man in front of her. Before she could reply, they had reached the landing, and Paul Bruckner. He was a shadow against the dark wood panelling, but at least here there was some measure of light. Genevieve blinked and tried to focus, only to lose her concentration when she had to strain to hear Bruckner's hurried whispers.

"It's no good, Rio. I got the horses, they're at Mack's saddled and ready."

"What do you mean, it's no good?" Rio interrupted, his voice hard and accusatory. "Kulkey see you?"

The vehement shake of Paul's head was clear even in the dark.

"No, as far as I know, no one saw me. Frank Covall, one of Buster's cronies, was on look-out at your hotel, so I had Lo Pau let me in the back way. But while I was at the livery, I heard Buster and Hank Murphy and a couple of the others planning an ambush. They figured you'd head for San Francisco."

"Damn!"

Rio flung Genevieve's hand away from him so violently that she lost her balance and had to grab the banister for support.

"What do we do now?" she asked in a tentative whisper, more afraid of the man than the answer.

"I don't know. I don't have any idea." He swore again, beginning to pace the tiny space of the landing. "Damn it, Paul, I knew I should have come with you."

"So you could get away without me?" Genevieve accused. "I told you that was the best thing to do two hours ago. Separately, we could make it."

"No!" This time he kept his profanity quieter, but she heard it just as clearly. "You can't go no place by yourself," he reminded her. "I swear, I shoulda took you back to St. Joe the minute I found out you was in that wagon."

He had sworn at her then, too, so loudly and violently that other men from the wagon train had gathered around in case there was a need to restrain him physically. But on that occasion, he had let the violence spend itself in verbal abuse, with hardly a word for her again during all the long months across the mountains and prairies.

She held her breath, letting her eyes strain to see the expression on his face, but the darkness was too

71

intense. His silence, however, did not last long this time.

"Did you get everything from that hotel room?" he asked Paul.

"Yes, everything. There wasn't much."

"How much cash you got on hand that you can spare?"

"Are you robbing this man?" Genevieve demanded.

"Hell, no, lady, I'm tryin' to get us as much ready cash as I can. We got a long trip ahead of us, and we're gonna need supplies."

The implication took only a second to reach Paul Bruckner, whose voice dropped to a whisper.

"Rio, you can't be thinking, not this time of the year . . ."

"How much cash, Paul? I got most of the five hundred you paid me, but that won't go far."

Again Genevieve interrupted. "Go far where? I am not setting foot out of this house until you tell me exactly what you are planning to do with me."

Rio turned so that the minimal amount of light on the landing caught in his eyes, rendering them the only points of brilliance in this whole shadowed world. Genevieve felt as though his gaze were a tangible thing, capable of physically caressing her as his eyes wandered up and then down to take in every invisible detail of her.

"I'm takin' you back to St. Joe the same way we come."

"Overland? This time of the year?" Paul asked. "Rio, for God's sake, that's suicide!"

Genevieve stood in shocked silence. What Paul Bruckner was putting into words had already gone through her mind. This was October, and though the weather in Sacramento was still warm and fine, the country Jackson proposed they traverse would already be mantled in winter's snow. She had heard

72

the tales of horror many times on her way westward through those mountains. Though the wagon train had left St. Joseph, Missouri, in plenty of time to miss the dreaded and deadly snows, there had always been a sense of urgency, as summer waned and autumn crept up upon them.

She was so lost in her haunted musings that she missed much of Rio's reply.

"Not for just two of us. If I had a whole wagon train, yeah, it'd be sure hell tryin' to cross in winter. But hell, the miners and the trappers been survivin' in them mountains for years, and the Indians long before them."

"But they were prepared for it. You've got no supplies, no equipment, no food."

"That's what the money's for. How much did you get?"

Genevieve heard the transfer of a satchel of coins from one man's hand to another. Already a thought was forming in her mind, the seed of yet another impulsive decision.

"It's a thousand dollars, all I could get my hands on quickly. Will it be enough?"

Rio hefted the sack, as though testing its weight would tell him how much he could buy with it.

"It'll have to be," he said with unconvinced resignation. Then, in a softer, more sincere tone, he added. "It's poor thanks for all you've done, Paul. I'm sorry, and I promise I'll pay it back, every red cent."

Frustrated that she could not see the faces of the men who were deciding her fate, Genevieve nevertheless drew a deep breath and firmly announced, "You'll pay back nothing, Mr. Jackson. I have no intention of going with you, so there will be no reason for the money to be spent."

"What the hell do you—"

"Your reliance on profanity is most distressing,"

73

she interrupted. This was becoming easier than she had expected, though the darkness still kept her uncomfortable and cautious. "However, that is no real concern of mine. As I said, I simply cannot embark on such an outrageous expedition and certainly not in the company of a man such as yourself."

"Now wait just a goddam minute!"

"An unmarried young woman does not travel in the company of an unmarried man if she expects to return to her family with any scrap of reputation intact."

"Jesus Christ, lady, what about six months with the wagon train?"

She sniffed disdainfully and gave him a scathing up and down stare even though she was not quite sure where he stood.

"I was in the company of a married couple and their children, not alone."

Rio snorted. "Hah! Like that makes a whole helluva lot of difference! Come on, we ain't got time to argue. Waitin' around for Kulkey won't do your reputation any good either."

The touch of a hand on her arm silenced her next retort. Her temper flared, but before she could either withdraw from Rio's firm grasp on her wrist or voice a protest, she heard the sound that had prompted his action.

Someone was prowling on the wide front veranda. The footsteps were slow, too slow to be sure if they belonged to just one person. A board creaked and the footsteps halted. A few seconds later, however, they approached the front door, down half a flight of stairs from where Paul, Rio, and Genevieve waited, unable even to breathe.

An unseen hand tested the door latch. The jiggle of metal against metal sounded loud in the silent, dark house, but no click of release followed it. Genevieve dared to let the air out of her lungs, slowly, carefully. She drew it in again sharply when the pressure of Rio's fingers around her wrist increased. Suddenly she realized he was pulling her toward the stairs.

She knew better than to argue this time and hurried only to obey the instructions Paul Bruckner whispered frantically to Rio as they groped their way through the house.

"There's a side door through Emmie's room," he told them. "It opens onto the garden. You'll have better cover."

If he wished them good luck or Godspeed, Genevieve never heard him.

The cover Paul mentioned consisted of a grove of enormous trees, which did indeed provide secure bulwarks behind which to hide from whatever eyes might be probing the midnight darkness. Those trees also created shifting, deceiving patterns of moonlight and shadow. More than once Genevieve stumbled. Rio's tight grip on her arm kept her from falling, and his continued silence kept her from making a sound of her own.

She lost track of everything: of time, of distance, of direction. For the second time in her life, and the second time in this one nightmare night, she was running blindly with survival her only goal and Rio Jackson her only guide.

Rio broke into her numbness of mind with a simple command.

"Wait here," he ordered in a tone that demanded obedience.

Piecing together details of her surroundings, Genevieve discovered she was inside a barn or stable. The warm smells of horses and hay, leather and grain tickled her nostrils. There was light, too, though only the faint glimmer from a lantern hung outside a door at the far end of the cavernous building. Still, it gave enough illumination for her to see Jackson emerge from one of the stalls.

He led not one but two horses, one the palomino stud he had relied on from Missouri to California. The other must be the mare Paul Bruckner had secured for Genevieve.

"We ain't got much time," Rio informed her succinctly. "You need a boost?"

She took the reins from him and tossed them over the mare's neck. The stirrups were almost out of her reach, but she was not about to become any more dependent.

"I can make it," she told him, though proving the truth of her statement wasn't easy.

"Mack sent some of Kulkey's boys in the wrong direction about half an hour ago, he says. How long they'll follow a false trail is anybody's guess, but it might buy us a little time."

They walked the horses out of the livery stable and into one of Sacramento's older and less fashionable neighborhoods. The sound and smell of the river drifted on the cooling night air. Genevieve shivered.

"Where did this Mr. Mack tell them we were going?"

"It's just Mack, no 'Mister' with it. He told 'em I asked for directions back to Frisco. So maybe they got their forces concentrated on that ambush and didn't send nobody in the other direction."

The other direction. Away from Sacramento. Away from San Francisco. Back across that trackless, endless waste to New Orleans, where she would face ridicule for her failure. Genevieve felt a sudden panicked urge to scream "No! I won't go!" but the words got somehow trapped in her throat, unable to escape and unwilling to be silenced. Tears of frustration and desperation welled in her eyes.

76

It was never supposed to end like this. Never.

They rode in silence through the dark, deserted streets along the river, until the streets ended and there was only a narrow, rough road visible in the moonlight. The night grew colder, forcing Genevieve to huddle in the saddle closer to the horse's body warmth and to conserve what little heat her own body generated. Exhaustion was a constant companion. Every few minutes, Genevieve jolted awake, and each time she swore she would not drift off again. The fear of falling off the even-gaited mare was not nearly as great as the worry that the mare would fall too far behind the palomino.

But she plodded steadily onward. With all sense of time lost, Genevieve was quite startled when the man ahead of her reined in his mount and said, "I think we beat 'em this far. Might as well camp for the night."

"Camp? Here? In the middle of nowhere?"

"You got a better spot in mind, lady?"

Of course she didn't, and he knew it. Well, she had slept out in the open before, though there had been the shelter of the wagon available if she needed or wanted it. At least a fire would be welcome, to drive away the threat of wild beasts as well as bring a little warmth back to her half-frozen limbs.

"Paul got us some extra blankets, but it might be a good idea to double up," Rio suggested as he swung down from the big stud. He had a feeling the prissy bitch who had gotten him into this situation wasn't likely to take him up on his offer, but hell, it was worth a try.

Genevieve gulped down a knot of shameless fear. What in God's name had she got herself into this time? Alone in the wilds with a man who, for all his past chivalry, might be every bit the lecherous slime that Buster Kulkey was.

77

"I think not," she replied haughtily to the idea that they share a single bed. "With an extra blanket and a good fire, I'm sure I'll be quite comfortable."

She had just swung her right leg over the mare's back but still had her left foot awkwardly stuck in the stirrup when Rio said, "Ain't gonna be no fire, lady."

"No fire?" she echoed, hopping on one foot as her startled mare took a step forward. "Whyever not? We'll freeze out here without a fire."

She pulled her left foot free and stood, trying to get Rio's attention. He seemed to take great pleasure in ignoring her. She could see him in the moonlight, dismounted, already loosening his bedroll from the cantle of his saddle.

When he whirled suddenly around to face her, she knew he had not been ignoring her at all.

"Look, lady, you got us into this. Now, I ain't any happier than you about these arrangements, but unless you got a better idea, I think you better let me make the decisions out here."

She was angry, almost too angry even to be afraid. Rio almost smiled with perverse satisfaction. It wasn't exactly the kind of satisfaction he'd like to have from her, but he savored it anyway.

"I got no idea how far behind us any of Kulkey's boys might be. Maybe they didn't even follow us. But I sure as hell ain't gonna light a fire this time o' the night. It'd be like hollerin' right at 'em, 'Here we are! Come 'n' get us!'"

He had a point. A good one. And she had no rejoinder.

Taking advantage of her silence, Rio hefted his bedroll to his shoulder. A yawn was sneaking up on him and he had no strength left to fight it. Or her.

"Look, lady," he said with a long sigh as he lowered the bedroll to his hip. "I got you outta that whorehouse and outta Sacramento. Now, I'm tired as hell and even if you don't want to admit it, you are, too. So why don't we call some kinda truce here and get ourselves a little sleep. Maybe, with a little luck, Kulkey won't find us, and then in the morning we can figure a way outta this latest mess."

He wasn't sure, but he had a feeling that was the longest single speech he had ever made in his life. As for the girl's reaction, she just stood there for a minute. It took him that long to realize she was virtually asleep on her feet.

She may not have appreciated his sentiments, but her utter exhaustion at least made her more cooperative about agreeing with him. She roused herself enough to help him unsaddle the horses and hobble them, then spread her own bedding on the ground. She did not, however, consent to his preparing a single bed for the two of them.

"Have it your way," he muttered when she had made herself as comfortable as she could under a stiff woolen blanket.

She was asleep before he had unrolled his own bed. Her breathing almost immediately settled into a deep steady rhythm. Rio watched her for a moment as he knelt to smooth the wrinkles from the saddle blanket that would provide extra insulation between himself and the chilly ground. He was amazed by the way sleep transformed her. In the fragile moonlight, the mask of pride and defiance slipped away, to leave behind the face of an innocent.

Rio rolled his eyes toward the star-studded sky and muttered a quiet "Damn!"

Chapter Six

Still wrapped in the dreams that accompanied the sleep of utter exhaustion, Genevieve only slowly became aware of the arrival of another day. After the long, steamy New Orleans summer, she welcomed the chill of an autumn morning. She drew a deep breath into her lungs to savor the brisk tang, but she did not yet open her eyes.

She let out that deep breath with a long sigh and a slight shiver. This wasn't the first time she had fallen asleep with a window left open. The thought of leaving her bed in order to shut that window, however, sent her burrowing deeper into the covers. There she found the warmth that would secure her another hour or two of sleep until Celine insisted her mistress rise and dress and come down to breakfast with the rest of the family.

But it wasn't Celine's soft voice that broke through the haze of Genevieve's wakeful dream-time. Instead, a deep-throated groan rumbled in her ear, and the warmth curling around her back shifted suddenly.

More asleep than awake, Genevieve managed to roll over to confront this interruption. In doing so, she became aware of the unexpected hardness of her bed, and her memory of recent events began to return. She knew that when she opened her eyes she would not see the yellow silks and green velvets of her room at home. She was on the trail, on her way to California, she remembered, thousands of miles from home.

Then she opened her eyes.

And came face to face with Rio Jackson, the source of that snug warmth.

A scream froze in her throat. She was fully awake now, and knew it would do her absolutely no good at all to begin shrieking her head off. That did not mean, however, that she had to submit to the uninvited intimacy. Hampered by tangled blankets and a body left stiff and a bit sore from the hard ground and the cold night, she struggled to free herself from the embrace of a man's strong arm thrown casually about her waist.

"Don't go," he suddenly whispered. "We got time yet."

His hand on her back applied pressure intended to bring her even closer to him. Though Genevieve resisted, he was too strong, and too determined, and he soon had her snug up against him. She tried to bring her hands up to push him away, but there was no room between their bodies. Instead, her right arm seemed to acquire a will of its own and snaked up to wrap itself around him.

"Good way to keep warm, ain't it," he murmured as he buried his face in the tangles of her hair. His lips nibbled her ear, then kissed a tingling trail down her neck to her shoulder.

Genevieve gasped for breath. She was no longer just warm; a searing, liquid heat suffused her. It began where his lips touched her skin, or maybe where his hand splayed so possessively at the small of her back, or maybe where her breasts pressed against the solidity of his chest. Wherever it started, it spread almost instantaneously, engulfing her in wildfire that raged beyond her control.

"Please," she pleaded in a raspy, scorched whisper. Her fingers clutched at the fabric of his shirt and tugged it in a futile attempt to push him away.

It was no use. Already she felt him pushing her back, easing his weight over hers. His mouth was at her throat, her head forced back to expose even more of her delicate flesh for his devouring kisses. He took her skin between his teeth, then ran his tongue softly along it until she whimpered, not in pain but in a strange unfamiliar kind of longing.

She tried once again to reason with him, but this time when she opened her mouth to beg him to stop, he silenced her with a kiss.

His lips touched hers softly at first, then moved to claim her mouth completely. With gentle insistence, his tongue probed the line of her lips until she found herself succumbing. Yet at the same time she experienced the wonderment of desire, her mind echoed with frightened questions. Why wasn't this a dream, instead of that memory of her bedroom in New Orleans? Why couldn't she wake up and find herself home, safe, secure, protected?

The cry of protest rose up from deep within her and finally burst forth. Genevieve slipped her hands between her and the strong body leaning over hers and pushed with all her strength. Twisting her head to one side, she severed the connection of the kiss but could not suppress a small gasp at what felt like a sense of abandonment.

"No," she breathed heavily. "No, no."

With a minimum of effort, Rio could have changed her mind. As he opened his eyes and gazed down at her, he knew that for all her protest, Genevieve Marie du Prés was as close to capitulation as any female of her stripe could be. A few more kisses, especially the kind he took great pride in being a master at, would have her trembling in his arms.

Something urged him to renew the attack. The taste of her was still sweet on his tongue, and the desire he had not quenched last night flared too easily. But however sweet might be the conquest of Miss Genevieve Marie du Prés, Rio Jackson was not prepared to live with the consequences. Not today.

In a single motion, he rolled away from her and got to his feet.

"You got fifteen minutes, lady. Don't waste 'em."

Without another word, he strode off into the concealing underbrush.

Deprived of his warmth, Genevieve shivered in the chill morning air. He had pulled the blankets away, but she did not reach for them. The cold was just what she needed to clear her head.

Nothing would have pleased Rio more than to have the girl ride in sullen silence the rest of the morning. He thought at first that she would, because she said nothing while they tied up the bedrolls and saddled the horses. Not a word, neither of reproach, anger, fear, nor even of curiosity.

She mounted just as silently, with a nod of her head to signal she was ready to continue the journey. A bit perplexed at this sudden change in her, Rio swung aboard the palomino and shoved his own curiosity out of his mind.

It wasn't until they had ridden out of the little pine grove and back onto the trail that Rio turned around to check on his charge and saw her almost doubled over on the saddle.

"Sweet Jesus, lady, why the hell didn't you tell me you were freezing!" he scolded as he jumped down off the big stallion and began to loosen the lashings on his bedroll. A blanket wrapped around her Indian-fashion might not be very elegant, but it ought to keep her from catching pneumonia.

When he handed the coarse blanket to her, she took it gratefully and whispered between chattering teeth, "Thank you. I'm sorry; I know I've been a bother."

"That's an understatement!" Rio laughed. "Look, if you need anything else, you gotta let me know. I'm a scout, not a nursemaid. I'll get you where you want to go, but other than that, you gotta take care of yourself."

They had had no more than four or five hours sleep, and by rights exhaustion and the comfort of being relatively warm again should have put Miss Genevieve Marie du Prés right to sleep in the saddle. A peaceful morning's ride, Rio estimated, should bring them to one of the myriad little mining towns that had sprung up in these mountains over the past few years. He only hoped the money Paul had given him would be enough for the supplies they needed to get all the way back to Missouri.

A peaceful morning's ride was not, however, what Miss Genevieve Marie du Prés had in store for Rio.

"I would like to know where you are taking me," she asked before the horses had gone another three strides.

He answered without turning around, "St. Joe. Don't expect to be there by nightfall though."

He thought she snorted at his attempt at humor. Lord, but she was sour in the morning!

"I meant right now. What is our destination for today?"

"As far as we can get. Look, lady, this ain't no

84

Sunday buggy ride. The towns in these mountains tend to sprout up kinda like mushrooms, overnight and in outta the way places. Last year, there was one up ahead a couple miles, a fairly civilized one where I ought to be able to get most of what we need without bein' mugged in the middle of the street. So just keep your britches on, lady and—"

"And stop calling me 'lady!' " she cried out, loud and shrill enough to make him jerk on the palomino's reins. This time the horse snorted. "I have a name, you know."

Rio danced the stallion around to face her. His good morning mood had fled, leaving a scowl on his unshaven face.

He gave her a mocking bow.

"Ah, bon jour, ma chère Mademoiselle Genevieve. A votre service. Nous allons aujourd'hui—"

The last thing she ever expected to come from his mouth was French, with an accent as pure as her own. It stunned her, and gave him both a sense of satisfaction and a sense of warning.

"Ain't got time for that kind of polite talk out here, lady. You want a name, make it short. And not Vi, 'cause I knew a whore in San Antonio named Vi once, and she tried to kill me."

He tugged the reins and headed the palomino up the narrow path that passed for a road once again. When the girl decided what she wanted him to call her, she could let him know, but he was damned if he was going to wait for her. And if she didn't come up with a name, well, maybe that was for the best, too. The last thing he needed now was for her to decide to get friendly.

Yet, he thought with a smile, he wouldn't turn her down if she did.

She said nothing for a while, just long enough for him to think he had finally silenced her. Maybe now they could make some progress.

It was a good morning to be setting out, clear, with no wind, though the temperature remained nippy. Overhead, the sky was a pale blue that would deepen as the day wore on. The haze that lingered through the early hours was destined to disappear, leaving maybe a few wisps of clouds, but thank God there was no threat of rain or snow.

Nor was there any threat so far from pursuit.

"Do you think we have escaped Mr. Kulkey?" the girl asked.

Rio rolled his eyes skyward and wondered if he dared to gag her.

"No. At best, we're ahead of him, but when we stop for supplies, we'll be leavin' a trail a blind man could follow. Not many men are gonna forget seein' a woman like you come through town."

The town scarcely deserved to be called such. A half dozen slapdash buildings made of whatever materials were handy at the time of construction — logs, lumber, stone — occupied a cleared area on the slope of a hill above a rushing stream. Between the buildings were half again as many tents, the hopeful precursors of permanent structures. Genevieve noted that at least four of the tents bore crude signs that simply said "Saloon".

There was, of course, no street, just a meandering path that more or less followed the course of the stream. Even so, traffic was busy, with several wagons headed toward higher ground upstream, and none of the businesses seemed to lack for trade, as there were men coming and going from nearly every establishment.

Genevieve did not see a single female in the crowd, not even an unsavory female.

She huddled more closely into the blanket and urged the mare abreast of the palomino.

"Are you certain this is less risky than my waiting outside town while you obtain the necessary supplies?" she whispered to Rio. "I feel rather— conspicuous."

Was that a chuckle she heard? Probably. He seemed to take special delight in proving a point.

"I told you you would. But this place isn't as bad as some; they at least got one cathouse here, so you're not the only girl in town."

"How do you know? I mean, which one is it?"

Good Lord, didn't the woman ever run out of questions?

"The last building. With a garter and a stocking on the sign, you can bet your sweet fanny it's a whorehouse."

Genevieve stared at the structure, repulsed and yet fascinated by it. But for a queer twist of fate, she would be in just such a house, albeit a bit more elegant in its appointments.

The thought sent a little shiver through her and brought her sharply back to the present. Rio was giving her instructions again.

"I want you to wait right here while I go buy us a mule. Keep your head down; don't go lookin' around. And whatever you do, don't talk to anyone. Understand?"

Before she could answer, Rio had already dismounted in front of a ramshackle barn with the single word "Livery" splashed across the front in fading red paint. He looped the palomino's reins around a hitching rail, then came back to take the reins from Genevieve as well.

"Don't talk to nobody, got it?" he asked again, looking up at her.

She nodded. With her hands free, she could hold

the blanket more tightly around her, but she took only small comfort from the added warmth. There was a strange chill in the air in this small cluster of buildings that called itself a town.

A corral beside the barn contained an assortment of horses, mules, and several small grey burros, as well as a pair of oxen. Rio strolled to the split log fence and folded his arms on the top rail to study the merchandise offered for sale. He stood, one foot resting on a lower rail, and waited patiently while a tall, gaunt man in filthy clothes and battered, stained hat shuffled from the barn door into the corral.

The liveryman kicked and shoved the animals out of his way as he crossed to where his customer waited.

"What kin Ah do fer yuh?" he asked with a remarkable lack of enthusiasm.

"Lookin' fer a mule," Rio answered, his drawl more pronounced, his words almost slurred. Without asking permission, he slipped easily between the rails of the fence and strode toward the animals.

There were five mules in the bunch, including a strapping white jack that Rio examined closely. He stroked the animal's shoulders and examined his hoofs and teeth.

"He's a strong 'un," the old man said. "If'n yer headin' far, he'll git yore gear there."

Rio had no quarrel with that assessment, but a few moments later agreed to buy a small dun jenny with one floppy ear.

"That's a nice-lookin' stud you got over there," the liveryman remarked while Rio counted out the coins to pay for the mule. "Don't think I ever seen one that big not hitched to a plow. He Mexican?"

Rio glanced protectively toward the palomino.

This old man wasn't the first to have cast greedy eyes on the golden stallion.

"Andalusian," he answered. "From Spain."

"Wouldn't like to sell him, would ya?"

Rio only shook his head and began counting the money over again.

"That's a shame. I had a guy in here just this morning said he was looking to buy a big yellow stud."

Rio's hands froze for a second over the coins he had spilled on the counter, but he recovered quickly and pushed a pile towards the liveryman.

"Sounds like my old friend Ed Cheever," Rio replied with a friendly grin. "Did he ask about Pat Kennedy? That's me."

The liveryman shook his head and scratched a white-whiskered chin.

"Nope, didn't ask about nobody. But I did get the feelin' he was lookin'."

As Rio took the mule's reins from the old man's hand, he added, "Well, if he comes lookin' again, you tell him Pat Kennedy went on up to the Emerald Lady."

Then he turned his back on the old man and led the mule to the corral gate. He had no idea how much he had just paid for the pack animal, because he had lost count of the coins so often. He could only hope he hadn't squandered too much of their limited funds and not worry much beyond that. He had other things to worry about.

Genevieve sensed the change in him as soon as he freed the two horses from the hitching rail. He tossed the mare's reins to her, but he did not mount the stud. Walking beside the big animal, he whispered further instructions as he led the way across the dusty street.

"You'll not be sayin' a word, understand? Not a

word," he ordered in an odd, lilting sing-song tone. "And you'll be keepin' your hands to yourself. Don't be handlin' the merchandise. I know what we need, and I know how much I got to spend. I'll not be needin' any help. Got it?"

He headed for one of two businesses advertising general merchandise for sale. They had already passed the smaller, housed in a two-story unpainted wooden structure. According to the crudely lettered sign in front of an enormous, weather-stained canvas tent, Rio had chosen to make his purchases at Spillman's.

This time, he allowed her to accompany him. Once inside, Genevieve found the place little different from any of a dozen or more such outfitters she had encountered on the way from New Orleans to California. Never before, however, had she been obliged to participate in the equipping. Now she looked around, taking in the myriad of goods offered for sale in what she would have thought was a barren wilderness.

For the most part, the merchandise was functional: tools for the gold seekers, cooking utensils, lanterns, guns, tinned food, ready-made clothing. Rio disappeared in the maze of shelves and tables, while Genevieve found following his orders to stay put rather easy for once. She found a bench in front of a pot-belly stove and sat down.

In three seconds or less, she had fallen sound asleep. And just as last night, memories of home invaded her sleep. When a hand on her shoulder shook her out of her slumber, she murmured a puzzled and haunted "Mama?" before relinquishing her hold on that comfortable other world.

"I ain't your mama," a gruff but now familiar voice growled. Genevieve came instantly awake, alerted by the tenseness in Rio's tone.

90

"C'mon. We gotta get outta here. Fast."

Wrapped once more in her awkward blanket, Genevieve followed him out of the tent store. "What's wrong?" she asked in a soft whisper as she struggled to keep up with Rio's long, purposeful strides.

He didn't answer her until they were outside the tent and untying their mounts.

"Somebody's on our trail. You heard that guy at the livery say someone was asking after me? Well, the one in there did the same thing. And I don't think he bought my story about a couple of Irish buddies."

To Genevieve's surprise, the little mule was already loaded with great canvas-wrapped bundles. Two similar but smaller packages burdened both the mare and Rio's stallion. Either Rio had worked quickly, or she had slept much longer than she thought.

"Do you think they've laid an ambush for us?"

He shrugged.

"I don't know. Could be." He mounted and turned the palomino back in the direction from which they had come. "If they did, they better have done it in the right place."

Rio doubled back on their path twice, then struck out across a rocky, ravine-like valley. Now there was no clear path to follow, only whatever directions Rio carried in his head. They rode the rest of the afternoon in dogged silence that not even Genevieve's curiosity could break. She was too hungry, and as the day wore on, too tired. Even when Rio stopped, in the first darkening of twilight, and made camp in another secluded pine glade, Genevieve could not bring herself to ask the questions plaguing her.

She did not question the lack of a fire, though her frozen body screamed in protest. She drank cold water from another icy stream and chewed strips of dried beef for supper, and then she collapsed on the hard, cold ground to shiver herself into a sleep that was more stupor than slumber.

Rio watched her from the corner of his eye. He ought to hate her for the situation she had got him into, but he couldn't. Her actions this afternoon had done nothing but earn her his respect. Though she had to be half frozen to death, she hadn't made a single complaint.

He leaned back against the tree under whose almost leafless branches they had chosen to make their meager camp. With his eyes closed, he shut out the normal night noises of the mountains to listen for the tell-tale signs of pursuit. It should have been an easy enough task, one he had performed countless times on countless other nights. This time, however, something interfered with his concentration.

The incessant bark and babble of the creek refused to fade out of his mind. Instead, it became the bright laughter of a young woman seated at a campfire, listening to the tall tales of a bunch of crazy young would-be prospectors. Rio squeezed his eyes shut to erase the sight and the sound of that memory, but it lingered stubbornly.

She had surprised him then, too, just as she had today. He had taken her for a pampered flower, pretty but useless, who would wither and wilt when the days grew long and hot and dry. He had never expected her to pitch in with the work, to get out and walk when the wagons had to be lightened, to join in with the simple and sometimes coarse entertainment that was so rarely afforded on the long and arduous trek.

But that one night stuck out so clearly in his mind, because she had done all the things he never expected. As an unmarried female, she would have been in demand under any circumstances on the male-dominated wagon train, but as an exquisitely beautiful woman, she became almost more precious than the gold so many of the pioneers were risking their very lives for. Yet when they had reached good water after three days' crossing a drought-baked plateau, she had joined in their celebration and danced with all the men, young and old, married and single.

No, not quite all, for one had hung back and watched from the shadows, afraid to approach the free-spirited creature who seemed to give herself to all men and no man at all.

Rio opened his eyes and shook his head. With a glance to where that stunning, puzzling creature now lay, he assured himself she had fallen soundly asleep.

He got to his feet without a sound. Twilight had almost given way to dark, but enough light still remained for him to scout their surroundings.

He did not expect to see anything so obvious as a campfire. but there were other signs a careless pursuer might not think to hide. Rio climbed over rocks and skirted awkwardly balanced boulders to reach a vantage point halfway up the slope they had just descended, then cut diagonally to the edge of the ridge itself. From there he could see both the narrow canyon they had crossed that afternoon and the deeper, broader valley they would enter in the morning.

No firelight glimmered amongst the rocks and ravines, nor did any train of men and horses march boldly up the trail. For a moment Rio dared to entertain the hope that no one had followed them from the nameless little town. His eyes slowly scanned the panorama spread below him and found only the rocks and trees nature intended.

But his ears, whether he held his own concentration or not, picked up a sound that did not belong. He could not identify it, could not even be sure he had heard it, but he let his instincts take over.

"Son of a bitch!" he whispered, angry but satisfied that his instincts had proven him right.

The sound was a man's sneeze, followed by an eerie echo of profanity. Before the echo faded, Rio had spotted the horses. Their riders appeared to be arguing, perhaps debating the wisdom of continuing to track their prey in the dying light.

Rio worked his way back to his own campsite as silently as before. No, there could be no campfire, no soul-warming coffee in the morning. But at least he was warned.

The next morning began much the same as that first on the trail, complete with the desperate dream of home and Rio Jackson's irresistible kiss. But there was no hot breakfast, only a few cold words and then they mounted their horses.

"You saw them?" Genevieve asked when they were well on their way. "How many men does he have following us?"

"I saw two horses," Rio answered. "That don't mean he's only got two on our trail, but it don't mean he sent an army, neither."

"Can we outrun them?"

It was a silly question, she knew, since the horses and mule barely maintained a crawling pace through the tumbled rocks that covered the slope. It would only get slower when they began the next climb.

"If by that you mean can we stay ahead of them, maybe. What we gotta concentrate on is losing them completely."

But he told her nothing of his plans to outwit their followers, and Genevieve was not sure she even cared to know his plans, if he had any. The sky that had been grey when she wakened remained grey, and an angry wind began to howl in the trees and swirl spits of snow.

The weather continued threatening the rest of that day and for the next two, while Rio and Genevieve entered another deep, silent valley and then began the long climb out. That day the first real snow started to fall. If Rio were following a path, it was one Genevieve could not see except for the hoofprints of the palomino and the dun mule in the snow ahead of her.

They were five days out of Sacramento when Rio called an early halt to the day's ride. The snow was heavier, cutting their visibility to a dozen yards or so. The sun was no longer even a pale glimmer behind the clouds; there was no telling how near it was to setting.

Nor was there any telling how near or far their pursuers were. Rio had seen no sign of the two riders for the past two days, though that did not guarantee the men had given up their hunt. Still, with the concealment of the snowfall, Rio consented to build a fire this night.

"If they find us, at least they'll find us warm," he told Genevieve as they huddled close to the flames and sipped bitter coffee with more delight than had it been the finest champagne.

Then, as the darkness thickened around them, they built the fire bigger and spread their single bed closer to it. And Genevieve knew that had it not been for the double layer of blankets beneath

95

them and above them and the body warmth they shared, they would have frozen to death that night.

Rio lay awake for several minutes, not moving, just savoring the warmth of the woman in his arms. The snow that had still been falling when they bedded down last night must have stopped shortly after they fell asleep, for only a light dusting covered the saddles and packs of provisions. Travelling would be easier without the snow in the air, but Rio worried that without something to cover their tracks, they'd be too easily followed.

And on this last day of the journey, he worried more than ever about being followed. Perhaps the unidentified trackers had given up days ago and headed back to Sacramento. Any man in his right mind would have, especially a man in unfamiliar territory who had brought no supplies with him. On all the occasions Rio had spotted the two men, he had never seen any sign that they were prepared for a long hunt.

It was never a good idea, however, to take anything for granted. No one knew better than Rio Jackson the lengths to which a man would go when a woman was involved, especially a woman he wanted but couldn't have.

That thought was enough to make Rio draw away from the woman curled up against him. Not that he didn't want her. He wanted her too damn much, and that was precisely the problem. Each night when he had wrapped himself up in the stiff new blankets with her snuggled beside him, he had sworn he wouldn't kiss her in the morning. Sleeping with her was a matter of survival, nothing more, though he had noted the disappearance of her resistance. He told himself she had merely accepted the seriousness of their situation and was doing what was necessary to stay alive on nights when the temperature dipped well below freezing.

But each morning, the temptation was more than he could resist. Her hair was lank and tangled, her face bore numerous smudges of dirt and soot, and her deep violet blue eyes had lost their lustre, but still his desire for her burned. He thought about stripping off his clothes and rolling in the pristine snow, but if that cooled his fever for a while, he knew it would only return later on.

He had to get this woman back to New Orleans as soon as possible, before she made him completely lose his mind.

Without kissing her, Rio crawled out of the pile of blankets. He stretched and pulled a deep breath of icy air into his lungs. In the clear light before the sun rose above the mountain tops, he surveyed his surroundings with a sense of satisfaction. From the white silhouettes of the mountain peaks to the shadowed valley spread out below, everything welcomed him with a sense of the familiar. Though he had never once doubted his ability to find this place, he still felt a surge of pride at having come to it without a single misstep.

Genevieve sat back in the saddle and gave the scene before her a careful study.

"It's not much," Rio was telling her, "but it's a roof over our heads."

Was there a roof? She assumed there was, since a stone chimney poked through it, though at a slightly crooked angle. She knew she should not have got her hopes up when her guide told her about the existence of a cabin at the bottom of the deep valley. Images of a quaint, cozy, thatch-roofed cottage had filled her mind, only to be dashed to smithereens when she realized that the jumble of unpeeled logs and mud-mortared stones was the eagerly anticipated cabin.

The first words out of her mouth were ungracious, but truthful.

"My God, Mr. Jackson, it has no door! The window is merely a hole in the wall! I believe we would be safer exposed to the elements; I'm afraid a sneeze would cause that *thing* to collapse and bury us alive."

And then, while he was still trying to think of a response to her hurtful words, she suddenly burst into tears.

Chapter Seven

Tears were not a technique Genevieve relied on, but she suspected when Rio ignored her that he was all too familiar with the weepy histrionics of many females of her social class. Her own mother had employed them frequently, and usually got the desired results, but Genevieve's tears were almost as distasteful to herself as they were to the man walking resolutely toward the dilapidated cabin.

How could she tell him it was a combination of exhaustion, hunger, and savage disappointment that brought on the spate of weeping? How could she tell him her imagination had conjured up visions of rustic architecture with all the comforts of civilized living? He would only laugh at her romantic notions, and she was certain she could not bear that.

Neither, however, was she certain she could bear to enter the tumbledown shack.

Rio clearly had no such compunctions. He tethered the palomino to a post just outside the gaping doorway and ducked his head to walk in. His first step raised a cloud of dust, and he sneezed.

The cabin stood.

He turned and called out to the forlorn figure on the mare, "It's safe! A bit dusty, but it stood up to a—" and he sneezed again.

He made quite a sight, leaning out the doorless opening in the wall. The lintel could not have been

99

much more than five feet above the ground, which meant he had to stoop to get that extra foot or so of his height through the door. Nearly a week's growth of beard gave him a disreputable appearance that was not helped by the condition of the building he proposed they inhabit.

And yet he could find it in him, under these appalling circumstances, to make light of the situation.

Genevieve sniffed and wiped a cold hand across her eyes and managed a ghost of a smile.

"If it can withstand one of your sneezes," she called as she dismounted, "I suppose it can withstand anything."

Levity helped. He led her weary mare to the same post and looped the reins through the rusty ring. Then, with a deep breath for courage, Genevieve ducked her own head and crossed the threshold.

She nearly burst into fresh tears.

A shutterless window let in sufficient light to illuminate the pathetic single room too clearly. All its filth and poverty was laid bare.

The floor was dirt, littered now with the droppings and refuse of birds and other animals that had wandered in and out. The furnishings consisted of a bedframe with only shreds of mouse-eaten rope left dangling from the holes, a table made from a single split log laid lengthwise across two stumps, and a chair made from a third stump. A shelf was set into the wall beside the stone chimney. Spiderwebs festooned it so thickly they might have been the only thing fastening it to the rough bark of the walls.

"The door's probably lying under the snow. If so, I can have it rehung in no time," Rio suggested. "We can always nail a blanket over the window to keep out the worst of the wind, and with a fire, it'll be as cozy as home."

Genevieve swallowed more tears. As cozy as home? He had no idea what he was saying, of course. But then, she had no idea what kind of hovel he might call home.

The fireplace was the one part of the cabin that seemed in passable condition. The fact that the hearth was blackened with the smoke of many fires proved its capability.

"Then perhaps I should begin laying a fire while you search for the door," Genevieve replied. She had to block from her mind the absurdity of what she had just said. If her voice was a bit unsteady, at least she had got all the words out in one string, without a gasp or a sob. "It's not much past noon, so we shall have light for several hours. Let us not waste it."

She probably used that same tone of voice when ordering her servants around her New Orleans mansion. Rio mumbled a sarcastic, "Yes, *ma'am*," and would have given her a mocking salute except that he had to duck his head to escape the suddenly close confines of the little cabin.

Genevieve stood to admire her handiwork. The snowy branches sizzled and steamed, but they burned. And the billows of smoke curled up the chimney, not out into the room. Perhaps there was a chance after all of spending a relatively comfortable night.

Before then, however, there was much to do. The mule was unburdened and the packs brought into the cabin. Rio finished his repairs to the door and hung it on new hinges. Rummaging through the cabin produced a handful of bent, rusty nails, but they were serviceable enough to tack a sheet of

101

canvas over the bare window.

That left only the light from the fire to dispel the gloom inside, but Genevieve did not particularly mind. At least now the fire was warming the tiny space within the walls. She could cook a decent meal, and then, with a full stomach for the first time in days, sleep snugly and alone, without the disturbing presence of Rio Jackson so close to her.

"It seems like a great deal of work for just a single night," she commented when Rio had finished covering the window.

"I thought we'd stay a couple nights, maybe three or four," he told her. In the gloom, he couldn't see well enough to judge her reaction, so he didn't bother to look at her. Or maybe it was his guilty conscience that kept his eyes trained on the work in his hands.

"Oh? But shouldn't we be getting out of the mountains as soon as possible? Before the snow comes?"

Three or four days in this cabin alone with Rio Jackson? Absolutely not. Genevieve busied herself over the kettle that sat precariously on stones placed in the bed of coals. She did not want him to see how alarmed she was at this unexpected turn of events, but neither was she about to spend an extended stay here with him.

"It might be too late already. I figured I could reconnoiter a bit this afternoon, while you stay here. If the passes are still clear, we can spend the night and get an early start in the morning. If not, we've got supplies and shelter for the winter, and we'll head on back to St. Joe come spring."

She shivered, as though someone had just walked across her grave. She recalled the way she had seen him in the Maison de Versailles, lounging casually at the back of the salon with a glass of whiskey in one hand. He was indeed no different from the other revolting animals in that room.

Brandishing the wooden spoon with which she had been stirring the contents of the kettle, Genevieve whirled to face this latest threat.

"You knew all along, didn't you," she accused. "You planned this, every step of the way."

Strewn with cooking utensils, an unopened sack of flour, and other provisions, the table lay between them. The woman had no weapon other than the spoon, but Rio doubted that would stop her from attacking him in her present state of mind.

"No, lady, I didn't plan it," he said, his hands raised in an attitude of surrender. "I wanted to take you to San Francisco, remember? If Paul hadn't overheard about Kulkey's ambush, that's exactly where you'd be right now."

"Do you expect me to believe that? Mr. Bruckner was probably your accomplice. How many times have you done this before? How many unsuspecting young women have you kidnapped and brought to this hideaway? And what did you do once you had finished with them?"

"You are crazy, lady. If I had anybody up here in the past three years, do you think it'd look like this?" He waved an arm to take in the shabby cabin and was gratified to see a light of reason enter her fiery eyes. "Do you think I had anything to do with that little show your Jean-Louis put on back in the Maison de Versailles? Think about it. All I did was try to get you out of a situation you had got yourself into. The rest of it ain't my fault."

"But you knew there was a chance we'd not be able to make it back to New Orleans."

103

He shrugged. She was being reasonable now that the first shock had worn off, but he sensed her wariness. And if he had forgotten his own feelings in the face of her anger, the guilt came rushing back very quickly.

"Sure, I knew there was a chance," he mumbled as he turned back to the window to examine the canvas. "That's why I headed up here. If it was already too late to beat the snow, at least we'd have shelter. There's plenty of game, and the creek never freezes. And if Kulkey followed us this far, he's gonna be spending some mighty cold nights in the open, 'cause there ain't nothin' but wilderness between here and that camp we went through two days ago."

When she said nothing in reply, Rio strode to the door and picked up the rifle he had leaned against the frame.

"It's gettin' late," he said without turning to face Genevieve. "I'm gonna do some scoutin' before dark, maybe bring in some fresh meat."

For a moment, while he held the door open, daylight flooded the tiny room and left him in sharp silhouette as he ducked under the low lintel. Then he was gone, quickly, silently, and the cabin plunged once more into darkness.

The overcast sun cast no shadows by which to judge the passage of time, but the sixth sense of experience told Rio he had only a few hours left until dark. He glanced at the sky to gauge the weather, not the time, then slipped the rifle into its scabbard and swung himself into the saddle. The palomino sidestepped impatiently before Rio turned him back in the direction from which they had come.

Though he had seen no sign of their pursuers for almost two days, Rio never let them slip from his mind. Now, while his charge was relatively safe in the shelter of the cabin, he could make one last reconnaissance.

He could also use the time alone to think without distractions.

It would be snowing soon, he knew. If not tonight or tomorrow, soon enough. He glanced over his shoulder at the still rising peaks of the mountains. Up there, the snow was already too deep to pass. He did not have to ride into them to be sure of that fact. If this sheltered valley was shrouded in nearly a foot of the stuff, there was no sense trying to get through the higher passes.

Recognition of that fact brought a twinge of guilt that Rio angrily shook off.

"It wasn't a lie," he said out loud to the silent, cold afternoon. "And if it was, it was for her own good. *I* knew we'd be stuck here 'til spring, so it didn't matter if she knew or not."

He retraced the path they had taken earlier that day and experienced a sense of relief when he noticed that there was no sign of their passing. The wind and the light but steady snow had blotted out all their tracks. Now only one set of hoofprints marked the trail.

An hour's ride took him to the opposite end of the valley from the cabin. He rode only a short distance up the increasingly steep mountainside, then, at a broad plateau, dismounted and left the palomino's reins dangling. After climbing to the top of a rocky ridge swept clear of snow by the incessant wind, Rio settled into a low crouch to peer over a granite boulder. Before him stretched another long, deep valley, one he and Genevieve had crossed at dawn this morning.

105

He spotted the tell-tale plume of smoke immediately. The dying daylight and the distance to the hunters' camp made it difficult for Rio to pick out the details, but eventually he determined there were still just the two of them. They were further behind than the last time he had seen them, but he had run out of room to run.

Scanning the lay of the land between his present position and the campfire, he contemplated several courses of action. The one that guaranteed freedom from pursuit also carried the greatest risk of discovery, not to mention half a dozen other dangers. The more he thought about it, however, the more he realized how little choice he really had.

He looked back at the patient gold stallion, trained so well not to stray when the reins hung loose against his neck. If Rio did not return, how long would the horse wait before wandering off in search of food?

"I'll be back," Rio promised, then began the long descent on foot.

Genevieve wakened to darkness and the muffled whinnies of startled horses. She had barely brought her mind back to consciousness and remembered where she was when the door of the cabin burst open. The faint light of a snowy dawn swirled in on a gust of wind before a hunched silhouette slammed the door shut again.

"Rio, is that you?" she asked as she struggled to extricate herself from a mound of blankets.

"Yeah, it's me."

She still could see nothing, but knew from the sounds that Rio was looking for her, fumbling around the tiny space of the cabin. He bumped into the heavy table and swore.

"Jesus, Viva, where are you?" he finally asked, and then she heard the pain in his voice.

"Right here. What's wrong? Are you hurt?"

Genevieve held her breath and listened for his. It was ragged and labored.

She groped her way to the fireplace and the stick she had used as a poker. Only a bed of ash and tiny coals remained, but the kindling she had brought in earlier was dry now and flamed to life the instant it touched the embers. Frantic, she piled on larger pieces of wood until the fire blazed strongly.

By the flickering light, she saw Rio stumble to the tree-stump chair and sink down upon it, then gingerly lift his left arm with his right hand and rest it upon the table. From elbow to wrist, the sleeve was darkened with a spreading stain.

Genevieve's stomach did a nervous flip-flop. "What happened?"

Rio grimaced and twisted the injured arm so he could see it better.

"I went hunting."

"At night? What can you hunt in the dark?"

"Skunks."

"Skunks? But we can't eat skunks! Why in heaven's name were you—"

"Two-legged skunks."

"Oh," Genevieve replied in a tiny, tense voice when she realized exactly what he meant. With a nagging sense of horror, she wondered if he had killed the two men who had dogged their trail the past several days, but she could not bring herself to ask. She was afraid what the answer would be.

"One of 'em thought I was a bear comin' to eat their horses and he took a couple of shots at me. Got lucky with one of 'em."

Now that he could hold the arm still, the pain

began to ebb a bit, but when he tried to unbutton his coat, another wave of dizziness washed over him. His eyes closed slowly and he swayed on the tree-stump stool.

Genevieve's heart skipped a beat. If anything happened to this man—it didn't bear thinking about. Rio Jackson was hardly the kind of man with whom she dreamed of being snowbound in an isolated mountain cabin—she was not sure she had ever dreamed of being snowbound with *anyone*—but he was her only hope of escaping those mountains and returning home to New Orleans.

With one arm around his waist, she steadied him, then with nervous fingers she reached to unbutton his coat. With his good right arm he pushed her away.

"I can get it," he snapped. "I don't need your help."

She backed away and watched as he struggled with the buttons. One by one he worked them free, then managed somehow to slip his right arm from the sleeve. But when it came to pulling the other arm out, the pain was too much.

Genevieve walked to him and gave him the assistance she knew he would never bring himself to ask for. He groaned when she pulled the sleeve over the injury, but he did not lose consciousness.

The bloodstain on his shirt was still wet and spreading.

"I'm going to heat some water so I can clean the wound," Genevieve told him. "And don't argue with me. You can't do it yourself, and it has to be done. This may be the only time you'll be glad I'm here, so be quiet and let me take advantage of the situation."

She filled the coffee pot from the canteens and

then set it amidst the flames in the fireplace. She was kneeling on the stone hearth, poking at the fire with her stick, when Rio finally conquered the pain enough to open his eyes again.

"I didn't kill 'em," he said.

She couldn't face him.

"I never thought you had."

"Yes, you did. You just didn't want to ask, afraid what I'd say."

She blamed the heat in her cheeks on the glowing fire. His accusation was too accurate.

"Well, I didn't kill 'em. Didn't even think of it. I snuck up on their horses and loosened a couple of shoes. They got a long walk home, but they won't be comin' after us."

He didn't like the taste left in his mouth by that angry telling of the truth. What Miss Genevieve Marie du Prés thought of him was unimportant, and it bothered him that he had felt so compelled to exonerate himself in her eyes. Had exhaustion and loss of blood affected his brain and made him care about her opinion?

He was exhausted, and he had lost a great deal of blood. Expending every effort to ignore the pain it brought, Rio began to roll up the torn sleeve to get a better look at the wound.

He almost passed out.

"Here, let me do that," Genevieve whispered.

He hadn't heard her approach or even been aware of her nearness. Now her slender fingers gently unbuttoned the cuff of his shirt. The touch of them against his hand and wrist sent a frightening quiver through him that had nothing to do with the pain from his injury.

He tried to pull his hand away but couldn't.

"Did I hurt you?"

He looked up and found himself staring into her

eyes just as he had that first morning when he kissed her.

His mouth suddenly dry, he croaked, "No. I mean, yeah, it hurts, but it wasn't your fault."

For days and days, she had relied on him for everything, and now he needed her. Genevieve knew she should have felt grateful for this opportunity to repay part of her enormous debt, but what she felt at this strange moment was more than gratitude.

She pushed the tattered, bloody sleeve up to his elbow, aware that her fingers ached to caress the exposed skin. Startled by her own reaction, Genevieve glanced to Rio's face, to search his eyes for some kind of explanation. She found only a reflection of her own confusion — and pain.

She refocused her attention on the wound.

"Another half inch and you'd have lost your arm," she said, wrinkling her nose at the sight of blood oozing from the jagged wound that ran from just below his elbow to a couple inches above his wrist. Instead of a neat, clean cut, the bullet had left a long, messy wound, with bits of shirt fabric and jacket leather stuck to the drying blood.

"Another half inch and he'd have missed me altogether," Rio retorted.

The hours of panic were slowly fading, to be replaced with a sense of relief and an almost overwhelming lethargy. Only the pain in his arm kept Rio from falling asleep. But he did close his eyes as he gave in to the ministrations of a dark-haired sprite who flitted about him on invisible wings. One moment she was dabbing a warm, wet cloth to the torn flesh on his arm, the next she placed a mug of steaming coffee in his right hand.

She gave him orders he thought he obeyed, to lift his arm so she could wrap some kind of bandage around it, to stand and lean on her if neces-

110

sary, to lie down and get some sleep. That one he didn't think he'd have any trouble with. There was something he thought he should have told her, but whatever it was would have to wait. After hours and hours in the freezing wind and snow, after scrambling up the slippery mountainside and then riding hell bent for leather back to the cabin, after fighting with the searing pain in his arm, Rio Jackson had reached the end of his endurance.

Chapter Eight

Genevieve sat down on the tree-stump stool and let out a long, weary sigh. A few feet away, Rio continued to sleep as soundly as a baby. He had hardly moved since collapsing on the pile of blankets at dawn; now night was falling again.

So far he had no fever, or at least Genevieve didn't think he had any. She had put her hand to his forehead often during the day and found it no warmer than her own. She knew little enough about medicine but believed lack of fever was a good sign.

She did not, however, think his continued slumber was a good sign, but neither was she eager to try waking him.

He saved her the trouble.

He stretched to the accompaniment of moans and groans and a cavernous yawn, then yelped as he rolled onto the injured arm.

"What the—?"

"Please, Mr. Jackson, don't start swearing," she pleaded. "In case you don't remember, you were shot last night. I did the best I could."

He shifted into a sitting position, suddenly aware that what he had thought was a flat, lumpy pillow was in fact his hat. He reached for it with his uninjured hand.

The pain in the left arm was still throbbing, but

not nearly as bad as last night. He poked at the hat with some success, then tossed it toward the table. It landed beside a pot from which a thin curl of steam was rising.

Rio's stomach grumbled loudly.

"I think you did quite well," he offered. "I smell beans and bacon and coffee, and there better be plenty of all of 'em."

"There is. Do you need some help?"

He shook his head. The arm ached, to be sure, but he was stiff and sore everywhere from last night's foray and then sleeping like a rock for so long on such a hard bed.

"I must be getting old," he groaned as he made it to his feet and stretched again.

The ceiling was too low to accommodate his height and the reach of his arms. His knuckles grazed the loose dirt of the sod roof and a shower of soil descended on his head.

Genevieve laughed.

Rio scowled.

"What's so funny?"

"I would have given just about anything to be able to reach that far. You do it with no effort at all and regret that the ceiling isn't higher yet."

He shrugged and walked to the table. Expecting to find a pair of tin plates and mugs on the rough wood, he was surprised to find the dishes laid out on rectangles of smooth white linen. The candle that illuminated the table had been stuck to a glittering lump of granite, and an extra bowl filled with pine cones and a few sprigs of red berries served as a centerpiece.

A nervous prickle ran down his spine. He let his gaze wander around the tiny cabin, afraid of what havoc Genevieve Marie du Prés had wreaked.

"You've been busy," he remarked.

She shrugged.

"I had to do something, besides watch you sleep."

She had even found a second "chair," an upended length of unsplit pine log dragged in from outside. Rio checked it for sticky globs of resin, found none, and then sat down gingerly. The chair didn't wobble.

At least he wasn't faced with an arsenal of forks and knives, just one of each.

He didn't wait for permission to eat. He grabbed the pot of beans and scooped a pile onto his plate. The aroma set his mouth to watering instantly, and he couldn't seem to fork the food into it quickly enough. He was aware that Genevieve sat across the table from him, her hands folded demurely on her lap, but nothing was going to stop him until that plate was empty—and his stomach was full.

Genevieve watched him, and blinked back tears. He had noticed the difference in the cabin; she could tell by the way his eyes had widened and then narrowed when he looked around the place. Obviously her labors were unappreciated, except in the kitchen department.

He must have felt her stare; he looked up, his fork halfway to his open mouth.

"You got a problem?"

She shook her head.

He ate the beans from the fork, then slammed it down on the table. "Aw, hell, Viva, don't give me that. Somethin's eatin' you, and you're not going to let me have a minute's peace until you have it eatin' at me, too."

His eyes were steady on her, blue as a forgotten summer sky, hard as sapphires. She could not escape them, nor the demands they made upon her. Yet she had demands of her own.

"We're not leaving here, are we."

He knew what she was asking, and he knew the

114

answer, but he was not going to give it yet. So he stared at her, as boldly and unblinkingly as she did at him.

"Of course we are. Can't get to New Orleans unless we do."

Sometime during the day she had found time to wash her face and pull a brush through her hair. Rio scratched his chin with its week's growth of beard and frowned.

"I mean now, today or tomorrow. We aren't leaving this cabin, this valley, these mountains, until spring, are we?" Now there was a questioning tone in her voice, and a little note of fear.

He had lied to her often enough before, but this time, facing her across the table, he could not dredge up a lie.

"No, not until spring," he whispered. He turned his eyes away from her and picked up the fork once more. There was still food to eat.

"You knew that when you brought me here, didn't you."

Again she stated it as a fact, not a question, but there was still a whisper of hope that he might deny it.

"I did," he admitted. "But we didn't have any choice." He nudged the pot of beans toward her. "Aren't you hungry? They don't taste so good when they're cold."

When she ignored the gesture, Rio rested his elbows on the edge of the table and leaned forward. The bandage on the raised left arm showed only a small dull brown stain; the bleeding had stopped long ago.

"All right, look, I told you I lied. I lied to Paul Bruckner, too, and that bothers me a lot more than lying to you."

Her eyes widened in surprise but she said nothing.

Rio continued, in a less antagonistic tone, "I knew we couldn't get through the mountains, not this late in the season, not without preparation. I wasn't even sure we'd make it this far, but we did. By the skin of our teeth."

"The men following us?"

"Yeah. I kept us out of rifle range, but the mule was slowing us down. Without her and the supplies, we'd never make it through the winter, but with her, we might not be able to stay ahead of them."

He pushed the pot of beans a bit closer, and this time Genevieve took some. Still, she toyed with them once they were on her plate, and she remained quiet and thoughtful.

"You knew about this place, though. You intended to come here when we left Sacramento?"

Satisfied that the girl was finally going to eat something, Rio returned to his own food before answering.

"I wasn't sure the cabin would still be here, but I figured there'd be enough of it left that we could put it back together. And it'd be better than nothing."

"So you *have* been here before."

He caught the accusation and it made him bristle.

"Ycah, I've been here before, but not the way you make it out. I found this place three years ago, after I made my first trip with a bunch of gold-crazy easterners. I figured what the hell, might as well give it a try myself, since I'd come this far."

He finished the beans on his plate and reached for the pot again. He was about to scrape it clean when he remembered his manners and offered more to Genevieve. She declined, so he helped himself to every last bean.

"I didn't have much luck. Either I was too impa-

116

tient or not stubborn enough, but when I didn't strike it rich after three weeks of panning in freezing water, I decided to head back to San Antonio."

"Is that where you're from?"

"Yeah."

He turned his attention back to the plate of beans in front of him, as though to erase any thoughts the mention of San Antonio brought.

Genevieve followed his example and finished what little supper she had taken. Then, leaving Rio to whatever black thoughts occupied him at the moment, she rose and walked to the fire, where the coffee pot steamed. She poured a little onto her dirty plate and swished it around, then set the dish aside to soak clean. There was enough left in the pot for at least two more cups, so she carried it back to the table and filled both her mug and Rio's.

He looked up at her, and smiled.

"Thanks," he said in a rather sheepish voice. "I was a real jack-ass last night, over a little scratch, and then I slept all day while you did all the work."

Genevieve looked down at the placemats torn from a clean petticoat Angela Bruckner had stuffed into a satchel. Most of the rest of that petticoat was tied around Rio's arm.

"No, I'm the one who should be saying 'thank you,' Mr. Jackson. I've been a great deal of trouble, and not very kind to a man who has saved my life several times in the past few days."

"Then let's call it even steven, okay?"

His grin was returned, and he toasted her with the mug of fresh coffee. Though the pine-log chair had no back, Rio relaxed, leaning forward to swirl the coffee lazily in his cup.

"Anyway, as I was saying, I headed back to San Antonio and got as far as this valley, only then it

117

was high summer. Viva, you gotta see this place in summer; it's like pure paradise. In the morning I'll take you down by the spring where there's this little waterfall, and — sorry."

She had never seen him so animated, nor so voluble. Was this a different side to him, or had he perhaps hidden a flask of whiskey inside his shirt? No, that wasn't possible. But the enthusiasm in his voice seemed contagious. Genevieve found herself mimicking his pose, elbows on the edge of the table, tin mug held in both hands. When Rio began his tale again, she drank in every word.

"There was an old guy camped down by the spring, all alone. He'd come west a few years before the gold rush with his wife and daughter. The wife died, and the daughter went back east to get married, so it was just him and a couple o' the orneriest Missouri mules you'd ever want to see."

"Like that big white one?"

"Yep, just like him. One of those son of a bitches bit me, and I swore I'd never own another. They're tough, but they're stubborn and meaner 'n dirt."

He swallowed another swig of coffee, then poured the rest into his plate. Checking the pot, he guessed it contained just enough for another half-cup each.

"No, I've had enough," Genevieve said politely. "Go ahead, finish it." She wasn't sure whether she meant the coffee or his story — or both.

"Thanks."

She was exhausted. The soft yellow light from the candle accentuated the dark hollows under her eyes. As guilty as Rio felt for keeping her awake when she should have been crawling between those blankets on the floor, he couldn't resist taking this opportunity to talk to her. Just talk. Nothing more.

When had a woman ever talked to him before? Or listened? He couldn't remember, and the effort of trying only dredged up other, unpleasant memories. He returned to that summer, one that he had truly enjoyed.

"I told the old guy—his name was Ernest Tibler—he was crazy to stay here through the winter without some kind of shelter. He suggested a stone cabin, and that's what we started to build, but it took too long with only the two of us. We finished it off with logs."

"So that's why it's half and half."

Genevieve glanced at the ceiling, with its exposed logs supporting the sod roof. She had no idea what this Ernest Tibler might have looked like, but her drowsy mind conjured up a vision of Rio Jackson, shirtless, laboring in the late summer sun. The valley was all green and gold and alive with the song of birds. While the shadowy figure of an older man shouted instructions, Rio lifted another log into position on the cabin's roof.

Standing on the top of the stone walls, he wiped the sweat from his brow and, hands on his lean hips, surveyed the valley and the mountains around him like a king. A satisfied smile slowly spread across his face.

"Viva? Viva? Are you awake?"

His voice broke into her dream like a lightning bolt.

"How rude of me!" she exclaimed, realizing she had indeed fallen asleep while he was still talking to her.

"No, how rude of me," Rio replied. He got to his feet and walked over to the fire, which was in need of additional fuel for the night.

"Rio?"

Her voice had a sleepy edge to it. Rio put more wood on the fire.

"Yeah?"

"Why did you call me 'Viva?' "

The word sounded softer on her tongue. It sent a flicker of warmth through him, stronger than the flames from the burning wood in front of him.

"It's a helluva lot shorter than 'Genevieve,' that's why," he grumbled. "And kinda for a good luck charm. It means 'alive' in Spanish; maybe it'll get us both out of these mountains alive at the end of winter."

He tossed a heavy log on top of the smaller branches that were burning ferociously, then got to his feet and stretched. Alive was what he felt now, alive with wanting her.

"Shouldn't've stayed up talking about a man dead and buried almost two years," he told her. "Now, you get yourself into bed there and get to sleep, while I make a quick trip outside to, uh, check on the animals."

The night was clear, the moonless sky filled with stars. A sunny day had melted most of the early-season snow, but with nightfall, the cold had returned. Rio shivered as he pulled the door shut behind him. He had left the coat behind intentionally, with hopes that a few minutes in the cold would chase away the insane desire that he had so far been unable to get under control.

"Why?" he whispered in agonized desperation to the stillness surrounding him. "Why me? Why her?"

The questions had plagued him almost since the instant he recognized her in the brothel. Or maybe it had been longer, maybe since the day she walked up to him and said she wanted to join his wagon train. He had experienced it then, too, the fierce, uncontrollable wanting, coupled with the sure and certain knowledge that this was not a woman for the likes of Rio Jackson. Again, it sent a rush of hot anger through him.

But this time he wasn't angry at her. She was blameless, as blameless as a spoiled, impulsive, beautiful woman can be. The fault was his, for giving in to the same impulses. He thought he had learned to ignore them years ago.

He shivered again. When he tried to roll down the left shirtsleeve, he found it stiff with dried blood. He swore bitterly, remembering that this had once been, not too many days ago, his best shirt. Now it was ruined, beyond salvage. Bitter, he grabbed the garment at the throat and ripped it open. As though the fabric itself burned his flesh, he couldn't get the shirt off fast enough.

He was about to shout his frustration to the pristine night, but a creak and the spill of yellow candlelight halted him.

"Rio?" Genevieve called softly. "Are you out there?"

She held his coat in one hand.

"Yeah, I'm here."

He turned his back to the cabin, trying to ignore her, but quiet footsteps on frosty grass drew nearer.

"You'll freeze," she whispered, as though afraid to break the stillness. "What happened to your shirt?"

Before he could answer or even tell her to leave him alone, the fire-warmed comfort of his coat settled about his shoulders. Survival instinct forced him to welcome it and turn toward the woman who had brought it to him.

Only starlight illuminated her face, raised now to his with a worried frown. Such soft light, fitting on such delicate beauty. No man could resist the temptation of those bright, innocent eyes, those sensuous, parted lips. Certainly not a man like Rio Jackson.

He wanted to gather her into his arms and crush her to him with all the passion that roared through him. How long had he craved her? How many nights had he dreamed of just such an opportunity? How could he not take advantage of it?

Gently, Rio took her face in hands that trembled from the cold as much as the barely controlled desire. She did not pull away; the only sign that she was even aware of his touch was the soft sigh she breathed and the slow closing of her eyes. He lowered his mouth to hers, still hesitant, still almost afraid.

But the instant his lips touched hers, all fear, all hesitation fled. This was no sleepy, half-conscious woman in his arms, accepting but unknowing. Now she returned the kiss, with a need almost as great as his own. Her lips parted, giving his tongue access to the sweet depth of her mouth.

At first it was his warmth that drew her, as the cold night air seeped through the blanket Genevieve had tossed over her shoulders. When she saw the strain, the exhaustion carved into his face, her heart had gone out to him. And when his strong, trembling fingers had circled her face, she looked up into eyes filled with invisible tears.

She closed her own eyes to the sight, but it was too late. She had seen his pain, his loneliness, and she could neither ignore nor forget it. When he kissed her, she was powerless to deny him — or herself.

Her arms slid around his waist, pulling her ever closer to him until their bodies touched. The sensation of his naked skin under her fingertips sent a flash like fuse-fire along her nerves; the explosion was inevitable.

She felt the swelling of her breasts against the

warm flesh of his chest, the rise of his manhood against her belly. A foggy warmth enshrouded her. Consciousness gave way to desire like dry grass before a prairie fire.

And then suddenly there was cold, bitter, biting cold. Angrily, Rio escaped her embrace and staggered back a step or two.

"No," he gasped, shaking his head emphatically. "No."

He turned so abruptly that the coat fell off his shoulders. Genevieve watched him stride off, not toward the cabin but into the starlit night. Shivering with the cold and confusion, she started to follow him but stopped. His name was on her lips to call him back, but she made not a sound.

She bent down to retrieve the coat and then walked on rubbery legs back to the cabin. Despite the cold night air that rushed in, she left the door open.

Rio stomped into the cabin just a few minutes later. His lips were a ghastly blue color, and goosebumps covered his back, arms, and chest. He slammed the door shut and shot the wooden bolt that secured it, then leaned back, rubbing his arms furiously to restore sluggish circulation.

"Shall I make some more coffee?" Genevieve asked.

Rio shook his head. His teeth chattered so violently he couldn't speak at first.

Finally, he managed to tell her, "Just heat up some water so I can shave and clean up a bit."

As the warmth from the fire began to seep into his frozen body, Rio stumbled to the corner where the saddlebags were piled. He knelt on the hard-packed dirt of the floor and began to rummage through his meager collection of belongings. From one pouch he pulled a clean but badly wrinkled shirt and a tight roll of black fabric that soon proved to be a clean pair of pants. Satisfied, he tossed that saddlebag back into the corner and attacked the second.

It produced a wooden-handled razor, a mug of shaving soap with a well-used brush, and a small, silver-handled mirror.

Rio took the items to the table and set them down almost reverently.

Sitting by the fire that was now a roaring blaze, Genevieve looked up at Rio and asked, "Would you like some privacy?"

He responded with a very puzzled expression that gradually gave way to a disappointed kind of embarrassment.

"Would I?" he asked in return, "Or would you?"

A little smile lit her face.

Rio sank down to sit on the crude chair and scratched at the whiskers on his cheek.

"I'm gonna shave, that's all," he said. "In the morning, I'll see if I can find the tub Ernest made, and then you and me can each have a nice hot bath, private-like, down by the spring."

"Outdoors?!"

"Sure, why not? Who's gonna see you, except me, and I won't look."

Genevieve turned her back on the man whose blue eyes seemed to read her very thoughts. Could he possibly know that the very thought of his seeing her while she bathed sent trickles of rekindled desire through her veins?

There was steam coming from the coffee pot; the water was hot enough for shaving, she supposed. Carefully she carried it to the table where Rio waited. She had the feeling he had not taken his eyes from her for a single second.

"I found a basin this afternoon," she told him.

"It's not much, but I'm sure it's better than the coffee pot. For shaving, at least."

She scurried away, to the shelf by the chimney where an assortment of utensils now rested. The china basin she brought to him was badly chipped but still recognizable as one Ernest Tibler's wife had brought from wherever they called home.

Rio poured a couple inches of water into the basin and said, "Sit down, Viva. Don't stand there like a scared rabbit. Haven't you ever watched a man shave before?"

The nervous shake of her head was an involuntary but honest answer, and it didn't surprise Rio at all.

"You better get used to it, then, 'cause I tend to do it once a day, when I can." He splashed hot water on his face and reached for the mug and brush. He didn't speak again until he had covered the black growth with thick white lather. "You don't look like you ever saw a man without a shirt on, either. That's another thing you better get used to."

Watching him draw the razor steadily across his skin, Genevieve wondered just how many other things Rio Jackson was going to demand she accustom herself to before this long winter was over. And winter had just begun.

Chapter Nine

They bedded down separately that night, for the first time since leaving Sacramento. If Rio noticed the difference, he made no sign, but fell almost immediately asleep. Genevieve, despite her exhaustion, lay awake for what seemed hours before finally drifting into troubled slumber. Whether she missed the security of Rio's warmth beside her or was disturbed by the events of the evening, she could not tell. She only knew that all her thoughts centered around the strange, puzzling man with the bright blue eyes.

Her dreams, however, brought two other men back to her consciousness. Twice she wakened herself from nightmares in which Jean-Louis paraded her through the streets of New Orleans as his bride, wearing nothing but a sheer white veil that exposed more of her than it concealed. Both times she opened her eyes to find the cabin dark, the fire burned down to a bed of coals. There was a tightness at the back of her throat that told her she had been crying in her sleep. She made her way to the fireplace and built the blaze once again, and swallowed the fear that now gnawed at her.

She had trouble falling asleep after the second dream and almost crawled under the blankets that covered Rio. With no logical reason for wishing to do something so impulsive, she returned to her own pallet on the floor.

This time she dreamt of a man in starlit shadows, who called to her and folded her in his arms against the cold. But when she raised her face for the kiss she knew would come, she found Buster Kulkey leering down at her. She screamed and struggled to escape, but his arms held her like bands of iron. Tears streamed down her face and her throat grew raw from hoarse sobbing.

"Hey, wake up, Viva!"

Rio's voice cut into the dream like a beam of bright white light. Buster Kulkey vanished, though the fear he engendered remained. Aware of a hand on her shoulder, Genevieve slowly opened her eyes. There, to her blessed relief, was Rio, his brows knit with concern.

"Bad dream," she mumbled, wanting to throw her arms around him and hang on for dear life. Instead, she rolled away from his concerned gaze and curled into a secure but forlorn little ball under her blankets and wiped her eyes dry.

"Musta been," he agreed, getting to his feet. "But it's time we got up anyway. Sun's up and it looks like we got enough of a break in the weather to get a few things done. Can't waste it; never know when the snow is gonna come back."

They breakfasted on coffee, then Rio outlined the day's chores. First task, he insisted, was to provide fodder for the horses and mule. When Genevieve questioned why the animals came first, he gave her a look of pure scorn.

"I don't know about you, but I have no desire to walk all the way to New Orleans," he told her. "That means we take care of the animals, since they can't take care of themselves. Even if it is just beans and coffee, we got food to last a while. They don't."

It proved to be back-breaking work. For the next

127

four days, they gathered every blade of grass they could find and loaded it on a contraption Rio called a travois, pulled behind the horses. The mare accepted hers placidly, but the yellow stud seemed insulted at having to drag tree branches across the ground.

The snow that had covered the valley on the day of their arrival melted under a bright October sun the day Rio lay recovering from his injury, and no more fell, leaving the dry, frosted vegetation exposed. But there was little of it, and that sparsity forced Genevieve and Rio to range farther and farther from the security of the cabin.

Each evening, after the early sunset ended their foraging, Genevieve trudged into the cabin to prepare a meager supper, while Rio turned his attention to the tree limbs, split logs, and scraps of half-rotten lumber piled behind the building. Working by the light of a small lantern, he slowly reconstructed a lean-to that would provide cover for both the animals and the store of feed.

There was no time for anything else. Though the days were short, both Genevieve and Rio worked frantically from sun-up to sun-down, and immediately after the evening meal, they collapsed onto their beds and slept like the dead.

But after four days of clear weather, the sky turned grey again, and the air filled with tiny flakes of snow. Sipping his morning coffee, Rio stood just outside the open doorway and considered the day's choices.

"It's not snowing very hard," Genevieve observed. "We should still be able to find grass."

Rio turned his gaze to the sky and pointed to the mountains at the other side of the valley.

"See, it's already snowing pretty heavy higher up. No telling when it'll come down to the valley. If we went out now, we could be stranded and never make it back." He took another sip of the coffee, then dumped the cold dregs onto the ground. "There's plenty to do here anyway."

Genevieve swallowed a groan. Where Rio Jackson was concerned, there was *always* plenty to do.

But to give him credit, Rio had managed to make some of Genevieve's labors easier. Under the branches and boards that became the lean-to, he found a considerable supply of useful items, including two sturdy oaken buckets twice the size of the little one they had bought. They made filling the big tin washtub—another discovery in the lean-to—considerably easier. Though heavier to carry from the spring some fifty yards from the cabin, the larger buckets meant fewer trips.

"What else have you uncovered out there?" Genevieve asked when Rio slipped in the door with his arms filled.

He dumped his treasures on the table with resounding clatter.

"A pair of shears, rusty but salvageable. A block plane in similar condition. A keg of nails, minus the keg. A double-bit axe with a split handle. A two-man bucksaw. Two pots, one skillet, four plates. And a crock of beeswax that I left sittin' outside."

Genevieve looked at the mess of rusty metal and broken wood that littered her table and almost ordered Rio to take his junk right back where he got it. But the past few days had taught her not to take anything this man did at its initial impression. Besides, there was such a look of pride on his face that she hadn't the heart to deny him.

She picked up a strange-looking block of wood with even stranger looking metal parts attached to it.

"What *is* this?" she wondered aloud. "And what do you *do* with it?"

Eager to demonstrate, Rio shoved the other items aside and settled the plane against the rough wood of the table. The blade was rusty but not too dull, and a good push sent the tool slicing down the plank. A long curl of stained pine twisted up from the plane and left behind a smooth, white path.

"Oh, Rio, it's beautiful! Can you do the whole table?"

"Sure, but it'll take some time."

Light in the cabin was limited, even in the middle of the day, but Rio saw by the reflection of firelight in her eyes that Genevieve was truly overjoyed by this simple demonstration. Her smile seemed to illuminate her whole face as she reached out a tentative finger to touch the sleek surface of the wood.

"What else is out there?" she immediately wanted to know. "Can I come out and help you look?"

This was the first time she had shown such enthusiasm, and Rio felt guilty at having to dampen it. But there was nothing else he could do.

"I got it all," he told her as gently as he could. Turning back to gather up the other tools, he explained, "The last time I was here, two years ago, Tibler was dying. I couldn't help him, so I just stayed with him 'til the end, then buried him up on the mountain, so he could look out over the valley."

A strange sadness had crept into his voice, as though he were describing the loss of a dear friend, not a man he had known only briefly.

"He wanted me to have this place, to stay here, but I couldn't. So I stashed what little he had in the back and pulled the lean-to down on top of it, hopin' it'd keep the animals out."

Rio, too, stroked the smooth strip of wood while a wave of memories washed over him.

After a long silence, Genevieve ventured to ask, "What did you do then?"

130

"Huh? Oh, I took his mules back to St. Joe with me and sold 'em. I was gonna send the money to his daughter, but I didn't know her married name or where she lived, and old Ernest had told me he wanted me to have everything anyway, so I spent it on myself."

On whores and whiskey, no doubt, Genevieve mentally snorted. But she couldn't blame the man. Not really.

"Well, if you aren't going to finish what you started, at least get these filthy things off my table and let me get to my own work."

He laughed, a warm genuine chuckle that brought a wide grin to his mouth and merry crinkles around his eyes. When Genevieve returned that grin she experienced again a sudden rush of awareness of how handsome Rio Jackson really was. But then he gathered up his old rusty, broken tools and marched back outdoors with them, and she shook her head clear of such frivolous thoughts. She had work to do.

Unable to get enough water truly hot, she settled for lukewarm and started the laundry. Rio had given her a cake of soap from which she carefully pared a few curls. Water was plentiful, but soap might well become a precious commodity as the months of isolation dragged on. She vowed not to waste it.

She washed her own things first, few as they were, and draped them over a length of rope stretched in front of the fire. Next came Rio's. Another queer feeling twittered in Genevieve's stomach as she picked up two shirts and dropped them into the wash water. She reached out to begin scrubbing them, but her hands refused to enter the water.

"You're crazy, Genevieve du Prés," she told herself in a shaky but audible whisper. She forced the words out in an effort to drown the others muttering in her thoughts. "They're ordinary shirts, made

131

of ordinary homespun. They're dirty and they need to be washed."

"But they touched him," those taunting little whispers in her mind snickered. "They lay against his skin, and you know what that feels like, don't you?"

Her fingers trembled with the memory and drew further from the water.

"Don't be ridiculous," she muttered. "What difference does it make that they've touched him? I have, too, several times."

With that she plunged her traitorous hands into the washtub and grabbed one of the shirts.

She was working up a lather and silencing the tormenting voices with hummed snatches of child hood melodies when yet another memory surfaced. It brought a bubble of laughter that erupted just as Rio burst in the door again.

"Look what I found!" he exclaimed.

This time he dumped an armful of shiny red apples onto the table.

Genevieve plopped the dirty shirt back into the washtub with a splash.

"Oh, Rio, where did you get them?" She wiped her soapy wet hands on her skirt and picked up an apple. "Not buried in the lean-to, I hope?"

"Nope. I'd forgot about Ernest's trees, 'til I was looking around for firewood and one of the apples fell almost on my head."

Genevieve gave the fruit a quick once-over, checking for worm holes, and then sank her teeth into it.

"Good, isn't it."

She could only nod, and take another bite. The apple was so cold it almost made her teeth hurt, but the sweet tang was delicious.

"I never realized how tired I was of beans," she said around a juicy mouthful. "Oh, Rio, this is wonderful."

With the back of her hand she wiped a trickle of juice from her chin. Rio watched the gesture and swallowed, his mouth suddenly dry. At this moment, her guard was down, and she was enjoying a sweet, simple pleasure he had given to her. He wanted her more than ever, yet at the same time he knew the complete foolishness of that desire.

"I don't know if there's anything left of the rest of the garden," he said, hoping words would cover his feelings. "The pears weren't any good, too small and stringy, and the peaches were all gone."

In his mind's eye, he saw her bite into a ripe, succulent peach, her lips pressed to the fuzzy flesh as she drank the sticky nectar. He had to blink the image away, though reality was hardly better.

"I'm not overly fond of peaches anyway," she told him, nibbling away at the core of the apple until there was nothing left but seeds and stem. "What else do you think might be out there?"

She tossed the remnants of the apple into the fireplace, where the flames set it to sizzling.

"Put on your coat and we'll go see."

Her coat consisted of a torn length of blanket draped shawlwise over her shoulders and then fashioned into sleeves with ties at the bottom made of rawhide thongs. It had been sufficient on the sunny days, but she doubted it would keep her warm now that the snow and wind were back.

The orchard had been planted a short distance up the mountain's slope behind the cabin, and in front of it, according to Rio's recollection, Ernest Tibler had planted his last garden.

Dried, dead grass grew there now, covered with a light dusting of snow. Struggling to keep up with Rio's long strides, Genevieve scanned the bleached brown tops of the weeds for a sign of anything familiar, but she knew she wouldn't have recognized anything.

Neither, apparently, did Rio. He kicked at a few

133

clumps and dug the toe of his boot into the frozen ground, but came up with nothing.

"Deer and elk would have got the carrots and turnips, I suppose," he mused. "And the rabbits. That stuff doesn't seed itself anyway."

It was Genevieve who spotted the odd weed first, with its top like a large prickly dandelion.

"What's this thing?" she asked as she pulled the three-foot long stalk from the ground.

Rio turned and smiled.

"Well, at least we got onions to flavor the stew."

Rio brought down the first game the following evening, a young elk. Hungry for fresh meat, they roasted chunks on green sticks over the open fire and devoured them. The next day, Rio taught Genevieve how to cut the remaining meat in thin strips, season it, and dry it slowly. He did not show her, or even tell her, of the old Indian method he had learned to turn the bloody hide into a sheet of soft, strong leather. That was his own chore, tended to outside.

Ernest Tibler's garden plot yielded a couple dozen onions, and that was all. The orchard, however, provided an abundant harvest of apples, though Rio had to hoist Genevieve to his shoulders to gather the uppermost fruits. The trees were still too young to have limbs strong enough for climbing, but at least they had borne fruit, and it would be a shame to let it go to waste.

While a kettle of stew simmered over the fire that evening, Genevieve sorted through the apples. Those with only small rotten spots or worm holes could be cut and pared for applesauce, while those completely unfit for eating could still be given to the livestock for a treat.

The idea struck her as a good one. Leaving the rest of the apples scattered on the table, she slipped her arms into her coat and took three apples. Rio was, as usual, taking care of the animals before coming in for supper, so she grabbed a fourth apple for him, and then ducked out the door.

The lean-to had changed over the past week. At first it had been little more than a roof, but Rio's labors had turned it into a substantial shelter. Dark had already fallen, but in the light of a small lantern, he continued to work.

He was brushing the palomino's coat, thickened and rough now with the onset of winter. Slowly, methodically, he stroked the stiff-bristled brush along the animal's side to remove bits of brush and dirt. He seemed unaware of Genevieve's approach, and for some reason she hesitated to make her presence known.

"I don't like it either, Cinco," he murmured to the horse, "but we're stuck here, and we gotta make the best of it."

The stallion shook his head up and down and let out a soft wuffling noise, just as though he understood exactly what Rio said and was agreeing with him. Genevieve almost laughed out loud, but she held her silence, fascinated by what she saw and heard.

"Yeah, I know, and it's all my fault," he continued. "But you didn't see her there, with those filthy bastards droolin' like dogs after a bitch in heat."

The strokes gained momentum, as the man's anger came out in his actions despite his effort to maintain control.

"I've done some pretty rotten things in my own life, but I never took a woman who didn't want to be taken, and if I hadn't got Viva outta that place, it woulda been the same thing."

Finished, he took a step back and looked the horse over before beginning the laborious task of combing through the long, wavy mane. As he

135

grabbed a hank of the coarse, cream-colored hair, a little chuckle escaped him, and he shook his own head. The horse turned to give him a quizzical stare.

"Damn it, Cinco, I gotta stop talkin' to you like this. I'm startin' to hear answers in my head and think it was you talkin' back!"

Genevieve knew she could hide from him no longer and took advantage of the opportunity to ask, "And were his answers intelligent?"

Rio spun around, all sign of laughter gone and a scowl now clouding his face.

"Where'd you come from?" he demanded.

Startled by this abrupt change, Genevieve hugged her meager coat more tightly around her. One of the apples dropped from her hand.

"I—I came to see if you were almost finished," she stammered as she bent to pick it up. "I thought the horses might like an apple, so I brought some out. Here's one for you, too."

She offered him the unblemished fruit and he took it, though slowly, almost cautiously. She could tell he was wondering how much of his conversation she had overheard, but she wasn't sure how to put him at ease without revealing the truth.

Rio said nothing, just continued to stare at her. Beginning to feel extremely uncomfortable, she pushed past him and walked up to the big palomino. She broke off a chunk of apple and laid it flat on her palm, then extended her hand toward the big animal's nose. As cautiously as his master, Cinco sniffed the proffered treat. His breath steamed in the cold air. The moist warmth of it against her hand sent a shiver up Genevieve's arm. Then velvety lips plucked the fruit and Cinco crunched down on it contentedly.

"I wouldn't get too close," Rio warned. "I don't trust him, especially around women. He's a stallion, and they can be, well, unpredictable."

136

Like you? Genevieve almost blurted out, but she stopped herself just in time.

She had never seen anyone change moods as quickly as Rio Jackson. One instant he was joking with his horse, the next he was back to his wary, closed self. She longed to ask him why, but knew that even if she found the courage to ask, he would never give her an answer.

"Then I guess I'll be careful," she agreed. "But it is time to come in. Supper's ready, and it's getting late."

Still he made no reply, nor did he make any move to leave the lean-to. Uncomfortable, and slightly embarrassed, Genevieve tore her gaze away from him and allowed it to wander while she tried to think of a graceful way to exit.

Then her eyes spotted something at the outer fringe of the lantern's light, something she knew they had not brought with them from Sacramento.

"Is that a trunk?" she asked as she took a step toward the object that had caught her attention. "Oh, Rio, why didn't you tell me this was out here?"

A crude but sturdy rail kept the horses and mule away from the trunk. Genevieve had to duck under the rail before kneeling in the dirt to examine her discovery. Cinco's curious nose pushed at her back, but she ignored it. The apples she had brought for the mare and the mule fell unheeded to the floor.

She ran her fingers nervously along the edge of the sadly weathered brass-bound box. She could see only one leather handle, and it had rotted like the door hinges. The wood was warped, too, until Genevieve was certain anything left within the trunk was undoubtedly as ruined as the outside.

A cry of despair welled up in her throat. What if the trunk contained clothes? They'd be ruined for certain by now. Genevieve felt their imagined loss like a blow. The few garments Angela Bruckner

137

had been able to stuff into a satchel before Genevieve and Rio fled would never last her through the winter. More important, she had declined Angela's offer of a heavy coat, expecting to find one when they bought other provisions. The fear of pursuit had chased her and Rio from the mining camp before she had had a chance to find a coat.

Genevieve thought of the two trunks, so hastily packed in New Orleans and now left behind, likely never to be seen again. She had been frustrated at being able to take only two of them when her search for Jean-Louis began. Now, trapped in a desolate cabin thousands of miles from the nearest dressmakers, she felt a stab of keen desire for those two trunks and their heretofore meager contents. And especially for the worn but heavy wool cloak.

"Ain't nothin' in it," Rio stated flatly.

In the very act of raising the lid, Genevieve froze. She had learned that when Rio slipped into that crude vernacular, it meant he was in a particularly unpleasant mood. He usually became very defensive, if he spoke at all.

"Nothing?" she echoed.

He shrugged and went back to brushing the stallion. This time, however, there was a nervousness to his movements, not the long, relaxed strokes of a man enjoying his labor.

He had no intention of telling her what was in the trunk. She would just have to see for herself, and be damned to what Rio Jackson thought. She lifted the lid and peered into the shadowy interior.

She really had not expected to find clothes, though the hope was always in the back of her mind. Beyond that, she had no expectations at all, so the dozen or so small packages wrapped in waxed leather were not so much disappointing as perplexing. Gingerly, she lifted the top one.

It was heavier than she had anticipated, and through the thick layer of wrapping, she could not

138

tell what exactly it was. The cord that bound the leather stubbornly defied Genevieve's attempts to untie the knot.

"Come on, let's go in and get something to eat," Rio suddenly urged. "Leave that old junk go. It ain't nothin' we can use."

He reached down and took Genevieve by the upper arm. At first she resisted, but she realized part of the reason she couldn't untie the leather was that her fingers were nearly numb with the cold. She got to her feet with Rio's assistance, but she did not put the package back in the trunk. Instead, she tucked it possessively under her arm and then closed the lid on the rest of the treasures.

Besides, in the cabin she had a knife that would make untying the knot unnecessary.

Genevieve led the way to the door, with Rio behind her carrying the lantern. Flakes of fresh snow drifted diamond-like in the light, but at last the wind had died. Still, by the time she pushed the door open, Genevieve was shivering.

Rio blew out the flame and hung the lantern on a hook by the door. The smell of hot food set his empty stomach rumbling. He watched as Genevieve walked to the fire, where the pot of stew simmered. Even in her makeshift coat and ill-fitting skirt, she taunted him, teased him, made him want to scream with rising desire.

He turned and pulled the door open again.

"Where are you going?"

"I forgot something."

"You won't be able to find it without the lantern."

"I can see well enough."

What was wrong with him? Genevieve lifted the pot of stew from its hook and carried it to the table, her brows knit with a puzzled frown. Rio hadn't acted this cold and closed for days.

"Come eat first," she insisted. "Whatever you've

139

left out there will keep until you've eaten. I can hear your stomach from here."

He *was* hungry, and the dark and cold outside grew increasingly less inviting. Besides, he asked himself, what was he going to do once he was out there? Eventually he would have to come back in anyway, and eventually she would confront him with the package.

Damn! he swore silently as he shoved the door closed once more. He let the latch fall into place with a quiet thunk. Only then did he turn slowly and cross the small room to the table.

The package from the old trunk lay right next to Genevieve's plate.

Genevieve ladled stew onto Rio's plate, then onto her own. Food, however, was far from her thoughts. Even the carefully wrapped package she had dropped on the table took second place in her curiosity to Rio's strange behavior.

Over the past few days, they had achieved a measure of civility that, at times, approached friendliness. There had even been moments, such as with the apples or the planing tool, when laughter and a sense of camaraderie filled the dreary little cabin. All that had gone, and Genevieve had no idea what had caused it.

She knew Rio would never respond to a direct assault. Thank goodness, she had long ago mastered the art of subtle interrogation. First her father, then her many beaux, had fallen victim: no one could keep a secret from Genevieve Marie du Prés.

Pouring coffee into Rio's mug, she did not look at him when she asked, "What kind of horse did you say yours is? I remember you told that old man when you bought the mule, but I can't remember what you said."

She knew perfectly well what he had told the old horse-trader, but Rio had no way of knowing what

140

she did and did not remember. So she filled her own mug and then sat down, and proceeded to level a bright, open stare at him, as though she had nothing at all to hide. Which, in fact, she hadn't.

"You better eat, or this is gonna get cold," he said, never once looking up.

How was she supposed to wheedle a confession from him if he wouldn't even look at her?

She tried a bite of stew; it was blessedly much too hot to eat.

"It's too hot. It needs a minute to cool off. And I just can't stand not being able to remember things. You said he was something like 'Alabamian' or 'Andaugustian,' but I know that's not quite right."

"Andalusian," Rio mumbled.

"Ah, yes, Andalusian."

The word rolled off her tongue like an endearment. It sent a shiver down Rio's spine.

"Did you get him in Spain?"

"No."

He was not cooperating at all.

"Well, then, where *did* you get him?" The exasperation was impossible to conceal.

Rio finally looked up, with black fire flashing in his angry blue eyes. "None of your business," he growled.

"Did you *steal* him?"

"I said it was none of your business! And what if I did steal him?"

She had no answer to that. Satisfied, Rio turned back to his meal.

"I don't think you stole him. I think you said that just to frighten me."

She wanted to lean back and fold her arms across her chest, but the stump that served as a chair had no back against which to lean. Genevieve instead bent forward, elbows on the table and chin on her upturned palms.

"You don't frighten me one bit, Mr. Rio Jackson."

But when he slammed his fist down on the table hard enough to make her plate bounce, Genevieve did indeed jump back in fright.

"You talk too much, lady," he growled.

"And you don't talk enough!" she wailed. "Oh, Rio, can't we just be friends? Do we have to go through this whole winter sniping at each other? All I wanted was to talk to you, to get to know you."

As though he were completely ignoring her, Rio continued to eat. If he stuffed enough food in his mouth, maybe he wouldn't make any more stupid remarks. Like telling her the truth about the palomino stallion.

But she had no intention of letting him get away with silence. She said nothing; she just kept staring at him.

He finished the last morsel of stew and looked across the table at her plate. The package Genevieve had unearthed still sat just inches from her elbow. Had she forgotten it? He doubted she had. He also doubted that talking to her would make her forget it. The best he could probably hope for was to delay her discovery. But for how long? An hour? Surely not a day. Women like Genevieve du Prés didn't go to bed until all the questions had been answered.

"You eat, and I'll talk," he agreed morosely.

Chapter Ten

"The truth is, I really did steal him," Rio began. "From my brother."

He was looking at his coffee when he spoke, but the stunned silence that greeted his opening remark brought his attention back to Genevieve.

"What'sa matter, lady? You don't think guys like me can have brothers?" he accused.

"No, not at all. It's just that, well, I think of you as so independent, so self-sufficient. It's hard to imagine you ever being a child, having a mother, a father . . ."

"You think I was *born* thirty-two years old? Hell, yes, I had a mother and a father. Jeez louise, lady." And he just plain ran out of words to express his anger—and his hurt.

But Genevieve had already recognized it.

"I'm sorry, Rio," she whispered, reaching her hand across the narrow table to touch his. At first she was afraid he would pull away from the contact. Beneath her fingers, his tensed, then suddenly relaxed. "I'm sorry I asked about the horse, too. You were right. It's none of my business. I spoke without thinking."

"You do that a lot," Rio said.

She took the charge gracefully, with laughter.

"I do indeed. Worse yet, I frequently act without thinking."

"Like when you marched into that whorehouse?"

"I didn't know that's what it was."

"What did you think it was?"

After a brief pause she admitted, "I honestly don't know! I never really gave it a thought!"

Her laughter was soft and quiet, but honest. For all his bitterness, Rio still managed to admit he believed her when she said she was sorry. He also, however, suspected it was the first time in her pampered life that Genevieve Marie du Prés was really sorry for anything.

He waited until she had eaten nearly half her meal before he asked, "You got any brothers?"

"No, nor sisters."

She was aware that control of the situation had slipped from her again. Instead of manipulating Rio Jackson to reveal his reason for concealing the old trunk and its carefully preserved contents, she was now the victim of his manipulation. That he had not planned this switch made no difference; Genevieve cursed her failure.

"Parents?"

"One of each," she muttered, unable to keep her own bitterness at bay.

"Oh, yeah, Angela said your father owned some bank."

Genevieve sniffed angrily.

"That wasn't quite true. Papa only owned half of the bank; Jean-Louis' father owned the other half. Idiots, both of them."

Well, that explained one thing.

"So you two were gonna get married and keep all the money in one happy family."

The topic of her engagement to Jean-Louis had never been an easy one for Genevieve to discuss, not even in the carefree days before the scandal. Now that her search for him had ended so disastrously, she was even less willing to talk about it.

"There were other reasons," she muttered.

"I take it love wasn't one of 'em."

She sighed and pushed her plate away.

"No, I don't suppose it was."

"Well, hey, I know it ain't none o' my business, but it didn't seem to me like the two of you made the most likely couple in the world."

Recalling the men on the wharf her first day in Sacramento, Genevieve let an ironic smile turn up her lips. They had been right, more right than they could ever have guessed. And Rio was right, too.

She shook her head sadly.

"The only thing I ever did in my whole life that I gave any real thought to before I did it was agree to marry Jean-Louis. Can you believe that? I turned down an English duke, an Italian prince, and every unmarried man in five parishes without so much as a moment's contemplation. But when Jean-Louis proposed, it was so businesslike, so unemotional, that I spent a full week going over all the considerations involved."

Rio had not forgotten his own anger, or his own bitterness, but he pushed them aside to watch the transformation of Genevieve du Prés from spoiled bitch to confused innocent. Nothing about her changed, except perhaps the expression in her midnight blue eyes, but his vision of her went through a metamorphosis that stunned—and frightened—him.

His voice unsteady, he asked, "You want some more coffee?"

She nodded, and he took advantage of the opportunity to wrap his hand around hers, to steady the tin mug lest she spill its contents.

She had forgotten the package, and for that Rio breathed a sigh of relief. He worried, however, that he had got himself into even deeper trouble.

"Look, you don't have to talk about it. I said it's none of my business."

Genevieve pulled her hand away from his and

brought the cup to her lips. The coffee was barely lukewarm, but she took a long swallow. Then, placing the cup on the still-rough table before her, she raised her eyes to meet Rio's.

"I know what you think of me. Since that day I forced my way into your wagon train, you've thought me a spoiled, impulsive brat. And don't try to deny it."

He couldn't, and she knew it. It was written all over his face, the slightly raised brow, the hint of a smirking smile, the lowering of black lashes to hide a twinkle in his eye. More important than denying the undeniable was the concealment of the other emotion that had taken a perverse and unshakable grip on his soul.

Spoiled and impulsive, oh, yes, she was indeed a brat. Stubborn, too. But even tonight, with her blue-black hair pulled back in a tangled knot, her cheeks smudged with soot and dirt, her slim, pampered body clothed in little better than rags, the woman he had dragged kicking and screaming from a Sacramento whorehouse was still the most beautiful creature he had ever laid eyes on. And Rio Jackson wanted her beyond all reason.

"I think," she said calmly, "it would be best if I *do* talk about it. After all, it was I who suggested we get to know one another."

"Yeah, well, I refused, so it's all right by me if you change your mind. Ain't women supposed to be good at that anyway?" He stood up, leaving his plate and cup on the table, and walked around to where Genevieve sat in a strange, icy silence. "C'mon, Viva, it's late and I'm tired. We can talk all this over in the morning, if it's still that important."

He stood behind her as he spoke, then gently placed his hands on her shoulders. After a moment, a heartbeat or two, he slid his hands down until he could grasp her upper arms. She seemed

146

almost unaware of his touch, which both pleased and disturbed him. Pleased, because he knew it was better, much better, for both of them if she did not react to him; disturbed, because something in him cried out for her response as though it would justify his own.

Slowly, the pressure of his hands conveyed a message to her body. She rose, her mind still on the words she needed to say. But the words drifted, like snowflakes on the wind, and refused to make coherent thoughts. She tried to keep Jean-Louis and his betrayal clear and sharp, only to have his face fade in her memory. Rio's replaced it, dark and passionate—and real.

He meant to guide her to the corner of the cabin where they had made their beds. Instead, he turned her to face him, his hands still gently holding her arms. She looked up at him, and for a moment he could see nothing in her eyes, nothing but a vacant bottomless depth he could not plumb. Then suddenly it was as if her soul had risen from that abyss.

She might have been seeing him for the first time, so intently did she study him. In so many ways, she knew, he was still a complete stranger to her. Then why did she want him so badly? Why did she wish she could tell him she longed for more than his hands on her arms? Why could she not stop her eyes from closing nor her lips from whispering his name in supplication?

His kiss was inevitable. Seeing her mouth form his name sent a flash of heat through him, a lightning storm of searing desire.

Softly, possessively, his mouth covered hers. At the first touch of his tongue on her lips, she parted them, giving him welcome access to the sweetness of her mouth. He tasted her innocence—and the passion that lay beneath it.

"Oh, God, Viva," he murmured, each word a

kiss against her cheek, her chin, her throat even as he pushed himself away from her. He held her at arm's length, well aware that his own muscles quivered with the strain. What he really wanted to do was crush her against him and never let her go.

Slowly, the long lashes lifted, revealing her eyes darkened with desire. The tip of her tongue slipped out to lick her lips, still parted. Rio let out a shivering sigh.

"Why do you call me that?" she asked in a breathy whisper.

She had wanted him to go on kissing her, but in the back of her mind she knew he was right to stop. At least he hadn't let go of her; her knees were so weak she was certain she'd fall if his hands were not still firmly clasped around her arms.

"God, woman, you really do talk too much!" he exclaimed, giving her a little shake. But there was a touch of humor in his voice, and no real anger. "C'mon, before we get carried away, let's get some sleep."

Rio was gone when she wakened. Somehow, she was not at all surprised. Neither of them had slept well, despite exhaustion. Genevieve's fitful slumber had been disturbed by eerie dreams she could not remember upon waking, but each time she opened her eyes, she felt aware of Rio's continued study. Once she had actually caught him looking at her, lying on his side with his head propped on one elbow. He had not tried to hide the fact, though he had silently rolled over and turned his back to her then.

Alone, she rose and tended to her personal needs, then set about cleaning up from last night's meal. The package from the lean-to still sat on the table, more mysterious than ever. It would have been a simple matter to take the knife and remove

148

the wrappings, but somehow Genevieve was reluctant to do so, though her curiosity was driving her almost insane.

A suspicion had grown, too, that Rio did not want her to open the package. Now that the excitement of its discovery had worn off, and that the night's passion had faded in the cold light of day, Genevieve confronted the facts she had willed herself to ignore last night.

First of all, Rio had obviously known of the old trunk's existence. Was it possible he also knew the contents of the package she had brought inside? She suspected he did.

She built up the fire to make coffee and heat water for washing. Wherever Rio had taken off to in the dark hours before dawn, he hadn't taken time to shave, and she knew he'd want to as soon as he came back.

Bundled as warmly as she could get herself, Genevieve carried the two buckets to the spring. This was one job she normally left for Rio, but since he had seen fit to take off without checking the supply, the task had fallen to her. The cold wasn't the worst of it, nor the pain in her fingers caused by the rope handles on the buckets. Standing just outside the door, she glanced down at her feet; the high-heeled shoes she had worn that fateful night were ruined, and would not last much longer if she had to make many trips to the spring.

For a change, the sky was clear, a bright, bright blue above the snow-covered mountains. The sun had barely risen beyond the eastern peaks, but even that was high enough to cast blinding light on the snow. With both hands full, Genevieve had to squint against the glare, almost closing her eyes as she trudged to the spring.

The pool was deep enough to dip the buckets into it, so Genevieve needed to stay only a few seconds. But after being shut inside the cabin so much of the time, she relished this time out of doors. She set the full buckets on a rocky ledge overhanging the spring, then shaded her eyes with her hands to survey the valley.

It was quiet now, and peaceful, as close to being untouched by human presence as a place could be. The cabin, the orchard, and the other signs of habitation occupied only a small portion of the space between the mountains, toward the northern end of the valley. The spring, which was south of the cabin, gave rise to a narrow but lively stream. There must have been other pools, Genevieve guessed, for she could see where at least one other stream joined this one and led southward to spread out into a small lake ringed with tall, dry reeds that swayed gently in the barely perceptible breeze.

Genevieve saw Rio emerge slowly from the forest of reeds.

What could he be doing? she wondered, almost aloud. Curiosity, and the surprising warmth of the sun, brought her to her feet and headed her in Rio's direction.

Rio added wood to the fire under the cauldron, then stepped back, wiping his nose against the smell. It was a good thing he had brought the kettle this far from the cabin; he would never have finished the process of tanning the elk hide if he had to breathe this gut-wrenching stench all the time.

He just hoped it worked.

Satisfied that the fire was going strong, he turned his attention back to the horse, and the travois he dragged disdainfully behind him. The stallion's brown gaze followed him.

"Don't look at me like that, Cinco. One more trip oughta do it."

He was about to set off into the reeds again

when he caught sight of the figure strolling toward him. She'd be frozen to death by the time she got to the fire, fool woman. To say nothing of her questions about the cargo loaded on the travois. And if she had opened Tibler's damned package—well, Rio flatly refused to contemplate that until he absolutely had to.

"Morning," he greeted.

"Morning yourself. Whatever are you doing all the way out here? And what is that smell?"

She coughed and tried to get upwind of the kettle's malodorous contents.

"Gathering cattails and leather."

She gave him a puzzled—and disbelieving—look.

"And just how does one 'gather' leather?"

" 'One' doesn't."

Leaving her to ponder his sarcasm, Rio turned and headed back to the frozen marsh. He was soon all but invisible in the mass of swaying reeds.

And Genevieve was soon frozen to the bone. The walk from the spring had kept her warm, but now the cold began to seep through her inadequate clothing. Her feet especially suffered. The crackling fire under the black kettle—which had every appearance of a witch's cauldron—beckoned those cold feet, but the stench soon drove Genevieve back from the warmth.

She looked at the palomino stallion, standing so placidly a few yards away. Did she dare try to mount him? At least if she got on the horse, she would no longer be standing on the icy ground. She whispered his name, and he swivelled his ears toward her. He neither stamped nor snorted nor showed any other sign of the unpredictability Rio had warned of.

In fact, he showed signs only of boredom. Shifting his weight from one hind leg to the other, he let his head droop and his eyes close. Genevieve was almost within reach of his velvety nose and

151

whiskered chin with its delicate tracery of icicles when a splintering crash, a splash, and a shout shattered the valley's stillness.

She ran as fast as her feet would carry her to the edge of the ice-bound marsh.

"Rio!" she shrieked. "Are you all right?"

"Don't come out here!" he shouted back.

"Are you all right?"

She envisioned him trapped in the frigid water, unable to climb out onto the ice. Even Rio Jackson could not survive long.

"I'm all right," he assured her. "Just don't come out here. The ice isn't as stable as I thought."

He lay face down on the ice, one leg soaked almost to his knee. The water at the edge of the beaver pond was no deeper than that, so he had been in no danger of drowning. But reaching solid ground again was not going to be easy. When his foot broke through the ice, it had sent cracks radiating in all directions from the hole. If he was to avoid another similar accident, he'd have to distribute his weight as widely as possible.

That meant crawling on his belly through the sharp cattails while his wet leg froze.

Then he heard the frantic rustling of the reeds that did not come from the wind.

"Get back, Viva!" he yelled. "I'm all right! I don't need your help!"

The rustling stopped.

Twenty yards away, Genevieve's heart stopped, too.

She knew from the sound of his voice that he had fallen, but whether he had crawled out onto the ice or still stood in bone-numbing water she could not tell.

"Are you out of the water?" she asked, afraid of the answer.

"Yes, I'm out. I only went in up to my knee."

That was good. His clothes wouldn't be completely soaked. And he had said "knee," not "knees." If he had got only one leg wet, she could wrap it in the blanket she wore for a coat.

She listened for the sound of his progress, and was rewarded with both the rhythmic swish of the reeds as he crept through them and the frightening crack and groan of the ice beneath him.

Realizing she, too, stood on the treacherous surface of the pond, Genevieve cautiously backed up, one slow step at a time. Not once, however, did she take her terrified eyes from the cattails in front of her.

Using his elbows, Rio pulled himself another six inches from the hole. The left leg of his pants had already frozen itself to the ice, but he was able to jerk it free without too much difficulty. The sudden movement, however, sent an undulation of groans through the ice. He paused, almost afraid to breathe, until the creaking stopped. Then he moved forward again.

Inch by inch he crept, aware that his elbows and forearms were growing numb, that he had completely lost feeling in the left leg. He could only tell it was still attached to his body by the way his boot caught on clumps of reeds and pulled at his thigh. Fortunately, he had not lost his hat when he flung himself face down; it protected his face from the slashing of the plants as he made his way through them.

There was nothing she could do. Heart pounding in her throat, Genevieve waited, afraid to move, afraid even to call out to him again. As long as she continued to hear the swish of the cattails, she knew he was coming closer. She prayed he would keep to a straight line and not go out further onto the dangerous ice.

Rio thought of calling out to her, to gauge his direction by the sound of her returning voice. His body would not cooperate. The exertion, and the fear, had him sweating, yet he knew half his body was nearly frozen. His mind, too, was beginning to suffer. Taking a moment to breathe deeply and slowly, he closed his eyes and refocused his mind. Even as he lay still, the ice shifted beneath him. Frantic, he pulled himself another foot closer to shore.

He could see through the reeds now, could see the girl waiting at the edge of the pond. There'd be frozen mud under him now, not water. Slowly, he commanded his legs beneath him and got gingerly to his knees. The ice cracked, but the ground beneath was solid.

"Is that you, Rio?" she called to him. "Are you all right?"

He stood, unsteadily. He wondered if it were only the frozen fabric of his pants that kept the leg from collapsing under him. Whatever the reason, it held. He took a single tentative step.

He did not remember crossing the last few yards. One moment he was walking on loose ice that crunched and gave way under him, the next he felt solid earth beneath his feet, and a sobbing, terrified woman in his arms.

"I wish I had some brandy for this," Genevieve said as she knelt down and handed a mug of hot coffee to Rio.

He sat on the cabin floor, leaning against his saddle, with every blanket in the place tucked around him. A few feet away, in front of the fire, his boot and wet pants steamed.

"You gotta stop fussin' over me, Viva. All I did was put my foot in a bit of cold water, for God's sake. Damn fool thing to do, but I'll live."

"I certainly hope so," she replied with a little more confidence than when she had helped him mount Cinco. For an unpredictable stallion, the animal had stood stock still while she boosted Rio

154

into the saddle and then managed to haul herself up behind him. "Now, what do you want me to do with all those cattail things?"

They had left the travois with its fluffy load in front of the cabin. When Genevieve would have left the ungainly contraption by the pond and spurred the palomino to get back to the cabin as quickly as possible, Rio threatened her with bodily harm if she lost so much as one spike of cattail. She had not argued with him after that.

Now, however, he sighed with what could only be described as monumental disappointment.

"It was gonna be a surprise."

Genevieve's smile of delight quickly faded. An odd shiver had snaked its way down her back. She shifted to a very unladylike crosslegged sitting position and stared at Rio until she blinked.

Whatever this surprise was, it had meant a great deal to him. And after his moodiness last night—which she suspected had a great deal to do with his concocting this surprise—Genevieve was inclined to humor Rio a little.

"Since I have no idea what use one could possibly make of a pile of dead swamp weeds, your surprise remains intact until you are able to complete it."

He turned his head suddenly to return her stare, his eyes narrowed now but brighter, more suspicious perhaps, but less defeated.

"Thanks, Viva," he whispered. They weren't easy words to say, but he had got them out.

At great cost to that enormous pride of his, Genevieve quickly realized.

"For what? For saving your life?" she laughed and patted his arm where it rested on top of the blankets. "I didn't do a thing but stand there, scared to death, while you pulled yourself out. Then, once you were safe, I started bawling like a baby."

They both knew his gratitude wasn't for anything she had done back by the beaver pond, but they also knew she was giving him a way to save face. And that, for a reason Genevieve didn't understand at all, was more important than anything.

"You got me up on Cinco," Rio pointed out. "I couldn't've done that by myself, and I couldn't've walked back."

He could very easily have thrown himself on the travois with all those cattails and told the horse to drag him back to the cabin, but Genevieve wisely refrained from pointing that out to him.

"In that case," she whispered, "you're very welcome, Mr. Jackson. And thank you, for saving my life more times than I can count."

She had meant just to pat his hand again, in a gesture intended to forestall any of his protests. Instead, she clasped her fingers around his rather tightly, then leaned down and kissed him softly on his whiskery cheek.

Rio slept until Genevieve wakened him for supper. He realized he had had nothing, except coffee, since the night before. After wolfing down two helpings of pan-fried rabbit, apple fritters, and the ever-present beans, he retrieved his boots and coat and disappeared outdoors. His parting words were something about the livestock, but he spoke most of them after the door was closed.

Genevieve did not go out to join him. She heard the sound of the travois being dragged around to the lean-to. And some time later, Cinco's hooves pounded by. That startled her, and she almost went to the door to call after Rio, warning him to be careful, but she pulled herself back. Still, she could not hold back an enormous sigh of relief a short while later when the horse returned, and she heard the familiar squeak of the saddle as Rio dismounted.

She thought he would come in. It was well past the time they normally went to bed, but she remembered he had slept nearly all afternoon.

She herself was exhausted. After settling the half-frozen Rio under the blankets that morning, she had gone to retrieve the buckets from the spring. They were, of course, frozen fast to the rock, so she had had to bring hot water from the cabin to free them. Several trips later, she was nearly as numb as the man sleeping — and snoring very quietly — on the floor.

He dreamed, too. Once or twice he had mumbled her name, she thought.

She stayed awake as long as she could, but still he did not come in. Finally, unable to keep her eyes open a moment longer, Genevieve separated her blankets from the pile where Rio had slept and made up her own little nest.

"You are crazy, Rio Jackson," Rio told himself as he stepped back to admire his handiwork. *"Y más que un* poco *loco,"* he added softly.

Behind him, Cinco nickered at the familiar accent.

The tools, like nearly everything else on which Rio was depending for his survival, were makeshift: a rusty nail for an awl, a sliver of elk antler for a needle. He had used his razor to trim the uneven edges of the skins, because he had no shears that would cut the tough, soft leather. Now that he had the rectangles pieced together, the difficult part began.

But it was late. He had stayed up nearly all night, after riding headlong back to the pond to fetch the precious sheets of leather, in hopes that Viva would honor her promise to let him have his surprise. She wouldn't stay locked up in the cabin another day, he was certain, and her curiosity was a dangerous thing anyway.

157

He looked at the carefully stitched leather and at the travois, still laden with cattails. Then he yawned. It had to be close to dawn. His leg ached, and his fingers were sore from pushing and pulling the needle. The rest could wait until later; he had to get some sleep.

He crept noiselessly into the cabin. The carefully banked fire, the only light in the tiny room, was little more than a red glow. Rio glanced at the meager pile of firewood beside the hearth and realized he should have brought more in, but there was enough to last until daylight. He settled a couple of logs atop the coals, then made his way to the corner where Genevieve slept.

The last thing he saw before closing his eyes was the package on the table, exactly where she had put it after bringing it in from the lean-to. He had an urge to get up and throw the thing into the fire, but he was suddenly too tired. He shifted to find as comfortable a spot on the hard earthen floor as he could, then pulled the blankets up. A small, warm weight settled on his shoulder. He was almost asleep before he realized it was Viva's hand.

Chapter Eleven

A blast of cold air and an explosive thud wakened Genevieve rudely. She sat up, only to be blinded by the sunlight coming in the open door. Rio, maneuvering some large object into the cabin, was a blurred silhouette against the brilliance.

"What are you doing now?" she asked, rubbing her eyes and stretching. As usual, her shoulders were stiff and sore from the hardness of her bed. He had told her she'd get used to it, but after three weeks, her shoulders flatly refused.

"Bringin' you a bathtub."

He kicked the door closed. Now Genevieve could see that the bulky object was the big cast iron cauldron he had been cooking his vile brew in yesterday. She did not ask what had happened to the stinky stuff, or what it was.

She did, however, sniff.

"I cleaned it out real good," Rio told her, a hint of feigned hurt in his voice. He set the kettle in front of the fire, then took the smaller one and dumped its steaming contents into the larger. "I'll get more water."

Before she could say another word, he was out the door again.

Genevieve got up, stared at the big black thing in the middle of the room and shook her head. If this was Rio's idea of a surprise, well, she was surprised all right. What it had to do with a mountain of bulrushes, she still had no clue. But the thought of a bath, even in a cooking pot, was too welcome to question.

The next time he burst into the cabin, she tried to stop him by pelting him with questions.

"Where did you get this kettle? And why did you have it down by the pond?"

He poured more water into the big pot and grinned at her over it. "You talk too much, Viva. Ernest left the pot out back, okay? and I found it there. What I been doin' with it is my business. Why don't you fix us some coffee?"

And then he was gone, leaving Genevieve, hands on her hips, to stare open-mouthed at his departure.

His grin faded the instant the door shut behind him. A frown of determination replaced it as he strode back to the spring. After just a few hours sleep he had wakened and set immediately back to work. If he paused to think about what he was doing, he wouldn't have the courage to go through with it. He had to keep going—or quit. And something about that crazy woman inside the cabin wouldn't allow him to quit.

When the cauldron was half-full, he hung the smaller kettle over the fire to begin heating the water for Genevieve's bath. She wouldn't really be able to bathe in it—the pot wasn't quite that big—but she could at least stand in it and pour warm water over her. The thought of her like that, her naked skin all wet and slick with soap and water while she stretched to pour a bucket of rinse water over her head, had a profound effect on him.

But it wasn't the first time he had pictured her in his mind. And his body's reaction was one he was all too familiar with.

He had been enjoying beautiful women and the effect they had on him—as well as the effect he

160

had on them—for a good many years. In most ways, Viva du Prés differed very little from the saloon girls, abandoned young wives, bored matrons, and painted prostitutes he had passed pleasant hours with. It seemed quite natural, therefore, that he should find himself aroused by her, especially when they had been thrown together and faced the prospect of spending an entire winter in the close confines of a desolate mountain cabin.

Until he kissed her that night, however, he had not known how deep his desire went. Even as his body responded and urged hers to do the same, his mind held back, wanting something more. By the cold light of day, he tried to convince himself that "something more" did not and could not exist. The package on the table lay between what he wanted and what she would expect in return, and no matter what else he did, Rio could not get that stupid bundle out of his mind.

The cattails, however, might go a long way to bridging the gap. And when the object of his desire had collapsed in his arms after he crawled out of the frigid swamp, the little kernel of hope began to sprout.

Eyes tightly shut, Genevieve opened the cabin door and shouted, "Rio, the coffee's ready! Are you coming in for it?"

He was at the door in seconds.

"I didn't peek!" she defended herself, backing away from his angry entrance.

"Good," he growled as he strode past her. "I don't like my surprises ruined."

He tested the water in the pot, found it still too chilly, but more was steaming over the fire. It wouldn't take too much longer.

"I brought the plane. Oughta be able to finish the table before the coffee's gone."

He never sat down. While Genevieve poured the coffee, he set the plane against the old wood and

161

soon had another of those graceful curls spiralling up from the blade. The pine was soft enough to work easily, and the table wasn't large. One after another, the wooden ringlets fell to the floor.

Nearly half the table was smoothed before Genevieve, her eyes alight with amazement, looked up from the work to gaze at the man who performed it.

"I thought you'd forgotten," she said quietly.

He did not return her gaze. There was still that damned package, glaring at him from its corner of the table. He'd have to move it, bring attention to it again after all these hours, and it was going to take a lot of courage to touch the bloody thing. He did not dare give in to any temptation to be interrupted.

"What's all this stuff in your hair?" Genevieve asked, plucking a feather-like substance from over his ear.

"Part of the surprise," he told her, bearing down on the plane as he came to a knotty place in the wood. "Now, quit askin' questions and move outta my way. Please."

Stepping away from him and moving to the other side of the table so he could finish, she picked up the leather-bound parcel and set it on the shelf by the chimney. She did not see how he watched her, or how he lifted his eyes to heaven in a quick and silent prayer of thanks.

Then she paused, and reached to take the thing down again.

"No!" Rio yelled before he could stop himself.

His voice seemed to echo in the tiny room, or else it was just the reverberations in her mind. Reverberations, not of sound, but of fear, almost of stark terror, that did not accord with the man Genevieve had come to know. Not believing what she had heard, she turned, and saw the same emotion in his eyes.

162

"Is something wrong?" she asked, barely aware that she clutched the parcel to her chest like a shield.

"I—I thought it was falling on you," he stammered, and immediately went back to his work.

Well, you jack-ass, you sure got her mind off that goddamn *thing,* he told himself as he leaned onto the plane and forced it past the knot. Be lucky she don't go and open it right now.

But she didn't. She put the package back on the shelf and walked cautiously away from the fire, around the table, to the cauldron. She felt better having it between herself and him.

Two more swipes and he had finished the table. His hands were shaking as he brushed the wooden shavings from them, then smoothed his palms along the surface of the table. Calm had, however, returned to his voice.

"It's not the greatest, but it's a damn sight better'n it was. Now all you gotta do is rub a little beeswax into it," he said. He set the plane down in the middle of the table, then headed abruptly for the door.

"Where are you going now?" Genevieve asked, almost panicky. This man was too much for her to handle, his moods more volatile and unpredictable than lightning.

"To finish your surprise. Water's warm enough for your bath; you holler when you're done."

At least this time he didn't slam the door on the way out.

"What a fool! What a goddamn fool!" Rio swore, kicking a pile of discarded cattail stems. In their little corral, the horses and mule stared dumbly at him but did not come any closer. Cinco lifted his head as a bit of errant fluff drifted by, but that was all.

163

Rio swore again, and kicked the pile harder.

Then he looked into the lean-to and the completed project. He wanted to rush in and tear the thing to shreds, cast the carefully gathered down to the wind, and forget this stupid idea had ever come into his head.

"Why'd you do it?" he asked himself for the hundredth time since leaving Genevieve inside. "Why'd you bother to think any of this would make any difference? You are crazy, Rio Jackson, soft in the head 'cause you ain't had a woman in weeks and the one you got sleepin' six inches away ain't the kind you can have. Forget her! And quit tryin' to change things that can't be changed!"

It was one thing not to try to change the situation, but quite another to forget the woman. Right now, she completely filled his thoughts, to the exclusion of all others.

What was she doing at this very minute? he wondered. She had had time to pour the hot water into the kettle; maybe she was taking off her clothes now. His mind strayed back to that first night, when he had seen her stripped to her corset and garters. That image alone was enough to send the blood rushing to his loins. He had had only a hint then of the soft flesh beneath, the proud breasts, the slender legs, the rounded bottom he had patted when he tossed her over his shoulder.

Had he done it all out of desire, rather than some misplaced sense of honor?

He looked out into the little paddock he had built for the animals. Cinco still stood, watching him. Despite his calm stance, the stallion was fractious, eager to be done with the confines of fences. As though to prove that, he tossed his head, sending his long mane flying.

Rio walked over to the fence and whistled. Cinco's ears swivelled forward, and he flared his nostrils to sniff for the familiar scent. Finding it, he

164

plodded over to where the man waited.

"I've done some stupid things in my life, old boy, but this is the stupidest." The velvet nose nuzzled his chest, pushing him backwards. "No, I don't have anything for you. *She* brings the apples, not me."

The stallion drew back at the hissed word.

"Hey, take it easy. I don't like this any better than you, maybe worse. But we'll get out of it somehow. We always do, don't we?"

Genevieve grabbed the thin cotton towel and blotted as much of the water from her body as she could. With her hair dripping all over her shoulders and down her back, drying was no easy task, and freezing wasn't a pleasant one. And until she had clothes back on, she would feel exposed and vulnerable, a feeling she hated almost as much as she hated being cold.

She also hated the suspense of Rio's surprise. At first she had enjoyed the game, and enjoyed the pleasure it seemed to give him. Heaven knew he had had little pleasure since she entered his life. Or he entered hers, depending on the way one looked at the situation.

The towel was almost as wet as her hair, but she wrapped it around her head anyway, to keep the drips from her skin. The last of the clothes Angela Bruckner had stuffed into the saddlebag—one of Paul's shirts and another of Angela's castoff skirts—lay on the freshly planed table. From the woolen blanket she had spread on the dirt floor, Genevieve had only a short reach to her clothes. She grabbed the shirt and quickly slipped her arms into it. As long as it was, and it came nearly to her knees, she felt considerably more at ease once the buttons were done up.

Then she stepped into the skirt and finally a pair

of underdrawers she had washed the day before. Though clean, her stockings were worn almost through at the heels and toes, and this was the best pair she had. Balancing on one foot at a time, she pulled the stockings on and walked over to the log stool to put on her shoes.

She lifted one and examined it sadly. Slippers like this had never been intended for rough wear, and certainly not day after day for weeks. She would be lucky if they held together until tomorrow. Beyond that, she had no idea.

Until she remembered the leather-wrapped parcel on the shelf. She glanced at it and wondered if the leather could be reused. First, of course, she would have to get beyond Rio's terror of the silly thing so she could open it.

"You know how women are, Cinco," Rio told the stallion, who was dozing with his head hung over the fence. "Shoulda known she'd take the whole damn day just to take a bath. And leave me standin' out in the cold after I damn near froze my butt just yesterday."

He reached up and pulled another bit of brush from the stallion's mane. If he didn't keep after it, he'd have a real mess on his hands.

"Yeah, I know, as usual, it was my fault. Shoulda watched where I was walkin'. But I knew the water wasn't deep and —"

"Do you always talk to your horse?"

He hadn't heard a sound, and whirled around almost in a crouch, as though ready to fight — or draw the gun at his hip.

"Don't do that, Viva," he breathed as he straightened. "I might've. . . ."

"Shot me?" she finished for him. "I don't think so."

She could see the relaxation begin at his shoul-

166

ders and then spread downward. With excessive casualness, Rio leaned against the fence and rubbed the palomino's nose.

"Me'n Cinco been friends a long time," he muttered.

"I can see that. Now," she said, sidling up to the fence herself, "before I strangle you for making me wait so long, what *is* this confounded surprise!"

He could easily have made her wait longer, just to give himself the joy of watching her. She really hadn't taken as much time as he complained to the horse she had, but regardless, everything was worth it.

Her hair wasn't quite dry, so it hung in curly little strands that feathered into individual hairs. He lifted one lock in his hand and wrapped the end around his thumb.

"Black as a crow's wing, soft as silk," he murmured. Then, shaking off the urges that threatened to overwhelm him here and now, he dropped the lock of hair and grasped Genevieve's hand instead.

He practically dragged her to the lean-to where, after the glare of afternoon sun on snow, her eyes took a moment to adjust to the shadows. She bumped into the low rail that kept the stock out of the stored feed, a rail Rio's long legs easily swung over. Without waiting for Viva to hike her skirt and maneuver herself to the other side of the fence, he placed his hands on her waist and effortlessly hoisted her up and over.

Then he turned her so her back was to him just the way she had been on the riverboat that first morning in Sacramento.

"That's it, right there. What do you think?"

For a long moment, she had no idea what to think. Her eyes were still struggling with the dimness, but what they could make out appeared to be an enormous shallow box on short legs. Inside the box rested something that looked like several large pieces of leather pieced together, but instead of lying flat in the box, they seemed to be covering something else, something lumpy.

And everywhere, on the box, on the leather, all around the lean-to, drifted bits of fluff like the piece she had seen in Rio's hair.

She took a step forward and placed her hand on the lumpy leather. Her hand sank down, down, down.

As understanding came, she cautiously turned and sat on the edge of the box, then swung her body onto the mattress. A slow, quivering smile spread across her face. Lying on her back, she let the tears trickle toward her ears to disappear in her still-damp hair.

"Oh, Rio, you nearly killed yourself—to make me a bed!"

The knot in his stomach tightened. He had seen her tears, as well as her smile.

Well, he asked himself, what did you expect from a selfish, spoiled little rich girl? That she'd invite you to—

"Aren't you going to join me?" she asked, interrupting his bitter thoughts. "It's certainly big enough for both of us."

She must have said it without thinking, the way she did most things. Reluctant to give her the chance to think about this decision, Rio still shook his head and backed away. After all, he had no right to be angry with her or to expect any more from her than what she had already given.

"No, I got work to do," he mumbled, growing angry at himself as he realized how far his imagination really had gone. "C'mon, you get up and I'll carry this thing inside."

Genevieve sat up and scooted off the bed. All trace of her earlier delight had vanished. Hands on her hips, she stomped up to him.

"*We* will carry this inside," she told him in a

168

voice that dared him to argue with her. "I don't know how or when you dragged that bedframe out here, but I am not going to risk having you laid up with a bad back."

Then standing on the very tips of her toes, she lifted her hands to his face and pulled him down for a quick, smacking kiss full on his surprised lips. "Thank you, Rio," she whispered, and kissed him again. "That was the best surprise I ever had in my whole life."

He swallowed an enormous lump in his throat but still couldn't find a single word to say to the raven-haired beauty who tugged on his arm. Then again, he didn't have to talk. She did enough for both of them.

"Now I know what you meant yesterday. Here, you take that end and I'll take this. We can set the mattress on the table for now, so it doesn't get dirty before we get the frame inside."

They hoisted the mattress over the rail and headed for the cabin door. Genevieve hardly paused for breath.

"I remember now I asked you what you were doing and what that awful smell was. You said you were gathering cattails and leather. I didn't realize you were answering both questions, so it didn't make a whole lot of sense then. Now it does. Wait a minute while I get the latch."

Once again the transition from bright daylight to interior dimness left them both nearly blind, but the lamp Genevieve had left burning on the table guided them that far.

"I never, ever would have guessed what you were doing out there. When did you take the old bedframe outside? I didn't hardly notice it was missing. I guess I thought you had taken it out to chop up for kindling or something. There, we can get the frame now, and then I'll get some more water heated up and you can take a bath and shave. I wish I had some nice crisp linen sheets. I just love climbing into a bed with freshly laundered sheets, when they smell like sunshine and soft breezes."

Just that quickly they were outside again, with Genevieve marching several steps ahead of Rio.

"I wondered what you had done with the skins of the elk you shot. I thought it was a shame to let it go to waste, but I had no idea how to tan leather."

"That's enough!" Rio suddenly barked when Genevieve reached the rail and had to take a breath before climbing over.

She stopped, one foot raised, and looked at him with a slightly hurt expression.

"You talk too much," he said quietly, but with a mollifying grin. "You wear me out just listening to you."

"I can't help it. I always talk too much when I get excited. You should have heard me the first night on the wagon train. Mr. Jensen threatened to stuff a rag in my mouth if I didn't shut up!"

They were standing at opposite ends of the empty bedframe, getting ready to lift it over the fence rail. A wicked gleam came into Rio's eyes, and he knew he was going to say something he'd regret, but the words refused to obey his better judgment.

"Don't worry, I'd never do that. I can think of much better ways to shut you up."

As understanding dawned, her jaw dropped, and her cheeks turned a brilliant pink. Instead of maidenly indignation, however, she responded with laughter.

"Then I guess I'd better start talking again, hadn't I?"

Though placed in a far corner of the cabin, the bed dominated the small room. Genevieve moved

170

the blankets and canvas ground covers that had served for the past weeks, while Rio leveled the frame. He tested the ropes woven across the bottom and tightened a couple before he helped carry the leather mattress from the table.

Standing on one side of the bed, Genevieve looked across it to Rio, and this time she had nothing to say.

She's thinking, Rio warned himself as he moved out into the middle of the room. Don't push her, and for God's sake, don't get your hopes up.

"Look, Viva, I'm gonna take some of this hot water outside and wash up, get this damn fluff off me."

And get myself out of here, he added silently, before we do something really stupid.

But as he headed to the fire where fresh hot water steamed in the kettle, Genevieve raced to cut him off.

"Don't you want a—a bath? I saved the hot water for you, and I can bring more from the spring."

He had given the idea considerable thought himself, only to reject it as absurd. Romantically absurd.

Standing so close to her he had to look down into her wide midnight eyes, he asked, "And where would you go while I'm standin' buck naked in the soup pot?"

Her blush told him she had forgotten that detail. He wished she would turn away, because he found himself totally incapable of it. His feet refused to move, and his arms wanted only to wind themselves around this teasing, perplexing, innocent creature and never let her go.

"I could feed the horses," she suggested. "That would save you having to do it later." When a raised eyebrow was his only reply, she added tartly, "I am quite capable of feeding two horses and a mule. Despite what you've said, Cinco seems as

171

gentle as a lamb. Rather like you, I suspect."

"Me? Gentle as a lamb?"

Oh, Christ, how he wanted to thread his fingers through her hair and hold her proud head still while he taught her a lesson in gentleness—and passion.

"Yes, you, Rio Jackson. Now, help me dump this cold, dirty bathwater and we'll get fresh for you."

He felt like a complete idiot. The water came barely halfway up his calves, which meant he had to bend over to wet the scrap of cloth Viva had given him as a washrag. Afraid to lock her out of the cabin in case some emergency arose, Rio kept one eye constantly on the door. If she came in before he was finished, he'd strangle her.

But it did feel good to be clean again. Not quite like that night in Sacramento when Lo Pau had scrubbed him, but still better than any night since then. He wondered, with an idle glance toward the bed in the corner, if the rest of the night would be an improvement also.

Pulling on the clean shirt and pants Viva had laid on the table for him, he shoved those thoughts firmly out of his mind.

He ran a hand along the smooth surface of the table. While they were waiting for the water to heat for his bath, he and Viva had rubbed some of old Ernest's beeswax into the raw wood. It wasn't enough to give the crude piece of furniture a glowing shine, but it did bring out the pattern of the grain, and added a soft golden tone. Rio couldn't help but smile, proud of his accomplishment.

He wasted little time on such indulgences, however. As soon as he had his boots on, he grabbed his coat and hurried outside. Poor Viva was probably frozen.

Not only was she not frozen, she appeared to be having a great deal of fun.

172

"See, I told you he was gentle!" she squealed, as Cinco dipped his head into the front of her coat and came up with a slice of apple crunching between his teeth.

Under his breath Rio muttered, "Lucky bastard!"

"What did you say?"

He was not about to repeat it.

She was sitting on the old trunk. She must have dragged it from the farthest corner to the apron of the lean-to, where the rail kept Cinco from just coming in and taking every slice of apple she had. Rio's stomach dropped down to his boots.

"Ain't it gettin' awful cold out here?" he asked, shoving his hands into his pockets.

The word was an instant warning signal. Genevieve's smile faded, and she pushed Cinco's questing nose away rather roughly.

"Yes, it is getting cold," she answered, with exaggerated calm. "But just as you allowed me time for my ablutions, I felt it only proper to return the favor."

He said nothing, just kicked at the dirt. Cinco strolled over and nudged the man's shoulder, looking for additional treats no doubt, but Rio ignored the horse. That surprised Genevieve even more.

"What's wrong?" she finally demanded as she slid off the trunk. It had made a fairly comfortable seat while she played with Cinco and the other animals, but she doubted it would last much longer. "Are you angry because I befriended your horse? If so, I'm sorry, but I never expected you to be the jealous type."

If only you knew, he thought, but at least that brought a ghost of a smile to his lips.

That was all she needed. His bad mood was gone as easily and quickly as it had come.

"Then come here and see what I found," she told him. Without waiting for his reply she knelt on the ground beside the old trunk and carefully lifted the

173

lid.

"I know what's in it."

The cold that seeped through her skirt to her knees was like warm sunshine compared to the ice in Rio's voice.

Turning so that she sat with her back against the chest, Genevieve looked up at him with total confusion on her face.

"You know? But how? All the packages were sealed. Mr. Tibler did a wonderful job; not one of them was ruined or damaged at all."

"Yeah, the old guy was good at stuff like that. Couldn't skin a rabbit, but he knew how to wrap a book so it wouldn't get wet."

He stared up at the sky, blue now but already changing to the slate grey of evening. A flock of geese or ducks passed high overhead, far beyond the range of his rifle. Besides, he had no dog to retrieve it, and he wasn't about to venture out on the ice again to fetch his own game. He had no desire—

Roughly, he grabbed the girl's arm and pulled her to her feet. She yelped and pulled away.

"Get your hands off me," she warned as she backed another step or two from him. "What in the name of heaven has gotten into you? One minute you're all scowls, the next you're all smiles, and now you act like you'd prefer to throw me in the beaver pond without caring whether I drowned or froze first!"

She sidled past him, the flash in her eyes warning him that if he approached her, she'd fight to the death. Then when he no longer blocked her way, she thrust her chin into the air and marched back to the cabin. He listened for the dropping of the bolt, but he heard only the click of the latch.

She sat on the floor, her head cradled on arms

174

folded on one of the stools. She must have cried hard for a long while; her body still shuddered with occasional convulsive sobs. Quietly, Rio closed the door and dropped the bolt home. The forlorn figure by the table didn't move.

Rio didn't move any closer.

"Viva?" He kept his voice to the softest whisper possible, but it still quivered with emotions he did not want to name. "Viva, are you all right? I didn't hurt you, did I? I swear to God, I never meant to hurt you. Never."

Slowly, she raised her head and turned to look at him over her shoulder. A curly curtain of black hair fell over one eye, but he still could see how swollen the other was.

"Oh, Rio, what am I going to do now?" she begged to know. A single glistening tear rolled down her cheek. She brushed the stray lock hair back from her face and studied the man with eyes open to the depths of her soul. "I think I've fallen in love with you."

Chapter Twelve

Without the door behind him for support, Rio was certain he would have staggered backward until he fell flat on his ass in the dooryard.

Amazed he was even able to speak, he said the first inane thing that came to his mind.

"You're upset, Viva."

"Upset?" she echoed. "Upset? Hell, yes, I'm upset!"

She was about to launch into a litany of the reasons for her distress when she noticed he carried something in his arms.

"I brought you your books. Where you want 'em?"

Genevieve sniffed and coughed, and wiped her eyes on her sleeve. The tears that had come in torrents a few minutes ago dwindled to a trickle, but they refused to stop completely.

"I don't care. Anywhere." When he stood stock still as though waiting for orders from her, she let out a long exasperated sigh and said, "On the table. And then, whether you like it or not, we are going to talk, Mr. Rio Jackson."

After dropping the stack of leather-wrapped parcels where she directed, Rio shrugged. He looked around for a place to deposit himself, but ended up choosing the other stool. There really wasn't any other spot. So as much as he would have preferred to sit as far away from his tormentor as possible, he sat down across the table from her.

"So, talk," he said.

Threatened with another onslaught of tears, Genevieve scrambled to her feet and dredged up all the anger she had ever felt toward any man. She remembered them all: her own father, Jean-Louis, Etienne Marmont, Buster Kulkey. If she could stay angry, maybe she wouldn't want to cry so much. The others, despite the things they had done to her, had never warranted her tears; why did Rio Jackson?

And why did she feel the way she did?

"You ain't sayin' nothin', lady," he drawled with maddening calm.

There was that word again, and that whole vulgar, uncouth way of talking. No matter how relaxed he might look, Rio Jackson was upset or nervous or worried—or something.

"Funny. Usually you tell me I talk too much."

"Usually you do." To add injury to insult, he pushed the stack of packages roughly out of his way so he could lean forward on the table and rest his chin on his crossed forearms. One of the books almost fell on Genevieve's foot. "Look, Viva, if you got somethin' to say, say it and get it over with."

The truth hit her like a blow. He didn't care. He just plain didn't give a damn that she, Genevieve Marie du Prés, *the* belle of New Orleans for more years than she could remember, had told this—this saddletramp that she loved him.

She could do nothing to retrieve those awful words, but she could salvage some of her pride, maybe.

As she brushed the dust and wrinkles and bits of

cattail fluff from her skirt, she said, "I'm sorry, Mr. Jackson, for behaving so childishly. You must think me a complete fool. I assure you such a thing will never happen again."

He was staring at her. She knew it without looking at him; she could feel the force of that blue gaze as surely as she felt the heat from the fire, the cold from the wind, the pain from her breaking heart. The tears gathered despite her stern insistence that they not, and one by one they overflowed her eyes and dripped to the dusty floor.

"Don't, Viva," Rio said softly. "For God's sake, don't."

Her sapphire eyes took aim at his.

"Don't what? Don't cry? I'll cry if I want to, Rio Jackson. I can't help it if *you* don't have any feelings. *I* do, and I'm not ashamed to show them." Again she had let out words she would have dearly loved to call back. Rio Jackson *did* have feelings. She had seen enough little hints of them. But the words were out, and the damage was done. "I *thought* you cared for me."

She was the impulsive one, the one who acted and spoke without thinking. She had got them into this mess, so it was up to Rio to rescue them both once again. Only this time he wasn't sure he really wanted to.

He knew damned well he didn't want to respond to her last statement. He could neither admit that he did care, nor lie and say he didn't. Instead, he changed the subject.

"Angela Bruckner felt the same way last year, after I saved her from drowning," he said calmly. "She was gonna leave Paul and follow me wherever I was goin'. After a few days, though, it wore off. Luckily, she didn't make a big scene of it." He made sure Viva understood exactly what he meant

178

by that, then concluded, "Me and Paul stayed friends, and they stayed married, and now they're gonna have a baby. All she felt was grateful 'cause I'd saved her life. Just like you are now. You'll get over it, too."

After just a moment's silence, Genevieve whispered, "You're lying. Start over and tell me the truth."

He met her eyes for an instant, felt their accusation, then looked away.

"I ain't lyin', Viva. I got no reason to lie," he lied. After taking a deep breath in a fruitless attempt to calm his racing heart, he managed to look at her again. The gemstone eyes hadn't blinked. "You think a guy like me wouldn't be glad to have somebody like you in love with him? But it don't work that way. Believe me, I know."

She blinked, once, and a pair of tears splashed onto her cheeks.

"You're lying to me, Rio. Why? If you don't love me, can't you just say so? But please, don't lie to me anymore."

He got up so fast he knocked the damn log stool over with a deep thud.

"What the hell makes you think I'm lying?" he roared. "God, woman, what is the matter with you? You act like you *want* me to love you."

Now he could meet her gaze. Now he could lean on the table, look down at her, and stare into those bottomless eyes and tell her the truth.

"I meant what I said, Viva. I stole that horse out there. Not quite so there's a wanted poster with my picture on it, but there's a man in San Antonio named Lawrence Whitmore Jackson, Jr., who'd hang me from the tree in his front yard if he ever caught me."

That much was the truth, and he saw the light

179

of belief flicker in her eyes. The tears, however, did not stop.

He knelt on the floor beside her and started to reach for her hand. Remembering, he drew back with a sigh.

"Jesus God, Viva, think about what I am. Everything I own, *everything*, I can carry in my saddlebags. I got nothin', and you're a rich lady from New Orleans. You said yourself you had the pick of every guy in Louisiana. Why'd you want to throw yourself away on a bum like me?"

She rose, not to stand but to kneel, facing him, so that their knees touched. When Rio tried to move away, Genevieve did what he had not been able to do. She took first one hand then the other in hers. As she lifted those rough, callused hands to her lips two tears fell and splashed softly on his palms.

"Rio, listen to me. And look at me when I'm talking to you."

Through her tears, she smiled.

He didn't.

She coughed and sniffed and began again.

"Rio, what a man carries in his saddlebags isn't what makes him whatever it is that he is. It's what he does, how he acts, how he thinks that's important."

"Like makin' a bed so he can seduce you in comfort instead of on the hard ground?"

"Is that what you were doing?" A little bubble of laughter forced its way though her tears. She tightened her hands over his lest he take them away. He responded instinctively, sliding his fingers into her hair to hold her firmly. Warmth began to coil inside her. In a slow, husky whisper she asked him, "Then what are we waiting for?"

No mortal man could resist, certainly not Rio

Jackson. His mouth was on hers in an instant, tasting the salt of her tears as he pushed his tongue past her lips and teeth to the deepest, sweetest reaches. He twined the soft, still-damp tendrils of her hair around his fingers with just enough force to let her know she would not escape easily.

She met him with her own fury, her own passion. At first her hands clutched his, molding his fingers around her head; then slowly, when she was certain he would not let her go, she eased her hands down his wrists, his arms, to his shoulders. Through his clothing she felt him stiffen. Afraid he would pull away from her, she slid the palms of her hands down his chest before wrapping her arms tightly around him.

And the tears continued to trickle from her eyes.

Abruptly, Rio broke free. Breathless, he held her at arm's length. His eyes, changed by passion to a smoldering, smoky blue, took in every detail of her upturned face, and if he had had any hope of stopping what she had begun, that hope died when her hungry, kiss-swollen lips again formed the words he did not want to hear.

"I love you, Rio Jackson. I love you."

He was crazy. He had to be. But he was also a man, a man who held a beautiful woman in his arms. His body wanted her desperately, and if his mind told him such desire was folly, he was beyond listening.

He kissed her again, this time pulling one hand free of her hair so he could wriggle out of his coat. He had barely got one sleeve off than she was helping him with the other. Her tongue teased his, eliciting gruff growls of pleasure, while her fingers fumbled at the buttons on his shirt. Then, when at last she touched his skin, a shiver rippled through him and broke the bond of their kiss.

181

Whatever they had started was beyond stopping now. She was no more in control than he. She did not want to be.

Yet she was aware of everything she did, everything Rio did, with an almost heightened sensitivity. When Rio pulled his shirt free of his trousers and lifted it over his head, Genevieve extended curious fingers to touch him. How warm his skin felt, how silky the dark, curly hair on his chest. With her little finger she traced a long white scar that ran just beneath his collarbone to the base of his throat. There, she could see each beat of his pulse.

Then she noticed other smaller scars on his side and shoulder, and one long, jagged slash of white flesh that started under his ribs and continued across his belly until it disappeared in the arrow of dark hair above his belt.

"Someone hurt you." she said, surprised.

"A long time ago. I don't even remember it anymore."

Nothin', not even a knife in the belly, is gonna hurt like lovin' you, Viva du Prés, Rio warned himself, but by then it was too late, much too late. Genevieve was already unbuckling his gunbelt.

He took her hands and drew her up with him so that they stood, the toes of her battered slippers just touching the toes of his boots. He leaned down to brush a light kiss across her lips while he finished undoing the buckle. The heavy belt, holster and revolver dropped to the floor.

Genevieve tugged at the buttons holding her borrowed skirt around her waist. In seconds it joined the gunbelt at her feet. The kiss deepened; Rio's tongue caressed the line of her lips until they parted, once again giving him access to the unbearable sweetness of her mouth.

182

She couldn't remove her clothing quickly enough. Every garment seemed a shackle, a barrier. Yet her fingers frequently strayed from the difficult buttons of her shirt to touch the man who did not hold her, whose only contact with her was his lips, playing so skillfully with hers.

Finally that shirt, the one Paul Bruckner had exclaimed over, came completely undone and, because she had nothing to wear under it, the removal of that single garment left her breasts bare. Not shyly, yet not brazenly, she stood still and waited.

First there was just the touch of his hands, cupping the fullness of her breasts with intimacy she had never known before. Then, slowly, gently, as though to break the bond too quickly would cause her pain, Rio released her lips and looked at her.

"So beautiful. So perfect."

His thumbs brushed across her nipples, and the delicate points of her breasts hardened even while she watched them. A sigh rippled through her, becoming a low moan as his hands curved themselves around her.

She had never guessed, never imagined, how exciting a man's touch could be. No, not a man's touch; just one man's touch, *Rio's* touch. Other men had touched her, not only the mauling paws of Buster Kulkey and the sadistic grip of Jean-Louis Marmont, but the tentative fumblings of the young beaux of New Orleans and the suave, practiced caresses of her more experienced suitors. None had ever thrilled her, delighted her, aroused her the way Rio Jackson did.

She tipped her head back, exposing her throat to his kisses, letting tiny cries of ecstasy vibrate under the tender nibblings of his teeth. The tears she had shed in heart-broken desolation a few minutes ago became tears of joy and exultation. Salty rivers trickled unchecked down her cheeks.

Rio slipped his arms around her and lifted her off her feet, far more gently than he had that night in Sacramento. And instead of slinging her over his shoulder, this time he held her against him, to bury his face in the wealth of her tumbled hair as he carried her the three steps to the bed.

There were no crisp linen sheets, just a woolen blanket covered with the remnants of a torn petticoat.

Abruptly Rio set Genevieve on her feet and turned away from her. He drew three deep, shuddering breaths before she could recover from the shock of his abandonment, but they weren't enough to destroy the ache of desire denied, the pain of arousal unfulfilled.

One small hand touched his back. The other must have been busy with the tie at her remaining petticoat. He heard it swish down over her hips. A moment later the increased pressure of her hand told him she was using him to keep her balance while she stepped out of her drawers.

Slender arms slipped around his waist. The warmth of her breasts, the nipples still hard, pressed against the smooth skin of his back.

He gave up fighting it. Maybe she was right; maybe thinking about things too long was wrong. Besides, who could fight when nimble fingers were fumbling at the buttons on his pants, each tiny movement sending bolts of lightning through him? With a groan of surrender, Rio pulled her hands away and nudged her backward.

She tumbled onto the bed with all the grace of innocence and passion newly awakened. An instant later, he had the last of his own clothing on the floor and lay beside her.

He said nothing. The look in his eyes just before he kissed her told her that there was now no turning back.

Everywhere, every way, he kissed her, touched her, caressed her. The deep probing kisses with which he plundered her mouth became softer, gentler, until he moved his lips to her cheek, her chin, then down her arched neck to that frantic pulsebeat at the base of her throat. Each time she felt that infinitely tender pressure against her flesh, she gasped. And each breath sighed out of her lungs with a cry.

With his left arm under her, he pulled her to him, and she knew the full wonder of his desire for her. She strained against him, seeking the ultimate possession, but he resisted.

"Not yet." he murmured against her ear. "Soon, but not yet."

His right hand wandered while he kissed her back from the brink. The palm swept across an engorged nipple that begged for his attention, the fingers traced random patterns down her ribs, the thumb stroked the sensitive point of her hipbone. Her legs parted to let him find that most secret place. He touched her gently, yet still the sparks exploded within her, setting fire to her need.

None of it, however, was enough. It was more, so much more, than she had ever known, but still not enough.

Then he was pushing her back, away from him until he covered her body with his. One arm around his neck, the other at his waist, she clung to him. The warmth of her, open, seeking, drew him inexorably.

He came into her easily, though he knew without asking that she was a virgin. He felt the resistance, and heard her gasp of pain, but then there was

185

only the sleekness of her around him, holding him. Her arms, her legs, the satiny sheath of her womanhood embraced him.

And for the moment, for both of them, it was enough.

"Rio?"

"Did I hurt you?"

He was propped on his elbows, holding his weight off her and letting the urgency subside a little. Nervous little strokes of her fingertips at the back of his neck relayed the intensity of her longing to him. But she could wait. He could wait. A moment at least.

"No. But I—"

"I didn't want to hurt you."

"You didn't."

"Good, 'cause I never—"

"Never?" she exclaimed. "You mean we were both—?"

His sudden burst of laughter drove him deeper inside her and drew a groan of pleasure from two throats.

"No, *querida,*" he murmured. He moved against her again, as desire regained control. "I just never had a virgin before. I wanted to make sure I did it right."

Lowering his mouth to hers to take unto himself any cry of pain, he entered her fully.

All that had gone before—the fights, the fears, the bitterness, the lies—was forgotten as Geneviève gave herself up to the sweet ecstasy this strange, unfathomable man brought to her. She responded with instinctive rhythm, as old as time, as new as her love.

Her awareness narrowed until only she and Rio existed in a universe of sensation: The heat of his body against hers, the power of his muscles under

186

her hands, the incoherent words he whispered in her ear, the taste of kisses filled with wild passion. And then suddenly that universe exploded. All feeling intensified a hundredfold. For one blinding moment every touch, every sound, every scent brought an exquisite flare of something akin to pain.

Ecstatic convulsions swept through her, accompanied by cries of astonishment and delight that she did not know came from her own lips. Rio was calling her name, over and over and over, raining kisses on her face and throat by the thousands, stroking the hair back from her forehead with an unsteady hand.

"I love you," she gasped as the world came back together.

She had fallen asleep, or at least into a dreamy afterhaze that allowed Rio to extricate himself from the tangle of her arms and legs. The fire was burning down, and though Genevieve had covered the bed, she had not brought blankets to cover the occupants. She moaned softly something that might have been his name, but he forced himself to leave her without even a kiss.

Lying on her side with one arm curled under her head for a pillow, Genevieve opened her eyes just enough to watch him. Muscle and bone moved in perfect harmony as he bent to pick up chunks of wood for the fire. She longed for her sketchbook, abandoned like so many other things in that Sacramento hotel room.

She remembered staring at the masterpieces of Michelangelo and thinking, with appropriate blushes that she refused to explain, that the marble was a poor substitute for warm, living flesh. She had dared to touch the stone and recoiled. Now, letting her eyes study Rio, she knew she had been right.

Satisfied that the fire would burn long enough for them to rest, Rio turned and walked to the pile of rumpled bedding. He found a couple blankets, shook them free, and draped them over one arm to carry to the bed. That was when he saw the reflection of the firelight in her eyes.

He froze, waiting for her screams, her tears, her tirade of self-recrimination. All she said was, "Oh, Rio, by all the saints in heaven, you are beautiful."

She slid from the bed and padded silently to him, unaware that she was as naked as he.

With no materials to draw him, she let her fingers trace every line and shadow, from his broad powerful shoulders, down the massive chest with its silky little curls of hair and the proud imperfections of his scars to the corded muscles of his belly. No ancient stone relic, no Renaissance monument could compare with this living, breathing magnificence.

He held his breath, wondering what she was doing, afraid she would stop.

"You go much further, lady, and you're gonna have a handful."

Reflex took her eyes where she knew she should not look, then shock brought them upward to his lazy grin.

They slept without making love again, because Rio warned her she'd regret it. So they curled together, her back to his front, and let exhaustion conquer desire. When they wakened, the fire had once again died.

An eerie wind howled, around the cabin and down the crooked stone chimney.

"Storm's comin'," Rio observed. He stretched, then laced his fingers behind his head. He could feel the warmth of Genevieve's body, but he dared not touch her. Not now, not yet.

Like him, she lay on her back, but with her arms stiffly at her sides.

"I'm sorry, Rio," she whispered.

" 'Bout what? The storm?"

"No. About, you know, making you do something you really didn't want to do."

"And what was that?"

"Um, what we just did."

Now he rolled over, on his side so he could look at her perfect profile, the sweep of her lashes as she blinked her eyes, the rise and fall of her breasts with each frightened breath.

"Give it a name," he told her. "Making love, that's what we just did. And there isn't a woman alive who can force me to make love to her unless I want to."

"But you didn't, not really. You kept trying to make me stop."

"Hell, yes, I did!" Now would come the remorse, the anger, the loathing, the hatred. He had seen it all before.

He threw back the blanket and got off the bed to grope for the discarded pants and shirt.

"What we did was wrong," he told her. Looking at her was the last thing he wanted to do, so he tended the fire, turned up the lamp, found his socks and boots, and filled the coffee pot. And all the while, he talked to her.

"You're gonna go back to New Orleans and pick up your life where you left off. Eventually you'll find some guy and want to marry him, and there'll be this thing that we did here standing in your way. Rich, proper men like to marry virgins, women

189

they know haven't been and likely won't be sleeping with other men."

"Men like Jean-Louis Marmont?" she asked, disgust filling her voice.

She had not moved, still lay staring at the crude ceiling when Rio dropped her clothes beside her on the bed.

"Well, not him exactly, but men like him. Men like, well, like your father."

A bitter little chuckle accompanied her sitting up and reaching for Paul Bruckner's shirt.

"Shows how much you know, Rio Jackson."

"And what's that supposed to mean?"

She pulled the shirt over her head and did up the buttons before pushing the blanket down and scooting off the bed. Aware of Rio's silent stare, she stepped into her drawers and petticoat and finally Angela's cast-off skirt. If Rio Jackson held all he owned in his saddlebags, right now she owned nothing, not even the clothes on her back.

Plopping down at the table, Genevieve looked up at Rio and sighed again.

"My father isn't a whole lot different from Jean-Louis. I have a feeling none of the men I ever knew were much different. Except, I thought for a while, you."

She stroked the smooth surface of the crude little table, amazed at how much pleasure she had derived from the fruit of Rio's labor. No one in her experience would ever have thought to do something so simple, so sweet for her. Certainly not Jean-Louis. Certainly not her father.

"My father and Jean-Louis' father were partners in the Louisiana Commercial Bank. They had inherited it from their fathers when it was just a small enterprise, and over the years they built it into one of the largest and most influential financial institutions in New Orleans. There were, in fact, rumors that Victor du Prés could have been governor, but it would have meant a loss of power."

Rio swallowed. If he took her all the way back to New Orleans, he was a dead man. Fathers like Victor du Prés didn't allow men like Rio Jackson to deflower their daughters.

"Etienne Marmont gambled. Heavily. And he lost just as heavily."

"Not a good trait in a banker."

"No. Nor in a banker's son."

"Jean-Louis?"

She nodded.

"You knew, and you were still willing to marry him?"

"I knew he gambled, but I didn't know how much until after we were engaged."

"I take it you found out."

Again, she nodded, and for a long moment said nothing more. Finally, when Rio sat down opposite her, she looked up into his eyes and a single tear fell from her eye.

"Etienne nearly ruined all of us. To cover Jean-Louis' gambling debts, Etienne gambled more himself. And he lost more. He had mortgaged their house and even sold his wife's jewelry, but it wasn't nearly enough. Finally, he stole from the bank."

"That's why Jean-Louis ran off? Why didn't he stay and try to work it out?"

"Jean-Louis didn't know how to work any more than his father did. Besides, there was more to the scandal than that. When my father confronted Etienne about the money, Etienne shot himself. Jean-Louis found the body."

"Jeez!"

"It was the stupidest thing he could have done, of course. There was no keeping a scandal like that

191

quiet, and once people got to talking, they would eventually have learned about the embezzlement. It was a considerable sum of money, but not beyond my father's capacity to make it up. He didn't gamble, not Victor du Prés, but he had other vices."

She swallowed and studied her clasped hands for a moment. The memory no longer embarrassed her, but it still angered her.

"He was arrested while sneaking out of the home of one of his mistresses. He had stolen several extremely expensive pieces of jewelry, some of which he had given her; others were gifts from her other 'gentlemen.' He spent two nights in jail and by then it was all over the city. Ironically, the woman had pawned the originals and what he stole were only cheap paste imitations, but we didn't learn that until after paying her a considerable sum of cash to drop the charges."

"So you ran away to escape the scandal? Or to make back the family fortune in the gold fields?"

She had to laugh.

"No, but I wonder if maybe you aren't just like Jean-Louis after all. That's exactly what he did. I went after him to make him face the music."

"Not because you loved him?"

"I never loved him."

"But you were going to marry him."

She stood and turned away from the accusation in Rio's voice and steady gaze.

"Jean-Louis was convenient. I had known him all my life. He wouldn't make demands on me, and before the scandal, I at least believed he wasn't marrying me for my money or position. He was boring, shallow, but manageable. Or so I thought, until that night in that awful place."

She tilted her head back to stop another rush of tears. A sudden warmth enveloped her as Rio's arms encircled her and turned her into his embrace. Silently he rocked her, willing the horror to go away. He knew he shared her thoughts, but it was she who put them into words.

Laying her head against his shoulder, she let the last of her fear subside.

"Oh, Rio, what would I ever have done if you hadn't been there that night, too?"

Chapter Thirteen

They ate a silent meager supper while the wind continued to howl around the cabin. Despite the roaring fire, the cabin grew colder. Genevieve was shivering before she had finished eating.

"Get into bed," Rio ordered as he pulled on his coat. "I'll check on the horses and be back in a minute."

When he opened the door, the icy wind nearly forced him back. Yet it bore no snow, and above the mountains he saw the bright silver disk of the moon. With a clear sky and this wind, the night would be cold indeed.

That near-full moon provided sufficient light for him to see that Cinco, the mare, and the mule were huddled together in the shallow shelter of the lean-to. If they had had water, it was frozen solid by now; they could wait until morning. Giving them feed would be a waste of time; the wind would blow it away before they ever ate it.

Inside the lean-to, the light did not penetrate except for a weak reflection from the snow. Carefully, Rio felt his way around. He knew exactly what he was looking for though he couldn't remember exactly where he had put it. Lacking gloves, his fingers rapidly grew numb, but one by one he gathered the few simple tools and materials he needed. Then, afraid he might already have suffered a nip of frostbite on his ears, he hurried back to the cabin.

The opening of the door and the accompanying blast of frigid air stirred Genevieve, but she did not waken. After he had set his things on the table, he found another blanket to lay over her, and he could not resist a kiss on the shining tumbled mass of her hair.

Reluctantly, he walked away from the bed and returned to the table. He had a long night's work ahead of him.

"Wake up, Rio! Didn't you hear that?"

Genevieve shook his shoulder again, then listened for the fading echo of the unearthly scream.

"Hear what?"

He had heard nothing before the girl's panicked whisper, yet in that instant he was awake and alert. Silently, he swung his legs out from under the blankets and groped for the boots left beside the bed.

When it came the second time, he froze. High, piercing, inhuman, the shriek split the cabin's silence. A moment later, he recognized Cinco's frightened whinny.

While Rio fumbled with the buckle of his gunbelt, Genevieve slipped her feet into what remained of her shoes and pulled her makeshift coat over her arms.

"You stay here," he growled.

"No, I'm going with you. I won't stay here alone and not know what's happening to you."

He wanted to argue with her, but another long, shrill wail told him he had no time.

The wind had died sometime during the night, and on its tail had come clouds. The hour was indeterminate; somewhere behind that thick overcast the sun rode, but Rio had no way of telling how high. It could have been any time between dawn and early afternoon.

Again the shrill scream shattered the quiet, all the louder and clearer and more soul chilling out of doors without the solid walls of the cabin to muffle it. Rio drew the revolver from its holster and handed the loaded rifle to the woman walking beside him.

"I can't shoot this!" she protested in a terrified whisper.

"Good. Then just hold it for me, and I'll do the shooting, if necessary."

In the paddock, Cinco was pacing in terror. Nostrils distended and tail raised to a snowy plume, the palomino trotted from one end of the enclosure to the other. Occasionally he snorted a challenge, then jumped and landed on all four hooves. In the shelter of the lean-to, the mare and the mule cowered.

Whatever was out there had to be an animal. Even though another of those blood-curdling screams rent the valley and echoed off the mountainsides like insane human laughter, Rio knew an animal had made them. He looked up, scanning the broken rocks and sparse trees for some sign.

Genevieve saw them first, on a ledge no more than a hundred feet above the cabin.

"There," she whispered.

The great tawny cat screamed again as it lashed out with one clawed paw. Behind her, a half-grown cub huddled against the face of the mountain. The youngster hissed, but together the cats were no match for the towering menace of the bear.

"He must have been drawn out of his den by the smell of the deer," Rio said as he reached for the rifle in Genevieve's trembling hands. "She dragged the carcass up there to feed in the sun and woke up the bear."

Standing on its hind legs, the grizzly growled again at the two cats. Between them lay the half-eaten doe the cougar had killed to feed herself and the cub. Rio shouldered the rifle and took careful aim.

"Damn!" he swore before the smoke of the single shot had cleared. He threw the rifle down and drew the revolver.

The bear must have dropped to all fours at the very instant Rio squeezed the trigger. Wounded, the animal let out an enraged bellow before it tumbled off the ledge.

With nowhere to run, the cat turned her back to the wall and faced the source of this new threat. Fangs bared, tail lashing, she prepared to do battle against another foe.

"Get inside," Rio ordered. He slid one bullet after another into the gun.

"Where are you going?"

"To finish off the bear. Now, get, and quit arguing."

"What about the mountain lion?"

"God damn it, Viva, when will you learn to shut up! The cougar's fine; she won't bother us if we don't bother her. Last thing we need is a wounded grizzly bargin' into camp. Now get inside before I shoot you first!"

Despite the clarity of the trail the bleeding animal had left, Rio tracked it slowly. A scree of tumbled boulders had broken the bear's fall from the ledge, the landing place marked by the amount of blood and the glaze of ice on the stones, where body heat had melted the snow.

The terrain was the worst possible, and Rio's lack of adequate clothing made the tracking an agony. His fingers were too numb to feel the roughness of the rocks, and before long he was leaving

197

his own trail of blood whenever he grasped a stone to keep his balance. Boots made for riding served poorly for climbing, though once the cold had seeped through and his feet were as unfeeling as his hands, Rio wondered if he might not have been better off barefoot.

He slipped the Colt into his left hand, to give the right a moment to flex and restore some circulation. Hoping to God he'd have enough feeling left in the fingers to pull the trigger, he took the gun back in his right hand. When he looked up, the bear stood no more than fifteen feet in front of him.

Genevieve hardly dared to breathe, yet she knew she could not stand at the door and stare at its planks forever. There was a fire to feed and food to cook. And a bed to make.

She could not bring herself to straighten the rumpled blankets just yet. The memories were still too fresh, the danger still too close. So she stirred the coals and added more wood, set coffee on to boil, and took down the kettle to begin the daily ration of beans and venison.

At the first gunshot she jumped and nearly dropped the kettle. At the second, she closed her eyes and held her breath. At the third, she prayed.

Only silence answered those prayers.

The body fell backwards, slowly at first, but by the time the head hit the rocks, the whole thing had begun rolling. Rio didn't lower the gun until the bear reached the valley floor and lay still. He watched, his finger still on the trigger, and waited. A man sprawled at such an impossible angle would surely be dead, but a bear might be different.

When a full minute had passed and there was no

sign of life, Rio began the cautious descent. Here
the path was a bit easier, less steep as well as less
rocky. Halfway down, he holstered the revolver and
used both hands to steady himself. A few flakes of
light snow drifted in the windless cold air.

If he left the carcass where it had fallen, there'd
be little enough of it left by morning. The animal
was old, and the meat probably tough as boot
leather, but still he hated to see it go to waste—or
to scavengers. It was too massive for him to move,
even with Viva's help; he'd have to use the mule to
haul it back to the cabin. Maybe he'd have time
for a cup of hot coffee before tackling that task.

Putting his hands in his pockets brought back
some feeling to them, but the increasing, snow
forced him to walk with head down to avoid being
blinded. Unable to see more than three steps in
front of him, Rio was totally unprepared for the
demon that flung itself at him.

"Omigod, Rio, are you all right? Are you hurt?
Did you kill the bear?" She touched his face, her
hands warm against his chapped cheeks. Then she
was checking his arms and shoulders for other possible injuries. "Oh, lord, your hand is bleeding.
You are hurt. Come inside and let me take care of
it. I was so worried. I heard the gun and then I
didn't hear anything and—"

"Hold on a minute!" He caught her hands in his
and that seemed to settle her down a bit, though
she still wanted to touch him everywhere at once.
"I'm fine, Viva. Cold, but fine."

"But the bear. What happened? It took you so
long, and three shots, and—"

There was only one way to silence her long
enough to get in out of the snow and cold. And
kissing Viva du Prés was not something Rio particularly minded doing.

Her lips were warm against his cold ones, her

199

tongue eager to tease and please. His hands found warmth within the luxuriant black hair, but nothing compared to the fire kindled when he brought her body up against his. He wasn't numb anymore.

When he lifted her in his arms and strode the last few yards to the cabin door, she grinned and whispered, "Oh, yes, you are just fine, Rio, more than fine!"

Rio laid out the stiffening grizzly while Genevieve unhitched the mule and led her back to the paddock. Made nervous by the scent of blood, Cinco continued to pace the tiny confines and blow twin plumes of steam into the icy air.

"Stay out of his way," Rio warned as he pulled out his knife to begin skinning the carcass. "The mare may be coming into season, and he's going to be one horny son of a bitch for the next couple of weeks."

A year ago, Genevieve Marie du Prés, New Orleans belle, would have had no idea what Rio Jackson was talking about. Now, pushing snowflakes out of her hair and warming her hands over a campfire, she blushed faintly and asked, "Could she get pregnant? Would that mean we couldn't take her back with us?"

"Depends. Probably wouldn't make any difference at all. She's dropped a foal or two, and she's pretty sturdy. Cinco's foals tend to be small, like he was. If we leave here by late April, she wouldn't be due until September, so we'd have plenty of time. Better turn your back now, if you don't want to watch."

She took one last look at the great hairy corpse. Without the stomach to watch the butchering, she still had refused to wait alone in the cabin.

"So Cinco was a small foal," she echoed bemusedly. "Then you've known him since he was little? You didn't just happen upon a beautiful golden stallion and decide to make him your own?"

He had known it would come to this. Telling her could be no worse, however, than facing the bear: inevitable, but once it was over, it was over and need never be dreaded again.

"I delivered that randy goat," he stated casually, though his heart pounded as the memories surfaced. Some were good, but most were unpleasant and were best left stored in the deepest cellars of his consciousness. "He was so little the old man spit on the floor and said he had wasted ten grand on a scrawny pony."

"Who's 'the old man'?"

"My father. I told you, I stole Cinco from my brother. My half-brother, that is."

Finally, after all the days and nights of wondering, she was going to learn just who Rio Jackson was. Whatever had happened between them the day before, it had changed him, opened him to her as nothing else ever had.

"Older or younger?"

"Master Lawrence is younger, by five years."

"Your mother died when you were very young then."

He laughed and drew the blade cleanly through the hide.

"My mother died six years ago. Master Lawrence's mother was married to my father; my mother was not. Which makes me, in polite parlance, a bastard. Master Lawrence, on the other hand, was the heir."

Genevieve shivered. The coffee in the mug she had set atop the fencepost was stone cold now. In a few more minutes there would be a rim of ice on the surface. Avoiding sight of the gory business

Rio labored on, she bent to pick up the coffee pot from the fire and filled her cup.

"Did he hate you as much as you hate him?"

Without hesitation, Rio answered, "Probably more. He *had* things; I *did* things."

Like stealing Cinco. Watching the magnificent animal canter around the paddock, she did not wonder why Lawrence Whitmore Jackson Jr. would be jealous of his older brother.

"How *did* you steal him?" she asked. "You can't have just ridden out of the stable with him."

"No, he was barely two years old then. He'd come a long way from that scrawny little foal, gave every promise of being all the old man had hoped for. But that night he was born, the old man gave him to me, told me I could have him if I wanted him. Sometimes I wonder if he thought some other stud had got the mare, and Cinco was a bastard like me."

"Then you didn't steal him. Your father gave him to you."

"Yeah, with half a dozen witnesses. But he never put it on paper." Peeling hide from flesh was a miserable, messy job. If there was any compensation, it was that the blood still held a bit of warmth. "And two years later, Cinco was worth ten times what the old man had paid for him. Junior wasn't about to let him go to the bastard son."

Once again he had lost all feeling in his hands. He'd have to get them warm again before he finished with the knife. After wiping the blood on a rag, he poured himself a cup of coffee and joined Genevieve at the fence.

"The old man never knew whether to hate me or not. When he wrote his will, he was between moods, so he didn't cut me out entirely, but he didn't make it easy for me either. He liked puzzles, the tricky kind you have to think real hard about only then they turn out to be really easy."

The coffee warmed him, but not as much as having Genevieve beside him. She snuggled against him, until he wrapped his arm around her shoulders and held her close.

"The boots keepin' your feet warm?" he asked.

She looked down at the calf-high leather moccasins she had found on the table after Rio pointed them out and told her he'd been up all night working on them.

"They're wonderful. I almost hate to wear them; I don't want to wear them out. Now, tell me how you got Cinco away from your evil half-brother."

He chuckled and gave her a little squeeze.

"The old man made my part of his will a riddle. I could have any five things not already bequeathed, provided I took them from different parts of the ranch, all at one time, and all in one hand."

"Just like the fairy tale!"

"I don't know about fairy tales. All I wanted was that damn horse, because I knew Junior wanted him, too. He, and probably the old man, too, figured I'd try to walk out of there with a handful of gold or something."

"Instead you picked up a mote of dust, a petal from a flower, a bird feather, a crumb of bread, and Cinco."

Rio looked down at Genevieve's triumphant smile and shook his head.

"Well, you got it right about Cinco, but I took two diamond rings, a gold watch, and one long strand of pearls before I walked out to the stable and grabbed Cinco by his forelock."

"Well, I was close."

He kissed the top of her head and pulled her around so she faced him, her feet in their elk-skin boots placed right between his spraddled ones.

203

"Delightfully close," he murmured with a smile. "But if you stand here much longer, I'm not going to get this bear skinned, and there's a lot more work to do after that."

Her worried eyes searched his face as she asked, "Will you be all right? Your hand doesn't hurt?"

"I'm fine, Viva. Now, go, and let me finish here. It's going to be dark soon."

And with the dark would come snow. Lots of it. After the girl had left him and returned to the cabin, Rio studied the sky for several long minutes. The clouds showed no motion at all, and the now steady fall of snow drifted straight down. With a concerned and somewhat doubtful shake of his head, Rio pushed himself away from the fence and returned to his work.

Genevieve sat down at the table with the stack of books and gingerly opened the first volume, the one she had taken from its leather shroud the other evening.

" 'Four Tragedies, by William Shakespeare,' " she read aloud. Her nose wrinkled. "I do hope Mr. Tibler saved us something more entertaining than Hamlet and King Lear."

After setting the Shakespeare aside, she took the second book from the stack and cut the thong. The leather wrapping was stiff and probably no longer fit for any other use, but she unfolded it carefully nonetheless.

"Ah, poetry. Herrick and Donne, Lovelace and Pope," she sighed with pleasure, running her finger down the list of contents. "I do not believe the good sisters would entirely approve of some of these, but Rio and I shall surely enjoy reading them together."

The third volume proved to be an elegant edition

of Machiavelli's *The Prince,* bound in a red leather cover whose intricate gold-leaf embossing shone bright in the lanternlight. The pages contained the text in the original Italian on the left and a modern translation on the right. Genevieve struggled over the first few lines, but her French provided little help to understanding the Italian.

"Well, Mr. Tibler certainly had an interesting library," she commented as she settled the Machiavelli atop the poetry.

The next package contained two separate books, the autobiographies of Benjamin Franklin and Benvenuto Cellini. Tucked between them, as though for added protection was an envelope with Rio's name written in beautiful copperplate on the outside. Genevieve turned the envelope over and smiled at the little lump of beeswax with a clover blossom impressed within it.

She was just getting to her feet to take the letter to him when the door opened and Rio himself entered the cabin.

Brushing a heavy dust of snow from his shoulders, he said, "I'm gonna need some help for a while. Can you—?"

The sight of her stopped him cold. The fragile lamplight turned her face to a golden cameo, her tousled hair to a veil of midnight moonbeams. One delicate hand rested on the open page of a book, the other held a piece of paper. What in the name of heaven ever made him believe a creature like this, so beautiful even in her cast-off clothing and hand-made shoes, could possibly love him?

The room was so small he crossed it in two long, angry strides. And with one angry sweep of his hand he sent the book flying, to land perilously close to the fire.

"Forget the goddamn books!" he yelled. "There's a blizzard comin', and we ain't got time for you to

205

sit on your ass readin'! Or do you expect me to play both lover *and* slave, takin' care of the horses, bringin' in wood, fetchin' water, while you sit here nice and toasty by the fire, and then hop into bed and service all your *other* needs half the night? Well, lady, I ain't nobody's fancy man, least of all yours!"

At first his outburst stunned her, robbed her of both speech and motion. Then, as his spiteful words sank in, she regained not only her tongue, but her defiance as well. His last insult was more than she would stand for, even from Rio Jackson. She brought her right hand up and slapped his insolent face as hard as she could.

"Don't you ever, *ever* accuse me of that again," she warned, her eyes flashing blue flames. "I came inside because you sent me here, not because I didn't want to work. And you know it."

He did, but he was too angry, too frightened, to admit it.

"I made your supper, and I heated water for you to wash. What more do you want me to do?"

Not waiting for his reply, she rose and took her coat down from the nail she had hung it on to warm by the fire.

"Where do you think you're going?"

"To bring in the wood. You're right; we are low. And then I'll get water from the spring."

"It's too dark; you'll get lost."

He grabbed her arm with one hand; when she tried to wriggle free, he caught the other and brought her face to face with him.

"You'd like that, wouldn't you," she muttered. Her lips, the lips he longed to kiss into silence, were a hard line, her eyes narrowed to mere slits of sapphire fury.

"Yeah, right, I'd just love it. That's why I keep riskin' my damn neck for you, makin' featherbeds for you to sleep on, and stayin' up half the damn night to sew moccasins so your dainty little feet don't freeze. Sounds like a great way to get rid or you, don't it?"

She wanted to hit him again and again, until he stopped reminding her how wrong she was, but this time her hand came gently into contact with his cheek and lingered.

He took her mouth in a savage kiss, without apologies, without tenderness. Demanding entrance, his tongue rasped along the edge of her lips, but she did not deny him long. With her free hand, she pulled off his hat and tossed it to the floor, while the fingers of her other hand threaded into the thick hair over his ears to hold him and keep him from breaking that kiss.

She tasted of coffee, bitter and strong, and of woman, sweet and wild. He tightened his arms around her, willing her to join with him. She did, her heat finding his. Afraid to free her mouth lest he—or she—say another angry word, Rio cupped the back of her head with one hand while with the other he struggled and fumbled to remove the barrier of clothing that separated flesh from flesh.

How fierce his passion was, how overwhelming her desire. It engulfed them in fire. The winds and snows of winter might rage outside this tiny cabin, but within the four rough walls, Rio and Genevieve generated a blazing heat. Sweat glistened on naked skin as they collapsed on the bed.

"Now, Rio, now," she begged, her lips forming the words against his own.

"Yes, now, now," he answered as he filled her, and his mouth never left hers.

Tenderness, gentleness had no place, only the fury of their loving. Wild, untamed, uncontrolled, it catapulted them into a fiery delirium.

Genevieve met each driving thrust of his hips,

opening herself to take him deeper inside. She arched her back to press her throbbing breasts more tightly to him. There was no existence beyond the craving of her body for the fulfillment of the blazing ecstasy Rio had kindled in her. The rhythmic moans she breathed into his mouth, the lascivious demands he murmured against her lips were the only sounds, the bursts of brilliant blindness behind her tightly shut eyes the only sights.

"Now, my heart, now," he urged. His hands stroked down the sides of her breasts, her ribs, her waist to her hips. He slid his fingers under her to cup her buttocks and hold her still more intimately. "Let it be—*now!*"

Then the explosion consumed them and they cried out in wonderment at its glory.

Rio lifted his weight off her, but did not leave her. His anger and his passion were well and fully spent, yet in the ashes of ecstasy glowed the throbbing coals of unquenched desire.

"Viva?" he whispered.

"Mmmm?" She could manage no other response. Sated, exhausted, she was content just to hold him within her and let the embers cool.

"Viva, I gotta go."

"No, not yet." Though her legs remained around his, she had not the strength to tighten the embrace.

Holding his weight on one forearm, Rio brushed the tangled strands of hair back from her face. She still didn't open her eyes, and he wasn't about to let her fall asleep.

"Yeah, now," he insisted. It was no easier for him to tear himself away from her than it was for her to let him go. "The wind's comin' up strong."

One deep blue eye opened, then the other.

"You talk too much, Rio Jackson," she mumbled, "but I suppose you're right. As usual."

No matter how hard she tried to hold on to it, the afterglow faded once Rio had left the bed. Once that sensuous luminescence was gone, all the harsh realities it had held at bay came flooding back like the darkness after the sun has set. She sat on the edge of the bed and took the shirt Rio handed to her, but she could not make herself put it on.

"You're gonna catch your death, you don't get dressed."

"I will, I will. I was just thinking."

He snorted as he buttoned up his trousers and buckled his belt.

"That's dangerous territory for you, isn't it? C'mon, Viva, it's really turning nasty out there. Listen to that wind!" He shoved one foot into a boot, then the other. "I'll get the water; you bring in the wood. Then we'll take the big pot outside, get it out of the way."

He slapped his hat on his head and picked up the two buckets. He had his hand on the latch, ready to walk out the door, when he suddenly turned and strode back to the bed.

"I'm sorry, Viva, I truly am. It shouldn't have happened, and it's my fault."

I wanted it, too, as much as you if not more, she wanted to tell him.

He leaned down to kiss a long curl that had somehow got twisted onto the top of her head.

"Get dressed, querida mía. We'll talk later."

He was gone before she could sort out her jumbled thoughts enough to look up.

The blast of cold air from the open door did, however, prompt her to pull on the shirt and finally the rest of her clothes. She could tell by the incessant whining of wind that it would be impossible

209

to keep warm even on the short trip to where the firewood was stacked along the side of the cabin. It would also be impossible to carry a lantern. She'd have to do it all with her sense of touch, unless some moonlight penetrated the storm clouds.

She took one last look around the cabin before stepping into the storm. On the floor, dangerously close to the fire, lay the open book Rio had so furiously swept off the table. It would be safe for a few minutes, until she had brought in some more wood. The fire was down now; she'd have to build it up again. She would rescue Benjamin Franklin then.

With the first armload of wood she brought in, she did just that. She set the book on the table, added logs to the fire, then braced herself for another trip outside. She had made three more before Rio came back with the water, the buckets dripping icicles.

She took them from him and dumped them into the kettle over the fire while he warmed his hands. If he saw the books and the envelope on the table this time, he gave no sign. Nor did he say a single word before going out into the blizzard again.

When he returned, she handed him a cup of coffee, but he could hardly hold it. The ice on his hands cracked as he tried to bend his fingers.

"Let me go this time," she suggested. "I'm sure I can find my way."

He shook his head.

"No, it's getting too bad out there now." His speech was slurred, signaling the danger he dared not challenge again. "You still got some supper left? If I ever get thawed out, I think I'm gonna be starved."

He tugged off his coat and hung it by the fire, then stood to soak up as much of the warmth as possible. Never in his life had he been so cold. Better men than Rio Jackson had died in these mountains, and Rio couldn't shake from his mind the possibility that neither he nor the woman he had rescued would ever see St. Joe again.

He must have been daydreaming, or even dozing, because Genevieve's voice startled him.

"It's on the table," she said.

He turned and walked to the stool at his place. Everything looked just as it always did: two tin plates, silverware, the placemats with their edges frayed for fringe, a skillet full of beans and venison. With a weary sigh, Rio reached for the skillet.

The envelope was propped against it.

He plucked the envelope out of the way and picked up the skillet.

"Aren't you going to read it?"

"Read what?"

"Your letter. Mr. Tibler must have written it before he died."

Rio scooped food onto his plate then set the skillet down with a thunk.

"If it's my letter, I can do with it what I want, right? And I choose not to do anything with it."

He dug his fork into the slightly dried out beans.

Because her own curiosity was gnawing at her worse than her own hunger, Genevieve nearly cried out in her frustration. How could anyone, faced with a letter years old, not pick it up and immediately rip it open to read? Surely even a man as methodical as Rio Jackson had some spark of curiosity in him.

But she said nothing, because she noticed as she reached for the skillet herself that an odd expression had come over Rio's features.

He seemed intent on his food, but he kept casting sidelong glances at the letter. It rested a foot or so to the right of his plate. the side with his name uppermost, but turned so that to him the writing

211

was upside down. With its elaborate swirls and curlicues, Ernest Tibler's handwriting was beautiful but difficult to read rightside up. Turned the other way, it would be nearly impossible to decipher.

Genevieve set the skillet down. She knew now why he hated the books so much, why he had feared their discovery.

"Read the letter, Rio," she urged. "I do so want to know what Mr. Tibler wrote to you."

"Nothin' he didn't tell me hisself before he died," Rio mumbled, his mouth full of food.

"But you don't know for sure. Go ahead, read it."

He slammed his fork down with a shaking hand.

"I said I don't want to. Now, will you leave me alone? Eat your own damn dinner."

"Why, Rio, why won't you read it? And why do you hate it, and the books, so badly?" She knew the answer, knew she was tormenting him by asking, but she would not let this stand between them any longer. "Is it because you—"

"Yes, goddamnit!" he bellowed. "I *can't* read it! Are you happy now? Any more secrets you want to know about me?" He ticked them off one by one on his fingers. "My mother was a Mexican whore who worked in Lawrence Jackson's kitchen when she wasn't on her back in his bed. I stole my horse from my own brother. And I couldn't read my own name if it was on a wanted poster."

Chapter Fourteen

She grabbed his arm as he rushed past her, headed for the door. When he tried to shake her off, she clung all the more tightly.

"Damn it, Viva, let me go."

"No, you stupid fool."

Three words she would have sold her soul to have back.

"Only an idiot would go out there," she reminded him, as though the other words had never been spoken. "Now, sit down, and eat."

Her own supper forgotten, Genevieve guided Rio back to the table. When he was once again seated and had, under her unblinking eye, taken another bite, she picked up the envelope and handed it to him.

"Open it," she ordered, standing behind his right shoulder. "If you don't, I will, but the result is going to be the same."

He used his knife to slash the fragile paper.

"Take the letter out, unfold it, and start."

He slammed it down on the table.

"You're really enjoying this, aren't you."

"What?" she mocked, stepping back so she could take in his stubborn profile. He didn't even glance sideways at her. "No 'ain't' this time?"

"And what's that supposed to mean?"

"It means that whenever you get touchy about

213

something, you fall back into a very vulgar patois. As though by sounding ignorant, you can fool people into believing there is nothing more to Rio Jackson than an unlettered wagon train scout. We'll forget the details of your, um, parentage, as irrelevant."

"You talk too much," he muttered, and stuffed his mouth with cold, dried beans.

"You're damn right I do, Rio Jackson, and I'm going to keep right on talking."

"Heaven help me."

"The only way heaven's going to help you is if there's a Bible in one of these packages and you start reading it."

After swallowing the glutinous glob, Rio looked up at this perplexing creature who lectured him, hands on hips, like some old maid school marm, and yet who still bore the traces of lovemaking in her tousled hair and smoky eyes.

"And why do you care?"

She threw her hands up in total frustration and emitted a sound halfway between a growl and a shriek.

"Because *you* care, you proud, stubborn fool. And don't tell me you don't. If you didn't, you wouldn't get so angry, and you wouldn't have tried to hide it."

At least he had not tried to deny it.

"So what're you gonna do, teach me?"

"Why not? We have nothing better to do for the next several months."

Rio lay awake for hours, listening to the keening wind and trying to push a thousand hated memories from his mind. He was certain Genevieve, curled beside him, was no more asleep than he. He

214

wanted her but tonight she was a temptation easy to resist.

She was crazy. Too many months away from the comforts and customs of civilization had addled her brain. What she had proposed to him while she sat at his feet was absurd. Preposterous.

And impossible.

"But it's not impossible," she had told him at least a hundred times.

He didn't like believing her. No, that wasn't quite right. He didn't like *wanting* to believe her.

"It'll be different this time," she blithely promised after he told her of his one other foray into a schoolroom. "There will be no other students to laugh at you, and *I* certainly won't."

Her explanation for his earlier failures made sense, though he warned himself that he *wanted* it to make sense. Because he wanted to hope she was right about the rest of it.

Every time Genevieve forced her eyes closed, they sprang open again of their own accord. A thousand ideas swirled through her head, chasing any hope of sleep. She had been her usual impulsive self again, only this time she had involved another person in her harebrained scheme.

What was the old saying about a silk purse and a sow's ear? There was a good deal more to making a gentleman out of Rio Jackson than teaching him his ABCs. Not that he had said anything about becoming a gentleman. In fact, she reminded herself, he hadn't even agreed to let her teach him to read. He had just finished his supper and then crawled into bed.

Best to take it one step at a time. Once he had learned to read, she could begin the rest of his education. The task promised to be difficult; Rio was proud and was very likely to fight every step of the way. Still, the result would be well worth every bit of trouble.

Wouldn't Fanchon LeFevre just fall dead when Genevieve Marie du Prés strolled through the Vieux Carré on the arm of Rio Jackson in his white linen suit, with his white beaver hat tilted at a jaunty angle? Of course, no social event would be complete without him, and any hostess who dared snub him would find her own name removed from every guest list in New Orleans.

Genevieve burrowed deeper into the comfy warmth of the bed and smiled. Tomorrow she would have to find pens and ink and paper, which wasn't going to be easy with a blizzard raging outside. But as she had told him earlier, they had nothing else to do.

The conditions left a great deal to be desired. The cabin's only window was boarded over to keep out drafts, but the boards also kept out the sun. There was, however, little time during the short daylight hours for lessons. At night, after supper, Viva lit the precious tallow candles and tried to remember how the sisters at the Ursuline Convent had taught her to read.

"We start with the alphabet," she intoned solemnly while Rio, elbows on the table, chin on his hands, pretended to pay attention. "First is 'A'." She wrote the letter on a pine shingle, using a pen made from a split reed. The ink, a concoction of lampblack, water, a drop of fat and a sliver of soap, was thick and lumpy but left a bold mark.

"Next, is 'B.'" She demonstrated the letter as well as the sound it commonly made.

"Aw, c'mon, Viva. I ain't five years old."

She did not so much as set the pen down.

"First of all, you will henceforth cease using that vulgar word 'ain't.' Second, until you can recite all the letters of the alphabet and distinguish them on paper, you will allow me to conduct this class after my own fashion."

He shrugged and let her continue.

"Fine. Wake me up when you're done."

"Don't you *dare* fall asleep while I'm teaching, Rio Jackson."

Only because he thought he heard the threat of tears in her voice did he acquiesce. Dutifully he repeated the letters and their sounds as she wrote them on the little slabs of pine. And he felt like an idiot.

An hour later, her voice little more than a croak, Viva set down the last of the twenty-six shingles. She rubbed eyes that itched and burned from the poor illumination.

"That's all for tonight," she whispered.

"But we just got started. All you did was teach me a bunch of letters."

"Yes, and tomorrow I'll teach them to you again."

"Again? What for?"

"To be sure you know them, and know them well."

"Aw, hell, Viva, how hard can it be to remember twenty-six lousy letters? When do I get to read words?"

She sighed and reached for her mug. The last swallow of coffee was cold and bitter, but it was wet enough to soothe her throat.

"Rio, it takes years to learn to read. You can't expect to do it all in one night."

"Years!" he thundered. "I thought you were

217

gonna do this in a few weeks, before we left here. You mean all I'm gonna be able to do is say ABCDEFG? Hell, I can do that now, and I'll bet I'll be able to do it tomorrow, too."

He stood and stomped the four paces it took to cross the room and then four more to return. Leaning on the table, he bored his bright, urgent eyes into her tired ones.

"You gonna teach me to read *words,* lady, or do we quit now?"

His impatience warred with his pride, and she did not know how to resolve that conflict except by falling back on her own experience.

"This is how I was taught, Rio. I don't know any other way."

"Then figure one out, 'cause I don't plan to leave this cabin 'til you do."

He broke the first nib, and splattered ink all over the thin slice of pine.

"This ai—isn't going to work, Viva."

She fitted another nib into the oak holder and handed it back to him.

"Yes, it is. Try again."

He wanted to strangle her, and had taken out his frustration on the split-reed nib instead. Nothing, it seemed, had the power to frustrate his teacher. If the past three days were any indication, Viva du Prés had the patience of a saint. No matter how often he gave up, she kept her temper and regained his.

"If I quit, I can't fail," he told her as he dipped the point in the ink again.

Genevieve shook her head and pushed another pine shingle in front of him.

"Quitting *is* failure," she insisted. "Now, start over."

218

He felt a complete fool, sitting there writing his letters like some five-year-old. Every few minutes he glanced over his shoulder, as though afraid someone was going to come through the door and start laughing at him all over again.

Viva did not laugh at him. She was, if anything, too serious about this whole affair. He wished she would lighten up a bit, before he began to take it seriously, too.

How in God's name could a man want something so bad and yet be so afraid of it that he'd do anything to keep from going after it?

He made one A, then another, then dipped the pen again.

"I thought I only had to learn to read, not write," he complained.

"You can stare at a letter for an hour and not learn it as well as writing it for a minute. Stop stalling."

A row of A's, followed by a row of B's, and a new nib. The reeds wore out quickly, but Genevieve refused to let minor problems defeat her. Or defeat her student.

Sometimes she did want to laugh, when he made remarks intended to turn the whole process of learning into a joke so he could set it aside. But under no circumstances was she going to quit, nor let him. If that meant being as stern as Sister Antoine Marguerite, then Genevieve Marie du Prés would be that stern.

"The G doesn't have a long tail like that," she scolded.

"What if I want to give it one? Tibler put all kinds of tails and ears on his."

"When you are able to make your letters with the skill Mr. Tibler had, you may give them all the tails and ears you like."

219

He got to her with that one. She coughed, but he knew it was really a snicker. The next G had an even longer tail. With a loop at the end.

It was time to teach him words.

"What do you mean? Why do you pronounce the 'A' in 'created' but not in 'heaven?' Who made up these crazy words anyway?"

"I don't know. It's rather like the T and H together; they don't sound anything like a T or an H." She moved his attention back to the well-thumbed Bible and had him repeat the first verse.

He struggled through "earth" and "void" and stumbled over the M's in "firmament" too many times for his own peace of mind.

"Well, hell for breakfast, if they meant 'heaven,' why didn't they just say 'heaven' and be done with it, and leave out a word nobody ever uses."

"I don't know," Genevieve sighed again. "Just read."

He plowed onward, steadfastly refusing to stop, though he paused for frequent questions, until he had finished the entire first chapter of Genesis. Then, while Genevieve stripped off her clothes and climbed exhausted into bed, he read it again.

There were days when the work of simple survival, which had to come before lessons, took so long that both of them were too tired to do anything but eat supper and crawl into the warmth of the bed.

The frigid weather that settled in the valley after that first blizzard took a tremendous toll. A constantly blazing fire barely kept the cabin warm; to let it die down even at night meant ice in the water buckets. Rio felled another enormous pine tree and wondered if it would be enough to see them through the winter. They rationed water as much as possible to save bone-numbing trips to the spring and even opened the door as seldom as possible, to keep the warm inside and the cold out.

The wind that howled almost nightly around the cabin did have a beneficial effect: it kept the snow from accumulating too deep in the open areas of the valley. The path from the cabin door to the spring remained relatively clear, and the fence around the paddock was never so buried by snow that there was any chance of the horses escaping.

On clear, sunny days, Rio took Cinco, who chaffed at the continued confinement, out to forage, and to hunt. Meat they had in plenty, for the valley abounded in elk, rabbit, partridge, and wild turkey, but what they needed were the hides. Slowly, laboriously tanned, the skins became gloves, moccasins that were warmer than boots, shirts to replace worn linen ones, even a jacket quilted with cattail down for Viva.

The bearskin, which took longer to cure than Rio planned, was intended for the bed, but Viva refused.

"For one thing," she told him when he finally brought it inside the cabin for its final drying and stretching, "it smells. And for another, I would have nightmares of that thing killing you if I had to sleep under it."

So the bearskin went in front of the fire, and they sat on it to warm themselves after a day in the numbing cold, to roast partridge on hand-held spits, to piece together soft rabbit skins, to read from Ernest Tibler's books.

Rio found most of them decidedly boring.

"Cellini thinks too much of himself," he com-

221

mented one evening between yawns. He was
stretched out on the bearskin with his head on
Viva's lap. A pot of coffee steamed on the fire; the
wind for once was still and all was quiet save for
the crackle of the pine logs and the rustle of pages
turning.

"That is the fifth or sixth time you've interrupted
me. If you aren't going to read it yourself, at least
have the courtesy to listen politely while I read it to
you."

"Why? What do I need to know about a gold-
smith who's been dead damn near three hundred
years for?" He rolled away from her and reached
for the stack of books piled safely away from the
fire. "What happened to *Moll Flanders?* She was a
good deal more entertaining than old Ben."

"I've created a monster!" Viva sighed, trying to
stifle a laugh. "Rio, you can't expect to read nothing but salacious novels."

"Why not?" He had found the book he sought
and was rapidly turning the pages. "This has the
same words, spelled the same, doesn't it? What difference does it make which I practice from?"

She had no answer. The truth she dared not tell
him. If he even suspected that she intended to
make him the darling of New Orleans society, he
would throw every book, pen, and probably herself
into the fire.

"Because I'm the teacher, that's what difference."

So he listened to Cellini's boastings because he
loved the sound of her voice, not because he gave a
damn what she said. When she began to yawn, he
told her it was time for bed, and she put up little
resistance.

"Explain what Cellini was talking about," Rio
asked when they lay together enjoying the warmth
that would be gone come morning. Their clothes

were hung by the fire, which was less damaging to them than being torn off during the night and left to lie on the floor.

Genevieve thought for a moment, then admitted, "I don't remember. Let me see, he received a letter, and he left Florence to go to Rome."

"But you just read it to me not fifteen minutes ago."

"I know, but my mind must not have been on Cellini at the time."

His hand found the fullness of her breast under the blankets, eliciting a soft gasp of expectation from her.

"What was it on? Not dear Molly and her amorous adventures, surely."

Genevieve's answering laugh was tinged with both drowsiness and arousal.

"No, not Moll's. My own perhaps?"

His thumb stroked her nipple to tingling hardness, yet he carried on the conversation as though they were seated in her mother's salon, sipping lemonade.

"But if Monsieur Cellini so little impressed you, my dear, whyever must we waste our time reading him? Would not the fair Mademoiselle Flanders offer a more practical education?"

Genevieve lay back with a sigh of resignation. If she had ever been able to remember Cellini and his letter from the Pope, Rio Jackson drove those thoughts and all others from her mind.

Over the weeks he had learned more than the letters of the alphabet and the words printed in Tibler's books. He had learned to read her, too, not only her moods but her needs and wants. And he had taken on the role of teacher as well, for if he had proven quick to grasp the intricacies of the written word, so too was she quick to learn the arts of passion.

This night he practiced gentleness, brushing her lips with little whispers of kisses. Sometimes the kiss was no more than a murmuring of her name or another endearment, sometimes he teased her with his tongue until she parted her lips in lazy hunger. When she did, he slipped his tongue in to touch hers with its very tip and then withdrew, pulling a sigh of longing from her.

She wanted it never to end. His caresses soothed her even as they aroused her, delighted her even as they made her hunger for more. How slowly, painstakingly he aroused her, with his hands, his lips, even the gentle but insistent pressure of his body beside hers. And how thoroughly he fulfilled her.

"Are you tired?" he asked, still stroking her gently from breast to knee and slowly back again.

Eyes too heavy to open, she whispered, "Yes, very tired."

"Do you want me to stop and let you sleep?"

"Mmmm, that would be nice." When he moved his hand away, she clasped it and brought it back to her belly. "But this is nicer."

She knew it was wrong to the point of being dangerous, but she could not stop loving him or wanting to make love with him. Someday the cold winter would give way to spring and they would leave this valley forever. Perhaps Rio would take her as far as New Orleans, perhaps he would leave her to make her own way from St. Joseph or St. Louis. But he would not stay. He would not be her pet, her toy, any more than she was willing to be Jean-Louis' trophy. And she could not bear the thought of being parted from this man who had not only saved her life but become her entire existence.

She cringed at the thought.

224

"Did I hurt you?" Rio's husky voice broke through the dream.

"No, I just shivered is all."

"Then I'll have to make sure I keep you warmer."

Rio tightened the ropes around the pine log and walked back to the mule's head. She nuzzled him affectionately and waited for his orders. When he took hold of the halter and slapped her rump, she leaned into the harness willingly, and the log moved.

"Blame Cinco for this," Rio told her as she hauled the dead weight slowly but steadily toward the cabin. "If he wasn't so horny for that mare, I'd put him to this."

He could see the stallion prancing around the paddock, almost unable to hold still for a minute at a time.

This was the first day in over a week Rio had been able to get away from the cabin. Snow squalls and bitter cold had kept him close. The sky hadn't exactly cleared, but there was some sunshine visible through a high overcast, and the wind had died.

The first chore was to bring in another section of the tree he had cut two weeks earlier. The two-man saw was difficult to operate without a partner, but he had managed it and hauled sizable limbs back for the fire. Now came the bigger task of getting the cut sections of the main trunk dragged from the edge of the woods at the head of the valley. The distance, no more than a quarter mile, could be walked in a few minutes in summer; it would take an hour or more now.

At least he had one major worry off his mind. When he noticed several days ago that Viva seemed more tired than usual and looked a bit pale, she had tried to ignore his concern. Persistence only got him tears and flushed cheeks and a hurled, "Well, at least I'm not pregnant!"

He vowed then that he would see to it they did not worry about that possibility again. If it killed him, if he had to sleep in the lean-to with Cinco and a mare in heat, Rio Jackson was not going to put a bastard baby into her belly.

He, after all, knew what it was like to grow up with that stigma. She didn't. A girl like her might find her reputation a bit threadbare, but embarrassments like unwanted fatherless children had a way of being taken care of when the family had money. There were foundling homes for those children, who would never know their parents, never know love, never know the finer things in life that they had lost through no fault of their own.

"C'mon, mule," Rio encouraged. "It's gettin' cold out here."

Genevieve pondered over the slab of smooth, waxed pine on the table before her. With a piece of charred stick, she had drawn a grid on the hand-planed board, and filled the squares with numbers.

In the first, which contained the number 25 in an upper corner, she wrote one word, then another in the second, and another in the third. She was puzzling over the next, chewing on the end of the stick to help her concentration, when Rio shoved the door open and just as quickly shut it.

"Did you get the logs?" she asked without looking up from her puzzle.

"Yep, all four of 'em. And something else, too." He came over to the fire behind her and lifted the coffee pot to fill the mug that sat on the table. "What's that?"

"A calendar?"

He leaned over her shoulder to try to decipher her charcoal scratchings.

"That's 'Sacramento,' then 'trail' twice. What for?"

"I'm trying to figure out what day today is. I've lost track of so many of them."

Rio took a long warming swallow of coffee and pulled his stool up next to hers.

"Well, we were three days on the trail before we stopped for supplies."

She filled in two more spaces, with "trail" and "town."

Silently Rio ticked off five more days on his fingers and pointed to the next square.

"That's the night I got shot."

One by one he gave her the details for each day since their arrival at the cabin, including the cattails, the bed, and the bear.

"How do you remember all this?" she asked, amazed at his powers of recall.

He swallowed the last of the coffee and shrugged.

"There are some advantages to being illiterate. When you can't write it down, you don't have any choice but to remember it." He set the empty cup down and winked. "You didn't put anything in for today. C'mon outside and see what today's memorable event is."

She tugged on her elkskin jacket and slipped her hands into mittens of rabbitskin with the fur on the inside.

Rio had put the mule away but left the logs lying in front of the cabin. Each was a good eight to twelve feet long, the shortest being also the thickest. One of the logs, however, had quite obviously not come from the tree Rio felled. It was hardly

227

more than a long stump, blackened at the top as though burned, and rotten inside.

Rio walked up to the rotten log and deftly kicked part of the pulpy wood away. The interior was filled with a cream-colored substance that shattered into tiny flakes when broken.

Genevieve's eyes lit with joy.

"The fifth day of December of the year 1853 will go down in history as the honeycomb day!"

Chapter Fifteen

Genevieve rubbed her eyes and wondered what had wakened her. The cabin was quiet, save for the omnipresent wind.

"Rio, are you still awake?"

He sat exactly where she remembered seeing him just before she drifted off to sleep: at the table, poring over one of Tibler's books. Only now the candle he had lit when she went to bed was burned down half its length.

This was the second time in a week he had stayed up to read well into the small hours of the night.

"Did you hear me? I said it's time to come to bed."

"In a little while," he answered without looking up.

"No, Rio, now. You'll ruin your eyes, and you need to get some sleep."

She was right. His eyes already ached, from staring at the same page for hours without comprehending a single word. Oh he was able to make them out all right, and he understood their individual meanings, but not a single ounce of his concentration lay on that page.

For three nights he had been able to think of nothing but the woman in the bed, the bed he had made to share with her, the bed he now dared not go near until exhaustion left him incapable of anything at all but sleep.

He had not touched her, not even so much as brushing his fingers against hers when they ate. When possible, he avoided being close to her. Had it not been for the bitter cold weather, he would have spent more time out of doors and out of her presence. It was the worst torment he had ever experienced, worse than when Pansy Arnett turned down his proposal of marriage. Pansy had laughed and destroyed his pride, but he had left San Antonio the next day and was never faced with reminders of her perfidy. Here, with Viva, the pain was constant.

Without one shred of success, he tried to find a reason to hate her, the way he hated Pansy. But the reasons he came up with always turned themselves around to become justifications for behavior he simply could not give in to.

The worst of all was the suggestion that he go back to New Orleans with her.

"Rio, what *are* you doing?"

His head snapped up. He must have dozed off, lost in dreams that could never come true.

"I'm reading. I want to finish this page first."

"Rio Jackson, I don't know what you're doing, but it isn't reading. You haven't turned a page in I don't know how long, and you are wasting those candles. Either you come to bed right now, or I am going to get up and drag you here."

Her threat had the desired effect. Rio pinched out the candle before closing his book. In the near darkness he was a fire and shadow specter, moving about the tiny room to add wood to the fire, remove his clothes, and climb into the bed. The stiffness to his movements bespoke utter exhaustion, something Genevieve had never seen in him before. Weariness, yes, but the healthy weariness of a body worked to its limits. This was exhaustion of the soul.

230

He lay, as usual, on his back, his hands laced under his head. In sleep he would relax, but he always fell asleep like this, often with Genevieve curled beside him, her head on his shoulder. This was the first time in several days he had come to bed before she was already asleep.

She rolled over to wriggle next to him.

"Don't I even get a kiss good night?" she begged as she rested her hand on his chest.

"I'm tired, Genevieve."

He had never called her that before. Never. Not in anger, not in passion. Even now, there was but an icy indifference. Stunned, almost frightened, she withdrew her hand and slid as far away from him as the narrowness of the bed allowed. Then, without making a sound, she cried herself to sleep.

"I have no idea what I did or said," Genevieve said aloud one morning several days later. Rio had already gone out to water the stock, leaving her alone within the tiny confines of the cabin. Talking to herself was better than talking to no one.

Wishing she had Rio's powers of recollection, she dropped her tattered underclothes into the kettle of warm water and proceeded to scrub them as gently as possible. Try as she would, no incident, verbal or physical, came to mind that he could possibly have construed as an insult. In fact, since the night he called her by her given name, she had gone out of her way to smooth whatever feathers she had ruffled.

All her efforts were futile. Day after day, night after night, he ignored her.

She wept silent, bitter tears and longed to know why.

As winter deepened, it was impossible for him to spend much time out of doors. Yet even in the cramped quarters of the cabin, he managed to make her feel shut out. He worked with his bone needles splicing rabbit skins into long sheets of leather or he sat at the table devouring the books Ernest Tibler had left for him. He had not, to her knowledge, read Tibler's letter.

Christmas came and went, then New Year's, both days unmarked save by notations on the calendar. As Genevieve propped the pine board on its shelf by the chimney, she realized how long it had been since Rio last spoke a kind word to her, or touched her, or gave her an affectionate, teasing kiss in the morning. A month. A whole month of Rio's hatred. At least this time she had not had even to worry about carrying his child. There had been no chance.

Almost dropping the heavy calendar on her foot, she gasped with another realization. "Oh, Rio, dear God I'm so sorry. I never meant it like that." But he was nowhere around to hear.

Rio examined the fodder in the lean-to and estimated it would barely last until the end of March. That wasn't long enough. There'd be little on the trail that early in the season, which meant they had to leave earlier than he deemed safe, so they could carry feed with them until they reached lower elevations where the animals could find sufficient grazing.

Ten more weeks. Seventy more days and nights of wanting that woman and not letting himself have her. He had thought it would get easier, as it had when he left San Antonio and Pansy. But Viva was there every day, her eyes, her mouth, her breasts within reach of his hand, her legs twining unconsciously with his while she slept.

"Stop it!" he ordered himself between clenched teeth, though his body paid little attention to words. "She's gonna go back to New Orleans and you're

232

gonna pick up another wagon train for Sacramento. After a while, you'll get over her. It's just gonna take some time."

And he would at least have pleasant memories of Viva du Prés, not only of the delight she had given him in bed but the pride she had shown in him, the determination to make him learn. He still didn't understand much of that Machiavelli's thoughts, but at least he could read the man's words.

As if anyone cared that a scout could read.

He need never again worry about being cheated, and the next time he signed his name to collect his pay at Bruckner's bank, he could add all the little flourishes and gingerbread curlicues he wanted. She had given him that, and never asked anything in return.

Except love.

That thought crept in without warning. Rio sternly reminded himself that what she felt for him wasn't love, it was gratitude and proximity. As for his own feelings, well, they didn't matter. Certainly not to her. Which was why he'd get over her sooner if he maintained his distance and didn't encourage her the way he had mistakenly done before. Just ten more weeks.

She pulled on the high moccasins and wriggled her feet into them but grabbed her old coat, the one Rio had made from the extra blanket. It was quicker to put on than the elkskin one, if not as warm. Still struggling with the leather ties on the front of it, she hurried out the door.

The sun on the windswept snow blinded her after the days in the dim cabin. Shading her eyes with an unmittened hand, she ducked her head into the wind and marched in the direction of the lean-to.

If he wasn't there, she'd go in search of him.

She'd nail his hide to a pine tree if that's what it took to make him listen. She was not going to spend another night frozen away from him because of a silly misunderstanding.

But when she saw him, leaning against the fence to talk to Cinco and rub the big stallion's nose, she lost a portion of her nerve. As much as she wanted to run to him and fling herself into his arms, she held her pace to a brisk walk and approached him cautiously.

The palomino caught her scent and alerted Rio to her presence. He turned, and immediately the relaxed attitude he had enjoyed with the horse vanished.

"What are you doing out here?" he demanded, yet there was neither concern nor anger in his voice.

The crystalline blue eyes studied him as she took one deliberate step after another toward him. She did not smile nor frown, but there was something so intense in those eyes, so determined in her strides, that he checked to make sure he had his revolver at his hip and had not left it in the cabin where she might avail herself of it.

He stood clear of the fence and let her come nearer. Still she said nothing, and the sapphire incandescence of her gaze froze him.

"Have you gone mad, Viva? What is the matter—"

So swiftly that he could neither stop her nor duck away from her attack, she slipped her cold, bare little hands behind his neck and pulled his head down for a ferocious kiss. Lips and tongue and teeth teased him, bit him, tasted and devoured him until response was instinctive. Then, just as violently and suddenly, she let him go.

"I love you, Rio Jackson, and don't you ever forget it," she announced as she laced those same cold hands around his waist and insinuated herself between his knees. "I am going to take you with me back to New Orleans and I am going to marry you and I am going to have two dozen of your babies. If one of them gets started a bit before the wedding, well that's just fine with me. In fact, I think we should start working on that right away."

At least he was reacting, if not speaking. The look on his face betrayed every bit of his confusion, and the ridge he couldn't conceal beneath his trouser buttons betrayed his lack of immunity to her advances.

He shook his head in a vain attempt to dispel this vision. He could not even put his arms around her, so afraid was he of capitulating after all his effort to resist her—and himself.

"Viva, stop it," he croaked. "Go on, in the cabin. You—you don't know what you're—"

She kissed him again, twice as hard as before. And this time she was in a perfect position to grind her lower body against his. If she felt guilty for ambushing him and taking advantage. she ignored the guilt in favor of pleasure.

"I love you," she crooned, more softly, more seductively. "I never meant I was glad I wasn't pregnant because I didn't want your baby. Oh, God, Rio, you have no idea how badly I do."

She was winning, breaking down all those horrible defenses he had built, though she still wasn't sure why he had done it. As though against his will, his arms rose, not quite enfolding her but coming closer and closer with every word she spoke.

"Did you think I didn't think you were good enough to be the father of my children? What kind of slut would that make me, to give you that which I can give only once, to welcome you to my bed and my body, and then loathe the product of that union?"

He ached with the wanting, with the hurt he had

235

given her, with the denial of all the nights they had lost. But he, who knew the consequences, had to remain strong, no matter what it took.

"No, Viva, I never thought that," he whispered. He had to hold her, to keep her from freezing. It wasn't an embrace; he just couldn't seem to keep his body from reacting as though it were. "I don't even want to hear you speak of yourself that way. Never."

The wind caught her hair, blowing strands of it across her face until he captured them and held them secure at the nape of her neck. From there it was only a breath and a heartbeat to another kiss, one that did not end until he lifted her in his arms and carried her to the cabin.

"I missed you," Genevieve sighed.

Above her, Rio shook his head with a rueful smile.

"I missed you, too."

"Do you promise not to leave me again?"

"Promise."

"Swear it."

"I swear. On my heart, on my soul, and the part of me you have taken rather secure possession of."

She giggled and squeezed him until he answered with a gentle nudge.

"We have a whole month to make up for," she reminded him.

"Do we have to do it all in one night?"

"We could try."

He had been a fool to think he could ignore her. He had been a worse fool to try. When they reached New Orleans and she was safely returned to her old world, then would be the time to put the distance between them. Vows made in a wilderness cabin would be forgotten with nothing more than a bashful blush. Genevieve Marie du Prés belonged there;

Rio Jackson did not. He had no right to her there, but here, while the idyll lasted, he would enjoy it.

If he could crowd a month of loving into one night, surely ten weeks was enough for a lifetime.

"We will try, Viva mia. We will try."

He began with a simple kiss, his lips just touching hers. No tongue, no mingling of panted breaths, no more than the sweet pressure of one mouth on another. Again and again, softly, until hunger demanded more.

"Just your tongue, querida." Rio guided. "Ah, sweet heaven, yes, like that."

They were birds meeting, touching, then flying away only to meet and mate again. Having quenched the thirst of the long draught, they could savor this second draught, drop by drop.

Little licks with the tip of the tongue, on her cheek, her ear, her throat, his eyes, his jaw. Caresses to her breasts, to bring the nipples hard once more against his palm.

"Do you know the first time I noticed your breasts?" he asked as he buried his face in her hair and circled his tongue in the sensitive indentation behind her ear lobe. "When you fell in that muddy little creek, flat on your face."

"That's why Mrs. Jensen was in such a hurry to get me back to the wagon before I'd even washed the mud out of my eyes. You were watching me, even then? But that was right after we left St. Joe."

"Mm-uhm," he agreed.

She felt his hand slide lower, to caress her hip into that timeless rhythm. There was no urgency now, only the deep desire that was its own fulfillment. The other had been a thunderstorm, violent, crashing, washing everything clean before its strength. This then was the soft, nourishing summer rain.

"You watched me all the way from St. Joe to Sacramento?"

237

"Every step of the way. Do you have any idea how good you feel right now? I think I could make up for the past month tonight. and start all over again tomorrow."

The wonder of it amazed her. Where before she had felt only the frenzy of their joining, she now experienced the satin cadence of skilled lovemaking. A subtle excitement began to build in her veins, spreading from the center of her femininity to every part of her body. Her hands, stroking the taut muscle of Rio's back and shoulder. began to tingle. Her pulse rate increased imperceptibly. Each breath she drew escaped as a sigh, then as a moan.

He was lost in her, in her scent, her touch, the seductive cries she made when he thrust deep into her. Notwithstanding the long abstinence, he still should have been able to hold back, to make the loving last and last. But with Viva, he lost all control. She invited unbridled passion, reveled in it, made him forget everything but the sweet madness she drove him to. No other woman had ever done that. No other woman ever would.

Ten weeks was such a short time, so short when compared to what waited for him afterward. Not forever, not even a lifetime. But it was all he had.

He should have told her right away, but he put it off another month. He hoped that there might be a change, that a mild winter would help the feed stretch further, that he had calculated wrong. That hope proved false.

The weather had been worse than he expected, with bitter cold and heavy snow that almost cut them off from the spring. Water was not as critical as it might have been, but the depth of the snow kept Rio from taking the horses out to forage. The three animals had grazed every blade of frozen grass

238

that could be found under the snow inside their paddock; they had only what Rio and Genevieve had gathered. And that was running out.

So he broke the news to her on the last day of January, while they sat at supper, a stew of dried venison and beans flavored with the next to last onion.

"You're sure?" she asked. "There's no way we can hold out longer?"

Rio shook his head. His hair had grown down to his shoulders, though he still kept his face cleanshaven. Over a shirt of supple elkskin he wore a vest of pieced rabbit fur. The homespun shirts had worn out weeks ago, and the leather was both stronger and warmer.

"With the mare in foal, six weeks is the most. Even our supplies are running low. We might be able to stretch the beans and corn meal into April, but just barely."

She was frightened, but she did not show it so anyone but Rio would notice. After a moment's thought, she straightened her shoulders and took a deep breath.

"Then we'll leave in six weeks. The ides of March."

The Rio Jackson who had watched her from a distance all those months from St. Joseph to Sacramento would have given her a puzzled look and then ignored her comment. The Rio Jackson he had become knew exactly what she meant.

They sat that night on the bearskin in front of the fire, her head on his shoulder, his arm around hers so he could stroke the long silken strands of her hair.

"I wish it could last forever," Genevieve whispered. "I know it can't, but I don't want to leave here."

"You mean you like a steady diet of beans and venison, lukewarm baths in a stew pot, toting water when the wind freezes it almost before you can get it to the cabin?" He gave her a gentle squeeze and kissed the top of her head. "No, you don't want a lifetime of this, believe me. Hell, *I* don't want it!"

"What *do* you want?" Resting one hand on his knee, Genevieve leaned forward to drop another log on the fire. Sparks rushed up the chimney and brightened the little room momentarily.

"I don't know. Get you to New Orleans, then pick up another wagon train in St. Joe. Same as always, I guess."

It was hard to express enthusiasm he didn't feel. But he had no choice.

"You couldn't go back to Sacramento. Not with Jean-Louis and Buster Kulkey waiting for you."

"They'll be over it by then."

Genevieve shook her head emphatically.

"Not Jean-Louis. You forget, I've known him since I was born. As easy as he always was to manipulate, he also had a stubborn streak, especially if he felt he'd been wronged."

Rio shrugged. A gimpy Frenchman with a mean streak was the least of his worries right now. "I don't have to go to California," he told her. "Might head up to Oregon Territory or down to Mexico."

Genevieve shifted position so she was kneeling, with her arms folded on his shoulder and her chin resting on her forearms. With one finger she skimmed his hair back from his ear, then gently touched the lobe with the tip of her tongue.

"Why not stay in New Orleans with me?" she suggested.

She felt the involuntary stiffening of his body. Any other man would have answered yes or no immediately, but not Rio. He would take at least a few minutes to think the whole thing over, even if he had been thinking it over for the past six months.

"No, Viva," he said a heartbeat later.

"No?" she echoed in disbelief. Rocking back on

240

her heels she added, "You didn't even think about it."

"Didn't have to." He reached for her hands and turned them over in his. Poor little things; they were chapped and raw to the point of bleeding. His were just a little more calloused than usual. "I can't go with you, Viva."

"Then I'll come with you. We won't go to New Orleans at all; we'll head up to Oregon. Or we could sail to Hawaii. They say it is like nowhere else on earth, a true paradise. I don't care where we go, so long as—"

"No."

He spoke so softly yet with such finality that she did not protest the interruption.

"You can't go with me, Viva."

"Why not?"

"Because you can't."

He unfolded his legs and stood with a long stretch. Genevieve did not rise with him, but he knew by the look in her eyes that she was not going to take his pronouncement without an argument.

"That's the kind of answer you give a child when you don't want to tell him the truth," she accused. "If nothing else, Rio Jackson, you owe me the truth."

He did, especially after hiding another truth from her for a month.

So he sank to his knees on the bearskin rug once more. They might have six more weeks in the cabin and several months on the trail to New Orleans, but tonight they were saying farewell. It would not be an easy parting.

He took her face between his hands and kissed her softly, briefly. Her eyes, brimming with uncontrollable tears, held his.

"I could lie and tell you I don't want you with me, but I have a feeling you'd see through that."

241

"You're damn right."

She blinked. Two enormous tears, struck to gold by the firelight, rolled down her cheeks. He stopped one with his thumb; the other he kissed off the edge of her jaw.

"Truth is, I *do* want you. I want you with me every minute of every day for the rest of my life, Viva. Wherever this Hawaii place is, I'd take you there, or China, or any place else, if that's what would make you happy. But it wouldn't."

"It would!" she insisted. "Just so long as I'm with you."

The tears dripped steadily now.

"Oh, God, Viva, why do you make this so difficult for me?"

"Because I don't want it to be easy!"

"Well, it isn't. But it has to be done. It has to."

"No, it doesn't. I love you, Rio. Doesn't that mean anything to you?"

He pulled her to him, crushed her in an embrace that couldn't halt her sobs. He felt every heart-breaking convulsion, and wondered, though only for a brief moment, if what he was doing was right. He knew it was. She was young and capable of loving again. As for him, well, he would survive.

"I love you, Rio, I love you so much."

"Corazón de mi corazón, I love you, too. That's why I have to leave. Because I don't want you to hate me. Ever."

She pushed herself away from him.

"I'd never hate you," she vowed. "Not unless you walk out on me the way you're planning to."

"Damn it, Viva, stop thinking with your heart and learn to use your head! I can't give you the things you're used to. You see what a couple months here has done to you. In another year, what do you think it would be like? Do you want to have your babies out here, all alone? Never read all the books you've

242

promised me are waiting back in 'civilization'?"

"I don't care about that."

"But you would, don't you understand? Love is wonderful, but it isn't enough to live on. And I can't give you anything else."

Hers wasn't the only heart breaking in that quiet little cabin.

"I wish I could. But I can't, and I won't destroy this wonderful thing we've shared."

"Then come with me, Rio. Stay with me in New Orleans."

He laughed, not at her, but at the shattering of the fragile dream he had once had.

"And do what? Ain't no wagon trains in N'Orleans, lady."

She slapped him. The crack of flesh on flesh rang loud in the sudden silence that followed.

Several breathless moments passed before Genevieve realized Rio had caught her hand before she could strike him a second time. Though his grip caused her no pain, he effortlessly kept her from escaping.

"You've given me more than any woman ever has, more than I ever deserved. Don't take it all away. Leave me my pride, for God's sake."

Chapter Sixteen

Genevieve contemplated her plan for two days, during which she did an inordinate amount of crying. Most of the tears were genuine; the ones that weren't came easily enough. All of them, however, served to put Rio off his guard.

Which was exactly what she wanted.

The weather, as though conspiring against them, turned even worse. The wind howled incessantly and seemed to pull every bit of heat from the fire right up the chimney. Logs burned twice as fast as they had before. Only lying in bed, swathed in blankets and with Rio's arms securely around her, did Genevieve really feel warm.

She could not have planned it better.

She tucked Rio's hands comfortably around her breasts and smiled with satisfaction when she felt the beginnings of his arousal. They had made love twice during the night and once already upon waking, but the inevitability of their parting seemed to have made both of them nearly insatiable.

"So soon?" she cooed.

"Always," he murmured against the back of her neck. "There isn't a moment of the day when I couldn't make love to you."

"Even outside when you're feeding the horses?"

"Even then." He stroked her nipples, bringing them tighter and tighter until she squirmed.

"At this rate I'll be as pregnant as the mare by the time we reach New Orleans."

His hands stilled.

"Don't say that, Viva," he warned. "I know you're not pregnant."

"You know I *wasn't*. That was four days ago. A lot has happened since then."

He threw back the blankets and got up. The chill air destroyed any desire he had felt, desire his own better judgment had never had any control over.

The oldest trick since woman discovered the power she held over man, and he had fallen for it. Of all people, he should have known better. He owed his very existence to it.

The cabin was freezing. He should have got out of bed an hour ago and revived the fire, but the blaze Genevieve kindled in bed was too irresistible. Angry at himself and at her, he pulled on his pants, moccasins, and coat; then, without tending the fire, he disappeared outside.

He was back five minutes later, lips blue, windblown snow in his hair, teeth chattering.

"You bitch."

She lay in bed, her eyes wide with worry, then with shock. He did not approach her, but went to the fireplace to stir up the coals and add more fuel. Calmly, without looking at her, he gave her the victory he knew she wanted.

"You spoiled, greedy, scheming little bitch. I'll give you credit for one thing: you're good. Real good. Maybe even the best I've ever come across, although to tell you the truth, I haven't had a whole lot of experience with high-class whores, the kind who don't take money, they just steal a man's soul."

Her reply was the very last thing he expected.

"Damn you to hell twice over, Rio Jackson."

Spoken with little inflection, those few words conveyed none of the fury building inside her. She had to keep it under control, no matter what, or she'd kill

245

him deader than the bear whose hide he knelt on right now.

"Me?" he asked as he turned and walked to the table, where the coffee pot contained the dregs from last night's supper. "Damn me? What for? What the hell did I do to you?"

It struck her that she ought to laugh at his absurd question, but she was too close to murder for mirth. With a sweep of her arm, she threw off the blankets and got to her feet. In an instant she was shivering violently, but that didn't stop her from striding across the room to stand stark naked in front of him and slap him as hard as she could across the face.

"It takes two to play that little game, Rio," she said, then smacked him again. This time there'd be no gentle caress to follow. She wanted only to hurt him as he had hurt her. "How dare you—how *dare* you blame me when you were the one who not ten minutes ago was fondling me and telling me he could make love to me in the snow! Where do you think babies come from, anyway? You think women do it all by themselves, with no help from you men? Then why, tell me please, is it that men do the most bragging when they find out their women are breeding? You take the credit, and we take the blame!"

She was cold, too cold even for her anger to warm her. But the tears spilling from her eyes were hot, and they burned like acid down her cheeks.

"You blame your mother, don't you? You think it was all her fault. What did she do, Rio? Did she fall in love with a married man? Did she try to trick him into marrying her?"

"Put some clothes on."

"Not until you answer my questions. Did she tie him to his bed and work her brutal seduction on him when he was helpless, the way I did you?"

"No, damn it, she didn't. Now will you get dressed or get back into bed?"

That was hardly the answer she was looking for, but she had at least got a response from him. And she could no longer hold the shivers at bay.

She took the shirt and elkskin skirt he held out to her and pulled them on, but not in silence. He had not behaved at all according to her plan; she'd have to fall back on instincts.

"Your father seduced her, didn't he?" she asked, seeking the truth desperately. "Was she already in love with him?"

He watched her in the simple act of dressing and wondered again why he bothered to try to hate her. Even when he was angry, even when he hurled hurtful words that he didn't mean at her, even when he knew she was going to destroy what little pride he had left, she shook his soul to its very deepest foundations.

How could he tell her about that woman who had brought him into the world? How could he separate the lies he had heard from the lies he had told? How could he make her understand the way a man understands those things, which is not at all the way a woman feels them?

"She went to work in the kitchen when Lawrence Jackson got married. The way the old man told it, his wife was too proper to enjoy a man's company very much, so he looked around. He found what he was lookin' for in the kitchen."

"Then why do you blame her? And me? And why do you continue to deny the possibility that by the time we reach New Orleans I might very well be carrying your child?"

"Because I don't want you to!" he thundered. He slammed his fist so hard onto the stones of the fireplace that the skin across his knuckles split, leaving blood on the stones. "What do I have to do to get you to understand? I don't want you to suddenly decide that this was all a mistake." He swept his arm to include the whole of the tiny cabin. "Once you get back there, you'll think about the dirt floor and the

247

sod roof and wish it had never happened, including me."

She shook her head emphatically.

"No, you're wrong, Rio. Not just about me, but about yourself. You learned to read, didn't you? Then don't you owe it to the child you might be creating to try, just try, damn it, to put a little polish on Rio Jackson? Because that's all I'm asking of you. I'm willing to give it all up; can't you at least try to take what's being offered?"

"And can't you ever let me make up my own mind?" he shouted in complete exasperation. "I'm not Jean-Louis Marmont, easy to twist around your little finger. Maybe Rio Jackson doesn't *want* to be a gentleman. Did you ever think of that?"

He was weakening. It had taken long enough, and her hand still hurt from the way she had smacked him. But he deserved it, for the things he had said about her. And if it brought him around to her way of thinking, a stinging hand was a very small price to pay.

February crept toward March. The days lengthened and, on the sunniest, some of the snow melted. At first it was just a dripping from the roof that resulted in enormous icicles at the corners of the lean-to. Then, as though nature delighted in thwarting dreams, the temperature dropped again and a fresh series of snowstorms swept into the valley.

Tempers shortened. Rio tried to dismiss the flares and fights as cabin fever, and fear of the date circled on Genevieve's calendar. One day at a time, one night at a time, it drew nearer.

One morning, while Genevieve was adding a spoonful of fresh coffee to the well-used grounds in the pot, Rio ventured to ask, "You ever eat snails?"

Knowing this was his way of making up his own mind, Genevieve suppressed a smile.

248

"Escargots? Yes, though they aren't one of my favorite delicacies, I've eaten them. Why?"

"I was just wondering how you get the little critters out of the shell, that's all."

She tried to teach him the intricacies of silverware, but after half a dozen fumbling attempts with crude wooden replicas, they gave up. Besides, they could find no substitute for the delicacies that required special utensils. Beans and johnny cakes didn't even need a knife. And just thinking about fresh vegetables and fruit, seafood and poultry brought painful pangs to their stomachs.

Though it brought a spark of laughter to their otherwise monotonous day, the incident also had an unpleasant effect.

"It's a little hard to learn fancy table manners out here," Rio observed while sweeping wooden shavings off the table into his hand before he threw them onto the fire. "Guess I'll just have to wait 'til we get to New Orleans."

Genevieve detected the note of disappointment and almost nervousness in his voice. She had to set his mind at ease without condescending. Now that he had accepted this course, she did not want him to find any reason to turn aside from it.

"We'll have plenty of time between St. Joseph and St. Louis, and then we can practice on the riverboat to New Orleans."

She dreamt that night of food, of sweet shrimp and spicy soups, of rich red wine and sparkling champagne, of strawberries in cream and lemon tarts. She wakened with tears on her cheeks and lay in the cold dark, afraid to sleep again.

They ate the last of the cornmeal on the last day of February. The apples had been gone for weeks, though there were plenty of beans left. Genevieve portioned out the flour for another fifteen days and hoped the honey would match it. They drank coffee as weak as tea to stretch that commodity to the end.

249

As the final days approached, Rio devoted more and more of his energies toward the preparations for the upcoming journey. With fewer supplies to pack out, they could take other things with them, the cattail mattress and bearskin rug among them, not out of sentimentality but out of necessity. There would be no convenient cabins on this journey.

Even their love-making took on a new character. More intense than ever, it lost all light-heartedness. Tears mingled with ecstasy and often lasted far into the night.

March came in like a lion, with the worst winds of the winter. Then, after four days of storms and snow, the sky cleared and a brilliant sun shone with real warmth. It might last a day, it might last a week. But when Rio made another inspection of the lean-to, he was sure of one thing: the feed would last no more than two days.

They spent the next day packing and spoke only when necessary. Rio had made the announcement simply, and Genevieve had accepted the news without comment. But that night, when they collapsed on the bearskin in front of the roaring fire, she let her fingers reach up to stroke his face, and the words would not be held back.

"I'll miss this place," she whispered. Rio lay on his side, his head pillowed on one arm while the other curled around Genevieve's waist to hold her against him. She traced the arch of one black eyebrow and then brushed the tip of her finger across the long lashes. "In spite of everything, I've been happy here. Sometimes I'm afraid I won't know how to behave when I go back to New Orleans."

She had been about to say "when I go home," but the last word stuck in her throat, as though the city where she lived all but the last year of her life were no longer home.

Eyes closed, Rio savored her touch, knowing that while she was trying to imprint every detail of him on her memory, so was he carving her image into his own.

"You didn't feel that way when we got here," he reminded her. Had she forgotten her horror at the sight of the dilapidated little cabin? He hadn't.

She did not laugh; she only smiled, and had he looked at her he would have seen the fond sadness in that smile.

"It grew on me. Like you."

The movement of his hand was almost imperceptible at first, but Genevieve felt it nonetheless. Slowly, with possessive tenderness, he pulled his hand from her hip to her belly and then let it rest there.

How could a man want something so damn much, and at the same time pray it never happened? She was right when she accused men of taking too much pride in an accomplishment they were only half responsible for. Or maybe even not that much. If she did conceive his child—if she already had—she would carry it within her for nine long months, a constant reminder of what they had shared, the good times, the bad, the tears, the laughter, the fights, the loving. And he would have nothing. Nothing at all. Only his memories, and his pride.

She smoothed her palm along the stubbled line of his jaw, down his throat, to the hard planes of his chest. She felt the sudden leap of his heart beneath her hand, the quick intake of his breath as she slowly circled her fingers around his nipple.

"Love me, Rio," she breathed, reaching lower still. "Love me now, tonight."

He leaned down to kiss her, his lips taking final possession of her command.

"Love me forever, Rio."

Tomorrow, after just one more brief night, they would leave this precious valley behind and embark upon another dangerous journey. Who knew what lay in wait for them along that trail? Here they had been safe. Rio had kept them safe, and for this last night she would cling to him and make the memories that must last forever.

She slipped her other arm behind him to pull him down to her. Arching her back she offered him the succulent globes of her breasts, the nipples already taut with desire, even as she parted her legs to cradle him between her thighs.

He drew away, breathless and barely in control. Her fingers still touched him, stroking him with quivering urgency. This might be the last time he ever made love to her and, like the first time, he wanted it perfect.

"Slow down, querida," he murmured. Deep breaths restored him; feathered kisses on her shuttered eyes calmed his raging need. "Don't make forever go so fast."

He loved her as if they did indeed have all of forever before them, not just this one night. And as desperate as she was to know again, perhaps for the last time, the soaring brilliance of passion fulfilled, Genevieve surrendered at last to the insistence of his hands, his lips, his tongue, his very flesh on hers.

With his face buried between her breasts, he curled his hands around the voluptuous mounds until only the dark peaks were exposed. The texture of his work-roughed thumbs on supremely sensitive flesh sent molten shivers through her. She thought she could not stand another instant of it, that she would succumb to this tantalizing arousal, but when he lifted his head and skimmed his tongue around just the very tip of her nipple, she cried out at the exquisite pain.

He took the crinkled nubbin into his mouth and suckled, drawing yet another impassioned shriek from her throat. She wrapped her legs around him, to find and fill herself with him, but he remained beyond her reach.

"Let it go," he whispered, his lips forming the words against her flesh. "Don't hold it back, amada mía."

"No, Rio," she gasped, "not without you."

252

He had wanted to watch her at the moment of culmination, as he had done before when they spent hours making love over and over until exhaustion claimed them. But now he, too, sensed the desperation of the impending dawn. Tomorrow would begin the long separation; tonight they must be together. This time, and every time until the night was over.

He came into her swiftly, with a single satiny thrust that elicited a gentle cry of triumph. But her victory was short-lived, vanquished by the final demands of ecstasy. Genevieve pressed her hips against his to force him deeper into her soul. He had brought her too close, aroused her beyond the point of holding back any longer.

"Now!" she cried, and let the storm sweep her away.

Genevieve took one final glance around the cabin. The small tools they wouldn't need on the trail had been stashed in the kettle, then covered with the table and the two log stools. The bedframe, looking forlorn with the mattress and even the ropes stripped from it, rested in its corner. There was nothing else. Swallowing a lump and refusing to cry, Genevieve stepped through the low doorway and took the reins from Rio.

He nailed two boards over the door, hoping that would keep the place secure from marauding animals. He said nothing, but when he had mounted Cinco and headed the stallion southward down the valley, Rio did not look back.

She did not ask him how he knew where to go; she had no choice but to trust him. Day after endless day she followed him, almost without a word, the mare plodding along behind the mule. They maintained a slow but steady pace, from dawn to dusk, on a trail invisible to any eyes but Rio's.

The sun blinded them and burned their faces. The wind numbed them. At night they dipped hardtack in weak coffee made from melted snow and chewed strips of dried venison as they fell asleep. The mattress beneath them and the bearskin over them kept in enough body heat that they did not freeze before they woke to start another day.

On the evening of the twenty-sixth day since leaving the cabin, in the purple glow of a spectacular sunset, they made camp overlooking a broad, flat valley. A river showing only a narrow strip of open water down the center of its course ran through the valley.

There would still be mountains to climb, but the worst of the journey was over. In the distance Genevieve could see a cluster of buildings enclosed within a log palisade. Tears stung her eyes as she recognized Fort Bridger, one of the old trading posts where the wagon train had halted on its way west.

They did not arrive until late the next afternoon. Though the fort offered few amenities, Genevieve and Rio felt as if they had just walked into heaven.

"A bath with a whole cake of soap," Rio said, expressing his first wish. "Coffee so strong you can eat it with a fork. A shave. Cherry pie."

Riding through the gates into the bustling heart of the compound, two buckskin clad strangers attracted little attention. This time of year there were few westbound travelers, but within weeks, Genevieve knew the fort would be teeming with emigrants, such as she had been last year.

In autumn the fort had been dry and dusty; now the dust was mud. But there was, thank God, no snow. It was, after all, the second day of April. Spring had truly arrived.

Genevieve had her wishes, too.

"A bath, first. With hot water. And a real bath, not the kind where you have to pour water over yourself to get wet." She hoped, however, that the bath did not come with a mirror. She wanted to delay seeing her reflection until *after* she had made some repairs to what six months in the wilderness had damaged.

"Then food. Potatoes. With butter. And eggs."

Her listing was interrupted by a sudden shout.

"Hey, is that you, Rio?"

A young man was waving to them from the boardwalk in front of the trading post, some fifty feet away. Rio reined Cinco to a halt, then turned the palomino in the boy's direction.

"By God, it is you!" In his excitement, the youth had apparently forgotten the thick, oozing mud that carpeted the area within the stockade's walls. One step into it, however, and he could only shrug and press forward. "What in tarnation you doin' out here this time of the year?"

"Lookin' for a bath and some hot food, Nat," Rio answered as he swung wearily down from the saddle.

"Sure thing. I see you got yourself a—" Whatever the boy had been about to say was swallowed back down his throat with an audible gulp. "Lord a-mercy, is that Miss du Prés?"

Too exhausted even to dismount, Genevieve sat still while Rio tied Cinco to the hitching rail. She shook her head with the sad realization that the boy Nat had mistaken her for an Indian squaw. When Rio came to help her down from the mare, she sagged into his arms until her feet touched the muck that passed for solid earth.

"We made it," was all she could whisper before dissolving into helpless tears.

The room was small and the furniture spare, but Genevieve almost wanted to kiss the plank floor and wrap her arms around the wooden bathtub. It was barely half full before she gave in to her impatience and stripped off her dirty, sweaty leather garments and plunged into the water.

Nat's mother, a plump widow who had worked at the trading post since her husband died there on the way to the goldfields four years earlier, brought two more buckets of hot water and poured them over a laughing Genevieve.

"Does everyone react like this to a bath?" she asked, turning her face into the cascade of steaming water. "I don't think I ever felt anything so good in my entire life."

Edwina Miller laughed.

"Some do. Most, though, they're either in a hurry to get on to California if they're going west, or if they're headed back east, then they're usually broke and disgraced, so they don't care too much about one thing or another."

Edwina set the empty buckets outside the door, then came back to lay out on the bed an assortment of brand-new clothing. Functional, unadorned under-drawers and camisole, a sturdy whipcord split skirt and flannel shirt, even black cotton stockings and a pair of boots.

"You're the last person I ever expected to see back at Bridger," Edwina commented as she smoothed the wrinkles out of the skirt. "I figured you found that boyfriend of yours and sailed back to New Orleans 'round the Horn."

The mention of Jean-Louis was like a pail of cold water thrown over her. Genevieve shivered and lathered the cake of soap on the tangled ends of her hair more vigorously, as though she could wash away the memories.

"Couldn't you find him?"

"Oh, I found him, all right," Genevieve answered, all her previous exuberance quenched. "I guess you could say absence did not make our hearts grow fonder."

Edwina clucked her own disappointment.

"I'm sorry to hear that. 'Course Rio there, he's probably tickled pink. That boy never took his eye off you the whole time you was here last fall." She bustled over to the little cast-iron stove that heated the room and turned the towels hanging over a chair beside it.

Satisfied that she had done everything she could, Edwina headed for the door. "You enjoy your soak, Miss du Prés. I gotta go help get supper ready."

The fur trade, for which Fort Bridger had been established more than a decade before the gold rush, had declined just when the waves of westward bound gold-seekers began washing across the continent. Within the stockade walls, the traveler was able to replenish supplies and rest for a while before beginning the long, arduous trek across the mountains.

For Genevieve, Fort Bridger offered another amenity: human contact. While they ate a sumptuous—to them—dinner of fried chicken, mashed potatoes and gravy, turnips in butter, and pumpkin pie, Rio watched as Genevieve chatted with everyone present, from young Nat Miller to the oldest and crotchetiest of the fur-trappers who still frequented the fort.

"You should have seen it!" she regaled a crowd of listeners far into the night. She sat on a bench pulled close to the massive fireplace, while the others either stood against the wall or sat cross-legged in front of the hearth. "It stood at least ten feet high, with hideous long yellow teeth. And the lioness was so beautiful, defending her cub. She was willing to give her life for him."

This was the second time Rio had listened to her tell the story of the grizzly. He felt a little foolish when she heaped more praise on him than he thought he was due, but nothing could compare to the embarrassment of her telling everyone how he fell through the ice while fetching the cattails for her bed. She was making him out to be some knight in shining armor or something, a role he felt decidedly uncomfortable in.

She, however, obviously felt more than comfortable in her role. The center of attention, surrounded by adoring males, she laughed and giggled, granted each of her admirers a smile surely meant for him alone, and never hesitated to pat a buckskin-clad arm or even tweak a dirty, scraggly beard until the bearded one blushed beneath his dirt and grinned a toothless grin.

Rio kept to a corner of the room, not too far away, but not terribly close, either. Genevieve Marie du Prés was coming back into her element; Rio Jackson could watch and admire her, even be in awe of her, but he could not join her.

And he wanted to. He had not known until this night, until he saw her surrounded by other men, how jealous he could be. Those lonely days in the cabin, where there had been just the two of them, seemed to grow more and more idyllic. The hardships faded, until he could think of nothing but her, and the way he had had to share her with no one.

One by one, the trappers and travelers, the employees of the fort and their families, drifted off to seek their beds. Edwina Miller bustled around the huge mess hall, snuffing candles and blowing out lamps. With a sudden realization of how exhausted she was, Genevieve stood and stretched and yawned. And looked for Rio.

He was gone.

Chapter Seventeen

Though not bitter, the night air was cold enough that Genevieve gave up her search soon after beginning it. Rio was nowhere in the trading post store or the mess hall, and she knew where nothing else was within the compound's walls. Nor did she possess a coat or shawl to keep her from freezing. Uneasy, she wandered back to the small room she had been assigned and opened the door.

For a brief moment she tensed in the darkness. The curtains were drawn across the window, blocking the moonlight that flooded the central courtyard of the fort. Genevieve left the door open until she had made her way to the table beside the bed and struck a match to light the single lamp.

The room was empty, as expected. Uncomfortably empty.

A bed, a table, a chair, a stove. Those were the only furnishings. And the room itself was so small even these few things seemed to crowd it. In the corner, Genevieve's saddlebags lay in an untidy heap beside her bedroll, reminders of the cold, uncomfortable nights on the trail.

She closed the door and leaned back against it. After the long-awaited luxuries of bath and good food, she had intended to collapse on the bed and sleep all night. But as she stared at the narrow cot with its skimpy pillow and threadbare blankets, a queer feeling settled in the pit of her stomach.

She had never imagined the sense of abandonment that assailed her at the thought of sleeping alone again after all the months of sharing her bed with Rio. He had made her no promises, and now, even if only for the night, he was gone.

While Cinco watched over the wall between the stalls, Rio pulled the brush through the mare's tangled mane. He had kept the pace to Fort Bridger relatively easy to save her, and she appeared to have come through in good condition. A few days rest and grain feeding ought to give her back any strength she had lost.

"She's not the prettiest filly you ever mounted, viejo," Rio tossed over his shoulder at the stallion, "but I think she'll throw a good strong foal."

Cinco whinnied and tossed his head, as though he understood exactly what he had been told. Rio laughed.

"Yeah, I was thinkin' the same thing. Either you're luckier than I am, or you got stronger stuff. Still, I guess it's just as well." He pulled the mare's forelock between her ears and smoothed it down her forehead. She butted her nose against his chest and knocked him a step backward. "One breedin' female at a time's about all I can handle."

Satisfied with the mare's grooming, he gently shoved her away. When she had settled back to munching the oats he had given her, Rio took down the lantern and walked out of her stall.

After leaving Viva still surrounded by her devoted admirers, he had gone to his room just three doors down the boardwalk from hers. The loneliness wrapped itself around him the minute he closed the door. He had felt smothered with it, until he pushed the door open and ran out into the night, struggling

260

for breath just as though someone had tied a blanket over his head.

He had never felt like that before in his life. And lord knew he had spent enough lonely nights in his thirty-two years.

But this would be his first night alone since Viva du Prés had entered his life.

"Get used to it," he muttered as he walked past Cinco's stall and picked up the bundle he had dropped on the floor earlier. The palomino replied with a snort.

Rio headed back out into the chilly April night, the canvas satchel now slung over his shoulder. Across the compound he could see a light in one of the guest rooms. Nearly everything else was dark, though the silvery moonlight made the muddy courtyard almost bright as day. Rio hesitated, staring at that yellow window for several seconds, before slowly making his way toward his own room.

He hesitated again when he approached the lighted window. Did he dare knock, ask her why she hadn't gone to bed yet when he knew she was exhausted? But what if she were entertaining one of the men who had listened with such avid pleasure to her stories of her time in the mountains?

Rio shook his head angrily. She wouldn't do that, not Viva. Not even if there had been an English lord, like the dandy who had once challenged Rio Jackson to a duel in this very same fort, would Viva have betrayed him so quickly. He refused to think that of her, no matter how insistent the voice that reminded him of other betrayals, other women.

He passed her door and her window without looking in and made his way to his own room. After dropping the satchel to the bed, he lit the lamp and gazed around the tiny chamber. It was only a fraction the size of the cabin, yet it seemed yawningly empty without her presence.

As for the bed, he could hardly even look at it,

much less get in it. Not without Viva. Not tonight. Maybe tomorrow night, when he had time to get used to the idea. But not tonight.

He took the canvas sack and dumped its contents on the bed, then selected one of the books at random. *"Pride and Prejudice,"* he read slowly aloud from the spine. "Sounds dull enough. Maybe it'll put me to sleep."

As he opened the large, expensively bound book, Rio wondered who had left it behind at the fort. An English tourist passing through on a journey of idle curiosity? A schoolteacher who never made it to California? By now it no longer mattered. Rio leaned against the wall beside the bed, then slid down to a sitting position on the floor, with the lamp above his right shoulder on the washstand.

They spent two more days at Fort Bridger before setting out again. The horses and mule had been shod, supplies replenished, and clothing replaced. For the first time since that horrible night in Sacramento, Genevieve wore a warm, comfortable cape around her shoulders.

Rio had spent little time with her prior to their departure. He was, he explained, busy. She noted at dinner, the only meal they shared, that he looked exhausted. She wondered if he, too, found sleep elusive. Her own nights had been ordeals of nightmares and tears and sleepless tossing on an unfamiliar and very lonely bed.

Being back on the trail seemed, in contrast, to restore him. Or perhaps it was just that once again they slept in each other's arms.

Four days out from Bridger, they camped just the other side of South Pass. At this altitude, the air was winter cold, and snow still clung to the frozen ground. Huddled around the campfire while a pot of stew simmered, Rio rummaged through his saddlebags and finally produced a small, neat canvas bundle, tied with a length of faded blue ribbon.

"What's that?" Genevieve asked as she leaned forward to stir the pot once again.

Rio's slightly wicked grin did not go unnoticed. Ceremoniously he untied the ribbon and unrolled the package. The contents clinked with an unmistakable sound.

"Silverware," he announced proudly, spreading the utensils out on the felt-lined canvas.

He had made his decision.

Travelling light, they made nearly thirty miles a day, twice what the wagon train had covered, and still camped early to spare the horses. The days slowly lengthened, and warmed, too. The grass on the prairie greened with spring's full arrival. Along the river, the trees spun webs of verdant lace before bursting into full leaf. Nights no longer brought frost, though days frequently brought rain.

"Won't be long now," Rio commented as they kindled their evening fire the day after stopping at Fort Kearny, the last major way-station before St. Joseph. The firewood was still wet from a three-day downpour and only reluctantly burned.

"It took nearly a month for the wagon train to reach this far. Would you say two weeks until we reach St. Joe?" Genevieve asked.

"Maybe, maybe a little less."

There had been days when she thought they would never get this far, when the rain pelted them and soaked through every garment they owned, when the mule threw a shoe and they had to wait until a passing wagon train came along to replace it. She had cursed each and every delay. Now, when the end of the journey seemed so near, she suddenly felt apprehensive.

She sensed the same unease in Rio. Since that night he had presented her with the bundle of silverware, he had demanded she drill him in every possible aspect of "civilized" behavior. His skill at mimicry proved to be much more than a convenient form of mockery; he could copy almost any speech pattern, any accent, after hearing it but once.

"That's how you managed that bit of French back in Sacramento!" Genevieve exclaimed.

But Rio shook his head. Determination had put a permanent scowl on his face.

"Nope. Learned it from a crazy Frenchman headed for the goldfields. Now, get me through these damn introductions again."

With a long, weary sigh. Genevieve began once more explaining the absurdities of etiquette.

St. Joseph teemed with activity on a bright, sunny morning in mid-May. The western edge of town was a town unto itself, a city on spoked wheels. Hundreds of covered wagons gathered here, waiting for the right moment to depart for points west. In the past few days, Rio and Genevieve had encountered more and more of the outbound vehicles. Now they wandered through a veritable sea of them.

Genevieve could barely bring herself to look at the people. They had no idea what they were heading into, the dangers, the hardships, the disappointments. And they would not listen to her, or to anyone else, for that matter. She knew. She had heard the arguments herself, and ignored them.

She remembered the day she had arrived, a year ago, filled with the same fervor and determination — and disbelief. Several people had tried to dissuade her, but most had given up after half-hearted attempts. Only one had persisted, the black-haired, blue-eyed scout whose wagon train she had wheedled her way into joining.

Following behind him now, she wondered if Rio was thinking of that day, too. If he were, he gave no indication, just kept weaving through the crowds toward St. Joe proper.

In the town itself, Rio continued his purposeful pace through the streets until he came to a tidy white frame house with a wide veranda across the front. Above the steps hung a neatly lettered sign.

"Grady's - Rooms to Let," he read aloud, then turned to Genevieve, who had pulled up next to him. "Easy, when you know how, ain't it?"

"It is," she agreed. "But what are we doing here? Shouldn't we be booking passage on a boat to St. Louis?"

Rio swung down from the saddle. The idea of sitting comfortably on a riverboat for the rest of the journey instead of straddling a horse for another thousand miles or so was mighty appealing. He was not, however, going to count his chickens before they were hatched. Or even laid, for that matter.

"We got things to do before we get on that boat," he informed her. "First off, we got to dispose of this mule."

"*What?*"

Genevieve's horrified shout seemed to hang in the morning air. Rio immediately glanced around to see if she had attracted any undue attention. The street, mercifully, was empty.

"I said, we need to find someone willing to buy the mule. I have no idea what it is going to cost for the two of us to sail in lazy luxury to St. Louis, but I do know we haven't got a whole lot of cash."

"You're not selling the mule."

He hadn't heard her right. He couldn't have. What he thought he heard made absolutely no sense whatsoever.

Then she said it again, and he knew he had indeed heard this utter nonsense correctly.

"Rio Jackson, you are not going to sell that mule."

He threw his hands up in exasperation and stared at her over Cinco's back.

"Why the hell not? Where else we gonna get the money?"

"I don't know. But you can't just sell her."

He walked around in front of Cinco and approached Genevieve, who had made no move to dismount. Even when Rio stretched up his hands to help her down, she sat adamantly straight in the saddle and would not even hand him the reins to tie the mare to the rail in front of the boarding house.

"You are being unreasonable," he told her in a low, controlled whisper. "Now get off the horse, help me take our gear inside, and then I am going to take the mule to an outfitter. She'll bring a good price and—"

"No," Genevieve cut him off. She swung down off the mare so quickly she would have kicked him in the face if he hadn't sensed her anger and backed away. "You're not selling her."

He took a deep breath and let it out in an explosion.

"Jeez, woman, what is the matter with you? She's a mule, a beast of burden, not a damned lap-dog pet. What do you plan to do with her when you get her back to New Orleans? Set her in the parlor and feed her bonbons from your own plate?"

She had no ready answer, but the set of her shoulders as she walked past him to tie the mare told him she had not given in. Not at all. But she was thinking. He decided to give her more to think about.

"All right I won't sell her to an outfitter, I'll make sure she goes to a good home."

"No. You couldn't be positive. Someone else might sell her to the first westward bound maniac who came along. You just can't do it, Rio."

Good God, she was crying! She was crying over a damn mule!

"Aw, Viva, stop it, will you, please?" Rio begged. "It's not like she's a human being. For crying out loud, she doesn't even have a name!"

266

"She does so!" To prove her point, Genevieve called firmly, "Veronica!"

The mule's ears twitched forward at a sound that was obviously familiar.

"You wouldn't sell Cinco, would you?"

Rio glanced instinctively at the big gold stallion. That glance was all the answer Genevieve needed.

Marching up to the boarding house stairs, she called over her shoulder, "I don't care if we have to ride all the way back to New Orleans and then swim across the Mississippi. We are not selling the mule."

Rio caught her just as she put one foot on the first step.

"Viva, for God's sake, will you listen to reason?" he pleaded as he took firm hold of her arm. She turned to face him, but did not try to escape his grip. "You can't keep the mule. You have no use for her. We *do* need the money."

She shook her head, sending the mass of black waves tumbling around her shoulders.

"No. I won't even consider it. I've already told you—"

"And I'm telling you, lady." His grip tightened just enough to let her know he was dead serious. "You may be willing to walk to New Orleans for all I care, but I'm not. I bought that mule with my money, and I'm gonna sell her and get it back. You can't save every animal from whatever its fate may be. Who knows? Maybe I'll find a preacher who only hitches her up on Sundays. But I *ain't* keepin' her, understand?"

She advanced a step upward, until she could meet his eyes levelly.

"You just don't understand, Rio."

Angry almost to the point of losing control, he let go her arm. He took two long strides away from her, then just as abruptly turned back.

"No, I guess I don't understand. But neither do you. That mule is not a pet, and neither, come to

267

think of it, am I."

A young doctor newly arrived in St. Joseph bought the mule later that afternoon, paying Rio just enough for passage on a riverboat scheduled to leave the day after next. Genevieve would have a cabin, though a modest one; Rio had slept worse places than the deck of a paddlewheeler in his life.

He did not tell her of the arrangements. For one thing, Agnes Grady, the spinster who, with her elderly father, kept the boardinghouse, did not allow visitors inside; and Rio was not about to tell Viva on the veranda he had sold her precious mule. She might have no compunctions about murdering him in public, but he did.

So he puzzled out the intricacies of a brand new steel pen and carefully scribed a letter, the first of his entire life. He delivered it that evening, handing it to Agnes herself. He did not wait for Genevieve's reply before he walked back to the livery stable where he would spread out his bedroll in the loft.

He gave serious thought to the idea of putting her on that boat and sending her home alone. It was, after all, what he had agreed to do back in Sacramento. She said she had an aunt or something in St. Louis, so even if he gave her none of the money from Paul Bruckner's bank draft, she should have no trouble getting the rest of the way home. Here in St. Joe he'd have no trouble at all signing on another wagon train.

But what had seemed a satisfying career a year ago now held no appeal. He had left San Antonio to get away from painful memories and all the reminders that kept them fresh. How could he ever make that trek to California and back again without seeing a thousand reminders of this wonderful, spoiled, impulsive, beautiful, soul-stealing, heart-breaking creature he had named Viva?

He couldn't. And he wouldn't. Neither, however, would he let her make a pet of him, as she would have the mule. He had lied when he told her he didn't understand, because in a way he did. She was trying to hang onto every tangible reminder of what they had shared, good times as well as bad, just as he was trying to erase everything. The future was so uncertain, because they had made it uncertain; she wanted only a little certainty.

Rio Jackson had none to give her. He had none to give himself. But what she had given to him in a cold, desolate mountain cabin, he could return to her: dreams.

Genevieve boarded the *Belle Jolie* breathless, just as the hands were about to pull in the gangplank. She had run all the way from Grady's boarding house.

Arms laden with everything she possessed, she stepped back just far enough from the rail to allow room for the gangplank. A uniformed man with a stub of a fat cigar clenched between his teeth asked for her ticket. She had to set down part of her load to find it.

The boat's whistle blasted the air with its announcement of departure promptly at one o'clock in the afternoon. Seconds later, Genevieve felt the craft begin to move. She turned back to the rail to watch St. Joseph, Missouri, slowly slide away.

Once again, Rio had disappeared.

This time, however, she had searched for him everywhere she could think of. Neither Cinco nor the mare were at any of the liveries; when Genevieve finally located the one where they *had* been, the owner informed her the man answering Rio's description had taken the animals away early that morning.

She had wandered through the hordes of wagons and travellers gathered at the western edge of town and had asked repeatedly if anyone had seen or knew

269

of Rio Jackson. She learned he was quite well-known, especially with the experienced guides and scouts, but no one had seen him since the day of his arrival.

Blinded by tears, she hurried to the dock where the *Belle Jolie* waited, paddle slowly turning to hold her steady against the current. There was no familiar tall silhouette waiting.

Stumbling under the awkward weight of her belongings and Rio's desertion, Genevieve found a porter to show her to her cabin. The man gave her more than one stare, but she ignored his curiosity. She found a coin to tip him, though she had no idea what denomination it was. Then, when she was finally alone in this tiny cramped space, she dropped her saddlebags and bedroll and other parcels unceremoniously to the floor. Unable to control the tears a second longer, she fell face down on the bed and sobbed.

"You took *everything,*" she wailed, as her heart shattered into tiny pieces. "The mule, the mare, even that stinking bearskin. Couldn't you have left me something?"

Tears still streaming from her eyes, she pulled from her pocket the note he had sent her. She could not read it, for she feared her tears would smear the neat but childish letters, but she could hold the page with its few short lines to her heart.

"Dear Viva," he had written, the words committed to her memory after so many readings, *"I have sold Veronica. It was the only way. Here is your ticket to Saint Louis. Many thanks. Rio."*

"Damn you, damn you, damn you," she wept, pounding her fist into the pillow. She must have repeated those same two words a thousand times before she finally fell into troubled sleep.

Standing outside the door to her cabin, Rio listened to her deprecations with only a twinge of guilt. In the morning, when he let her find him, then he'd decide if he needed to feel really guilty. For now, he felt a smug satisfaction. He would allow himself to revel in it for a day or two only, because once they reached St. Louis, he'd know only fear.

She spotted him the minute she walked out onto the main deck. There was no mistaking the broad shoulders, the hat shoved back on his head, the lazy confidence in the way he leaned on the rail. At first she hesitated, unsure of his reaction, but after the horrible night she had spent mourning his abandonment and the dreary hopelessness of the morning, her hesitation lasted only seconds.

Still, the resounding kiss she gave him left a few doubts.

"Am I forgiven then?" he asked when she finally released his mouth, though her hands were still locked together at the back of his neck.

"Yes. And no." She pulled his head down to plant another smack on his all too willing lips. "Yes, for selling the mule. You were right; I was being childish. No, for letting me think you had left me. Don't you ever do that again, Rio Jackson. Ever."

The third kiss did not catch him by surprise as the others had. Knowing it might be a long time before he had such an opportunity again, Rio wrapped his arms around the slender creature who so frequently drove him to the point of madness and returned her welcoming kiss full measure.

The matter of the mule behind them, they still found plenty to argue about. The matter of accommodations once they reached St. Louis provided fuel for a flare of tempers later that same afternoon.

"You'll stay with your Aunt Cecilia," Rio insisted. "You have a reputation to re-establish. Staying in a hotel, however elegant, will only make people ask questions. And it's only for a few days."

"A week is not a few days. It's almost forever. And Aunt Cecilia is an ogre. If you call on me, she'll sit there with us—*between* us—and never let us have a

271

moment of privacy. You might just as well have me stay in a convent."

Rio shrugged. They were sitting at one of the tables on the upper deck of the riverboat, where the stiff breeze played havoc with the stack of blank paper Rio had brought with him. He wrote the word "privacy" on the top sheet, not in the block letters of a child but in a tight, slightly unpracticed cursive. His fingers were liberally stained with ink.

"A convent might not be such a bad idea. Now, give me another problem."

"We aren't finished with this one! I am not staying with Aunt Cecilia."

Two days later, despite continued protests, Genevieve stood on the front porch of her Aunt Cecilia Haliburton's home in St. Louis.

A brief spring thunderstorm had drenched them on their ride from the dock, but now the sun had come out once again, leaving the air heavy with warmth and damp. Genevieve looked so bedraggled, Rio almost felt sorry for her. However, neither her pleading sapphire eyes nor the seductive pout of lips he had kissed whenever the opportunity presented itself would sway him now.

The house was a comfortable one, separated from the street by a neatly trimmed yard enclosed by a decorative wrought-iron fence. Two immense trees shaded the yard, and also partially shielded the couple on the porch from the curious eyes of passers-by.

Still, Rio turned to watch until an open carriage passed out of possible hearing.

"Look, Viva, I'm gonna tell you for the last time. Go in there and make peace with your aunt. I'm not abandoning you, I promise. I'll be back this evening."

"But how am I supposed to explain how I got here?"

"Tell them the truth. As much or as little as you think they can handle." He rested his hands on her

272

shoulders and risked one last kiss. The further he allowed himself to sink into this quagmire, the more difficult it was going to be to extricate himself. "I got to go, Viva."

She was watching him walk down the flagstone walk to the open gate when she heard a door creak behind her.

An instant later, a crisp voice ordered, "Get off this porch!"

Genevieve slowly turned, with no smile of recognition though the voice was as familiar to her as her own mother's.

"We don't allow any—Miss Genevieve?"

The tall, gaunt housekeeper took one hesitant step across the threshold and onto the porch. Raising long-fingered black hands to her cheeks, she repeated the question.

"Miss Genevieve? Is it really you?"

"I'm afraid it is, Mercy," Genevieve sighed. "Is Aunt Cecilia home?"

Disapproval quickly replaced surprise on the housekeeper's face, and she moved her hands from her face to her hips. Genevieve suddenly realized Mercy was nearly as tall as Rio, and twice as menacing in her anger.

"Yes, Miss Cecilia is home. And I have a feeling she is going to be just as put out as I am with your appearance. Lord, child, what have you done to yourself?"

Chapter Eighteen

Rio ignored all the guilty whispers from his conscience. He had done what needed to be done. If he put the money to a use other than what Paul Bruckner might have intended it, well, money could be repaid. In fact, the whole crazy plan was designed for that express purpose.

And there was always Tibler's gold. It might take a while to recover from where the old man had hidden it, but Rio had no doubt he knew the exact location. The instructions in the letter were perfectly clear.

For now, however, he was in St. Louis, two thousand miles from the valley where Tibler had found and then hidden his treasure.

After depositing Genevieve at her aunt's house, Rio had headed immediately for the bank where Paul Bruckner's father was president. He had recognized the older man at once; Paul took after him right down to the smile and invitation to dinner. But as in Sacramento, Rio begged off the invitation. This time, however, he had much different reasons.

He wondered, as he walked up to the Haliburton house in the evening cool after another brief shower, if Genevieve would even recognize him. He had hardly recognized himself when the tailor Gerrard Bruckner recommended had finished with him.

Rio had no doubt he would be admitted to the Haliburton house, unless, of course, Genevieve had told her aunt and uncle too much of the truth. Then, they might be waiting for him with a gun. The thought was enough to slow his steps, but not stop him. He mounted the stairs, crossed the veranda, and ignored the brass knocker in favor of a sharp rap with his knuckles.

The appearance of a tall black woman in starched apron and cap came close to destroying his confidence.

He doffed his new gray hat and introduced himself.

"Mr. Rodrigo Jackson, to call on Miss Genevieve du Prés," he said with a slight bow.

If the woman staring almost at eye level with him was the celebrated Mercy Genevieve had told him about, then she was the most misnamed creature on God's earth. There was nothing merciful in the baleful glare she lavished upon him.

"So," she snorted. "You're Rio Jackson. Come on in, then. Miss Cecilia and Mister Blayne are in the back parlor with Miss Genevieve. I believe they have been expecting you."

Rio quelled an urge to wipe his sweating palms on the fabric of his new charcoal coat. Mimicking the aristocrats of San Antonio when he was a child was one thing; it had come easily and he had never done it in front of the people he ridiculed with his imitations. Nor had he ever tried to sustain the act.

What if he couldn't do it? What if everything she had taught him was a lie, done to humiliate him? What if it was the truth, but he couldn't remember any of it? What if they laughed at him, the way his brother's friends had laughed at him that day at school?

What if *she* laughed at him?

He stared at Mercy's ramrod stiff back and wondered if he could escape without her catching him.

* * *

Genevieve had heard the quiet knock on the door. It sent her heart leaping to her throat, and her hands, folded nervously on her lap, began to perspire. Brown and roughened from weather and work, they looked absurd against the skirt of her butter yellow muslin gown. Aunt Cecilia's constant lament, in fact, was that her niece had returned from The West—one could hear the capital letters in Cecilia's voice—minus her beautiful ivory complexion.

Her niece did not mention other physical assets she had lost since leaving for California.

With her eyes still lowered, Genevieve nevertheless managed to watch her aunt and uncle during those nerve-wracking few minutes while she listened to Mercy's and someone else's footsteps on the polished parquet of the hallway.

Blayne Haliburton, trim, white-haired, with a luxurious silver mustache he stroked whenever deep in thought, had carried the after-dinner conversation almost singlehandedly. Genevieve tried to pay attention but failed miserably. All evening she had been waiting for that knock on the door, listening for it, praying for it. Now that it had come, she understood that Blayne's chatter was as much an outlet for nervousness as Cecilia's patient embroidery. They, too, paused, he in mid sentence, she in mid stitch.

Mercy entered the parlor first. Usually Genevieve could read the woman's face like a book. Not this time. Or perhaps, she thought in a fleeting second, Mercy is just too confused to make one of her instantaneous judgments.

"Miss Cecilia, Mister Blayne, Mr. Rodrigo Jackson, of San Antonio, Texas."

Genevieve barely stifled a gasp.

The height, the breadth of shoulder, the lazy yet poised stance, all were unmistakable. As he stepped into the parlor, where the glow of lamplight shone on the blue-black hair and glittered in the sky-blue eyes,

Genevieve blinked, recognizing him but still not quite believing. In pale grey trousers and darker grey coat over a black waistcoat and snow-white shirt, he looked every inch the Creole gentleman.

"Mr. Jackson, welcome to St. Louis," Blayne said, rising to greet his guest. "I understand we owe you quite a debt for bringing our niece back safe and sound from her adventure."

"I was glad to be of service," Rio replied.

His mouth was dry as the Utah desert in July, yet trickles of sweat slithered down his back. How much had she told them? How close was he to being shot? He wanted to look at her and find answers in her eyes, but he didn't dare. He was afraid the answers wouldn't be there.

But he had got that one glance of her, just as he came into the room. It had taken every ounce of will power he possessed not to turn tail and flee like the impostor he was. On any other woman, the soft yellow would have washed all the color from her skin; on Genevieve, it brought out the sun-kissed roses in her cheeks, the gilding of a few freckles across her nose. And her eyes, oh God, they were like the pond back in the valley, when the moonlit summer sky reflected on its undisturbed stillness and a man could be drawn to drown himself in the midnight depths. Those eyes, with their ebony frill of lashes, and that mouth, open now in surprise just waiting for his kiss. She touched the tip of her tongue first to her upper lip and then her lower. The memory of how that little tongue felt against his sent the blood surging through Rio's veins, ringing with every pulsebeat in his ears.

"Genevieve said she wasn't certain where you would be staying, or we would have issued an invitation to dinner, Mr. Jackson. You will, please, join us tomorrow?"

Rio wondered how much of Blayne Haliburton's chatter he had missed and hoped it was nothing important. He hadn't intended to stand there and stare at Genevieve, but damn it, a man can resist only so much temptation.

She was beautiful and she was home. Or close enough to it that he could see she belonged here. Bathed and perfumed, her glossy black hair pulled into a simple but elegant coiffure, she was every inch a wealthy young woman. Eventually the calluses would be smoothed from her hands and her nose would lose that charming spatter of freckles, and no one would ever know she had spent an entire winter making love in an isolated cabin in the snowy mountains of California. No one but Rio Jackson, and what claim could he make on her?

"I'd be honored to join you and your family, Mr. Haliburton," Rio answered, not knowing where he found the breath to speak.

"Good. Maybe you can fill in some of the blanks in Genevieve's story."

Genevieve lay in a pool of sweat in her bed. No breath of breeze stirred the curtains at the open window though quiet rumbles of distant thunder warned of another storm. She paid it no mind.

She could not remember a single thing Rio had said. He had stayed, she thought, no more than fifteen minutes, during which time he had not addressed a single word directly to her, nor had she spoken directly to him. But that had not stopped her from feeling that unconquerable rush of desire the instant she saw him.

Had he felt the same way? She couldn't tell. She had been in a state almost of shock upon seeing him so completely transformed. No doubt he had taken the letter from Paul Bruckner to his father's bank and then used the money to buy the clothes. She had no idea how much he might have spent on his new ward-

278

robe, but surely there couldn't be much left. Would it be enough for their fare to New Orleans? No, that didn't matter. Blayne and Cecilia would pay their niece's passage home, whether Rio saved enough of Bruckner's money or not. That wasn't the point. The point was, did Rio intend to go with her?

Genevieve rolled over, trying to find a cool spot on the sheets, and admitted Rio had probably made a wise decision in adopting the accoutrements of a gentleman, regardless of the cost. But why had he told her nothing of his plans? And what other plans might he have made and kept from her?

Rio lit a thin, dark cigar from the lamp flame, then turned the wick down until the light went out completely. He had stripped off his coat and vest and shirt and hung them carefully on the back of the chair. Had the expenditure been justified? he wondered as he walked to the open window and stared out over the city. A flash of lightning lit the sky, but he would have preferred a cooling breeze. Rain in St. Louis only meant more sticky heat.

He laughed quietly and shook his head. A few short months ago he had been freezing his ass off in the mountains, and now he was complaining of the heat.

Besides, he could do absolutely nothing about the weather, and he had to direct his efforts toward the things he could control. Or at least do something about.

Genevieve had not said a word to him in that elegant parlor where she looked so at home, yet she had never taken her eyes off him either. Was she appalled at his appearance? Had the tailor dressed him too outlandishly for her tastes? Or had she simply hoped never to see him again, no matter what he wore?

He puffed slowly on the cigar and reasoned his way

out of his fears. In the days before he could read, Rio
Jackson had relied on his powers of observation and
memory to get him through. They enabled him to
recall with perfect clarity every trail he had ever taken,
though some he had been on only once. They also
allowed him to take careful note of the people he saw.
Since formulating this outrageous plan, he had been
studying much more than the books he picked up
wherever he could find them. He had also been studying people.

On the four mile walk from his riverfront hotel to
Blayne Haliburton's home, Rio had discreetly eyed
everyone he passed, comparing not only their clothes,
but the way the well-dressed gentlemen walked, tipped
their hats to ladies, halted at a busy intersection. By
the time he reached his destination, he was confident
that he would attract no undue attention.

It was only when he was in her presence that his
confidence faltered. Because then it meant so much.

He had wanted to talk to her alone, but knew he
didn't dare ask. Not yet. Tomorrow, after dinner, perhaps the Haliburtons had a garden and he and Genevieve could sit in the shade of a tree and talk. And
maybe he would be able to tell her all the things he
wanted to.

Then again, maybe he wouldn't be able to say a
thing.

His discussion with Gerrard Bruckner had to remain a secret. Taking another deep pull on the cigar,
Rio forced his thoughts away from Genevieve and
concentrated on the plan he intended to put into motion on Monday morning. Just two more days. And
by the end of the week he would know if he had any
hope of succeeding. If not, he would leave St. Louis,
and Genevieve du Prés, without a farewell.

"Miss Cecilia sent a letter to your mama this morning," Mercy informed Genevieve while the latter sat at her dressing table and allowed her hair to be brushed and then twisted into a knot on the top of her head. "Miss Marie-Claire is gonna be one happy lady when she hears you're safe and sound and coming home."

Mercy did not often slip into the Louisiana patois of her birth. That she did so warned Genevieve that her aunt's lifelong companion was harboring a secret.

"My mother will faint dead away," she said bluntly.

"Oh, no, Miss Cecilia sent the letter by way of Miss Leonore, so she can break the news gently."

Genevieve groaned. Her father's widowed sister was the greatest gossip in New Orleans and was very likely to have half the city turned out for the prodigal's return.

Such a prospect dashed all Genevieve's hopes of a quiet arrival and gradual reentry into society. There was no time in the remaining four days until her departure to prepare herself, let alone Rio, for a grand and very public welcome.

He had amazed as well as puzzled her these past few days. He had joined her and the Haliburtons for dinner Saturday evening, then accompanied them to church Sunday morning. Genevieve wondered how much he knew of the formal rituals of the Catholic church and how much he parroted from those around him. Still, his performance had been flawless. She had to give him credit for that much.

Nor had he overstayed his welcome. He had tried to decline another dinner invitation but Blayne pressured him into acceptance. This time there were other guests, the Haliburtons' daughter Charlotte and her husband Dennis Melrose, who edited one of St. Louis' daily newspapers. If Rio was as nervous as Genevieve, he did not show it. She, on the other hand, dropped her fork twice and could hardly eat a thing.

He gave her an indulgent but slightly mocking

smile. She felt her cheeks turn beet red.

They had only a few minutes alone, on the veranda as he was leaving.

"Are they treating you well?" Rio asked, his voice as serious as his eyes were teasing.

"Yes, they are. You know they are."

She wanted to touch him, run her fingers through his hair, smooth her palms down his naked shoulders and chest. And yet she was afraid, too. Had it all been a dream, the passion they shared, the intimacy, the friendship? Or was this now, this present, the illusion?

"Are you happy here?" he asked, and this time he was serious.

"No, I'm miserable. Where have you been? And why can't you come to tea tomorrow?" She was pouting and acting like a spoiled child again, and she knew it. She didn't care.

He touched her then, stroking a curled index finger down the side of her cheek. She leaned into the caress, hoping for more, for a kiss, but he withdrew. Her only satisfaction lay in the tremor she saw in his hand.

"I told you, querida, I have things to do. We'll talk tomorrow, at dinner."

And then he was gone. Again.

Now, sitting impatiently still while Mercy readied her for her first evening away from the Haliburton house since her arrival, Genevieve wished for the hundredth time she could just have stayed at the cabin forever.

The reflection in the mirror told her, however, that she did not entirely mean that wish. Civilization had its advantages, hot baths, scented soap, and new dresses among them. And the sooner these freckles faded, the better she'd like it.

She turned her head to one side and then the other, taking stock of the reflection. Not once in all the years she had reigned over the balls and cotillions of New Orleans had she ever worried about her appearance. Geneviève Marie du Prés simply took it for granted that no one could compare. Every eligible man — and some not so eligible — had paid her court as though it were due her.

And she had rejected every one of them.

"You look just fine, Miss Genevieve. Nobody will notice the freckles, and if you want this old woman's opinion, I think that bit o' sun did you some good. Put some color in your cheeks."

Genevieve caught Mercy's reflection in the mirror and smiled.

"I am inclined to agree, Mercy. Now, help me into this new dress and I will be on my way."

"That's more like it. No sense going to dinner with a nice young man like Mr. Jackson and putting on a sour face like you've had the past couple days. A man like him wants smiles, and lots of 'em."

Mercy's enthusiasm almost dampened Genevieve's. She hadn't forgotten that air of mystery that seemed to hang around the old woman's every move, every word. It cropped up again in her smile as she walked to the bed and lifted the exquisite gown of pale pink silk.

"Now if Mr. Jackson doesn't ask permission to come calling on you after he sees you in *this*," Mercy said, "then that man doesn't have good eyes in his head. And from the way he's been looking at you, I don't think there's a thing wrong with his eyes."

Genevieve lifted her arms so Mercy could drop the gown over her head.

"Oh, Mercy, I do hope you're right," she whispered into the muffling folds of silk and lace.

Blayne, having a shorter walk from his law offices on Second Street, was waiting at the restaurant when

283

Genevieve and Cecilia arrived in the Haliburton carriage.

"Mr. Jackson isn't here?" the older woman asked while she straightened her plum-colored skirt.

Taking a slip of paper from his coat pocket, Blayne shook his head.

"He sent word to my office that he might be a bit late, depending on the business he was taking care of. Here, Genevieve, this is for you."

She managed not to snatch the folded, sealed piece of paper from him too greedily, but she wasted no time breaking the waxen seal.

"Dear Miss du Prés," he had written in a tidy hand that had lost all traces of hesitation. "I beg your forgiveness in advance if I am tardy this evening. Please be assured that the very instant I have concluded my business this afternoon, I will join you at the appointed place."

"Not bad news, I hope?" Cecilia asked.

Genevieve could only shake her head.

"Well, then, let's go inside. I'm sure Mr. Jackson will be along any minute."

With his usual gallantry, Blayne offered an arm to each of the women, then led the way through the wide doors and into the opulent lobby of St. Louis' grandest restaurant.

Genevieve had hardly the time to take in the crystal chandeliers, the gilt moldings, the heavy velvet draperies, when seemingly from nowhere an entire crowd appeared. Young women in gowns of pink and green, turquoise and lilac all crushed around her, squealing and chattering so that she understood not a single word.

Four or five gentlemen reached out to her, as though they would fight for the privilege of being first to take her hand. She turned from one face to the next, striving to make some sense of the babel of conversation. But everything was happening too fast.

The faces, even those that registered with some familiarity, melted one into another. The bodies pressed closer, and each touch on her arm or shoulder felt like a blow.

Then out of the tumult, a single voice rang clear.

"Give her some air! Can't you see you're smothering her?"

Rio pushed his way through the crowd. A storm of fury darkened his eyes and knit his brows. Genevieve barely had time to breathe his name before she fell limp into his arms. Her last thought was to wonder why he looked so angry.

She had not completely lost consciousness, but came close enough to it that she let herself be lifted into Rio's arms and carried amidst cries of concern to the private room her uncle had engaged for the evening. While several waiters were sent scurrying to find a chaise, Rio continued to hold her.

His "What the hell did you think you were doing?" came through clenched teeth.

"I knew nothing about it!" Genevieve protested in a hoarse whisper.

"It's your birthday!"

"My what?" She blinked and thought for a moment, then said in a somewhat chastened tone, "Oh, yes, so it is. But for heaven's sake, Rio, did you think I would be so vain as to throw a birthday party for myself?"

No, he didn't think that. But arriving at the restaurant to find not the three people he had agreed to meet but a whole throng of strangers, and Genevieve in their midst looking as pale and terrified as she had that night in the Maison de Versailles, he had acted almost without thought at all. And it was just like her to spring a public celebration on him when he was just getting comfortable in his new role.

At least he could not blame her for the splitting headache that had helped shorten his temper. Gerrard Bruckner might be the direct cause, but Rio had undertaken the task willingly and therefore accepted the blame as well. If only Paul's father didn't have such pinched handwriting!

The waiters returned, carrying a gold brocade upholstered chaise, onto which Rio gently deposited his burden. Aware of the dozen or more people jostling behind him, he stepped back from the elegant little lounge. When he addressed the other guests at this disrupted little party, however, he kept his eyes steadfastly on hers.

"I believe she's quite recovered now," he announced. "Just a bit over surprised."

A collective sigh rose from two dozen throats.

"And she's not the only one," he added quietly so only Genevieve could hear.

She also heard a hint of sarcasm in that whisper.

The sarcasm and the disapproval that spawned it, remained with him the rest of the evening. As he mingled with the guests. Rio adroitly steered clear of Genevieve. He watched her, just as she watched him, but even when the dancing started after a sumptuous meal and a huge, three-tiered birthday cake, he avoided her.

"You certainly gave us a scare," Blayne gently scolded his niece when he led her out on the dance floor for a celebratory waltz. "Though I suppose it is partly our own fault."

"It is," Genevieve agreed, not at all ashamed to lay the blame where it belonged.

"But you always loved surprises, and Cecilia thought it would be such a wonderful way for all your friends to welcome you home."

"You could have invited them to the house for a Sunday barbecue."

"But then there'd have been no surprise!"

They made a complete circuit of the tiny dance floor before Blayne spoke again.

"Your Mr. Jackson seemed quite upset at your fainting spell."

Genevieve detected a curious hesitation in her uncle's question and answered cautiously.

"Yes, he was."

"Yet he hasn't paid you much attention since."

So Blayne had noticed. She wondered who else had.

"He hasn't had much chance. You and Aunt Cecilia have hovered over me, and everyone else has seen to it I'm very well taken care of."

Blayne nodded his best courtroom nod but seemed immune to her assurances. Genevieve began to fear her uncle guessed, or at least suspected, the whole truth that lay behind the incomplete sketch she had given him of her adventure.

His next remark came as close to confirming her fears as anything short of a full accusation could.

"Robert and Emmeline Cramer have plans to visit family in New Orleans early next month. Why don't you delay your departure until then and let them escort you? You really shouldn't be travelling in Mr. Jackson's company alone, you know, Genevieve."

She said nothing. No argument, no persuasion, would sway Blayne Haliburton. Aunt Cecilia, for all her bluster, had on occasion displayed some flexibility. Her lawyer husband, who was more conscious of what people thought and said than his wife, never bent at all.

Though her impulse was to defy Blayne's strictures simply because she did not care to be bound by them, Genevieve thought out her reply before speaking and chose each word with utmost care.

"Uncle Blayne, I appreciate your concern. You know I do. But I have been away from home a full year, and I cannot delay returning."

287

The next turn of the dance gave her a full view of the rest of the room, and whatever she said next, she would never remember. For there, in plain sight, stood Rio Jackson, surrounded by five young women whose adoring expressions could not be mistaken. And for the first time since Genevieve saw Rio that evening, he was actually smiling.

Chapter Nineteen

Rio laid the pen down and rubbed his aching eyes. The clock chimed five times to signal the end of his fourth and final day in the employ of Gerrard Bruckner.

"Well, how did I do?" he asked the banker, who sat across the paper-strewn table from him.

Gerrard picked up the piece of paper Rio had been writing on and scanned it with experienced eyes. The gentle nodding of his head while he read indicated more than just approval.

"Not bad. Not bad at all. Your analysis of the railroad situation is a bit different from most I've heard, but it makes perfect sense. Better than the others, to tell the truth."

Rio let out a long sigh of relief, then flexed cramped fingers. At least, he noted with satisfaction, he had learned not to get ink all over himself.

"You realize, of course, you won't be able to walk into a position of any authority without first proving yourself on the job, as it were," the older man cautioned as he pulled a cigar from the rosewood humidor on his desk and offered another to Rio. "But your knowledge of the trail of westward migration and of California especially will be of immense value. I daresay I'd be happy to employ you here, if things don't work out in New Orleans."

Rio declined the cigar and pushed his chair back

to rise and stretch more cramped muscles. Sitting all day in a chair was a hell of a lot harder on a body than riding the same number of hours in the saddle.

"I appreciate the offer, Mr. Bruckner. And thank you, for everything."

With a wave of his hand to indicate the scattered sheets of paper, Gerrard Bruckner smiled and said, "No, Rio, thank you. Your reports on California will repay my 'investment' in you a thousand times over. Besides, the joy you brought my wife when she read the letter from Paul is payment enough. Now, I believe you said there was to be a *bon voyage* dinner at Blayne Haliburton's. You'd best not be late."

Rio consoled himself during the walk from the bank to his hotel and, after bathing and changing into clean clothes, from his hotel to Haliburton's with the knowledge that at least he would not be surprised. Genevieve had demanded and received promises from her aunt and uncle last night that there would be no repetition of Monday's extravagance. Only the Melroses and the Cramers—Emmeline was a cousin to Charlotte—had been invited to this final dinner before Genevieve and Rio departed on the *Henry Dart* in the morning.

He wished he could have kept the party smaller still. Since arriving in St. Louis, he had had less than five minutes alone with Genevieve, and those few occasions had been strained, to say the least. He was beginning to wonder if she preferred it that way, and didn't like the thought. He pushed it out of his mind as he walked up the now-familiar pathway to the Haliburton house.

The Cramers had arrived before him, which drew a mild but silent curse from him as he followed Mercy through the house to the back veranda. Once again, his hopes for speaking privately with Genevieve were dashed.

Then, just before he reached the open french doors that gave onto the porch and the garden beyond, Genevieve entered through those same doors.

He saw her first, while her eyes were still blinded from the outdoor light, and the vision set him back a step.

Breathless with laughter, she halted and held onto the doorframe for support. The white muslin of her dress strained across her breasts with every gasp. Instead of an elaborate coiffure, she wore her hair simply, the sides pulled to the top and fastened with a lavender bow, the rest hanging loose and free down past her waist. A long wiggle of it fell over her left shoulder. Rio could not resist reaching out to lift it and flip it back where it belonged.

In coming that close to her, he could smell the soft, fresh scent of her. No heavy perfumes, just the fragrance of the waxy white gardenia tucked behind her ear. He let his hand linger on the hank of ebony hair for a long, silent moment while she caught her breath. Then, hesitating as though unsure of her reaction, Rio brought his fingers to her cheek, and finally to her chin, to tip her mouth up for a kiss.

She nearly cried out at the touch of his lips on hers. A week of being with him and yet never with him at all had driven her nearly insane with pent-up desire. Now, touching him, tasting him, meeting the questing tip of his tongue with hers, she wanted him even more. And knew she could not have him. Not now. Not here.

With a stifled cry, she turned her head away. She could not even look at him for fear the passion that always smoldered in his eyes would ignite hers beyond extinguishing.

"Viva?" he asked in the softest of whispers. "Are you all right? Is something wrong?"

"No, nothing's wrong," she insisted with a stubborn shake of her head. That long hank of hair fell forward again. This time she did not risk his touch, but tossed it back herself. "Blayne and Aunt Cecilia are on the veranda with Robert and Emmeline. We were wondering where you were."

She did not expect an answer. Every day, she had asked him how he spent his time, but he never told her. Nor did he make any effort to appease her curiosity with lies. "Business," he had told her, as though he expected her to be satisfied with that vague response.

He had clearly spent considerable time — and money — at a tailor's. Each time she saw him, he had some new coat or waistcoat on. This evening, for instance, he wore an elegant dark blue coat over black trousers and the deep wine-red waistcoat he had worn last night to the theatre. She could not fault him for his taste, and the admiring looks he garnered from every woman he passed made it painfully clear that Genevieve du Prés was not the only one who approved of the way his clothes fit his magnificent body.

"Dennis and Charlotte should be here any minute. They are always late, so Aunt Cecilia tells them to be here an hour before the other guests, in hopes they'll be on time, but it rarely works," she went on, fully aware that she was babbling. She wished she could remember what it was Robert had said that made her laugh so hard; forcing a smile when what she wanted was a kiss almost brought tears to her eyes. "There's lemonade on the veranda, unless you want something, uh, stronger."

I want you, he almost told her, but he swallowed the words and said, "Lemonade will be fine. It was a long walk from the hotel."

"A long walk?" she echoed, a tremor in her voice. She glanced again at his clothes, and knew

292

they were expensive. "You didn't—"

"Didn't what?" he asked when she stopped abruptly without finishing her question.

Now, at last, she raised her eyes to his. There was no sadness in them, no emotion at all save a mild curiosity. But then, he had disposed of the mule with no regrets either.

She moistened her lips with her tongue and finally got the words out.

"You didn't sell Cinco, did you, Rio?"

A smile broke through the concerned frown on his face. Again he ran a curled finger under her chin, though this time he did not risk a kiss.

"No, I did not sell Cinco. Or the mare." Before her relief could turn to more questions, he gently took her elbow to guide her through the open doors to the veranda. "But I did walk, and I could use that lemonade."

He was on his third glass of the cold, refreshing beverage before Charlotte and Dennis arrived, and by then nearly a dozen other friends of the Haliburtons had "dropped in" to say farewell and godspeed to Genevieve and the man they clearly considered her new, if more than slightly mysterious, beau. Dinner was delayed again and again, to Rio's increasing discomfort. He had not eaten since noon, and sunset was long past with still no announcement for the evening meal.

An empty stomach did not improve his mood. Though he had, over the past few days, grown somewhat comfortable with Blayne and with Dennis Melrose, Rio disliked Robert Cramer intensely. He disliked Emmeline even more.

She possessed a fresh, youthful prettiness, with her soft, blowzy blonde hair, pert nose, and childish falsetto voice. Behind that image of innocence, however, lurked a devious, selfish brat.

293

Emmeline flirted shamelessly, a trait her husband apparently found endearing. Robert encouraged her, not only by smiling at antics so brazen they threatened to bring a blush to Rio's cheeks, but by urging the object of his wife's attentions to sit beside her.

Emmeline immediately placed her hand on Rio's thigh and fluttered her pale eyelashes at him.

"Tell me again how you killed the bear, Mr. Jackson," she cooed at him.

"Oh, please," Charlotte Melrose protested, her own impatience with Emmeline obvious. "We've heard that story three times this week!"

"But I do love it so!" Emmeline exclaimed with an infantile pout. And a squeeze to Rio's leg.

When Robert added his imprecations, Rio looked to Genevieve for help. But she, as had happened too many times in too few days, had turned away to chat with another guest.

In his world, in the San Antonio saloons, the Sacramento bordellos, the fortified trading posts along the trail, Rio would have gone after her. But this was St. Louis, her world, and he had to play the game by her rules, whether he understood them or not.

While he was telling the story of the bear and the cougar one more time, it actually crossed his mind that both Robert and Viva were in cahoots, trying to foist Emmeline on him. Lord, but he'd be glad to get away from these people! Unless, of course, the folks in New Orleans were even worse. He refused to think about it.

Dinner, delayed two hours, was a dismal affair. Emmeline giggled constantly, and her right hand was more often to be found holding Rio's arm than holding a fork. By the end of the meal Genevieve wanted to scream. How could Rio pay court to that simpering, whining tart? Why had he stayed at Emmeline's side, letting her twine her ankle seductively around his, while Genevieve waited, alone, in the farthest corner of the moonlit garden? Didn't he know she had left the gathering in expectation of his following her? Or did he prefer Emmeline's puerile adulation to the passionate kisses Genevieve ached to lavish upon him?

She shook her head and pushed her untouched dessert away.

"Excuse me," she mumbled, rising unsteadily from the table. "Blayne, Aunt Cecilia, I think I'll retire now."

All the gentlemen rose, but only Rio threw his napkin on the table and walked toward her. A single icy glance halted him before he reached her, and silenced the words on the tip of his tongue.

"Good night, Mr. Jackson. I'll see you in the morning?"

With Mercy's help, Genevieve finished her packing the next day. A single small trunk and one valise were enough to contain the new gowns and accessories Aunt Cecilia had purchased for her, but Genevieve's almost incessant ranting made the packing process take three times as long as it should have.

"He humiliated me!" she wailed as she threw stockings and underthings into the valise. "He sat there and let that woman *pet* him like a lapdog all evening!"

Mercy retrieved the wadded articles and laid them out on the bed for careful folding.

"I believe Mr. Jackson was merely trying to be polite, Miss Genevieve."

Genevieve rounded on the housekeeper.

"How dare you defend him! You saw what he did! It's bad enough I have to travel all the way to New Orleans in his company, unchaperoned, but then to have him slobber over that—that—"

"Watch yourself, Miss Genevieve. Emmeline Cramer is your family."

Genevieve grabbed a stack of neatly rolled stockings and flung them to the floor.

"I don't care if she's my sister," she said with icy, controlled rage. "She's a common slut. And he has no right to ignore me all day long and then worship at her well-tended shrine."

"Miss Genevieve!"

"It's true!"

Mercy moved the valise beyond Genevieve's reach and began rerolling the stockings.

"That may be, but ladies don't talk about other ladies that way, no matter how true the truth be," the black woman cautioned. "Now, if I was you, and I'm glad I ain't, I'd be taking a good long look at that man."

Chastened, and touched by Mercy's concern, Genevieve flopped backwards onto the bed, oblivious to the new green travelling dress she crushed beneath her.

"I would gladly take a good long look at him, if he were ever around," she wished aloud. Overhead the canopy rippled in the cooling breeze that surged through the room. It was still early morning; that breeze would die long before she had boarded the *Henry Dart* and begun the last segment of her journey home. "Where can he possibly spend all his time? Mercy, he doesn't know a soul in St. Louis, except for Paul Bruckner's father, and I know for a fact he took care of his business with the bank almost as soon as we arrived."

Mercy shrugged and began folding lacy chemises.

"He was late the night of that birthday party, too," Genevieve continued. "I tried to tell him it wasn't my fault, that I knew no more about it

296

than he, but he wouldn't listen."

"I heard all about that party. Seems to me you had a pretty good time."

Restless, Genevieve rose from the bed and walked to the dressing table, where she began to pull a brush through her hair.

"What would you have had me do? Walk out in protest, and humiliate everyone?"

She watched Mercy's reflection in the mirror, and once again the black woman shrugged and went on packing.

"Like always, you had a choice," she pointed out. "Maybe you made the wrong one. Maybe you humiliated the wrong person."

Dressed once again in practical, comfortable whipcords, soft linen shirt, and boots, Rio boarded Cinco and the mare in the still cool hours just before dawn. The mare disliked the gentle roll of the deck and had to be coaxed to put all four hooves on it, but Cinco took no notice. When they were settled in their stalls and had given their attention to generous rations of grain, Rio made his way to his modest stateroom.

The *Henry Dart* was primarily a freight-carrying side-wheeler, with only limited passenger facilities, an argument Cecilia Haliburton had used when trying to persuade Genevieve to delay her departure from St. Louis. The Robert Cramers could not change their plans for sailing in June due to Robert's employment as professor of Latin at Washington University, and Cecilia staunchly insisted they would provide the chaperonage essential for Genevieve to retain her reputation.

To give her credit, Rio had to admit Genevieve had stood up to her temporary guardians and gone ahead with the plans Rio had made to take the less elegant *Henry Dart* and leave as soon as possible, Friday morning. He'd have left her for good if she accepted Emmeline Cramer as escort.

If he applauded her actions in that matter, why could he not even begin to understand half the other things she had done in the past week? Like freezing him with that icy glare last night when he wanted so badly to follow her.

Genevieve would not arrive until nine o'clock, half an hour before the *Henry Dart* was due to depart. He would wait until her aunt and uncle and any other well-wishers had left and the boat was underway before he confronted her. He couldn't go all the way to New Orleans without some answers first.

"But what do I say to her?" he mused aloud to the four bare walls. "Lay my heart on a silver platter in front of her and ask her why she put me on display like a caged bear for the past week?"

He recalled with a mild shudder her outrage over his sale of the mule. Was she truly capable of making a pet out of a human being? Did she think she could make him dance like a trained dog and then expect him to beg for favors?

No, he refused to believe that. He had known her too well, too intimately to think her that shallow.

But, warned the voice of reason that had guided him for many more years than he had known Viva du Prés, what did he know of her outside the environment of the wilderness? Did he himself not put on different masks, different attitudes when he changed situations? The Rio Jackson who had postured for the unmarried ladies of St. Louis at Viva's birthday dinner was a far cry from the Rio Jackson who fought his way out of the Maison de Versailles in Sacramento.

"You're thinking too much," he told himself, and

298

then lay down on the bunk to sleep until Genevieve came aboard.

Genevieve spotted Rio waiting on the dock just as the Haliburton carriage came to a halt. She couldn't help sighing with relief. For once she didn't have to go looking for him. And, she admitted freely, she had had her doubts as to whether he'd be there at all.

His appearance brought a silly grin to her face. Gone were the elegant coats, the fancy waistcoats. Once again he was the Rio Jackson she remembered.

"You waited 'til the last minute, I see," he said after greeting Blayne and Cecilia. No one else, he was pleased to note, had come to see Genevieve off.

"You can blame Emmeline Cramer for that," Cecilia explained with clear disgust in her voice.

Rio raised an eyebrow in curiosity, but Cecilia did not come forth with the rest of the tale.

"But we are here at last, and the boat hasn't left," the older woman went on. Then, taking Genevieve's face gently between her gloved hands, Cecilia kissed her niece affectionately on either cheek. "Now, go, child. You go with my blessing, if not my approval, which is more than you got the last time you left my house. And you, Mr. Jackson."

Cecilia gave him a scathing glare that travelled from his wind-ruffled hair to his slightly muddy boots and back again. Genevieve was certain a tirade simmered behind that glare, and if it were anything like the diatribe Cecilia had launched at Emmeline Cramer, the crew and passengers of the *Henry Dart* were in for a theatrical performance.

But Cecilia surprised her. And Rio.

"Take care of her, Mr. Jackson," the older woman said in a subdued voice. "And of yourself."

Blayne's farewell was just as brief, except that he gave his niece a hearty embrace before allowing Cecilia to usher him back to the carriage.

The final whistle blasted the air, sending Rio and Genevieve hurrying up the gangplank just before the crew hauled it in.

They remained at the rail for several long minutes, until the boat was well out into the river. The muddy, spring-swollen water churned beneath them as they watched St. Louis slowly recede. Genevieve waved to Cecilia and Blayne as long as she could see them. When they were finally out of sight, she turned to face Rio.

Her gaze, too, took in every detail of his appearance. She wasn't sure she liked his close-cropped hair, cut to meet the standards of current fashion. She reached up to touch it, surprised to find what had been thick waves were now springier and tighter curls.

But she did like his leaving off the fancy new clothes. As handsome as he had looked, she liked him better this way.

"I missed you," she whispered.

He wasn't exactly sure what she meant, but he welcomed her kiss just the same. While her arms tightened around his neck, he wrapped his around her waist, lifting her to the very tips of her toes. He brought his mouth down gently on hers, well aware of the struggle facing him to keep a long week's worth of desire under control.

"I missed you, too," he replied when she tilted her head back and broke the kiss. "But people are watching us, you know."

A wicked smile turned up the corners of her mouth, inviting another kiss.

"I don't care if the whole world is watching. I haven't kissed you for a whole week, and I intend to start catching up right now."

He splayed one hand at the back of her waist to press her closer. Ah, God, how good it felt, her soft willingness moving instinctively against his arousal. He ached with wanting her, but it was a delicious ache, one he could control now because he knew it would soon be satisfied.

"We have four days," he murmured against her throat. "And four nights."

Questions, recriminations, fears, and anger were all pushed aside as the *Henry Dart* made its steady lazy way down the Mississippi. Rio linked Genevieve's arm through his, then led her without a moment's hesitation to the cabin he had reserved for both of them.

"Are you awake?"

The question floated through a languid haze of exhaustion. Genevieve murmured, "Yes, I think so."

The cabin was dark, and the damp coolness spoke of midnight, or later. Rio wondered what had wakened him, but could recall no sound, no change in the motion of the riverboat. Perhaps it was just the knowledge that this was their last night aboard the *Henry Dart*. By noon they would dock at New Orleans.

Twelve hours, maybe more, maybe less. Genevieve, weary of counting the hours and yet unable not to, slid closer to Rio on the narrow bed. She lay neither on her belly nor on her side, but with her right leg stretched out straight and her left drawn up so her foot rested on his knee, her calf on his thigh. Pillowing her head on Rio's shoulder, she draped her arm across his chest.

"It won't be long now," he said, aware of the tightening of her embrace as he spoke.

301

"Don't," she whispered. "We agreed not to talk about it."

To enforce his promise, she slid over him, twining her legs seductively around his. She lowered her head to take possession of his mouth and found him waiting for her kiss.

How many times had they made love in these past four days? She had lost count. How many different ways had he taught to make love? More than she had ever imagined possible. Yet each time seemed like the first, for the thrill of possessing him, and being possessed by him, never diminished.

She refused to think that each time could be the last.

This time, however, might well be.

She took him into her easily, without haste. All the wild hunger had been satisfied; only this languid desire now remained, a desire to hold him, to love him, to keep him part of her forever.

"Ah, Díos mío, but it is good," Rio sighed as her silken warmth surrounded him. "You are enough to make a man pray the sun never rises again."

He curved his hands around the sides of her breasts, crushed now against his chest. The gentle kneading of pliant flesh sent the slow molten flow of arousal through her veins once more. Rising above him, she gave his thumbs and fingers access to her already tightening nipples, while her lips and tongue teased his into silent submission.

She could not halt the tide of passion. Slowly, in-exorably, it mounted, though she held it back as long as she could. With Rio's hands stroking her back and buttocks until she lay still on him, she tried to calm her racing heart and take full deep breaths of air into her lungs in an effort to savor each and every moment, each and every sensation.

The calluses on his hands, the stubble of beard on

his cheek. The brandy and coffee that flavored his kisses. The heady, clinging fragrance of magnolia and jasmine that drifted on the river air to mingle with the sweat of passion.

The planes of his face under her blind, trembling fingers. The heat of bitter tears behind her eyelids. The strangled cry of loss and fulfillment that burst from her throat when the little death claimed them both in the same instant.

The first light of dawn penetrated the slatted shutters on the single window. Two sated, naked bodies lay motionless on the tangled sheets. As the light slowly grew, and the night sounds gave way to day, the bodies still clung to each other. They did not sleep, but they did not move, and their tears made not a single sound.

The noon sun shimmered behind a thin haze as the *Henry Dart* approached the Canal Street Levee at New Orleans. At the riverboat's rail, the two dozen passengers who had accompanied her load of freight down river waited in lethargic silence. Somewhat apart from the others, Rio and Genevieve watched as the dock drew nearer. Their eyes were dry now, but they could not bear to look at each other.

She wore the yellow dress and had taken the time to pin her hair atop her head. One curl refused to obey her wishes and hung from the otherwise tidy chignon to trail along her shoulder. Rio took it between his fingers and lifted it to his lips.

"It's not the end, Viva," he whispered, though he wasn't sure he believed his own words.

"Then why am I so afraid? Why do I feel as though I'm going to my own execution?"

He laughed and kissed the bare skin at the back of her neck. All the hours he had spent loving her

303

hadn't been enough. He was exhausted from lack of sleep, and the heat sapped what little energy exhaustion hadn't taken, but still he wanted her.

And he knew she wanted him.

"Are you afraid of *them?*" he asked, meaning the people whose lives — and society — she was reentering.

"No," she said firmly, then changed her mind. "Yes. It's as though what didn't matter before suddenly matters now."

"Because of me?"

Finally he straightened, and his eyes demanded a reply from hers.

But her only answer was a look of such confused emotions he could not determine which was strongest: passion, love, fear, or regret. She turned away.

The *Henry Dart* rounded the last bend, bringing the dock into view. The other passengers cheered, glad to be almost at the end of their journey.

The levee was crowded, as usual, with stevedores tending to freight, with carriages waiting for arriving passengers, with merchants and urchins and shoppers. Amongst the throng, Genevieve spotted the blue du Prés landau. It was still too far away for her to make out who was sitting in it, but she was certain that green parasol belonged to her mother.

"Is that them?" Rio asked, following the direction of her steadfast gaze.

"I think so. Yes, I'm sure of it."

A lump rose in her throat, and her heart began to pound with a strange mixture of excitement and apprehension.

"That's Tomás driving. He once let me have the reins and I nearly turned the whole equipage on its side. Yes, and that must be Marcel riding post. He has grown so! He'll be taking the reins from his grandfather one of these days."

304

The steam whistle cut off her next comment, but only for a moment.

"And that's Papa!" she cried. "Oh, Rio, he'll be furious because I took him away from the bank during business hours."

She had threaded her arm through his and squeezed him unconsciously in her excitement. He laid his other hand over hers, waiting, praying.

The *Henry Dart* slowed to a crawl. Deckhands scurried about, ready to toss ropes to the dock to make the boat fast. Their activities distracted Genevieve for a moment, and when she looked back, the people on the levee had grown that much nearer.

"That's Aunt Leonore, Papa's other sister, beside him. Aunt Cecilia wrote to her first. The women on that side of the family are so much more sensible than on Mama's. Poor Mama would have been prostrate for a week if Aunt Cecilia had told her directly."

A twinge of guilt silenced her, as she thought of what her departure a year ago must have done to Marie-Claire du Prés. There would be many long and tearful apologies, on both sides.

"Someone else is in the carriage, sitting next to Mama, but I can't see who it is," she observed, standing on tiptoe to get a better look.

While she watched, the postboy jumped down from his perch and set the step for the ladies to alight from the landau. First Leonore, in the lavender and grey of old mourning, descended, followed by her brother. The riverboat's prow nudged the dock with a slight bump.

Victor du Prés then turned to take his wife's hand and assist her. Rio noted two things in the gesture: Victor was clearly impatient, as though eager to get this family business over and return to his precious bank; and that Genevieve's mother leaned heavily on

305

her husband. She clutched the parasol in one hand, with the other dabbed continually at her nose and eyes.

Finally the fourth person descended. There was no need to recognize his face or his form. The gold-headed walking stick that preceded him identified Jean-Louis Marmont beyond a doubt.

Chapter Twenty

A wave of dizziness washed over Genevieve as she watched Jean-Louis walk toward her. She gripped Rio's arm and would have slumped in a dead faint if he had not supported her and whispered reassuringly to her.

"It's all right, Viva. I'm here. I won't let him hurt you."

It was a nightmare, worse than anything she could ever have imagined. And from the smug look of triumph on his face, Jean-Louis was well aware of her reaction.

"What do I do?" she asked Rio, unable to keep the panic from entering her voice. "My God, he can't think I'll ride in the same carriage with him, can he?"

"I'm sure he does," came Rio's bitter reply. He was having difficulty keeping his own emotions under control. If Genevieve was terrified of the man with the ivory cane, Rio simply hated him. They had a score to settle, and Rio could almost thank Jean-Louis for giving him the opportunity.

Revenge, however, demanded cool thought. Rio tamped down the rage and concentrated on reason.

"Does the offer to stay with you still stand?" he asked.

Genevieve breathed a sigh of relief, though she did not ease up her death grip on Rio's arm.

"Yes, of course! Even if that weren't Jean-Louis, the offer would be open. Dear God, Rio, what can he be thinking? That I'd still agree to marry him, after what he did?"

But she knew the answer to that question. Jean-Louis had had months to perfect a tale that would be accepted as gospel by now. He would have told it over and over and over, until no one would doubt but that it was the truth. He had probably made himself believe it as well, like the lie about his limp.

But what was the tale he had told to explain his reappearance? She had no idea, and the fact that she could not combat what she did not know filled her with more fear. What lies might he have told about her? Or about Rio?

"Don't try to second-guess him," Rio warned, as though he had read her very thoughts. "You can't. He's crazy, and the minds of crazy people don't work like ours, so we can't even begin to understand them. It's a waste of time to try."

"But we can't just do nothing."

"No, and we won't."

An insane idea came to her, a lie as great as any Jean-Louis could ever have told.

"We could tell him we're married," she suggested. "He couldn't do anything to us then."

Rio drew in a deep breath, partly in surprise, partly to collect the thoughts scattered at her announcement. How many minutes remained until they would have to join the people who had come to meet them? Ten at the most. Not nearly enough time.

But he would take the time to tell her this much.

He raised her hand to his lips and kissed her palm gently, revelling in the feel of her fingers curving to cup his chin.

"No, Viva, we can't lie to them. I think I'd sell my soul to have you for my wife, corazón de mi cor-

308

azón," he murmured, "but not as a lie. Let him lie, and be caught in his own web." He kissed her hand again, this time never taking his eyes from hers.

Then, with a final reassuring squeeze of her hand, he released her.

"Now, you run into your mama's arms and hug her and cry, and I'll introduce myself to your father as best I can."

Her first steps were hesitant as she edged away from him down the slanted gangplank from the deck of the *Henry Dart* to the dock. Twenty feet away, the two men and two women who had come to greet the returning prodigal halted, and that was when Genevieve threw her arms wide and ran.

Rio watched her, wondering if he had done the right thing. For a few moments, she would be beyond his protection, except for the revolver he still wore at his hip. He flipped back the edge of his new coat and rested his hand on the familiar grip of the Colt. It was a gesture intended for Jean-Louis to see, and Rio had no doubt the Frenchman took note.

Satisfied that he had made his meaning clear, Rio strolled down the gangplank himself to join the others.

Though Rio would have preferred to sit in the open landau with Genevieve, Cinco was too rambunctious to allow Marcel to ride the stallion. The boy instead took charge of the mare, riding bareback just behind the lavishly appointed vehicle. The palomino pranced impatiently beside it.

Genevieve, animated as always when excited, seemed unable to stop talking for more than a breath at a time. Rio wondered how much of her ebullience was genuine, and how much was forced for Jean-Louis' benefit.

"And so, Papa, you simply must not allow Mr.

Jackson to take a room in some dingy hotel," she pressured her father. Seated between her parents, she held tightly to their hands, squeezing for emphasis. "You must *insist* that he be our guest for as long as his business keeps him in New Orleans. You cannot imagine how wonderful he has been to me, getting me through the mountains in the dead of winter. The same mountains, did you know? where that tragic party suffered so terribly a few years ago."

Rio had to admire her. She was playing her part as though her very life depended upon it.

Perhaps it did.

He also had to give Jean-Louis credit for telling a lie so simple no one would fail to believe it. Instead of concocting an elaborate fabrication, the French-man claimed never to have seen Genevieve since the day he left New Orleans. Of the Maison de Versailles and Buster Kulkey, he had said nothing. They might never have existed.

Yet he tossed a glance at Rio that proved the lie, and at the same time dared the interloper to challenge it with the truth.

Rio ignored the challenge, and let Genevieve rattle on. His instructions to her had been to keep anyone from asking her too many questions, and her incessant babbling was doing just that. She even managed to make the oft-told tale of the cougar and the bear fresh. Rio was relieved that this time she was telling the story, not he.

Old Tomás held the matched chestnuts to a sedate walk down Canal Street, which left Rio busy with a palomino stud who wanted to run. The stallion's antics, combined with his majestic appearance, drew the attention of pedestrians and riders alike along the wide boulevard and then down the quiet side streets.

Rio would have preferred anonymity.

He would also have preferred that the du Prés

home be something less than a palace.

Recalling the spacious adobe compound where he had spent his youth, he knew Lawrence Jackson's San Antonio house was but a cottage in comparison to the mansion Victor du Prés had built on Third Street in what Genevieve explained was called New Orleans' Garden District.

The two and a half story edifice reigned over a full city block of lawns and gardens, trees and arbors, fences and hedges. Each room of the upper floors was graced with a balcony of black ironwork that contrasted to the white-washed stucco walls not at all unlike the black lace on a harlot's white chemise. Rio dropped behind the landau as it wove up the curved driveway beneath the moss-draped branches of ancient oaks. The house was seductive, almost compelling, but the streamers of moss, the garlands of vines that climbed the walls reminded him too strongly of a spider's web.

He felt a sense of not belonging creep upon him like a fog from the swamps that surrounded New Orleans.

That feeling intensified when, after leaving Cinco in Marcel's care, Rio followed Genevieve into the house.

In the vastness of the Sierra Nevada, under the unlimited sky, he had never felt so insignificant. Here, the gaudy decor, the ostentatious embellishment with gold and marble and elaborately carved wood, crowded in on him. Though the immense foyer, with its grey and white marble tiles, was light and airy, Rio experienced a sensation of imprisonment he had never known in the tiny confines of Ernest Tibler's cabin.

Genevieve, too, paused just inside the wide double doors.

"It's so good to be home," she whispered.

Then why, she wondered a moment later when she

311

followed her mother and father and aunt into one of the parlors, do I want so badly to run away again?

Genevieve displayed absolutely no emotion when her mother assigned Rio to the most insignificant of the second floor guest rooms. She was simply glad Marie-Claire had not thrown up a wall of propriety and insisted her daughter's lover move into a hotel. That Marie-Claire had guessed at least part of the truth Genevieve did not doubt.

She wondered just how much information Aunt Cecilia had imparted to Aunt Leonore.

The room was still palatial, by the standards of some of the places Rio no doubt had lived. A massive mahogany wardrobe occupied one wall; a desk in the same elaborately carved style sat under one of the two tall windows overlooking the back gardens. Dominating the room, however, was the enormous four-poster bed, its canopy a full ten feet above the floor. The voluminous mosquito net billowed in the breeze like a specter's winding sheet.

"Fit for a Medici," Rio commented with a lift of a rather disdainful eyebrow.

Genevieve remembered he had had no great love for Machiavelli's vaunted Florentines.

She responded with an understanding wink and said, "I'm so glad you like it, Mr. Jackson. You'll have a view of the stable area," she added as he walked to the window to pull aside the velvet drapery and look out. "I'm sure you'll want to refresh yourself, so Claude will bring you a hot bath immediately, and then we'll have luncheon in the garden."

He had no time to reply before Claude arrived with tub and hot water.

Genevieve discreetly ducked out of the room on her mother's heels.

"Wherever did you find him?" Marie-Claire whispered as soon as the door was closed and they had walked far enough down the hall to be out of his hearing.

"Mr. Jackson?" Genevieve innocently asked. "I told you, Mama, he was on the wagon train I took to Sacramento. Why?"

Marie-Claire halted at the top of the white marble staircase and faced her daughter with a very stern expression.

"This family has endured five scandals in the past year. I do not think it will stand another," she warned. "Your gratitude toward this person had best not exceed what is right and proper for a young woman of your station."

Genevieve stiffened.

"Do you not approve of Rio, Mama?" she asked. "Is he less acceptable than, say, Jean-Louis?" She longed to tell the truth, all of it, but held back.

Her mother's face reddened slightly, but Marie-Claire continued without a stumble, "Jean-Louis behaved foolishly, but he still has much to recommend him. Your behavior, on the other hand, may not be so easily forgiven."

A cold, hard weight settled in the pit of Genevieve's stomach. She understood exactly what was left unsaid: a resumption of the engagement between herself and Jean-Louis would go a long way to repairing the damage to their individual reputations and the family's. No doubt Jean-Louis had made the proposal the instant he learned of Genevieve's survival.

She wondered if he were disappointed.

Putting on a smile to cover her fears, she gave her mother a spontaneous hug and said, "Oh, Mama, I am only just come home. Please, let us not quarrel so soon."

She then skipped merrily off to her own room, where a bath already waited.

The temptation to soak away a thousand fears was

313

great, but Genevieve was too nervous, too full of frightened energy to lounge in the steaming, jasmine scented water the way she used to do. Nor did she like being parted from Rio for even a few minutes. She would bathe and dress as quickly as possible, then rejoin him. Apart, they were vulnerable. Together, they were invincible.

Celine, who had been her personal maid almost as long as Genevieve could remember, helped her out of the yellow dress, petticoats, corset and chemise. Genevieve immediately stepped into the tub and sank beneath the mound of bubbles.

"So you done decided to come back," the soft-spoken Celine said while gathering soap and wash rag to hand to her mistress. "And with a man yet."

"Gossip travels quickly in this house," Genevieve observed with a smile.

"Oh, it does, 'specially when it's man-woman gossip."

Genevieve lathered the cloth quickly, eager to be clean after four days aboard the riverboat.

"And what else does the gossip say now that I've been home almost half an hour?"

Celine chuckled and poured a pitcher of warm water over Genevieve's back-tilted head to wet the mass of blue-black curls.

"The gossip say that man you brought with you, he be a *real* man. Gonna open some eyes around this town. Make a few hearts skip a couple beats maybe."

Genevieve scrubbed her arms and neck while Celine lathered her hair. If the maid noticed the blush that rose to Genevieve's cheeks, she said nothing.

"I have a feeling you're not telling me everything."

Again Celine laughed, and there were secrets in that laugh.

"Gossip say maybe you know just how much a man that man be."

And with that, Celine gently pushed Genevieve's head beneath the water to rinse the soap from her hair.

If Celine had more gossip to relate, she kept it to herself. Genevieve finished washing, then stood to have a final pitcher of cool water poured over her to erase the last of the soap. The maid first wrapped the long hair in one towel, then handed another for Genevieve to wind around her body before she stepped from the tub.

The trunk containing her clothes from St. Louis still stood in the middle of the room, unpacked as yet, but Genevieve ignored it to walk to the wardrobe where she had left so many beautiful clothes over a year ago. A quick inspection produced a quiet gasp, for there, in with the gowns abandoned when she fled to California were those she had taken with her—and been forced to leave behind in Sacramento.

She whirled to face Celine.

"Where did these come from?" she demanded. "How could Jean-Louis say he never saw me if he brought these back with him?"

The black woman cocked her head to one side, her brows knit in obvious confusion. She wrung out the wash rag and picked up the extra towels before walking to join Genevieve at the wardrobe.

"Mister Jean-Louis brought nothing with him. Long before he came back, the trunks they came alone. Miss Marie-Claire told me to put everything away, just like you were expected any day now. But somebody took that pretty blue satin. Everything else was there, 'cept the blue satin."

Genevieve slumped onto a small white brocade upholstered chair. It wasn't Rio Jackson who caused her heart to skip a beat this time, it was simple fear. She wondered if she would ever be free of it.

"Paul Bruckner must have sent it," she mused aloud. "Celine, when did the trunks arrive?

Do you know if a letter came with them?"

The maid shook her head.

"I only know what Miss Marie-Claire told me."

"What about the gossip? Did it have nothing to say about two trunks arriving here from California without me?"

Again Celine raised her shoulders in a gesture of futility.

"The trunks didn't come here, to the house. They come to the bank. Mister Victor, he brought them home in the middle of the day. Stayed home two days from the bank, too. Maybe a letter come, but I don't know."

If Jean-Louis had not brought them himself, Genevieve was certain Paul Bruckner had sent the trunks on the first available ship back to New Orleans. It was possible, therefore, that he had also unwittingly sent her the tool she needed to pry the truth from her former fiancé.

Her momentary shock conquered, she got to her feet and went back to the wardrobe to select a gown for the afternoon. After deciding on one of her old favorites, a pale pink muslin with tiny satin roses at the waist and shoulders, Genevieve began to fire more questions at Celine.

"Does Mama know the blue satin dress is missing?"

Shaking her head, Celine answered, "No one knows, just me."

"Good. As soon as I've gone down to lunch, I want you to take a note to Madame Savriere, the dressmaker. I want an exact duplicate of that gown. And no one, not even the gossip, is to know about this one."

Catching the spirit of conspiracy, Celine dropped the pink dress over her mistress' head.

"Not a soul, Miss Genevieve," Celine agreed with a smile.

Despite her haste, Genevieve did not arrive in the garden as quickly as she wanted. Rio was already ensconced in a comfortable rocker, taking what comfort there was to be had in the shade of the rose arbor. Little breeze entered the bower, but at this time of day the air hung almost perfectly still anyway. Bees hummed overhead, drawn by the thousands of red blossoms. And pervading all, the cloying fragrance of the flowers. Not only the roses, but the last of the magnolias, crepe-myrtle, jasmine, and the potent gardenia lent their perfume to the sultry afternoon.

Rio had also availed himself of a tall cool drink. He stood at her entrance and gallantly took her hand to lead her to a chair beside his own. Aware of her parents' disapproving scrutiny, she flashed him a flirtatious smile.

He shot back a warning glance that she did not understand. With enough other puzzles demanding solutions, Genevieve ignored the questions raised by Rio's caution.

"Where is Jean-Louis?" she asked boldly as she sat down and gracefully spread her skirt. "I expected him to join us."

"He had a meeting with his attorney," Victor du Prés answered. "Lemonade?"

She nodded and took the glass he filled for her.

"Is he in some legal difficulty?"

That question earned her a rivetting glare from her mother, but again it was her father who supplied the response.

"Quite the contrary."

Victor leaned back in his chair and took a long pull at his julep. Like his daughter, he was dark-haired and blue-eyed, but virtually all resemblance ended there. Tall and portly, he moved methodically,

317

an indication that he had rarely done anything impulsive in his entire life. And when he had, he immediately regretted it.

"Jean-Louis stands to become a very wealthy young man. The money his father embezzled was put into some extremely unsound investments, as you know. When Etienne, uh, died, he left a will giving me, the surviving partner, ownership of all those investments." Victor coughed discreetly, as though speaking of money was somehow impolite, especially in the presence of a stranger. "Most of the investments were, of course, quite worthless. A few, however, proved successful."

"Enough to pay back everything Etienne stole?"

Again Victor coughed.

"Yes, with considerable profit left over. When Jean-Louis returned several months ago, I felt it only fair to return his father's portion to him. After all, he would have inherited."

Genevieve sipped her lemonade thoughtfully. This must have been part of what her mother meant by Jean-Louis' other recommendations. No doubt the bank had suffered severe reversals following the scandal of Etienne's embezzlement—and Victor's abortive attempt to recoup. The windfall success of Etienne's investments would probably have allowed Victor to continue operating the bank and taking a lucrative salary from it. To have to share with Jean-Louis might mean the end of the Louisiana Commercial Bank.

The question burning on the end of Genevieve's tongue was beyond even her audacity, at least as long as Rio was present. She was saved having to find a circuitous way of asking by the timely announcement that luncheon was served. She was famished, and curiosity could wait until hunger had been satisfied.

She expected to claim Rio's company, but to her

surprise, he offered his arm to Marie-Claire, and let her lead the way to the buffet that had been laid out in another part of the garden.

"So, you are from Texas, Mr. Jackson?" the older woman asked.

He sensed the first tiny crack in the wall of animosity. Marie-Claire du Prés would not be as easy a conquest as her sister-in-law Cecilia, but Marie-Claire was still a woman. Rio knew few of them who were not susceptible to flattery, and the attention of a man.

"San Antonio, as a matter of fact," he replied.

"And from San Antonio you went to California, and now all the way to New Orleans. What brings you here?"

What might have been meant as serious interrogation had slipped into innocuous polite conversation. She even went so far as to smile up at him, and blush.

"Business. Investments."

Marie-Claire paused just long enough to give him a quizzical look that spoke volumes of disbelief, but her smile remained.

Rio took advantage of it.

"As a matter of fact, I must beg your indulgence, as I have an appointment this afternoon with a party of prospective investors."

He wished he could turn and see Genevieve's response to this announcement, but to do so would give away too much. From the sound of it, she was deep in conversation with her father. Though Rio wanted to listen, he concentrated instead on his conquest of Marie-Claire.

The arrangement of places at the intimate table for four in the shade of one of those moss-shrouded oaks suited his designs perfectly. He held the older woman's chair for her, then took the place beside her—and across from Genevieve.

319

He was taking his first spoonful of spicy shrimp etouffé when he felt a small foot reach out to graze his ankle. He could not even hazard a discreet glance to verify that it was indeed Genevieve's caress, nor did he dare return it, for fear that little foot belonged to someone else. Hating the necessity for his own subterfuge, Rio ignored the gentle rubbing.

Marie-Claire resumed the conversation almost immediately after the first dish was served. "Perhaps Victor might be of some assistance to you, Mr. Jackson," she suggested. Then, by way of explanation, she added, "Mr. Jackson is in New Orleans looking for investors, Victor."

Rio nearly choked.

"I could not dream of imposing on your hospitality," he managed to say without an audible tremor in his voice. His assumptions about the du Prés bank appeared correct, which was all the more reason for his steering clear. "And certainly not so soon after you have just welcomed your daughter home after a long absence."

That seemed to give Marie-Claire something to think about. She ate without paying much attention to the food, as though lost in thought. Her expression was much the same as Genevieve's, brows knit, lips pursed, except that the daughter's eyes were narrowed, and their gaze focused across the table rather than at some nebulous point in space.

Genevieve was frightened, and confused, and there was little he could do right now to allay her fears or dispel her confusion. To divulge the details of his plans would be to destroy their purpose; the last thing he wanted was her help, or even her father's. The unexpected presence of Jean-Louis posed a threat, yes, but also a challenge. Rio knew he had to emerge victorious in both contests, not just one. In that respect this latest was different from any other challenge he had faced: life was an all or nothing proposition.

After a few moments of silence, it was Genevieve who picked up the conversation with questions about friends and neighbors and relatives. There was a hesitancy in her tone that Rio detected immediately, and when he caught her puzzled glance, he did not smile but merely nodded his approval. The intensity of her excitement returned.

"So Aurore LeBecque married a sugar planter and moved to the Cane River. Who would ever have guessed!"

"And she is the mother of twins," Marie-Claire added.

Leaning her elbows on the table drew a horrified expression from her mother, but Genevieve ignored the silent scolding to continue her questions.

"What of Rémy Montague? Did his father pay his debts, or was Rémy forced to sell his property?"

Marie-Claire nervously toyed with her napkin while answering.

"Rémy Montague was a rogue of the very worst type," she said without looking up from the square of linen on her lap. "He sold the quadroon girl who was his mistress to a Red River plantation owner they say that abolitionist woman wrote that awful book about."

"But surely that wasn't enough to pay what he owed."

Victor leaned over to touch his daughter's arm and said quietly, "Rémy's body was found three weeks ago in Lake Pontchartrain."

Genevieve's face paled.

"Rémy's dead?" she whispered in disbelief. "But Rémy would never take his own life. Never."

She understood the truth when Marie-Claire finally picked up the napkin and dabbed at one eye.

"Murdered?" The very word stuck on Genevieve's

321

tongue. She shook her head slowly, trying to deny the truth.

"His Aunt Clothilde died last spring and left him everything. He was a very wealthy man, who refused to pay his gambling debts. Someone," Victor said with a telling shrug, "collected what was due."

The tale of Rémy Montague plagued Rio the rest of the day. Ignoring the suffocating afternoon heat, he saddled Cinco and rode the worst of the stallion's fractiousness off, but his own remained. The narrow streets closed in by buildings on all sides, the heavy, musty air, the sense almost of stagnation made him long for the freedom of the wilderness.

He made his stops at the banks to deliver the letters Gerrard Bruckner had written on his behalf. At the Plaquemines Bank on Royal Street, he spoke briefly with the president, a voluble Creole named Antoine LeFevre, who, it turned out, was an admirer of fine horseflesh. Antoine took an instant fancy to Cinco and would probably have made an outrageous offer to buy the stallion had he not been called to a meeting.

With his business completed, Rio turned Cinco back in the direction of the du Prés home. He took a long, circuitous route, partly to familiarize himself with New Orleans and partly to delay his return to that magnificent monstrosity on Third Street.

He rode through the narrow streets of the Vieux Carré, fascinated by its beauty and its decadence. Several young beauties waved to him from their wrought-iron balconies, but Rio never knew which were pampered, protected Creole daughters and which were prostitutes soliciting the evening's business.

A single clap of thunder was all the warning he received before a sudden downpour struck. He quickly dismounted and took shelter under one of those overhanging balconies while the rain came down in solid sheets. Across the street was a tiny, dark tavern, but even that short distance would mean a drenching. If this storm were like the others he had witnessed, Rio knew the sun would be out in just a few minutes.

He could barely see through the curtain of teeming rain, but a movement in the open tavern door caught his eye. A man had stepped out just far enough to whistle shrilly, then ducked back inside. A carriage pulled up a moment later, the black driver huddled under an inadequate umbrella. The man from the tavern swore so loudly the oath carried through the rain to Rio. The voice struck a familiar note, and Rio strained to watch as the man dashed from the tavern door to the carriage and jumped inside.

Anywhere else, he would have dismissed the familiarity as coincidence brought on by nerves stretched too tight. But having already seen Jean-Louis Marmont, Rio was unwilling to dismiss the resemblance between the tavern patron and a Sacramento bully by the name of Buster Kulkey.

Ten anxious minutes later, the rain stopped as abruptly as it had begun. Rio waited only long enough for Cinco to shake like a wet dog, then he swung into the saddle with no regard for his very wet seat. His route to the du Prés mansion was direct this time.

Chapter Twenty-one

On Sunday morning, after walking back from Mass, Genevieve tried to excuse herself from a conference with her mother, but Marie-Claire deftly herded her into the small parlor. She had known this meeting must take place, especially after the ball they had attended at Régine Roffignac's Vieux Carré mansion last night.

"But, my dear, we simply *must* have a party," Marie-Claire insisted, continuing the discussion begun on the way home from Régine's in the pale light of dawn. "People have already been asking me when it will be; they expect it, under the circumstances."

She took a seat on the settee and invited Genevieve to sit beside her. Genevieve, exhausted after a night of partying, feared she would fall asleep the instant she sat down. She shook her head and chose to remain standing, leaning wearily against the doorframe.

"Rio doesn't like parties," she said. "I told you what happened when Aunt Cecilia surprised me for my birthday."

Marie-Claire waved her hand in dismissal.

"Nonsense. That was because *he* was surprised, and newly arrived. He has had almost a whole week now to meet our friends, and we will give him plenty of 'warning,' if you will, of our intentions."

"If," Genevieve said with a grimace, "he stays around long enough for us to give him the warning."

He had done the same thing in St. Louis, disappearing for nearly the entire day and giving her no explanation, or at most a cryptic single word: "Business." Each time she asked him, he deftly steered the conversation in another direction, or simply walked away.

Marie-Claire, however, was quick to defend him.

"Mr. Jackson is a very busy man, Genevieve. He did not come to New Orleans on holiday; he came to conduct business."

He had obviously won her over completely. Genevieve was about to point this out to her mother, but Victor's entrance prevented her saying something she would probably regret.

Rather than spend the rest of the morning in sullen silence while her mother sang Rio's praises, Genevieve sought to escape to her room and perhaps catch up on some of the sleep she had lost to last night's ball. But when she turned to leave the parlor, she found Rio himself blocking her way.

It was no wonder nearly every woman in the Cathedral had stumbled over her prayers this morning. Fashionable clothes, a rakish haircut that left a single errant curl forever drooping over his forehead, and a special, indefinable sense of mystery made Rio Jackson irresistible. Halted in mid-flight, Genevieve herself could not keep from staring at him, and the old fire began to sizzle once more in her veins.

"Did you want something?" he asked when she stood still for a very long time.

"Did I want something?" she stammered. "No, nothing."

It was a lie, because she knew very well she wanted something. Explanations, answers, to begin with. And she wanted him. Wanted him so badly she had to clasp her hands together to keep from touching him.

Then, before she was even aware of it, he had taken her by the arm and was leading her through the house, to the back door that gave onto the veranda and then down the steps, into the garden where the only sound was the incessant drone of the bees—and the pounding of her own heart.

For a brief instant, their eyes met, hungry and questioning. When that hunger became unendurable, Rio cupped her face in trembling hands and held it still so he could lower his mouth to hers.

What was intended to be only a reassuring kiss quickly went far beyond. As lips parted and tongues twined sinuously, bodies strained to achieve the intimacy denied by layers of clothing. Genevieve slid her arms under Rio's coat to wrap around his waist and pull him to her, but that was not enough. The swell of his arousal throbbed against her belly, starting a liquefying heat in her own loins. Her fingers ached to touch him, to caress his passion-fevered skin, to stroke the hard, satiny flesh of his desire until he cried out and possessed her completely.

Gasping for breath, she threw her head back to escape his demanding mouth.

"Stop it, Rio," she begged, knowing her body betrayed her plea. "Not here, not now." And if he had insisted and pushed her to the dew-damp grass, she would not have fought him, so strong was her need of him.

His lips were at her throat, then his teeth nipped at the taut skin.

"When?" he asked. "Where?"

She could not think, could hardly breathe. He had moved his hands down her neck to her shoulders and now was smoothing them over her breasts. So well remembered were those skillful hands that she could almost feel the calluses through her clothes. Her nipples hardened to such a sensitivity that the friction against her chemise brought sparkling pain.

"When?" Rio repeated, his low husky voice demanding an answer.

She pulled deep breaths of air into her lungs in an effort to regain control. Slowly, in gradually receding waves, the passion ebbed, until Genevieve was able to push herself free of Rio's relaxed embrace. Still unnerved by the power of her desire for him, she turned her back and walked several steps away. Only then, when he was beyond her reach, could she face him.

"Never," she said, pain and unshed tears in her voice.

"Never? What do you mean?"

She put out a hand to stop his approach, a hand that trembled and seemed more to be seeking than denying.

"No, Rio, don't come any closer. I can't stand this any more."

"Can't stand what?" he asked, taking one more step toward her.

Her lower lip quivered. She tossed her head back to contain the tears, and for a while at least she was successful. Then it was she who closed the distance between them, with three determined strides.

"Don't play so innocent with me, Rio Jackson," she hissed. There, anger was replacing the other emotions, and anger she could control for her own purposes. Passion, or whatever that fire was that flared between them, always took on a life of its own. "I don't know what you're up to, but I refuse to be a part of it."

"What in hell are you talking about, Viva? You aren't making any sense at all."

"Where were you Friday? And Thursday? And Wednesday?"

Her blue eyes skewered him. He turned away from that dagger gaze, knowing it would see right through his lie.

"I told you, I had business to tend to."

Hands on her hips, she walked around him until he had to look at her.

"And just what kind of 'business' can a man have who's never had any 'business' of any kind before? And in a city where he knows no one?"

Tell me the truth, she begged silently, unaware that despite her anger, tears dripped steadily down her cheeks.

He wanted to tell her, but knew he couldn't. Not yet. In another week, two at the most, when he was sure of his position with LeFevre's bank, then he would break the news to her. To tell her now, before the victory was in his grasp, would only make her want to take a hand in it, and this was something he had to do on his own.

But he had to tell her something.

"It's Cinco," he said casually. "I've been looking for breeders with good mares. He's never been bred to blooded stock, and I thought—"

"Liar!"

She was shaking with fury, and breaking into little pieces at his easy betrayal. There was no holding back the tears now, or the painful sobs that racked her body. She wanted to run, but her knees felt as if they would give out at the first step.

And when he made no defense, she knew her accusation was correct.

"I don't know where you go every day, but I know it doesn't have anything to do with Cinco. You never bring anyone here to see him, and I think that's the first thing a breeder would want to do, is see this stud you're trying to sell."

Each word was like a knife, cutting pieces from her soul, but she could not stop them any more than she could stop the tears.

"And last night, at Regine Roffignac's, for half an hour you talked to Arthur Montgomery, one of the foremost authorities on horses in Louisiana, and not once did you mention your palomino stallion. *Not once!*"

"How did you know that?"

"Because I watched you," she answered. Her voice was but a shrill whisper, not the scream she wanted to hurl at him. Screams would bring others to the garden, and how was she, Genevieve Marie du Prés, who had scorned nobility, to explain her tears over a half-breed Mexican? "I watched you all night, Rio. And you never so much as glanced my way. You never asked me to dance, not once. And after the way you've ignored me all week, you can't imagine how badly I wanted to be held in your arms, even if only for a few minutes on a crowded dance floor. A dance, Rio, that's all I wanted."

Still he said nothing, neither in the way of defense nor explanation. Through tear-blurred eyes, she saw the cold bitterness come over his features that she had not seen since those first days out of Sacramento. He had hated her then; she wondered if he had ever stopped.

With eyes closed against the unstoppable torrent of tears, she swallowed the last of her pride.

"You thought you could drag me off to the garden and beg me to make love with you, like a common whore, but you wouldn't give me the honor of

329

a dance. *That's* what I can't take anymore, Rio."

She refused even the handkerchief he held out to her. Making her way through the maze of the garden, she disappeared without another word, without a backward glance.

Rio threw the square of neatly folded linen to the ground with a growl of helpless rage.

True tragedy, he had learned from Shakespeare, contains a kernel of irony.

He had not wanted to go to the ball last night. He had, in fact, made repeated excuses, not the least of which was that he knew no one and that he was exhausted. He had hoped Genevieve would take the hint, but instead she had pressured him to accept her mother's invitation.

It might have made a difference if he had reminded Genevieve, while she hurled her accusations at him, that she was far from blameless. She claimed to have watched him all night, but how was that possible, when she spent nearly the entire evening on the dance floor, being whirled in someone else's arms? Or, when she wasn't dancing, she was surrounded by a swarm of admirers, to whom she granted countless smiles.

And Rio could do nothing about it. Had he been introduced as her lover, he might have had some claim on her attention. Propriety, however, required that he play the role of the kind stranger who had guided her safely home. Yet even a businessman should have had the right to claim a dance. He could not fault her logic on that point.

The problem was, Rio Jackson didn't know how to dance.

A poultice of crushed cucumbers and cream relieved most of the swelling around Genevieve's eyes, and a long afternoon nap in a dim, quiet bedroom restored her calm. Nothing, however, could take away the pain of Rio's desertion.

That evening she allowed Celine to dress her in another of her favorite gowns, this of blue silk with flounces at the neck and hem of heavy white Belgian lace. After pinning Genevieve's hair into an elaborate confection of curls and tendrils, the maid festooned it with tiny blue silk bows and freshly cut delphiniums the exact shade of Genevieve's eyes.

"You just pull that neckline a mite lower, and not a man at that party will be able to take his eyes off you," Celine said, looking over Genevieve's shoulder into the cheval glass.

But Genevieve did not pull the neckline lower, nor even slip the lacy sleeves off her shoulders.

She rode in the carriage silently, paying more attention to the steady drum of rain on the roof than to the conversation between her father and Rio. She caught the words "railroad," "telegraph," and "California," all mentioned rather frequently, but they had no meaning out of context.

Obviously Rio preferred to talk business with Victor du Prés than converse with her. She swallowed the beginning of a lump in her throat. There would be no repeat of this morning's tears.

The soiree to which they had been invited was to be a small affair, unlike the ball of the previous night. The Champleur family were welcoming home their youngest son, Armand, from a year-long tour of Europe. Genevieve remembered him as a brash youth, too aware of his good looks, who had once stolen a kiss from her.

"My goodness," Marie-Claire exclaimed as the du Prés carriage pulled up behind a rather long line of vehicles in front of the Champleur mansion in the

Vieux Carré. "If this is Marguerite Champleur's idea of a 'small gathering of intimate friends,' I should hate to see what she considers a large party!"

Genevieve glanced first at her mother, but Marie-Claire's attention was directed out the window. The tone of the older woman's voice, however, clearly hinted at surprise and puzzlement. When Genevieve hazarded a cautious glance toward Rio, she found him every bit as perplexed—and concerned—as she.

He had not wanted to come. Pleading an early morning meeting with one of his potential investors, he had tried to avoid attendance at yet another social event, but Marie-Claire insisted. She had assured him this party would be nothing like the lavish ball at Roffignac's; Marguerite and Samson Champleur had just come out of mourning for her father, and so the gathering would probably be nothing more than dinner followed by conversation, including the obligatory recitation of his travels by Armand.

Why then were there so many vehicles ahead of them, all discharging guests headed for the Champleur home? An instinct for self-preservation nudged Rio's hand toward the familiar weight of the gun at his hip, except that tonight the weapon was not there.

He muttered an involuntary "Damn!"

Marie-Claire, seated across from him, reached to pat his arm apologetically.

"I am so sorry, Mr. Jackson. Armand is a very eligible young man, and it appears a great many mothers have brought their daughters to welcome him home."

Genevieve caught the oblique look her father cast in her direction. Did he consider her one of those daughters as well, to be paraded once again before

332

the "eligible young man" who might catch her fancy? Instead of tilting her chin higher in defiance of that possibility, she lowered it, and returned her father's glance with a glower.

Once she was inside the house and had gone through the formality of greeting Armand and his family, Genevieve realized that her father had not entirely misread the situation. He had, however, pointed to the wrong man as the target of the matchmaking mothers.

Though some practiced a bit more discretion than others, they all made sure that their daughters were brought to the attention of the handsome, mysterious stranger Marie-Claire du Prés had presented last night at Roffignac's. Among the most eager were Armand Champleur's younger sister Eulalie, and Genevieve's childhood friend, Fanchon LeFevre. Fanchon had the unmitigated gall to thank Genevieve for bringing him.

Left to her own devices, Genevieve wandered from the scene of such flagrant pandering and made her way to the courtyard around which the Champleur mansion was built. The rain had finally stopped, leaving behind a silver mist glittering with the droplets that fell from flowers and vines, gallery railings and roof tiles. Not eager to ruin her gown, Genevieve stood in the shelter of an overhanging balcony, where the flagstones were dry, to calm her nerves and gather her thoughts.

She did not blame Fanchon or Eulalie; she remembered the days not so very long ago when she had been just like them. Their world was so narrow, so predictable, that any new diversion grabbed their immediate and total attention, especially a new face in their carefully limited social circle.

But how did that excuse Rio? How could he—how *did* he—justify lying to her, then abandoning her? And why was she bothering to look for reasons? Hadn't she learned to trust her instincts over any thought-out, considered rationale?

No, not with Rio. He threw her instincts into turmoil.

She leaned back against the solid bulk of a stuccoed wall. The light of late afternoon cast a seductive pall over the quiet courtyard. Only New Orleans had this greyish rose light that made everything dream-hazy, everything beautiful. Wrapped in the mist and the warmth and the light, Genevieve knew she should have felt content. All this was home and familiar, and she had missed it so much.

This was what Rio had brought her back to, just as he had said he would.

Was everything to be a reminder of him, even the things that should have had no connection to her life with him?

She closed her eyes and swore, violently but softly.

"My, my, that's no way for a lady to talk."

At the soft-spoken scolding, Genevieve opened her eyes. She watched, suddenly tense, as Jean-Louis emerged from the shadow of a circular iron staircase. He walked slowly, to make the limp less noticeable, or perhaps just to emphasize his presence.

"Or are you no longer a lady?"

As he approached, she realized she could not escape him. The home of Marguerite and Samson Champleur was a far cry from the Maison de Versailles, but Genevieve felt the same kind of panic rise within her. Behind her was the wall, and to her left a trellis supporting a rampant bougainvillaea. Jean-Louis came at her from an angle, trapping her in the corner between the wall and the sharp-thorned plant.

"No, you probably are no longer the lady you were when you left New Orleans," he answered his own question. Leaning on the walking stick, he reached out a confident hand to curl a finger under her chin. "Don't turn away from me, Genevieve. We are, after all, still engaged, you know. Now that we've returned from our adventures, don't you think it is time we set a date for our wedding?"

"You must be *mad*," she finally managed to whisper. "I would never marry you, *never.*"

Jean-Louis shook his head sadly.

"Do not say 'never,' my dear Genevieve. It is such a frightfully long time. And I rather think you will marry me much sooner than that."

His confidence warned her to be careful. The man she had agreed to marry had not exhibited that kind of sureness except when he possessed information no one else did.

"How do you expect to force me?" she asked him bluntly in a voice not intended for confidences. Someone must soon come looking for her, or at least come out to the courtyard, and she wished to be heard.

"Force you? I prefer to think of it as reasoning with you, Genevieve. Your parents' comfort in their old age ought to be of some concern to you, for instance, and I hold that comfort in the palm of my hand."

He turned his hand palm up, drawing her attention involuntarily. Then, with a lightning movement she never expected from him, he grabbed her arm and pulled her close.

"I swore I'd make you pay, you spoiled bitch," he hissed, whiskey-laden breath like a strangling fog in her nostrils. "What your father stole from mine I will now take back, with interest. The bank will be

335

mine alone when I'm through with Victor du Prés. And so will you."

Had he tried then to kiss her, which was clearly his intention, Genevieve would have kicked away the support of the walking stick. But she, and Jean-Louis as well, heard approaching footsteps. He let go her arm and moved as though to escape into the misty shadows, only to stumble and then be halted by the figure that materialized out of the shimmery light.

"Monsieur Marmont," Rio greeted with a mocking bow. "We meet again."

Awkwardly trying to regain his footing, Jean-Louis turned his lips up in a sneer.

"Mr. Jackson, the scout turned businessman." He gave Rio an assessing look and chuckled. "What a shame you weren't in New Orleans for Mardi Gras. You'd not have needed a masquerade."

Rio's reaction was reflex, born of years of defending himself against such insults. But this time, he merely fell into another.

"Reaching for a gun, Mr. Jackson? Tut, how barbaric!" His balance and dignity recovered, Jean-Louis drew a handkerchief from his pocket and passed it delicately beneath his nose, as though some foul stench had assailed him. "Some of us, Mr. Jackson, see right through your veneer of respectability. And it would be so easy to strip that veneer from you and expose the *real* Rio Jackson to those businessmen you've so carefully cultivated these past few days."

"Don't pay any attention to him, Rio," Genevieve warned.

Jean-Louis turned to her then, his face contorted with the effort he made to maintain his own facade of civility.

336

"Foolish advice, my dear, when you know what hangs in the balance. But the choice is yours." He seemed to regain his control, straightened the wrinkled sleeves of his coat, and took a hesitant step away from her. "By the way, if I were you, I wouldn't look to Mr. Jackson for assistance," he added as an afterthought. "The 'gentleman' has been seen in the company of Mademoiselle Fanchon LeFevre *very* early in the morning."

"You son of a bitch," Rio growled, aware that his hand once again reached for the non-existent revolver.

"You see, my dear, he does not deny it," Jean-Louis said with a Gallic shrug, "because he knows it is true."

Genevieve leaned back against damp, clammy wall, afraid her knees would give way beneath her. She could not speak, could not plead with Rio for a denial she knew in her heart would never come, could not accuse Jean-Louis of lying because she knew he spoke the truth.

Rio had no such difficulty.

"Get the hell out of here," he ordered Jean-Louis. "Gun or no gun, I'll strangle you with my bare hands."

Again the Frenchman shrugged.

"As you wish. But remember, my dear Genevieve, running away this time will hardly solve your problems." He bowed deeply, mockingly, then slipped away into the darkening mist of the courtyard.

Silence hung in the heavy air after the tap of his footsteps faded. Stunned, Genevieve tried to find a way out of her hidden little corner, but just as Jean-Louis had blocked her way earlier, Rio now prevented her escape.

He took a hesitant step toward her and said,

"It's not what you think, Viva."

"How do you know what I think?" she shot back, tears of rage, of betrayal, falling to her cheeks. "My God, Fanchon was my best friend. How could you?"

He turned away from her for a moment and stared into the fading silver light. She was waiting for an explanation he wasn't ready to give her, or for a denial he couldn't.

"You gotta trust me, Viva," was all he could tell her.

"Trust you? And how am I supposed to do that? You won't tell me what you do with your time all week, and then you tell me to trust you? You walk into Armand Champleur's party and immediately surround yourself with all the unattached females who were invited for Armand's perusal, just like you did last night, and—"

"No, Viva, there you're wrong," he interrupted.

He turned to face her again, and in doing so took another step in her direction. Though she stood in shadow and the light was fading rapidly, he could still see the devastated expression on her face. She had caught one of those carefully twisted curls on a bougainvillaea thorn and pulled the silken ebony lock free just enough to hang over one eye. It beckoned his touch, but the look in that sapphire eye warned him back.

Did he dare tell her the truth? She might not like it, but at least she could not accuse him of lying again.

"The young ladies weren't, uh, invited to see Armand," he began. "They were here to see me."

"What?"

"Don't laugh," his pride prompted him to snap. "Anyway, it's a compliment to you. You apparently did such a good job with this old sow's ear that

338

every mama in New Orleans is pushin' her daughter in front of me. With, I might add, your own mother's encouragement."

"That doesn't excuse your seeing Fanchon early in the morning," Genevieve retorted. He was not going to get away with changing the subject. As tears spilled again, she begged, "Can't you even try to explain?"

She loved him, dear God, how she loved him. Couldn't he see that? Couldn't he tell his silence was breaking her heart?

"Can't you even try to trust me?" Rio asked in a voice as cold, as bitter as the Sierra wind. "Or is it easier to take the word of a 'gentleman' like Jean-Louis Marmont than a half-breed scout like me?"

The bright blue eyes narrowed, and hardened to ice. Closing the gap between them, Rio lifted a curled finger to stroke her tear-wet cheek with the knuckle, to push aside the drooping lock of hair that covered her eye. The tenderness in his touch did not disguise the underlying anger.

"I told you I wouldn't be a toy, Viva. Or a pet, to come when you whistle. You trusted me with your life that night in Sacramento; all I'm asking now is that you trust me a little longer."

The pain in her questioning eyes and the quiver of her lower lip nearly melted his resolve. But she was the impulsive one, who acted on instinct and emotion alone; he had to rely on the carefully constructed plan already in motion, and hope that if and when it came to fruition, she would understand and forgive.

"I want to, Rio, you know that, don't you?" she whispered. He tilted her head a notch higher, and she knew he was going to kiss her. When he did, she would give in to him, because she could not help herself, but before that, she wanted every reas-

339

surance she could wrest from him. "It was so different before, when it was just the two of us. We didn't have any secrets then."

With mesmerizing slowness, he lowered his head until his mouth was half an inch from hers.

"Don't think of it as a secret."

She felt the warmth of his breath, tasted the words he used to tease and tantalize her, but she could see nothing, for her eyes closed in anticipation of the fulfillment of this promise.

He ran the end of his tongue along the fullness of her lower lip, then brushed it across the bow of her upper. The sharp intake of her breath sent a tremor through him, an earthquake of longing.

"Think of it as a surprise," he murmured, and then he possessed her mouth completely.

Chapter Twenty-two

Genevieve found sleep elusive Sunday night. She lay in the darkness of her room for hours, reliving every detail of the way Rio had made love to her in the shadowed recess of the courtyard.

There had been nothing romantic in their coupling. With their mouths still joined in a fevered kiss, Rio had lifted her skirt and wantonly caressed her until, aroused beyond all reasoning, she squirmed against his hand. Never had she known such frantic desire, such frenzied need.

Was it the risk they took that someone might find them that drove her to such heights? Was it the almost brutal way Rio touched her, sought her secrets, probed within her and demanded her response? Was it the rough wall behind her, preventing her escape, making her surrender unavoidable?

She did not know why, only knew that she could not survive this assault. Hampered by the bulk of skirts and petticoats bunched between their bodies, she fumbled to unfasten his trousers and free the swelling proof of his own desire.

He had groaned into her mouth as her fingers grasped his rigid flesh. There was no retreating now; she had committed both of them to the completion.

She stroked him slowly, reveling in the feel of his need. Each rhythmic pulse that surged through him triggered a tightening in her own body. The culmination was close, hovering just beyond her reach.

Then suddenly he withdrew, and seemingly in a single motion grasped her buttocks and lifted her bodily onto him. His hungry mouth captured her cry of surprise as he plunged all the way into her with a single urgent thrust.

He held her tightly for a moment, then deftly turned so it was he who leaned against the wall. She alone could move, to find her own satisfaction and to bring him his.

"Now, Viva, now," he whispered hoarsely.

"Yes, Rio, now, now, *now!*"

The explosion of his climax triggered her own. She cried out at the force of it, as shock wave after shock wave assaulted her senses.

She would never be quite sure what happened next. She vaguely remembered a rush of embarrassment when she realized it would be impossible for them to return to the party in their more than disheveled condition, but the haze of fulfilled rapture eased even that humiliation. Somehow she found herself seated beside Rio on a wrought iron bench, and across from them sat Fanchon LeFevre.

It was Fanchon, the same best friend as ever, who promised to provide an excuse. She would tell everyone she had found Genevieve in the courtyard, ill with a headache, and Mr. Jackson had agreed to take her home.

"Dear Fanchon," Genevieve whispered in the dark hour before dawn. "I will have to find a way to thank you, especially after thinking the worst of you."

After a few hours of dreamless sleep, she wakened to the sound of angry voices in the corridor outside her room. She recognized one as her mother's, but the other was too low, too indistinct. It might have been her father, and arguments between her parents were not unusual enough for Genevieve to give the matter a second thought. She rolled over and, recalling with a pleasant blush the erotic adventure of the night before, drifted back to sleep.

But later that day, when Genevieve discovered a subtle change in the atmosphere of the house, she began to wonder about the nature of that argument. In the glow of passion and its aftermath, she had pushed Jean-Louis' threat out of her mind. Now it came back to her, its terror stronger than ever.

She went looking for Rio, though something told her she would not find him.

In answer to her questions, no one in the household had seen Rio since he brought her home last night, but there was ample evidence of his presence. His bed had been slept in, and the silver tray beside the bed contained the ashes of at least one thin cigar. But Cinco was gone from the stable.

Rio might be able to blend into the fabric of New Orleans, but a palomino stallion like Cinco would surely have aroused some curiosity. Genevieve determined to set out in pursuit of the elusive Mr. Jackson by means of tracking down his horse.

"I have several errands to run this afternoon," she told Celine while the maid brushed Genevieve's hair. "I'll stop a few places on the way and ask if anyone has seen Cinco."

"You sure that's a good idea?" It was as much a warning as a question. "Mr. Rio might not like it if you ruin his surprise."

"I don't like surprises anymore."

Celine stepped back so Genevieve could see her

reflection in the mirror. The look of disbelief on the black woman's face was unmistakable.

"Since when? As long as I've known you, nothing pleased you better than a big surprise."

Recalling the mattress Rio had made for her, and the moccasins, Genevieve wondered if she was lying when she replied, "Since I saw Jean-Louis waiting for me when I arrived home. Now, hurry with my hair. I want to have as much time as possible to look for Cinco before my fitting at Madame Savriere's."

With a clatter, Celine dropped the hairbrush, a handful of pins, and the long twist of hair coiled at Genevieve's nape.

"Whatever is the matter?" Genevieve snapped. She twisted around on the dressing table stool to stare at her maid.

Celine knelt on the floor, her face averted, and swept up the pins.

"I forgot," she mumbled uncharacteristically. "Madame Savriere sent word she would bring the blue gown here for the fitting. This afternoon. You better stay here and not go out."

Rio wiped his forehead with an already soaked handkerchief. The air in Antoine LeFevre's office seemed saturated with sweat. Even the papers strewn on the enormous desk felt limp.

Sitting across the sea of papers from Rio, Antoine LeFevre let out a dejected sigh.

"There's nothing here," he said as he leaned back in his chair.

"Nothing," Rio echoed. "Damn! I wish to hell I knew what to look for."

"Even if you did, I don't think you'd find it. I don't think it exists."

Rio was inclined to agree. Over the past few days, and especially the past several hours, he had come to trust the bald, bespectacled little Creole. Antoine had gone out on a limb for him, getting these papers from his son-in-law, who happened to be one of the attorneys working on the settlement between Victor du Prés and Jean-Louis Marmont.

"You think he's bluffing."

Antoine shrugged and said, "What else can he be doing? Bluffing, or lying, that's it." He waved a hand to include the disaster that covered the desk, then lifted the long sheet of paper that sat separate from the others on one corner of the desk. "This is the list of the investments Etienne Marmont gambled on. I got it from Victor last year, after Jean-Louis had disappeared, when I thought I might buy him out."

"And we went over every one of them."

"We did. There isn't a single one that could give Jean-Louis enough money to control the bank. You saw that." Antoine grabbed a handful of papers and waved them in front of Rio. "You've enough experience to recognize worthless stock when you see it."

For the first time that day, Rio laughed.

The fitting should have taken an hour at most. It took three. Frustrated, Genevieve stood in chemise, stockings, and shoes while Madame Savriere and her two assistants restitched three seams, removed a lace ruffle and sewed it back on, and took Genevieve's measurements at least three times.

"Can't you do that back at the shop?" she complained when the delays mounted.

Madame Savriere, short, plump, and usually very jovial, shook her head and did not look up from her work.

"It is most unusual for me to have so much work this time of the year," she said. "I sent one of my girls home to be with her maman, because I could not afford to pay her. But now this party has brought me more orders, and I cannot fill them all unless I work every minute."

"Are there no other seamstresses you could hire?"

This time Madame looked up, with a disdainful scowl.

"I do not hire just any seamstress off the street," she sniffed.

Resigned, Genevieve stood at Madame's order and allowed the blue satin dress to be dropped over her head for another trial. And yet she wondered, though she supposed it would be futile to ask, why Madame brought both of her assistants with her, when there should have been so many other dresses to be working on.

They did not leave until five minutes after Celine informed Genevieve that Rio had returned to the house.

Wakened by a thunderstorm in the small hours just before dawn Tuesday morning, Genevieve rose from the airless confines of her bed and walked out to the back veranda to enjoy the fleeting respite from the tropical heat and humidity. She enjoyed the tumult of the storm, the brilliant flashes of lightning, the violent thunderclaps, the intermittent splats of the first raindrops before the deluge. She had even ventured to stand in the downpour in the hope the refreshing rain would wash away the hurt that had become her almost constant state of mind since returning to New Orleans.

It didn't.

346

It merely hid the tears that began just as dawn turned the sky a murky grey.

Rio had hardly spoken to her all evening. He claimed to have a splitting headache, and she agreed that he did look exhausted. His eyes were red, which might have come from too much to drink, but she detected no scent of liquor about him. After a silent, hasty dinner, he retreated to his room.

The light was still burning at midnight, when Genevieve peeked out into the hall and saw the sliver of yellow under the door to his room.

She had gone to him then. Whatever he had done during the day, whatever secrets he kept from her, she still wanted him. She wanted to be with him, as they had been together in the mountain cabin, as they had been together on the riverboat from St. Louis. Let him have his surprise for her; she would give him one of her own tonight.

Tiptoeing down the corridor lest she wake any of the other occupants, she began to untie the ribbons that fastened her nightgown. Tonight there would be no clothes between them, only passion as hot and sultry as the Louisiana summer.

She was within ten steps of his door when the light beneath it abruptly went out. Though surely he could not have been aware of her approach, that sudden darkness seemed a curt dismissal. Then again, she thought as she silently crept back to her room, perhaps it was just as well. She remembered how tired he looked at dinner, how he had eaten without his usual relish and seemed almost preoccupied. He had had no more sleep than she, and she knew she was exhausted.

Now, drenched to the skin and shivering, she climbed back onto the porch and tried to bring her weeping under control. She was leaning over the rail to wring out her dripping hair when she heard the door softly open and close.

Rio walked right past her. He was dressed like any other businessman on his way to a day's work, but no one left for an office at this hour. Torn between wanting to follow him and being afraid to learn his destination, she waited only long enough to see him leave the stable, mounted on Cinco, five minutes later.

She ignored all Celine's warnings and cautions. No matter how painful the truth, Genevieve was determined to learn if Rio was indeed visiting her best friend at this ungodly hour of the morning. She dressed hurriedly and, accompanied by a vociferously protesting Celine, marched out of the house within half an hour of Rio's departure.

New Orleans never truly went to sleep, so the two women, one white, one black, were not alone on the streets. Late revelers staggered from casinos and taverns; lovers crept out of their mistress' apartments; slaves and servants began the day's errands. Genevieve saw none of them.

She saw only the squalor, the filth, the mold and mildew and rot.

The rain had stopped, but the streets were wet and filled with puddles that gave off a noxious odor in the increasing heat. Too many doorways sheltered sleeping — or unconscious — drunks. Weeds grew in cracks in the sidewalks. Garbage littered the gutters. A whore, on her way home from a night-long assignation, argued loudly with the driver of the carriage she had hired for the ride.

Genevieve closed her ears to the vulgar mixture of French and English, heavily laced with obscenities, but she could not close her eyes to the dismal sights. Was this the New Orleans she had known and loved all her life, or had the city undergone a

348

horrible change in the past year? Genevieve shivered, not so frightened by the change itself as by the thought that perhaps it was she, not the city, that was so different from what she remembered.

Once again, Rio invaded her thoughts. *He* had caused this change in her, in the way she saw her world. He had become a part of her, and the thought of losing him brought a lump to her throat. She swallowed it, closed her mind's eye to the decadence around her, and pressed on.

Twice, within a few streets of the LeFevre mansion in the heart of the Vieux Carré, she halted and turned back. Did she truly want her worst fears confirmed? What, she asked herself, would she do if she saw them together, Rio and Fanchon?

She would not, like Fanchon, be content to share. Fanchon's liaison with Calvin Hood, an American hotelier, was hardly proper, acceptable behavior. Hood had been married when they met, and he showed no inclination toward divorcing his wealthy wife. Antoine LeFevre's fortune was not sufficient to divide amongst eight daughters and leave each of them independently wealthy, so Fanchon had faced the fact that in order to live as she was accustomed to live, her relationship with Calvin was doomed to be a clandestine one of stolen hours and secret nights.

And yet there was no denying she had betrayed that relationship. Genevieve ducked into the shelter of a covered doorway when she heard the screech of a gate opening across the narrow street. Her heart rose into her throat to cut off the scream of protest that tried to escape, but nothing could stop the torrent of tears.

Barefoot, dressed in a plain cotton frock, Fanchon pushed the old gate open. Behind her, Rio led Cinco.

"Until tomorrow," he said, bending over her hand. A wide grin split his face when he straightened.

"Tomorrow?" Fanchon echoed, with laughter in her voice. "I must submit to this abuse again tomorrow? After this morning, I am sure I shall not be able to walk for days."

Unable to listen to another word, Genevieve pushed past Celine and ran toward home.

Breathless, Fanchon LeFevre collapsed onto one of the ballroom's gilt chairs. Pale blonde ringlets, turned dark with sweat, clung to the side of her face; and she pressed a hand to her heaving bosom. A merry laugh escaped her as she stuck her feet out from under the edge of her simple grey cotton frock and kicked off her shoes.

"Oh, please, Rio, that is enough!" she gasped. "Now, where did I leave my fan?"

Rio spotted the dried palmetto leaf on another chair and retrieved it for her. Grey eyes closed, she began fluttering a breeze upon her face.

"That'll be all, William," she said, with a blind gesture to the fiddler who stood beside the piano.

"No, wait," Rio called as he strode to the black musician. "Here, for your trouble."

He dug into a pocket and found a silver dollar to press into the man's hand. William grinned.

"You got any friends need dancin' lessons, Mr. Rio?" he asked.

"Just me. I don't think Miss Fanchon wants any more pupils like me, either."

She didn't reply to his self-deprecatory remark until after William had gone and Rio was alone with her in the big, empty room. The tempo of her fanning slowed.

"Come, Rio, let's go down to the courtyard. I'll have someone bring us lemonade." She offered him her hand and he pulled her gently to her stockinged feet. "Unless you'd prefer something stronger?"

"Not at nine o'clock in the morning. Lemonade's fine."

He glanced at her shoes, but she shook her head and walked to the door without them.

"I avoid the things whenever possible," she told him. "I only wore them as protection for the top of my feet while dancing."

"Was I that bad?"

She stopped and looked up at him with blond brows knit together.

"Bad? Mr. Jackson, you were *terrible*. I meant what I said the other morning about not being able to walk. Shall I show you the bruises you left me?" She resumed her resolute striding from the ballroom to the outside gallery and then down a curved corner staircase. "Fortunately, I am an excellent teacher, and you are an above-average student. With one more day's practice, you will be the beau of the ball Saturday evening, and not just for your looks this time."

With a smile and a shake of his head, Rio followed her down to the courtyard.

Over the past four days, he had learned a great many things about this youngest of Antoine Le-Fevre's eight daughters, not the least of which was that she said exactly what was on her mind, whether compliment or insult, and she never apologized for either. Her porcelain coloring, inherited from an English mother, gave the impression of fragility, but Fanchon was singularly robust,

351

energetic, and—when she wished—stubborn.

It was no wonder she and Genevieve were best friends, which was why Rio had felt relatively safe asking Fanchon for dancing lessons. The risk of jealousy seemed minimal, or so he thought until he caught sight of Genevieve spying on him two mornings ago. He had been plagued with a combination of guilt and smug pride ever since.

They found chairs at a small table in the shade of a vine-covered wall, and a moment later a black servant appeared with a tray bearing glasses and a pitcher. Fanchon waved the woman away, then poured a drink for herself and another for Rio.

"Is Genevieve still jealous?" she asked after taking a long, thirst-quenching swallow.

" 'Fraid so," Rio admitted. "You should have let me tell her the truth Tuesday."

"And ruin our surprise? Never! Besides, until you get to the bottom of Marmont's scheme, both you and she are much safer if he thinks he has the upper hand."

That had, in fact, been part of the reason Rio cultivated the friendship with his employer's daughter: as long as Jean-Louis believed Rio's affections lay elsewhere, the Frenchman would probably leave him alone. And as long as Genevieve remained the object of Jean-Louis' quest, she, too, was unlikely to be harmed. Still, Rio disliked maintaining this charade. Lying, especially when he saw the pain it brought to Genevieve, made him uncomfortable.

"Well, if I don't find something pretty soon, he's gonna have the upper hand for good."

Genevieve picked at her breakfast. After another almost sleepless night, she had no appetite. If she had, seeing Jean-Louis once again at the breakfast table would have destroyed it anyway.

352

"Are you not feeling well, my dear?" he asked.

"I'd feel a great deal better if you weren't here," she snapped back.

"Now, is that any way to talk to the man you are about to wed?"

He had been saying the same thing all week. With Rio making himself scarce and her parents increasingly controlled by Jean-Louis' threats, Genevieve stood alone against him.

Even her best friend had deserted her. The memory of that discovery still had the power to bring tears to Genevieve's eyes, but she blinked them back rather than let Jean-Louis see. She would deprive him of that victory at least.

"You must keep up your strength, my dear," he prattled. "We wouldn't want you not to be able to dance with your intended at your betrothal party now, would we?"

For the first time since joining him at the breakfast table, she looked up. A thousand memories poured into her brain, each one making her more and more ill. Dancing with Jean-Louis at their first engagement party, watching Rio flirt with every female at Roffignac's, listening to his silence when Jean-Louis leveled the accusation of infidelity, seeing him ride through the entrance to the LeFevre mansion and wave good-bye to Fanchon.

She may have lost Rio, but she would not give herself to Jean-Louis. Somehow, there had to be a way to stop him. With or without Rio's help, she would find it.

"I'll never dance with you, Jean-Louis. I'd sooner rot in hell."

The household rested during the heat of the day. Victor frequently even came home from the bank during the hottest days of summer, to find a brief respite from the debilitating weather. That he had remained in his office every day this week gave Genevieve a clear indication of how seriously he took Jean-Louis' threat.

Her mother, too, had been deeply affected. Marie-Claire took most of her meals in her room, claiming to have developed a slight fever. When she did join the rest of the family—and Jean-Louis— for dinner, she frequently glanced wistfully at Rio, a gesture Genevieve at first discounted, until it became too frequent too ignore.

But although Rio continued to pay flattering attention to Marie-Claire, the older woman did her best not to return the compliments. Her enthusiasm toward him seemed to wane, or perhaps she was simply being forced to quell it. Twice since the Champleur party, Marie-Claire had excused herself early from dinner, and she addressed her excuses to Rio.

Nothing made sense. Lying in the mosquito-netting shrouded bed, Genevieve tried to find a logical explanation for everything, but failed miserably. Why would Rio sneak off at dawn to visit Fanchon LeFevre? She had no idea. Why had Fanchon betrayed a lifelong friendship? Again, this made no sense. Saturday evening at Roffignac's, Fanchon had expressed a desire to leave early so she could meet her lover. But Saturday was the first time Fanchon had been introduced to Rio.

Genevieve rolled over and tried to focus her thoughts on Jean-Louis and ways to thwart his plans. She had beaten him once before, when the odds were much greater against her. She could not let him win this time.

But with thoughts of Jean-Louis came thoughts of Rio. He was never far from her mind, for everything seemed to remind her of him.

Why had Marie-Claire swung from loyalty to Jean-Louis to infatuation with Rio and back again? No doubt Jean-Louis had impressed his threats upon her, and Marie-Claire, unlike her daughter, was not one to take risks.

The most difficult question to answer was why had Jean-Louis suddenly become so sure of himself. All his life he had been arrogant, protected as he was by the wealth and power of his father's position. But he had always confined his bullying to those weaker than himself, and when he came up against resistance, he backed down.

A chill ran through Genevieve despite the afternoon's sultry heat. The first time Jean-Louis had stood up to her own resistance was in Sacramento, when he had the brute force of Buster Kulkey to back him up.

What reinforcement could he have here in New Orleans? And what would happen if Genevieve Marie du Prés decided to defy him once again?

Chapter Twenty-three

The du Prés house glittered like an enormous yellow jewel. Lanterns lined the long curving driveway and illuminated the facade; a crystal chandelier hung from the veranda ceiling sparkled over the open door. Inside, every room was ablaze with light and alive with merriment.

The ballroom hummed with conversation. Guests had begun arriving late in the afternoon, some from as far away as Baton Rouge up the river. Marie-Claire, resplendent in a gown of gold satin, moved easily through the crowd, introducing people, directing them to refreshments, answering questions on the latest gossip. Watching from the second floor gallery, Genevieve experienced an unfamiliar nervousness.

"I can't go through with this," she whispered to Celine, who stood just behind her.

"Nonsense. This is your party, and folks would wonder if you didn't show up."

It might as well be my funeral, Genevieve thought, for all the pleasure I'll have tonight.

"Besides, if you don't go, you'll be giving Monsieur Marmont exactly what he wants."

Capitulation. For a bully like Jean-Louis, that was the greatest triumph. Victory without a fight. She would not, could not, give that to him.

He had told her, earlier that morning, that he

would greet her at the stairs at precisely seven o'clock. He said no more, as though he believed that if he told her nothing, she would guess nothing. After glancing at the clock on the landing to ascertain that it lacked yet fifteen minutes of being seven o'clock, Genevieve scanned the crowd below her.

She spotted Rio immediately. His black evening clothes made him an easy target in the center of a dozen pastel-gowned young women, but somehow Genevieve knew she would have been able to find him anywhere. She remembered how she had looked up at him the morning of her arrival in Sacramento and been struck by his masculine beauty. It struck her again, and more deeply this time, because she saw him not only with the appreciative eyes of an artist, but with the adoring gaze of a broken-hearted lover.

And beside him, in a mauve silk gown cut daringly low, stood Fanchon. Someone in the group said something amusing, and as Fanchon broke into laughter, she placed her hand on Rio's arm for just a second.

Genevieve started down the stairs. She would not give in to Jean-Louis; she would not give up Rio.

"She's coming," Fanchon whispered, but Rio did not need her warning. He had been watching Genevieve ever since she appeared on the gallery.

Tonight would end it, once and for all. The waiting, the worrying, the lying would stop. The past week had been hell for him, and he knew it must have been even worse for her. In another hour, perhaps less, it would all be over, one way or another.

He excused himself from the gaggle of schoolgirls and turned a deaf ear to their pleas and pouts. Making his way carefully through the crowd, he begrudged every greeting that delayed him but kept Genevieve in sight. She had descended only five or six of the stairs, as though timing her entrance. Taller than most of the other guests, Rio could easily see over their heads, but he worried that Genevieve still might reach the bottom of the stairs before he could reach her.

The members of the small orchestra hired for the occasion began tuning their instruments. A subtle change came over the crowd as they prepared for the dancing. Something cold slithered down Rio's spine and his palms began to sweat.

He had stood up to Buster Kulkey and a grizzly bear, had survived a winter in the Sierras, and had conquered the mysteries of the written word, but the idea of taking the hand of Genevieve Marie du Prés and leading her onto the dance floor suddenly terrified him.

An elbow dug into his ribs, bringing him out of a momentary daze.

"Beautiful, isn't she?"

Rio turned toward the heavily accented voice. A tall, hawknosed Creole gentleman of some sixty years peered in Genevieve's direction through his pince-nez.

"Yes, she is."

"I almost married her mother, thirty years ago," the grey-haired man continued. "Marie-Claire Lamargue was a beauty, but I do believe she must yield to the daughter."

Manners were one thing, but Rio had no time to waste listening to an old man's reminiscences. He pushed his way through the crowd, ignoring murmurs behind his back. He was sure Genevieve had seen him; he could almost feel her eyes seeking him out.

Yet when he finally reached the foot of the stairs and looked up, he discovered her sapphire eyes stared fixedly in another direction. Before he could follow that gaze and determined what had so captured her attention, a mild disturbance at his left answered the question for him.

Jean-Louis Marmont shoved his way rudely between Rio and the young man at his left, the same Armand Champleur who had recently returned from Europe.

"So, we meet again," Jean-Louis muttered under his breath. "But I think this time will be different. Very different."

He reached out a hand to the young woman in blue satin who had paused some half a dozen steps from the bottom of the wide staircase. She seemed frozen in mid-stride, like a doe confused as to which way to run.

This was not possible. Genevieve stared at the outstretched hand in its immaculate white glove, then glanced over her shoulder and up the stairs to the clock. Seven o'clock was still five minutes away.

Rio did not offer his hand as Jean-Louis did; he stood, stock still, as though waiting for her to make the choice.

"Come, Genevieve," Jean-Louis prompted. "I believe the first dance is to be a waltz."

She turned back to face him, her eyes studying first his greedy smile, then his cold, pale eyes. He did not mask his hatred, did not even try. He wanted her to be afraid of him, the more, the better.

"And *I* believe," Rio interposed in a soft, velvety drawl that instantly drew her attention and that of everyone else within hearing, "that Mademoiselle du Prés has already promised the first dance to me."

359

The hand he held out to her was bare and brown and callused, but she grabbed it and held on desperately. She had seen the look of murderous rage cloud Jean-Louis' face as he stepped back to make room for her and her partner.

The crowd parted, with murmurs and whispers, and cleared the floor for the dancing to begin. Other couples paired off, young and old, but still Genevieve had the feeling of being utterly alone with Rio in her arms. A hundred pairs of eyes were staring at her, most of them envious, and she reveled in the sensation.

"Is this the surprise?" she asked as she rested her left hand on his shoulder and let him gently clasp her right. The touch of his hand sent a cascade of tingles through her that manifested themselves in a shudder of anticipatory delight.

"Wait 'til the music starts," he answered through clenched teeth.

His voice held no warmth, no excitement, none of the emotions she had expected. And there was a certain stiffness to his body under her hand that communicated to her his unwillingness to go through with this.

She tried to draw away, only to have his hand at her waist tighten and hold her firmly against him.

"It isn't necessary," she whispered. "You don't *have* to dance with me."

For the first time since taking her into this stylized embrace, Rio looked into her eyes.

"Oh, yes, I do," he insisted. "Fanchon put me through hell this week, and I—"

The rest of his comment was covered by the introductory strains of a waltz. Determined not to dance with the man who had not only betrayed her but betrayed her with her best friend, Genevieve planted her feet firmly and closed her ears to the lilting, irresistible music. Rio took just one hesitant step and stopped.

Squeezing her hand to let her know he would not put up with any more foolishness, he lowered his head to whisper in her ear, "Damn it, Viva, people are startin' to stare. Dance with me, please? I can't promise I won't step on your toes, but—"

She tilted her head back so quickly she almost bumped him in the nose.

"Oh, my God," she gasped, lifting her left hand from his shoulder to cover the grin that was spreading across her face. Unbidden tears seemed to accompany the grin, and the dawning of very welcome truth added a searing blush. "Fanchon was teaching you to dance!"

"Yeah, so let's get to it," Rio growled as he moved her hand back to his shoulder.

If he trod upon her toes, she never felt it. If he lost the rhythm and missed a step, she never noticed it. All that mattered to Genevieve was that Rio Jackson once again filled her arms and her heart. Proud, stubborn Rio, who had done everything to avoid admitting he couldn't read, would have been just as diligent in hiding another gap in his education. At least to her. But he had swallowed his pride and gone to the one person he thought she would trust, her best friend, and submitted to Fanchon's instruction.

Genevieve wanted the dance never to end. In bringing Rio back to her arms, it had brought back all the joy to her life. Nothing else mattered.

But the music did end, leaving only vibrant echoes in the air. Still smiling, still with tears blurring her vision, Genevieve refused to release the man she had chosen to be her partner.

A hush fell over the ballroom.

"They're starin' again," Rio whispered, but this

time he, too, grinned.

"Let them. Oh, Rio, that was a wonderful surprise! Cruel, but wonderful!"

Finally he was able to ease her away from him, though he could not bring himself to let go her hand. Her dark eyes glittered with tears that he ached to kiss away; her lips, softly parted in a smile, begged for more kisses. The middle of a crowded ballroom, however, was not the place to begin making love to her.

The orchestra began another tune, and as couples once again crowded onto the floor, both Genevieve and Rio knew they could not stay. Genevieve cast a glance to the second floor gallery, then lowered her eyes seductively.

Reading her thoughts, Rio shook his head and said, "No, querida mía, not yet. We have to talk, and if I took you within sight of a bed, I'd never get a word out."

God, but he wanted her. The past week had indeed been hell, a hell of desire unfulfilled, of unintentional anguish inflicted on an innocent. He had seen the hurt in her eyes, the questions, the disbelief, and all he wanted to do now was chase it all away.

"The garden," she whispered. "No one will be there yet."

Rio had been feasting his eyes on her, oblivious to everything else around him. As he tucked her arm around his and began to lead her to the beckoning privacy of the garden, he looked up, and scowled.

Jean-Louis Marmont, minus the gold-headed cane, was weaving his way through the dancers. The limp was less pronounced, as though he made the effort to conceal it.

"Why, Mr. Jackson, surely you would not be so

rude as to deny me this one dance?" he asked, slipping his arm sinuously around Genevieve's waist.

There was a threat behind that innocent question. Jean-Louis had not known the man who invaded his fancy Sacramento whorehouse, but he had had plenty of time to find out the truth about Rio Jackson. Knowledge glittered in his pale eyes, and Rio understood the threat. He could care less what anyone in New Orleans thought about him, but he'd not let Genevieve be forced to defend him. Not even with a dance.

"I believe Miss du Prés is feeling ill," he told Jean-Louis in a low voice, "and would like some fresh air."

"Then I insist upon escorting her to the garden."

Genevieve felt the pressure of the gun's barrel against her ribs at the same time she felt the pressure of Jean-Louis' hand at her waist.

The dance had now begun in earnest, and none of the dancers paid the slightest attention to three persons leaving the crowded floor. No one noticed the metallic gleam of the little pistol, or the pale, pleading look of panic on Genevieve's face.

"Oh, you need not accompany us, Mr. Jackson," Jean-Louis hinted as they made their way out of the ballroom. "I can take care of Miss du Prés myself."

The wide double doors to the back veranda and gardens had been thrown open to admit the evening breeze. Outside, lanterns glimmered in the trees though night had not yet fallen. Later, when the ballroom became overheated, the garden would provide a cool retreat. Now, it was virtually abandoned.

"But I insist," Rio mimicked.

Jean-Louis half led, half dragged her down the porch steps, always careful to keep her body between him and Rio. Had he noticed the instinctive movement of Rio's hand? Or had he put it down to old habit? Rio took another long, slow stride in persistent pursuit and felt the familiar secure weight of the revolver against his thigh.

They had reached the most secluded spot in the garden, beyond the rose arbor and into the shade of a massive, moss-festooned oak. A single lantern swayed in one of the lower branches. Jean-Louis, his face now marked with pain, leaned back against the enormous trunk.

Sweat plastered the Frenchman's hair to his forehead and stained the collar of his shirt. He was breathing hard, and each breath seemed to bring a wince of pain. Holding Genevieve tightly in front of him, he could not relieve the pressure on the knee.

"I am a much more patient man than you, Monsieur Marmont," Rio drawled, "and in better shape for a long chase."

Soft maniacal laughter filled the bower beneath the oak.

"But I have, shall we say, reinforcements," Jean-Louis boasted.

He whistled, just the way one would call a faithful dog.

Rio heard the footsteps and mentally breathed a sigh of relief that they came from the shadows to his left, not from behind. That relief was short-lived.

Genevieve saw Buster Kulkey at the same instant. Only force of will kept her from screaming in outrage.

"Gimme the girl, Frenchy," Buster growled. "I got the carriage waitin'."

"Give her to you? Oh, no, Mr. Kulkey. I shall be accompanying you."

The pale eyes never left Rio, even while Jean-Louis conversed with Buster Kulkey.

"Whaddayou mean? I bought the girl; she's mine. We don't need you around."

A grin spread across Jean-Louis' face as he reminded both Buster and Rio, "On the contrary, Mr. Kulkey. You only *rented* her. She still belongs to me."

Genevieve could not stifle a groan.

"And I wish to play with her for a while myself, before I allow you to enjoy her pleasures."

Rio flexed his fingers and calculated each move more diligently than the old men who played chess in the park. Buster wore a gun, but he did not look as though he used it well. There *might* be time to get a shot at the Frenchman and still have time to take out Buster, but Rio hesitated to draw until he was certain. Though his aim was instinctively accurate and his speed born of survival, he was no gunfighter. And at the moment, Jean-Louis provided a chance for increased advantage.

"You see, my dear Genevieve, I suspected you would not play along with my little game, so I had to, shall we say, load the dice."

"You won't win," she muttered through teeth beginning to chatter with fear and tension. She hardly dared to breathe.

"But I already have! Look at Mr. Jackson. His fingers are fairly itching to draw a revolver he doesn't have. Such a gentleman!" Jean-Louis sneered. "Mr. Kulkey, on the other hand, does have a gun, but he won't draw it, for fear of harming the one thing in this world he wants above all else, namely, my dear, you."

Genevieve stiffened. She had indeed seen Rio's hand move as though to draw a weapon. She had also danced with him and had felt the bulk of the

365

familiar Colt against her own thigh.

"Quit stallin', Frenchy," Kulkey whined. "Somebody's gonna come lookin' for her."

Buster was afraid. Rio could smell his fear, see it in the sweat that ran down the man's temples, hear it in the nervous quiver of his words. But Buster was also confident. He had believed Jean-Louis' assurances that the half-breed would be unarmed; otherwise, Buster would surely have answered his procurer's whistle with weapon already drawn.

It was just another advantage, and a big one.

But the bigger advantage was the shattered knee. Did Genevieve know how badly it pained her captor? Rio wanted to signal her, but he dared not. Any communication between them must be kept beyond Jean-Louis' knowledge.

Continued stalling, however, might offer an opportunity for subtle hints to be dropped.

"You'll have to leave New Orleans again," Rio observed. "That'll mean leaving behind a whole lot of money."

Listening to Rio's slow, methodical drawl, Genevieve wanted to scream. What was the matter with him? Why didn't he pull the gun and—

She knew why. She was the reason, blocking any real shot at Jean-Louis. A wounding shot meant nothing; the little silver gun still pointed at her heart.

So Rio stalled, and as she felt Jean-Louis try to shift his weight behind her, she understood the subtle strategy.

The Frenchman laughed again, but she felt the shiver of agony slice through him. It was only a matter of time. If he gave up his game and dragged her off to the waiting carriage, he would no doubt kill Buster Kulkey and have her for himself. Her only hope was to help Rio delay that escape until the old injury toppled her captor.

"You could have taken over the bank," Rio went on. "You could have ruined Victor du Prés the way he ruined your father."

"He will be ruined anyway. He signed the papers this afternoon to give me the money my father's investments earned. It is more than the bank can afford. Victor du Prés is a pauper."

Genevieve closed her eyes. She should have known he would never go back on his vow for revenge. No matter what she had done, whether she married him, became his mistress, or suffered the ultimate degradation in his brothel, Jean-Louis would never have stopped the suffering.

He had made her powerless, and that, she suddenly realized, was what he had wanted all along.

"C'mon, Frenchy, let's get goin'," Kulkey begged again.

"When I'm ready!"

That outburst was his last.

He had turned to shout at Buster, and in doing so, shifted the gun he held to Genevieve's side an inch, no more. She felt the deadly pressure ease.

It was as if they moved with a single reflex. Genevieve raised her foot and kicked at the leg behind it, while Rio finally went for the Colt. She saw him crouch, saw the hand flick back the tail of his coat, and then she threw herself on the ground. Jean-Louis' howl of agony ended in an explosion of light and smoke.

Genevieve refused to be sequestered in her room.

"This is my party," she insisted to her mother and Fanchon LeFevre while Celine divested her of the blue satin gown. A huge bloodstain had ruined the skirt, and one sleeve was torn where Jean-Louis had grabbed it in his deathfall. "I have much to celebrate, not the least of which is that I'm alive to celebrate at all!"

"But how will we explain *his* disappearance?" Marie-Claire, fluttering a lacy fan to ward off another fainting spell, wanted to know.

"Leave that to my father," Fanchon answered. She was sorting through Genevieve's wardrobe in search of a replacement for the blue satin. "He and Victor were the only ones who heard the gunshot, thanks to a very enthusiastic group of musicians. No doubt Papa will enlist the aid of some of my brothers-in-law to keep everything very quiet. Now, do you prefer the pink and white striped, or the yellow?"

A door creaked open and a low, masculine voice drawled, "The yellow."

Genevieve pushed past Celine, ignored Marie-Claire's protests, and flung herself into Rio's waiting arms.

"The yellow it is," she whispered, gazing up at him through tear-filled eyes. "Whatever you want, querido mío."

Though Marie-Claire threatened another fainting spell if her daughter dressed in Rio's presence, Genevieve refused to make him leave.

"Besides, Mama, he has seen me in less," she admitted with a great deal of what could only be called pride.

"It still isn't proper. On the trail from California, that is different, but here—"

"Mama, we spent five months in a one-room cabin. We crossed two thousand miles of mountain and desert together. We shared a stateroom on the riverboat from St. Louis."

Understanding slowly dawned. While Marie-Claire turned a brilliant shade of scarlet, Genevieve

368

gently chased her and Fanchon and even Celine from the room. She had to be alone with Rio before she faced the crowd again.

For a long time, he just held her, stroking her hair, caressing her bare shoulders, murmuring words of endearment in half a dozen languages. Her tears began with a quiet whimper until finally she was able to let them all out. Sobbing, she let him lift her and carry her to the bed.

"C'est fini, ma vie," he crooned, cradling her on his lap. "Over and done with. He can't hurt you anymore."

He wiped her tears away with the heel of his hand, and when her sobs subsided, he pulled out a large handkerchief for her to blow her nose.

"It is over, isn't it?" she asked, with a big sniffle.

"Do you mean is he really dead? Yes. Está muerto, querida, y tú y yo vivimos."

She looked at him with curiosity in her red-rimmed sapphire eyes.

"He's dead, my love. He's dead and we're alive and . . ."

"And what?"

Rio tucked her head against his chest and held her tightly, not wanting her to see the doubts that he knew filled his eyes.

"And we're going to be married and go back to California just as soon as we can arrange it." When she struggled in surprise, he held her still and added, "If that's what you want, of course."

She squirmed free of his embrace. After another sniffle into his handkerchief, she studied his face, taking in every detail of his expression, trying to read into the mystery of his furrowed brow, his steady eyes, his nervously flared nostrils. A thousand questions bubbled up inside her, but the first to make its way to the surface was the silliest, the least important.

"That was your surprise, wasn't it?"

His response wasn't an answer, but another question.

"Does that mean you're not saying 'No'?"

She had to think about that for a minute, and the minute gave Rio enough confidence—or enough terror, he was never sure which—to pour out the rest of the surprise.

"When we were in St. Louis, I went to Gerrard Bruckner and asked him if he could show me enough about being a banker that I could get a job when we reached New Orleans."

"Why a banker?"

"Don't interrupt me, Viva. It's a long story, and if you want to get back to the party, you're going to have to let me get through it."

He took a deep breath and swung his booted feet up on the bed, then tugged the netting securely down.

"It didn't matter to me what I did, so long as I could do something to stay with you. Paul's letter to his father gave me the chance, and you teaching me how to read gave me the means. I figured I'd be a fool to pass it up."

In as few words as possible, he told her of Gerrard's resistance and his own insistence, which ended in a frenetic course under the tutelage of a stern but effective teacher.

"But why didn't you tell me? I could have had Papa give you a position with his bank."

Rio shook his head almost angrily.

"That's what I was trying to avoid. I didn't want charity, or even help. I had to do it on my own."

"Stubborn."

"Yep, but I did it. Antoine gave me a job, but

he saw through me right away. I had the knowledge, but not the experience. He called me into his
office to chew me out and I told him the truth."

Her tears dried now, Genevieve slid off Rio's lap
and snuggled beside him. While he talked, she proceeded to unbutton his coat and then went to work
on his shirt.

"Hey, what the hell are you doing?"

"Oh, I figure after you finish telling me about
this whole surprise, we're probably going to want
to make love, and if we aren't ready, it'll take so
long we won't get back to the party in time to an-
nounce our engagement. Now, go on with your
story."

It was difficult to talk while she was methodically undressing him, but Rio persevered.

"I had a feeling he was ready to give me the
boot right then, but he got this funny look in his
eye and pulled a whole stack of papers out of his
desk. It was maps and letters from California. It
seemed Antoine's bank had staked one of Etienne
Marmont's investments, a huge land deal in California right after the gold strike. Antoine wanted
me to take a look at it and see if I could tell what
it was worth."

He leaned forward to let Genevieve work his coat
and then his shirt off. She flung them unceremoniously off the side of the bed.

"Well, what was it worth? Anything?"

Knowing she was right, at least about the inevitability of their making love, Rio tugged his boots
off and let them clunk onto the floor, too. If they
gave a signal to anyone as to what was happening
in Viva's room, he didn't care. Maybe discovery
would hasten the wedding.

"Eventually, probably millions."

"Millions?" she echoed. "Of dollars?"

371

He nodded sagely, then slipped his hands around her face to capture her astonished mouth for a swift, ferocious kiss.

"Millions of dollars," he affirmed, amused at the roundness of her eyes, the stunned "o" of her mouth despite his kiss.

He lay back against the pillows and went on while Genevieve recovered her composure and proceeded to unhook the unnecessary corset she had worn under the blue satin gown.

"Etienne must have thought he was buying mining claims, but what he got was an old Spanish land grant property, most of it around Monterey, some up north of San Francisco. It's farmland, ranchland, rich and fertile with good water. But it needs managing, someone to live on it and see it's taken care of and parcelled out for sale."

He paused and held his breath for a moment. When he spoke again, his voice was hushed, yet husky with the passion he no longer tried to control. "I love you, Viva du Prés, and I'd do almost anything you ever asked of me. But, damn it, woman, I hate this town. I wasn't cut out to be a Creole gentleman, and I sure as hell wasn't cut out to work in a bank. Antoine offered me the job of managing the California property, and I told him I'd take it—if you'll come with me."

Looking into his impassioned eyes, she remembered the clear blue of the mountain sky, the fresh tingle of the air, the openness, the newness, the wild freedom that had exhilarated her no matter how dangerous or threatening the situation she found herself in.

"I wasn't cut out to love a Creole gentleman," she whispered, "but, Rio, we just got here. You want to go back to California already?"

He shook his head. It was getting more and

more difficult to think straight. Genevieve had removed corset and chemise and now was fumbling with the buttons on his trousers, something he found eminently pleasurable but not conducive to serious conversation.

"It's too late to head back now; we'd never get across the mountains before winter, and I won't ask that of you again. Besides, there's more I gotta learn from Antoine, and your father's bank is involved, too, so it'd take time to sort everything out. We could leave in the early spring, February maybe. Or March."

He waited for her reaction, but she didn't look at him. With her hand still resting with seductive innocence on the outside of his pants, she seemed to be thinking. He had seen that same concentrated expression before, when she was calculating how long their supplies would last. He did some quick calculating of his own. An involuntary grin split his face.

"What's the matter?" Genevieve asked suddenly, resuming her ministrations. She slipped the last button and freed the warm, satiny hardness of him into her hand.

He gasped at the surge of pleasure her possession sent through him, and touched a fingertip to a bare nipple to tighten it into a dark, pearl-hard nub. Then he ran his palm over the crinkled jewel, down her ribs, and under the waistband of her underdrawers to her belly.

"I think you got a surprise of your own, Mademoiselle Viva du Prés who is about to become Mrs. Rio Jackson."

She flushed, from those rosy-tipped breasts to the roots of her tousled black hair. He knew her too well, too intimately, and she had seen him mentally ticking off the weeks.

"I'm only three days late," she confessed. "It could be anything, the strain of travel, the excitement, the worry about whether or not you were carrying on an affair with my best friend."

He used his other hand to undo the knot in her drawers, then slid them down over her hips until she could kick them wantonly off. Only her stockings remained, and his pants. Both were quickly done away with.

"It could also be a baby," he suggested, resting his hand once again on her stomach.

"Mmm, it could be."

"I don't want him to grow up a bastard like me."

"Then shall we get married tomorrow?"

"Would that be proper?"

"Why not?"

But the answer to her own question came unbidden. A man had died tonight, no more than an hour ago, and Rio had pulled the trigger on the gun that killed him.

"Always impulsive," he murmured, leaning over her to kiss her willing mouth while one hand cupped an eager breast. "Hell, Viva, nothin' about us has been proper since the night I hauled you out of a Sacramento whorehouse. You find us a preacher who'll say the words tomorrow, and we'll do it."

Then, without another word, with only laughter and sighs of exquisite pleasure, he slid himself inside her. If there wasn't a baby yet, he was going to make damn sure there was one pretty soon.

Epilogue

The last of Rio's surprises was more than a year in coming to fruition.

The valley hummed with life, from the summer breeze in the waist-high grass to the rasping cry of an eagle soaring from crag to crag. Fish jumped in the beaver pond, and birds sang in the green cattails that grew around the water's edge.

Viva, her hair pulled back and tied with a bright red ribbon, raised five-month-old Nicholas to her left shoulder and shielded her eyes with her other hand. Rio, as expected, was on the beaver dam, fishing.

They had reached the valley three weeks ago, after an uneventful trip with a freight wagon train from Independence. Over everyone's objections, they had set out barely two months after Nicholas' birth, in order to have this belated honeymoon before Rio was to take over management of the LeFevre-Du Prés properties.

"Catch anything?" Viva called to him as she walked closer. The distance from the cabin seemed so much less when it wasn't bitter cold and snowy.

"Not yet," Rio answered.

Approaching closer, Genevieve could see he didn't appear to be fishing according to any notions she had of the activity. His pole lay beside him, along with several other tools including a hammer and a chisel. The can of bait worms sat up-ended and empty on top of a crinkled, yellow piece of paper. And Rio himself was in the process of shifting from a sitting to a prone position. He then immersed one bare hand and arm into the frigid water.

"May I ask what you are doing?" she asked, halting on firm ground rather than taking the baby onto the precarious and uneven dam itself.

"Fishing," came the strained answer.

"For what?"

She couldn't see the expression on his face, but something in the way the muscles of his back tensed told her he had found whatever it was he was "fishing" for.

He pulled three times before it came free of the mud and muck. Hanging onto the stout metal pole with numb fingers, he hauled it to the surface. From the muddy end dangled a length of chain that disappeared into the water.

He set the pole on the ground, making sure to hold it fast with a booted foot, then picked up his shirt to dry his arm and shoulder.

"I swear that water is as cold now as the day I put my foot through the ice," he remarked as he dropped the garment to the ground again. The water might be cold, but the August sun was warm on his skin.

He retrieved the piece of yellow paper and carefully tucked it into his hip pocket. Then he grasped the pole again and began dragging it with its chain off the dam. Genevieve could see that the metal rod was some five or six feet long, a good inch or more thick, and rusty but still sturdy.

Nicholas squealed as soon as he saw his father coming toward him. Naked arms flailed in the welcome sunlight that turned his cap of fine curls to a brilliant blue-black.

"Just a minute, son," Rio told the boy, who did not like being ignored and set up an angry wailing and squirmed so frantically Genevieve had difficulty holding onto him. "I got a little wedding gift for your mama here."

There was just enough chain to loop around the mule's pulling harness. Rio walked to her head and grasped the bridle, then led her forward.

A great length of chain began to emerge, rusty, muddy, and weed-entangled. A good twenty feet of it stretched between the mule and the water's edge when something else appeared, a small metal box attached by separate rings to the chain. Ten feet later, another box, coated in mud and stringy weed, broke the surface of the water.

It was mid-afternoon when Rio first found the pole; it was suppertime before the mule — a temperamental black jenny Viva had named Veronica like the other — hauled the last of the thirty-two metal "fish" to the shore.

"Rio, will you tell me what is going on," an exasperated Genevieve demanded. "I am hungry, my nose is sunburned, and Nicholas is soaking wet. You and your surprises."

He grinned, kissed her on her sunburned nose, and said nothing except, "Five more minutes. I'm gonna cut one box free and leave the rest 'til tomorrow. There's a half dozen nice trout in the bucket over there for supper."

Using the chisel, hammer, and a flat rock, Rio separated one mucky box from the chain and tucked it under his arm. He kept it there while he unhitched the mule, lest Viva pick the thing up and start shaking it or trying to open it. And he didn't say another word until they reached the cabin.

By then Nicholas was cranky, and pawing at the front of Genevieve's dress.

"I'll put the mule away, feed the stock, and then bring this inside. You go ahead and feed Nick."

"Surprises, surprises," she muttered as she turned her cheek up for her husband's kiss and then walked into the cabin.

Inside, she took pleased note of the changes they had wrought in their three weeks' occupancy. The bed was back in its corner, but now had a bright cathedral window quilt covering its crisp sheets and down-filled mattress. The table sported two chairs as well as a hand-painted vase full of slightly drooping wild-flowers. The dishes on the three new shelves by the fireplace were fine china, not tin, and there was also a walnut chest filled with silver.

The original shelf bore Ernest Tibler's books, and more than a dozen new ones.

Nicholas' cradle sat beside the bed, with Genevieve's rocker at the foot. She trudged over to it and sank down wearily. Nicholas was screaming now, and there was no doubt about the health and strength of his lungs.

She had to fight his little hands away so she could unbutton the front of her dress.

"Just like your father," she sighed.

He found the nipple and stilled his screams to suckle noisily.

Bathed in the fragile light and shadow of late afternoon, mother and son presented an irresistible tableau when Rio stepped through the doorway. He paused for a moment, afraid to disturb the dream. But it was no dream. Genevieve looked up and smiled.

"What did I ever do to deserve this?" he wondered aloud as he walked across the little room to stand beside the rocking chair. Then, kneeling so his head was level with hers, he ran the knuckles of a closed fist down the swell of her exposed breast.

Something cold and hard fell out of his fist and landed just above her distended nipple. She could feel it, but couldn't see until she gently pushed his hand out of the way.

It was a flat lump of yellow metal the size of her fingernail.

She stared at it, then into Rio's bright blue eyes.

"That's gold, Rio," she said, astonished at how stupid the words sounded.

"Yep. And here's some more just like it."

He raised his fist and let a handful of nuggets, most of them smaller than the one on her breast, rain down on her and the sleeping infant. One struck Nicholas on the forehead, but instead of waking he simply resumed sucking at her other breast.

When the shower of nuggets stopped, Rio took the piece of paper from his pocket and opened it.

"Ernest Tibler's letter!" she whispered in awed surprise. "I thought you'd lost it!"

"Nope. Now, be quiet while I read it.

"He starts out thanking me for everything I did for him, and makes a big deal about how one of these days I'd find out what I was missin' by not bein' able to read. 'Like this letter. You're the only one who knows about the gold, and you won't find it until you can read this, or you're fool enough to let someone else read it for you. I hid the gold so nobody but you can find it. It's under Lucinda's mirror, wrapped in the fur coat she never got.'

"Lucinda was his daughter, the one who went back east. She used to call the pond a mirror, 'cause it'd be so still in the mornings, and that chain was from a trapline old Ernest never had the heart to set out."

They sat in silence for a few minutes, contented, half drowsy, half lost in thoughts and memories, until Genevieve asked, "Did you ever wonder about the gold? Did you know he had hidden it and put the clues in the letter?"

"Oh, I wondered about it, after he was gone, but he never told me a thing. I knew about the letter, of course. I helped him wrap up those damn books and put them in the trunk, but I had no idea he put anything in it about the gold."

"When did you finally read it?"

Rio laughed and sat down crosslegged on the floor. Here at least he didn't have to sit on dirt; he had laid in cut granite flagstones so the rocker would have a level base.

"The first day I got beyond 'In the beginning.' "

Genevieve turned so sharply that Nicholas wakened, and a dozen glittering nuggets fell to the stony floor.

"All that time? You've known about this gold for over a year and you said nothing?"

Picking up the scattered bits of metal to drop them back in the leather pouch Ernest Tibler had stored them in, Rio chuckled and said, "Wouldn't have done any good. When we left here, the pond was frozen over, and I sure as hell wasn't going to dive into it lookin' for gold. I figured I'd get back here after I took you home. It just took a little longer than expected."

"But you didn't tell me!"

Rio grinned and reached to begin collecting the treasure he had poured onto his wife's lap.

"A man's gotta have some secrets! Besides, I know how you like surprises."

She rolled blue eyes upward and lifted Nicholas so Rio could finish picking up the scattered pieces of gold. The baby gurgled and stretched his sturdy legs,

380

then reached out to grab a handful of his father's hair.

With a teasing yelp, Rio snatched the boy from his mother and lifted him high overhead. Nicholas squealed with delight and dribbled a stream of milky saliva down the front of Rio's shirt.

Genevieve watched her husband and her son play in the fading afternoon light. Contentment, and pride, filled her.

"We did such a good job with this young man, Viva, I think we ought to try for another."

Bright blue eyes met sapphire ones.

The adventure was beginning all over again.